The Seed
of Deception

The Seed
of Deception

Marino Scott

Library of Congress Control Number: 2020923424
ISBN: Hardcover   978-1-6641-4404-0
                   Softcover   978-1-6641-4403-3
                   eBook   978-1-6641-4402-6

Print information available on the last page.

Rev. date: 11/24/2020

To order additional copies of this book, contact:
Xlibris
844-714-8691
www.Xlibris.com
Orders@Xlibris.com
815504

CHAPTER 1

"Mr. Ali, once again, welcome to the show. You have within your mind a story that the world is waiting to hear. Will you be kind enough to tell us what really happened that night?"

"Well, Oprah, just like my attorney Mr. Gaines said in court, it was a beautiful fall night, October 31, 1979. I don't think there has been a night as beautiful as it since. Nothing under the moon that you can imagine could have shared the serenity. Mr. Gaines did such a magnificent job relating the story to the jury that I went to give him the privilege to tell the story to the world, as you put it."

"Well, Mr. Gaines, the weight has been shifted to you. Will you share the story with us?" Oprah asked as she looked over at him.

"I can do my best. Like I told the jury, a couple and their two young children were traveling home from a family reunion, taking full advantage of the pleasant night. Tired and sleepy, Samson Ali, the head of the small family, asked his wife, Shanda, 'Baby, will you please drive the rest of the way?' Looking like he was a little under the weather, she was happy to oblige him. As she was traveling through a small town in Tennessee, Teller County, she passed a sign that read Memphis Tennessee 95 Miles. Captured by the serenity of the night, she reminisced about the good time they had shared with her parents in New Jersey. With a smirk on her face, she turned briefly to check on their children as they lay sleeping in the backseat. Within that short and quick glance, she noticed a police car traveling close. Before the thought registered, the car lit up with red and blue lights.

"Unable to pull over onto the shoulder because of the small trench that ran alongside the one line highway, Shanda drove a little farther, looking for a place to pull over. After about a mile and a half, the opportunity was presented. She turned her hazard lights on. The officer took a minute before he exited the car. Seeing him through her side mirror closing the car

1

door and heading her way, Shanda Ali grabbed her purse to retrieve her driver's license. As the officer walked toward the driver-side window, she pulled her license out from an inside pocket in her purse, and she waited for the approaching officer to make his way to the driver-side door. Once he reached the door, she pushed the power button downward until the window came to a complete stop.

"The officer leaned over and looked around in the car. Once his eyes landed on Samson Ali, he quickly pulled out his flashlight and shined it on him as he lay there asleep and unaware of the stop.

"Shanda Ali looked and noticed the name that read George Fuhrman below his badge. With an evil look on his face, he asked 'Is everything okay?' 'Yes, sir,' Mrs. Ali said.

"Thinking nothing of his spontaneous action, she handed over her driver's license without being asked. After receiving it, Officer Fuhrman walked toward the back of their automobile and signaled for his partner with a nod. Watching his every move through the rearview mirror, she sensed something was wrong by the expression on the two officers' faces. Immediately she tapped her husband's leg and called his name. 'Samson! Samson! Samson,' she yelled, 'wake up! 'What! What!' he said.

"Before he could sit up, the officer that now we know as Mike McClain shouted as he pulled the passenger door open. 'Put your hands up, n——— and get your black ass out the car. If you think about moving the wrong way or doing anything, I'm going to blow your fucking head off.'

"Both officers stood there with their weapons pointed at Mr. Ali as he stepped out of the car with his hands raised above his head. 'Turn around and face the car, n———, and spread your legs, Officer Mike McClain said. 'If this n——— make a move, shoot him," Officer McClain added before he placed his .38 revolver back into the holster and frisked Mr. Ali. 'He's clean,' he told his partner. 'Move to the back of the car,' Officer Fuhrman said as he motioned with his pistol.

"Mr. Ali did as he was told with his hands raised high. Officer McClain pulled his weapon from its holster and pointed it at Shanda Ali. 'Bitch, turn the car off and pass me the fucking keys—now—I said.' Hands trembling from fear, she pulled the key from the switch and passed them to the officer. 'Don't do anything stupid,' he said before closing the door and putting the keys into his front-left pants pocket. 'This is a big n———, bro. What are we going to do with him?' Officer McClain asked his partner, Officer George Fuhrman. 'We are going to teach this n——— a lesson,' Officer Fuhrman said. 'What do you want me to do?' asked Officer McClain. 'Kill him if he tries to resist.' 'Turn around and put your hands on the trunk of the car," Officer Fuhrman said before instructing his partner to shoot and kill Mr. Ali if he took his hands off the car.

"Once Mr. Ali had done as the officer commanded, Officer Fuhrman placed his sidearm back into the holster and pulled out his nightstick. With all his might, Officer Fuhrman struck Mr. Ali with a fearless blow to his lower back. The force behind the blow sent pain through Mr. Ali's whole body, causing his knees to bend as his body fell forward into the trunk of the car. The officer followed up with another powerful blow to Mr. Ali's lower back and then one to his right thigh.

"Officer McClain thought that his partner had their victim subdued. He placed his weapon back into the holster. After receiving another blow, Mr. Ali noticed that Officer Fuhrman was out of breath as he held the nightstick loosely in his right hand. He recuperated instantly from the pain and responded with a deadly swinging elbow to the right side of Officer Fuhrman's head.

"The impact from his elbow knocked him off his feet and onto the pavement. Before Officer McClain could get his sidearm out the holster, Mr. Ali rushed him and knocked him backward with the weight of his body. The two fell to the ground and rolled over and over as they tussled for Officer McClain's weapon. *POW!* A single shot sounded out. The bullet entered upward through the right side of Officer McClain's face. He was killed instantly.

"Officer Fuhrman, dazed and not sure of his whereabouts, slowly stood to his feet and went for his sidearm. Before he could get it leveled, Mr. Ali pumped one into his right shoulder at close range, knocking him backward into the highway. The impact of the bullet forced him to drop his weapon. His handgun slid one way, and he went another, looking from Mr. Ali to his weapon underneath the squad car. Unsure of what to do, Officer Fuhrman pleaded for his life as the pain started to set in, 'Please! Please! Please don't kill me.'

"Being a man of compassion, Mr. Ali looked over at his family out the corner of his eye and noticed the fear and tears in their eyes. Their looks brought tears to his eyes and gave him a reason to spare Officer Fuhrman's life.

"'Get up,' Mr. Ali said as he stood back allowing Officer Fuhrman to get to his feet. Holding the gun on Officer Fuhrman as he ordered him to walk toward him from out of the highway, Mr. Ali told him to put his hands on his head. 'I can't! I can't move my arm,' Officer Fuhrman said. 'Turn around and walk over to your squad car.'

"Once over by the squad car, Mr. Ali then ordered him to get down on his knees. Once down on his knees, Mr. Ali walked up behind him and took the handcuffs from Officer Fuhrman's left side. After handcuffing his hands behind his back, Mr. Ali sat him down beside the passenger-side door of the squad car.

"Mr. Ali called his wife. With tears in her eyes, she came running to his aid. 'Bring me the car keys,' Mr. Ali said. 'I don't have them,' she said. 'What do you mean you don't have them?' 'I don't have them. He took them,' she said as she looked over at Officer McClain's lifeless body lying on the ground. 'What did he do with them?' Mr. Ali asked. 'He put them in his front pocket.' 'Will you get them out of his pocket for me?' 'No, baby, I can't,' she said. 'He's dead. He can't do anything to you,' Mr. Ali said. 'Please don't have me do that," she asked. 'Okay, I'll do it,' Mr. Ali said as he walked over to check Officer McClain's pockets.

"After he pulled the keys out of the dead man's pockets, he handed the keys to his wife. 'Look in the trunk and get a big towel out and put it on his shoulder for me. I'm going to call for help from their radio.' 'No, baby, you get the towel out and put it on him. I will call for help,' Mrs. Ali said after seeing the look that Officer Fuhrman had in his eyes. 'Okay,' Mr. Ali said, agreeing with his nervous and frightened wife.

"Mr. Ali went on and got the towel from the trunk of the car and pulled Officer Fuhrman's shirt half open and placed the towel on the bullet wound, hoping to stop some of the bleeding.

"'You will live. The bullet exited out the back of your shoulder,' Mr. Ali said, looking Officer Fuhrman in his eyes. 'I'm nothing like you. If I was, I would kill you, so if you believe in a God, you need to thank Him." Officer Fuhrman just looked at him with hatred in his eyes. 'Hello, can anyone hear me?' Mrs. Ali asked. 'Yes, go ahead,' the dispatch said. 'We have two officers down. One is presumed dead, and the other has a gunshot wound to his shoulder,' Mrs. Ali said as she called for help. 'Where is your location?' the dispatch asked. 'We are about ten miles east of Exit 2 on Highway 470, at Mile Marker 11,' she added.

"Within minutes three cars of Teller County sheriff and an ambulance were on the way to their location. Mr. Ali heard the sirens from a distance, turned to see where the sounds were coming from, and saw the red and blue lights flashing as they became closer. He placed the weapon he took from Officer McClain on the hood of the squad car and stepped over to the trunk of his car and then told his wife to get back in the car.

"Within seconds, the help arrived. Hopping out their cars with guns in their hands, they were unable to see any officers because one lay dead in the grass and the other one was handcuffed on the ground against the squad car. 'Where are the two officers?' one of them asked.

"Mr. Ali pointed to Officer McClain first and said, 'He's lying over there, and the other one is up against the car.'

"Once the paramedics saw that the area was safe, they exited the ambulance. 'Over here,' one of the officers said as he held his hand up to get the paramedics' attention. 'I think he's dead,' the officer said as the paramedic checked for a pulse. 'Why the fuck are you cuffed?' the officer asked Officer Fuhrman. 'That n—— over there did it. He killed Mike and tried to kill me too. Get that, motherfucker. Kill him,' Officer Fuhrman ordered.

"All the officers rushed. Just as they rushed Mr. Ali and started beating and kicking him, a black unmarked car pulled up. Two men with black suits got out with their badges in their hands. 'FBI,' they said as they held up their badges. As the Teller County sheriffs were kicking, they stepped in. 'Step back! I said step the fuck back now!' one agent said.

"Slowly, one by one, they stepped back from Mr. Ali. 'Turn over,' one of the FBI agents said to Mr. Ali so that he could handcuff him.

"Once the handcuffs were on him, he helped him to his feet and walked him over to their car. Once safely inside, the two agents looked around. The both of them walked over to the car where Mrs. Ali and her two children were and motioned for her to roll down the window. For a minute, she just looked at them. They identified themselves by showing their badges. 'We are FBI,' one of the agents said. 'Could you please roll down your window?'

"Mrs. Ali then rolled the window down. As the agents looked into the car, I'm sure that they could see the fear that she and the children had in their eyes. 'My name is Agent Woods. What is your name?' 'Shanda Ali.' 'Are those your kids?' 'Yes, sir, they are.' 'What are you doing here?' 'I was pulled over,' she said. 'Is that man we have in the back of the car with you?' 'Yes, he's my husband.' 'Where were ya'll headed?' 'We were headed home.' 'Where is home?' Agent Wood asked. 'Memphis . . . Memphis,

Tennessee.' 'Here, take my card. Call me. I will let you know what's going to happen with your husband. You can go now,' he said.

"Luckily the FBI was in town investigating the cases of the missing women along that part of the highway. I don't want to imagine what might have happened to Mr. Ali and his family. If the FBI saw that there was a need for Mr. Ali to be transferred from Teller County to Jackson, Tennessee, and held there, that alone should give us something to wonder about, I added as I walked over toward the jury box presenting the case." Mr. Gaines unconsciously drifted into the story.

"For my closing arguments, I would like to use the time, ladies and gentlemen of the jury, to paint you all a picture—a picture that any God-fearing person can identify with. Here, we have a black man with a white woman, traveling through an all-white town filled with racism and hatred. I ask that you—the people of the jury, the ones who have the power—to make the right decision."

"All it takes is twelve independent thinkers to open their eyes and see the big picture. The picture for what it truly is. I know you all can see through this very shallow case that the district attorney has pumped up so he could try to steal a conviction. As you all can see, my client, Samson Ali, and his family are the true victims in this matter. Please! Please! Just don't look at this case and make your determination from a black-and-white standpoint. The only true witness other than the ones we have here in this courtroom are Shanda Ali, my client's wife, and their two kids.

"Thanks to Officer Fuhrman and his friends, they went to their home in the middle of the night, burning crosses and threatening to kill her and her children if they ever catch her in Teller County."

"Objection! Objection, Your Honor!" the District Attorney Hernzberg hollered. "That's pure speculation and hearsay."

"Objection sustained. I ask that the jury disregard that remark and it be stricken from the record. Mr. Gaines, don't make any more remarks like that in my courtroom," the judge said.

"Yes, Your Honor."

"You may continue, Mr. Gaines," Judge Turner said.

"Thank you, Your Honor," Attorney Gaines said with a smile on his face as he turned back and walked from the jury box. He then made eye contact with his client, Sampson Ali, and turned back around.

Forcing the jury to give him their undivided attention as he walked up close to them, he continued, "We all know what is going on here. This is a case filled with hatred toward a man who had to fight for his life and his rights to be married to a white woman. America is supposed to be the land of the free. If that's true, why is this black man"—he pointed his finger at Samson Ali—"on trial for protecting himself and his family? Ladies and gentlemen of the jury, does it make us above the law or righteous because we wear a badge or work for the sheriff's department? I don't think so. What makes us righteous is when we do the right things for the right reasons. I pray not only for myself but for Mr. Ali as well in hopes that we picked a group of God-fearing people to determine what is the truth and what is falsehood. You all will be doing just that if you acquit Mr. Ali of all charges. Thank you, all," Mr. Gaines said as he closed.

"Mr. Hernzberg, are you ready to present your closing argument to the jury?" Judge Turner asked.

"Yes, sir, Your Honor, I am," he said with surety and wasted no time to hop to his feet.

"Ladies and gentlemen of the jury, Attorney Gaines's story sounded really good but only to himself. What I would like to present to you are facts."

"October 31, 1979, wasn't the nicest and most peaceful night as Attorney Gaines dressed it up to be. In fact, it was the total opposite. It was a night filled with pain and agony—a night when one officer of the law was murdered in cold blood and another one shot trying to make a routine traffic stop.

"Mr. Gaines gave you a long drawn-out story about what happened on that unforgettable Halloween night that took a great officer, father, husband, and friend from us. He told you a story of some alleged person who isn't here. That should lead us to believe that his story was fabricated by Attorney Gaines and that defendant," said Herzberg while pointing at Samson Ali.

"It's simple, people. If there were any other witness, they would be here. Where are they? Do we have to look for them outside, under the tables? I know where they are. They are only in the minds of the defendant and his attorney.

"Once again, facts, good people. On that so-called night that Mr. Gaines claimed was filled with serenity, a law-abiding citizen and member of the Teller County Sheriff's Department for thirteen years was shot in the line of duty. His partner, a ten-year veteran, murdered because that man didn't want to be pulled over," he said as he pointed his finger at Samson.

"As I look into the eyes of each and every one of you, I can see that all of you are good, God-fearing people. The facts show that this murderer is guilty as charged. I am not going to hold you, good people, up any longer from finding this murderer guilty. That's all and thank you all for your time," Mr. Herzberg said as he looked at Samson Ali and Attorney Gaines with a smile on his face.

"Ladies and gentlemen of the jury, we have gone over all the instructions in open court, and everyone agrees that they understood them. So I ask that you all carefully look over all the facts in this case. Take all the time that's needed to come up with a verdict. This court is adjourned until a verdict has been reached by the jury in the case of the *State of Tennessee v. Samson Ali*."

As soon as Judge Turner finished his closing statement, the bailiff of the court stood up and said, "All, stand. This court is adjourned until further notice."

"All we can do now is pray and hope that they at least come back with lesser charges," Attorney Gaines said as he looked at Samson.

"Prayer is good. As you know, Mr. Gaines, if something is meant for you, it will never pass you by. And if it's not meant for you, you will never get it. After all, it isn't what you or anyone knows. It's what you can prove. For what we had to fight with, I feel you did a very good job, Mr. Gaines. That really was an excellent effort, and I'm very pleased with your work," Samson said.

"Thank you, Mr. Ali. You must have known I needed that."

"Truthfully, Mr. Gaines, it shows a little in your eyes," Samson said. "You see, I was dealt a pretty messed-up hand, and without the grace of God, it will be over for me."

"That's true," Attorney Gaines said as he shook his head.

"I must keep in mind, Mr. Gaines, that the God that I serve is all-powerful. If I claim to believe in Him and think I will not be tested, that means I'm not a true believer. I know what type of people we are dealing with. I pray and ask God to allow me to prevail in this situation. How He wants me to prevail, I don't know. What I do know is, I must keep my faith in Him and prepare myself for the worst that He will allow these people to do to me. I am a true believer in the one and only creator, the creator of all life. He is the only one that I will ever submit my will to. Mr. Gaines, this situation isn't my greatest test. My greatest test is to stay away from anything that will cause His wrath to be upon me. He is the only one that gives life, and He is the only one that can take it away. So why should I be afraid of what they think that they can do to me? From Him, we all came, and to Him, we will all return. Then and then alone will we all be rightfully judged for the things that we did in this world. I thank God for you. He is the one that put it in your heart to represent me to your best ability. I saw you stand up for the truth even if it costs you your life. That's a good thing. This day and time, it is hard to get people to stand up for what is right."

"You are so right," Attorney Gaines added.

"I need to pray. Will you please get the bailiff to allow me to go into one of the holding cells for a few minutes, Mr. Gaines?"

"Sure," Attorney Gaines responded. "While you are praying, I will be back in about thirty minutes."

"Okay, see you then God's will," Samson said.

"Excuse me, Bailiff," Attorney Gaines said as he walked up to the heavyset middle-aged white man who stood with his arms crossed over the top of his stomach protruding out over his belt line.

"Yes, how can I help you?" the bailiff asked.

"My client would like to be put into one of the holding cells for a few minutes."

"Okay, no problem."

As the bailiff walked over toward Samson, he grabbed the keys that hung on a chain at his right side. He motioned at Samson with an upward motion of his head. Samson got up and went over to the door that's next to the door that the judge uses. The bailiff opened the door for Samson and locked it once he was on the inside of the holding cell.

Once Samson was in the cell and the bailiff locked the door behind him, he stood there with his arms crossed, his right hand over his left, and he started reciting the Al-Fatiha, a surah [verse] from the Qur'an.

"In the name of God, the Most Gracious, the Most Merciful, all Praise and thanks are due to you. The Cherisher and Sustainer of the Worlds, the Most Gracious, Most Merciful, Master of the Day of Judgment. To You we worship, and your aid we seek. Show us the straight way, the way of those on whom You have bestowed Your grace, not those who have earned your wrath and have gone astray. Amen."

When Samson was finished doing all his regular physical routine positions and reciting the verses from the Qur'an, he made his supplications, something that he had become accustomed to doing after each of his five daily prayers. He stayed there after his prayer with his hands on his lap over his knees and said, "Lord, I ask that your will be done in my life, and I ask that you allow me to stay strong in the presence of the ungodly. I know, Lord, if you are with me, nothing can stand against me. You are the greatest."

Samson stopped as he heard the keys enter the lock.

"Excuse me . . . Mr. Ali," said the bailiff respectfully.

"Yes, sir."

"The jury has returned."

"Already?" Samson asked.

"Yes, already."

"How long did they take?" Samson asked.

"About thirty-five minutes," the bailiff answered. "This time, I have to handcuff you. It's their policy."

"That's no problem. Is my attorney back?"

"Yes, he's out there. I don't think anyone got a chance to really take a break. The jury was finished deliberating almost ten minutes ago. That's not a good sign to be truthful with you," the bailiff said.

As Samson walked out into the courtroom, he said to himself, *All praise are due to You, Allah [God],* making eye contact with his best friend and brother in faith sitting as the back of the courtroom. Samson and the tall nicely built white gentleman with a closely cut goatee smiled at each other as they nodded. Samson placed his right hand on his chest over the heart then held out his index finger with the handcuffs on his wrist.

"Allahu Akbar [God is the greatest]!" Samson said in a low tone of voice that could be heard across the calm courtroom.

"Allahu Akbar [God is the greatest]!" the gentleman said from the back of the courtroom.

Quickly the whole courtroom all at once turned to see who it was giving a response to the foreign language. Within seconds, the judge entered the courtroom.

"All stand, the Honorable Judge Turner is presiding." Everyone stood to their feet and waited for the judge to be seated. 'You may be seated,' the bailiff said.

"Ladies and gentlemen of the jury, has a verdict been reached in the *State of Tennessee v Samson Ali* case?" the judge asked.

"Yes, Your Honor," the foreman for the jury said.

"Bailiff, will you please collect the verdict slips?" the judge asked.

The bailiff approached the foreman and reached out his hand to receive the verdict slips that the foreman extended out to him. Making sure the wind didn't blow them out of his hand, he clenched them tightly as he walked up and passed them to the judge. The judge counted the slips as he looked over them. When he was finished, he passed them back.

"Will the defendant please stand?" the judge said.

Samson and his attorney Fred Gaines stood up at the same time.

"Foreman of the jury, will you please stand and read off the verdict?" the judge asked.

The foreman stood up and looked around but wasn't able to look over at Samson before he started reading their verdict.

"In this case, number 79-CR-0133 *State of Tennessee v. Samson Ali*, we the jury finds the defendant guilty on count one, murder in the first degree, in the case of Officer Mike McClain. In count two, attempt to commit murder in the first degree on Officer George Fuhrman, we find the defendant, Samson Ali, guilty."

"Hang that n——!" one man yelled from the back of the courtroom. Others in the courtroom made racial outbursts.

"Order! Order! Order in the court!" the judge said as he hit the gavel down repeatedly.

Samson stood there with his head up high and didn't even flinch.

"Alhamdulillah [All praise are due to God]," he said in a low tone before he leaned over to his attorney and said in his left ear, "I knew it, and I'm okay with it. God is the greatest."

Once the courtroom was back in order, the judge said, "Mr. Ali, you have been found guilty by a jury of your peers. This court will set a sentencing date on this matter thirty days from today. Mr. Gaines, is that enough time for you to be ready?"

Attorney Gaines looked over his notes and then said to Samson, "I don't think that will be enough time for us. What do you think?"

"If you don't think thirty days is enough, ask for what you need," Samson said.

"No, Your Honor, I don't think thirty days will be ample time to properly prepare for sentencing," Attorney Gaines said.

"Why not, Mr. Gaines?"

"Your Honor, the state is seeking the death penalty in this case. I will need at least ninety days to have everything professionally drawn up."

"Mr. Hernzberg, do you object to Mr. Gaines's request?" said the judge.

"Yes, Your Honor, I do. That is way too much time for someone to prepare for a sentencing hearing."

"Good enough. Mr. Gaines, I am going to meet you halfway. You have forty-five days to have everything prepared. This court will set a sentencing date for September 11, 1980, at 9:00 a.m. This court is adjourned," the judge said before stepping down and walking out.

"I will be over there to see you later today, so we can start on some kind of strategy," Attorney Gaines said.

"That will work. I will see you then God's will," Samson said.

"Mr. Ali, all you have been through today, I know you don't want to see any news reporters," said the sheriff escorting Samson from Jackson, Tennessee.

Samson smiled and said, 'I sure don't."

"They are waiting for me to bring you out that door. I have a trick up my sleeve. I'm going to take you out the back and around the courthouse. I moved my squad car on the north side earlier, hoping we could avoid them."

The townspeople noticed them walking out behind the courthouse and started shouting. "Hey, hey, everybody, he's trying to sneak the n——— out the back," quickly grabbing the attention of the reporters and other townsfolk.

The news reporters ran around in full speed, like they were in a race. The townspeople stood there, yelling all kinds of racial remarks. The news reporters looked forward to having the opportunity of getting a word or two from Samson, who maintained his story that he acted in self-defense.

"We have to move a little faster," the Sheriff said.

The news reporters met them at the squad car located on the north side of the courthouse. Within seconds, news reporters and the townspeople surrounded them.

"Mr. Ali, how——"

"Kill that n———"

Out of nowhere, a Coke bottle flew past the sheriff's face and Samson's head as the sheriff was putting Samson into the car, causing the reporter to stop her question and move out of the way. Acting quickly, the sheriff closed the door behind Samson, then ran around, and jumped in the driver's side, blowing his horn as he pulled off, making the people get out the way.

"Did you see that bottle fly by your head?" the sheriff asked.

"No. I heard it and felt the wind from it," Samson responded.

"Whoever threw it wanted you to take it with you," said the sheriff with a smile.

"Thanks but no thanks," Samson said. "I know one thing. It made the news reporter get back," he continued.

"That's true. It did. One of them was trying to ask you something, but she couldn't get it out," said the sheriff.

The two talked as the news of the verdict spread across the state of Tennessee like a wind-propelled wildfire. As the two were talking, the sheriff looked into his rearview mirror and noticed that a black unmarked car was following them closely. He sped up a little to make sure there was enough room in between them and the suspicious car.

"I see we have a tail," the sheriff said, knowing that Samson was being held in the Jackson County Jail because his life could be in danger. Keeping his eyes on the car trailing them at a nice distance, the sheriff drove the twenty miles back to the Jackson County Jail. As he pulled into the county jail carport, the black car pulled into the jail's visitors' lot.

Two white men in black suits exited the car with their badges pinned to their suit coats. They looked over at Samson and the sheriff as they waited to get into the carport.

CHAPTER 2

Shortly after Samson was escorted to his cell, his name was called for a special visit just when he had lain down and closed his eyes. He sat up when he heard the key entering the lock to his cell.

"Mr. Ali, you have a special visit," the jailer said.

"What do you mean by special visit?" Samson asked.

The jailer smiled and said, "The FBI would like to speak with you."

Samson was escorted from his cell to a room used for attorney's visits. The room was one or two feet larger than is cell. The only difference is that the walls didn't have writing all over them and a moveable table and chairs took the place of his two-in-one stable concrete table/chair and bunk. Samson pulled out one of the chairs from the table and sat down. Minutes had passed while he sat there thinking to himself. The sound of keys made him look over at the steel door with a small window. Within seconds of hearing the keys, the door opened and the same two FBI agents who saved his life at the scene the night of the shooting walked in. The two identified themselves as they stepped through the door.

"Mr. Ali . . . how are you doing, sir?" one agent said.

"I'm good. All praise due to God."

"My name is Agent Woods, and this is my partner Agent Sanders. We are with the Federal Bureau of Investigation. We would like to talk to you."

"Are you going to read me my rights first?"

"There is no need to. We are not looking to charge you with anything. We just would like to know more about what happened that night," Agent Woods said.

"With your cooperation, Mr. Ali, it might be possible that we can get you off the hook. After what happened to you today, I'm sure that you will take our offer," Agent Sanders said, talking about the verdict that Samson received in court earlier.

"That sounds good, but I think that it would be best for me to wait until my attorney gets here. He should be here any minute now. Speaking of him, there he is," Samson said as he smiled and leaned back in his chair as Mr. Gaines walked in.

As soon as he walked through the door, he said, "Pardon me, gentlemen, my name is Attorney Fred Gaines, and this is my client you are talking to. Looks as if you are violating his rights by not allowing him to have his attorney present while you two are questioning him."

"It's not like that. We are here to offer our help. If you would, Mr. Gaines, we would like for you to join us," said Agent Woods in a very polite manner. "Like we told him, we are not here to charge him with anything. We are hoping that he can help us, and in return, we will be able to help him. Maybe even get him out," Agent Woods said clearly.

"How will you go about doing that?" Attorney Gaines asked.

"We believe that he was just in the wrong place at the right time. Things could have gotten really ugly that night," said Agent Sanders.

"We are not here to blow smoke up your behinds. If Mr. Ali can provide us with the proper information that we need, we will be able to help him. At this point, he doesn't have anything to lose. The district attorney of Teller County will get what he wants," Agent Woods added with a sure look on his face.

"Mr. Ali, it is your call. What do you want to do?" Attorney Gaines asked his client.

"I'm okay with it. One thing about it, it can't hurt. Pretty much like they are saying," said Samson.

"Okay then, let's do this." Attorney Gaines said.

"Good choice, Mr. Ali. I looked closely into your background. I see that you were a lieutenant in the naval air station of Memphis. That base is located in Millington, Tennessee, right?" Agent Woods asked.

"Right," Samson answered.

"At the time that this happened, you had been enlisted for fifteen years. Did you actually fight in the Vietnam War?" Agent Woods asked.

"Yes, sir, I did," Samson responded.

"Me too! That was war, wasn't it?" Agent Woods said.

"Yes, it was, one that I wouldn't want to fight again," said Samson Ali.

"I agree. Neither would I. I read your statement. Are you sure you didn't leave anything out?"

"I'm sure I didn't," said Samson.

"You stated that your wife woke you up right before you were forced out of the car at gunpoint."

"That's correct," said Samson.

"It really would help if we could talk with her as well. We had someone to follow her home that night to make sure she got there safely. I gave her my card and waited for her to call, but she never did. A few months ago, my partner, Agent Sanders, and I went by there, hoping to talk to her. However, we weren't successful in doing so. We spoke with the neighbors. They informed us that the KKK ran them off the night after the shooting. They said that the Klan burned a cross in the front yard, called her all kinds of racial names, like n—— lover, etc. They told her if they catch her in their town again, they were going to kill her and the kids. That same night she packed up and moved out and took only a few of her things. Do you know anyone she may have moved in with?" Agent Woods asked.

"No. I talk to my best friend at least once a week, and he hasn't heard anything from her. I have a brother who also lives in Memphis. I keep my family away from him."

"Why do you think that she wouldn't go there?" Agent Sanders asked.

"Because she knows that I don't approve of my children being around anyone who lives the way he does."

"Do you have an address on your brother?"

"No . . . no, I don't. The last place I saw him was over by Gaston Park on a street called Patton. I don't know the address."

"Did you say this place was in Memphis, on Patton Street, by Gaston part?" Agent Sanders asked.

"That's correct."

"Is it an apartment or house?" Agent Sanders asked.

"A house," Samson said as he looked at Agent Sanders taking notes.

"Mr. Gaines, according to the story that you gave the jury, you talked to her. How did you manage to do that?" Agent Woods asked.

"I went by the house and noticed that it was boarded up. So I talked to the neighbors. They told me the same story that they told you about the KKK. So after talking to them briefly, I gave them my business card. It wasn't long before she called me. She related the story to me over the phone, all that happened on the night of October 31, 1979, and also what happened the night following. She wouldn't tell me precisely where she was. She did say she and the children were okay and in a safe place," Mr. Gaines said.

"We really need to talk to her. We are going to go by this place. You gave us in hopes of locating her. If we are successful in doing so, we will be back."

"Likewise, if you find out anything before we do, here is my card. Call me," Agent Woods said.

"We will do so," Mr. Gaines said when he received the business card from Agent Woods.

Samson stood up and shook both agents' hands tightly and firmly as he looked them in their eyes. After they shook Attorney Gaines's hand, they walked out the door.

"Mr. Ali, I have a few questions to ask you myself, if you don't mind."

"Mr. Gaines, you can call me by my first name. By you saying Mr. Ali, that makes me feel old."

"Okay then, Samson, you understand that the DA is asking that you be put to death, right?"

"Yes, but I don't believe that it will happen. He could ask for whatever he wants, but God has the last say when it comes to me. So, Mr. Gaines, don't give him that power. He is only a man."

"Before I get into the questions, I would like to get a bite to eat. I saw the sheriff of this county pulling up just as I was coming in. They must have called him when the FBI showed up. John . . . John Harris is a good friend of mine. He and I are old friends. I don't know about you, but I'm hungry. If you are too, I will see if he would allow me to grab you something from Burger King."

"I'm due for a bite to eat," Samson said. "What would you like to have?"

"A whopper with cheese and some french fries. Have them put everything on the burger for me.

"What about something to drink?" Attorney Gaines asked. "Just a cup of cold ice water will do."

"If you don't mind, I'm going to tell them to leave you in here until I get back. I don't mind," Samson said.

"It shouldn't take me no more than fifteen minutes at the most," Attorney Gaines said while walking out as he requested that the jailer leave Samson in the visiting room until he returned, if it would not be a problem.

"No, it's not a problem," the jailer said.

"Okay, thank you," Attorney Gaines said.

"You are welcome," the clean-cut young white jailer said.

Samson sat there with his elbows on the table, with his hands over his face, and said to himself, *God, please keep me strong and my family safe. Lord God, help me to overcome the trip that has been set for me by Satan. All praise is due to You, Lord. I ask for Your forgiveness. I will hold fast to the rope that you have extended me if I have to hold on to it with my teeth. I know that you are the one who accepts repentance and who is most forgiving. I will remember being on the brink of a pit of fire, and you saved me from it. There is none worthy of being praised but you and you alone. Amen.*

After he prayed, it renewed his whole way of thinking; and it gave him back the strength that he had at the beginning of the day.

Within the time that Attorney Gaines said that it would take to return, he walked through the door with a big bag in his arm. Samson looked up with a smile on his face. The glow made Attorney Gaines ask, "What did I miss?"

"Why would you ask that?" Samson asked.

"The glowing smile that you have on your face."

"I'm just thankful. God is the greatest."

Attorney Gaines smiled and shook his head, and he said to himself, *This man is strong in his faith.* Attorney Gaines then reached into the Burger King bag and pulled out the whopper Samson ordered.

"The french fries are pretty hot. I know you don't want me to sit them on the table. So I'm going to tear this bag in half and lay it on the table," Attorney Gaines said.

While the french fries were still in the bag, Attorney Gaines ripped the bag down the side and opened it up, allowing the fries to sit on top of the torn bag between them and the table. The two of them sat there quietly as they finished eating their food. Once Attorney Gaines was finished, he looked up at Samson and said, "This has been my biggest case. To be truthful with you, at first I didn't think I could do it. People I have been knowing all my life talked down to me about taking this case, even some of my closest friends. I went through a lot, and I still am going through quite a bit about this case. I have learned a whole lot, and this has been quite an eye opener for me," confessed Attorney Gaines.

"I feel the divine cause, but before that calling, I was going to just sell you out. Get this case out my hair as quick as possible. After getting to know you and looking into the case, God gave me a change of heart. All of a sudden, I felt inspired to help. The drive to Memphis helped a lot too. Seeing what had happened to your family, it was a hurting feeling. One would think those days were over. When your wife called me and told me the story, I knew then that money was no longer my motivation. It's like I'm on a quest for righteousness now. Believe me, it's a good feeling. I thank God for allowing me to meet you. Don't get me wrong. I don't like the way we met," Mr. Gaines continued.

"Mr. Gaines, God is the best of planners. He is in charge of everything. If this wouldn't have happened to me, it would have happened to someone else. Most likely, it would have probably been worse. God knows best," Samson said.

"That may be true."

"Are you okay, Mr. Gaines?"

"Why do you ask that?" Attorney Gaines said.

"You look like you can use some rest."

"I do. Is it that noticeable?"

"Oh yes. You are starting to get rings around your eyes," Samson said.

"Let's cover some of the things that might help us at the sentencing hearing first. Then I will think about going home to get me some sleep. Okay, Samson, the sentencing phase is supposed to go like this. First of all, the DA will try to convince the jury that you are a cold, heartless killer, who has no remorse for what you have done. Our job is to get the jury to split or just don't come up with one agreement for you to receive the death penalty. We have an all-white jury, seven females and five males. We can bet our last dollar that all five of the men are racist," said Attorney Gaines.

"I'm not a gambling man, but I agree with you 100 percent," Samson replied.

"If we can get one or two of the females to side with us, we will be all right," Attorney Gaines said.

"Mr. Gaines, all that sounds good, but it's up to God. I place all my affairs in his hands."

"Samson, I understand you and respect your faith. You still must realize that your faith lies in the hands of the people sitting to your right in that jury box. We are dealing with people who hate blacks and really don't know why. It's something that's deeply rooted into their hearts. You remember telling me something out the Qur'an? It went something like this—man, I hope I don't say this wrong, so correct me if I'm wrong. You said, 'God said he isn't going to change the condition of the people until they change the condition of themselves.' Am I right?"

"You're right," Samson said.

"That stuck with me, along with the other saying you shared with me.

You also said, 'God didn't put us on this earth for us to hate one another but to learn from one another.'"

"Are you sure I told you that, or have you been reading from the same book that I have?" Samson asked.

Attorney Gaines just smiled.

"Samson, I understand if God is with you who can stand against you. God also wants us to tie our camel, if you know what I mean by that. That's why I am willing to stand out firmly for justice if it is against myself. That's the God fearing in you," Samson said. "Keep me in mind, Mr. Gaines. God is a better protector than anything you can think of. I can't put my faith or full trust in men. Most people follow the lust of their hearts. They avoid justice by refusing to give it. God is well acquainted with what we do. I understand that I must tie my camel. I also understand the people we are dealing with. They will be judged according to their deeds. I pray that somewhere deep in their hearts they still hear the word of God. Whatever you say, Mr. Gaines, will not change what God has predestined to happen."

"You're right. Where did you grow up, Samson?"

"Why do you ask that?" Samson asked.

"Seems like you had a good upbringing."

"I was born in Memphis but was raised in Mississippi by my grandmother from the age of eight to seventeen."

"Did you finish high school?"

"Yes, sir, I did."

"Any college?"

"Yes, I was working on my PhD in medicine when I was arrested."

"Did you start college immediately after school?"

"No."

"Why not?"

"Because I wanted to enlist into the air force, and that is what I did," Samson explained.

"Where were your parents during the time you stayed with your grandmother in Mississippi?"

"My parents were killed in a car crash when I was eight years old."

"Sorry to hear that."

"My siblings and I moved to Mississippi with our grandmother right after that."

"How many siblings are there?"

"Two. I have a brother who's two years older than me and a sister who is eighteen months younger than me."

"Is your grandmother still living?"

"No. She passed away in May of last year."

"Do you have anyone who will be willing to speak on your behalf at the sentencing hearing?"

"I have been maintaining contact with my sister living in Colorado Springs, Colorado. I wouldn't put her life in danger by asking her to come down here. She is all that I have now as far as family is concerned. I have a lot of brothers on base who I can have to come. I can get officers, sergeants, and most of all my best friend and brother in faith, who's a captain. All of them will be more than happy to come. My brother, Captain Brandon Morris, was the one in the courtroom today."

"The tall white guy who was sitting in the back of the courtroom?" Attorney Gaines asked.

"Yes, that's him. He will be here tonight, God's will, to see me."

"All the ones willing to come, have them call me."

"Yes, sir, I got that covered," said Samson. "Oh yeah, Mr. Gaines, they only allow me to use the phone once a week. See if your friend the sheriff can change that."

"I will talk to him on my way out. He told me that you haven't been a problem, and he needs more inmates like you. So he shouldn't have any reason not to."

"That's good to hear. Thanks"

"No problem, Samson. Anything I can do to help out, I will do it for you."

"I need to call my sister and let her know what happened today. Also, get to rounding up all the brothers," said Samson.

"Good because I will be looking forward to getting some calls. I will be back to see you before this week is gone. If you need to talk to me before then, you have my number. Oh yeah, before I forget, Samson, since we can't locate your wife and children, is there any way by chance you can get a picture of all of them together? If you have one."

"Yes, sir, I have some wallet-sized pictures of them here. Why?"

"Because I know the male jurors wouldn't like seeing you with a white woman. The females just might get some enjoyment from it. Most of all, I would like for them to see your family so I can stress the point that you two have been together over eleven years. God's will, that will knock a lot of the stereotyping down that they have about blacks. Most of them have never been around blacks. All they know is what they heard or been taught. Once we take that wild-animal picture out of their minds and show them that you are human and also a family man, it might be what we need. In between time, Samson, stay strong and pray, and I will keep you and your family in my prayers. Also, I will be praying that the FBI will find them."

"Thank you. I appreciate that very much. I will keep you and your family in my prayers as well."

"God's will, I will see you later, Samson."

"God's will, I will see you later, Mr. Gaines."

CHAPTER 3

Visitation time came quickly for Samson as he waited for the jailer to come and escort him to the visiting room. The jailer, who was in charge of watching over Samson five days a week, opened his cell.

"How are you today, Mr. Ali?"

Samson was caught off guard by the young jailer's ability to finally speak.

Samson smiled and looked at the clean-shaven young man. "I'm blessed and highly favored, thank God," said Samson. "How about yourself?"

"Okay, just trying to get through another day of work. Can I ask you a question?"

"Sure," Samson said.

"After all the stuff that you are going through, how can you still have a smile on your face?"

"Simple. I have my faith in something that is greater than men," Samson said.

Unsure of how to respond to Samson's answer, the young man, who stood about five feet nine inches, looked up at Samson, who stood over six feet, and said, 'You must have been a highly respected person before you were locked up."

"Why do you say that?" Samson asked as he looked at the talkable young gentleman.

"Everyone who comes to see you, mostly servicemen, all have good things to say about you. They also ask me to keep an eye on you. I also noticed something else."

"What have you noticed, young man?" Samson asked with a smile on his face.

"You and the captain who's here to visit you now—Captain Morris is his name—you two don't ever salute when you enter into the visitation room. Why is that?"

Enthused about the young man's questions, Samson said, "He is not just my ranking officer. He's my big brother."

A strange look formed on the young jailer's face.

"Don't look like that. He is not my biological brother. We share the same belief. With us, it goes even deeper than that."

The jailer shifted his head in an up-and-down motion as though he understood Samson.

"Is that why you two hug every time?"

"That's part of it," Samson said.

"Out of all the people who come to visit you, I have only seen one colored man. The way all of them interact with you shows that they have a lot of love and respect for you."

What was usually a short quiet walk to visitation room turned out to be one filled with questions.

"Make sure you have a nice visit," the young jailer said as he stopped at the visitation door.

"Hopefully, I will. Thank you."

"Captain Brandon Norris, as-salamu alaykum [May peace be upon you]," Brother Samson said as he walked into the visitation room.

"Wa alaykumu s-salam [And may peace be upon you]," Captain Mooris said to return Samson's greeting.

"Alhamdulillah [All praise are due to God]. My Muslim brother is still glowing."

"Why shouldn't I be?" Samson asked. "Allah is Akbar [God is great]."

"I know it hurt me to sit there and listen to them pass judgment on you like they did."

"I will be okay, Inshallah [if it's God's will]."

After the two embraced each other, Captain Morris said, "You need to start eating. You have lost a lot of weight."

"Have I?" Samson responded while looking down at himself.

"Oh yes, you have."

"I need to lose a bit myself."

"You have lost more than a little. You are small, brother, so small that I'm beginning to start worrying about you."

"No . . . no . . . no. Brother, don't allow those thoughts to enter your mind. I stress myself sometimes thinking about Shanda and the kids, but other than that, I'm okay. That's my word, brother. Allah is still at the forefront."

"I pray so."

"The stress is there because I don't know if they are alive or dead."

"I thought that she would have called me by now. If she is alive, I know she has seen the news. I have received a lot of calls and messages since I left the courthouse earlier. Come to think of it. I went by your house the other day. Someone had moved in. Come to find out someone sold the house to them."

"Do you think it was Shanda?"

"Who else could have sold it?" the captain asked.

"The people I talked to said that they are renting to own. They didn't know who Shanda was. They went through a real-estate company to get the house."

"That's crazy. Anyway, how's your wife and daughter doing?"

"They are doing pretty good, thank God. I just haven't been able to spend time with them."

"That's nothing new," Samson said. The both of them started laughing.

"You're right. You know that they love you. They were so hurt today after seeing you all over the news they couldn't wait for me to get home to bomb rush me. They have been asking me to bring them down here to see you."

"Why haven't you?" Samson asked.

"I didn't think it was a good idea."

"Man, brother, you know how I feel about them. They are my family, and I would love to see them."

"I will tell you what, brother, I will make sure I bring them down here the next time I come. Is there anything else I can do for you?"

"I need you to pick those books up that I have been asking you for," Samson said.

"I apologize. It really slipped my mind. I know it was something I was supposed to do for you. I just have so much to do. I will make sure I make it my business to get those books for you. Samson, brother, I just need you to stay strong."

"Everything is going to work out for the best. I have my faith in Allah, brother," Samson said.

"I believe that. I'm just letting you know I love you, brother," Captain Morris said.

"I love you too. Make sure you tell Lisa and Fatimah I said I love them. Make sure you have them with you next week."

"I will, brother. You know I got you. Salam [Peace]."

"Salam [peace]. I know," Samson said. The two hugged.

"I hate to leave you in this place."

"I know you do. Inshallah [if it's God's will], I will see you next week."

"Inshallah [if it's God's will], we will be here," Captain Morris said before walking out the door.

Samson walked out behind him. The jailer was right there to escort Samson back to his cell. The jailer wasn't in any rush to get Samson back to his cell.

"How was your visit?" the young jailer asked.

"I enjoyed it."

"How long have you two known each other?"

"For about fifteen years."

"I see that you and he are very close."

Samson smiled. "We are. I thank God for the man every day. He has been a great brother and friend to me. No one could ask for a better person to be a friend. He's the one who introduced me to my wife nearly twelve years ago. I have pictures of her and our two children in the cell. You are more than welcome to see them. You might not like what you see, but you are welcome to see them."

"Why would you say that?"

"My wife is white. Not just that, she's very beautiful. She's five feet nine inches, 135 pounds, with blonde hair and dark-blue eyes. They sometimes turn green."

"When they first moved you into this jail and told me what you were here for, I prejudged you. Over the past eight months, I have had the opportunity to learn a lot from just watching you. You are a human being just like me. I don't know what to call it, but it is something good. Like a good spirit, you have always shown me respect. I'm only twenty-one years old. There is a lot of stuff I still have to learn and most of all learn to deal with. Judging people by the color of their skin is my biggest one. If you don't mind, I would like to see the pictures of your family."

Samson walked into his cell, and the jailer closed the door behind him. Samson reached under the head of his mattress and grabbed the pictures he had under there. Then he turned back around and walked over to the bars where the young jailer was waiting.

"The first picture was taken two years ago," Samson said as he passed them through the bars.

"That's all four of us."

Samson stood there looking to see the expression the young man would show. The jailer smirked and asked Samson, "How old are your children?"

"On that picture, they were nine and six. Now my son Adam is eleven, and my daughter Verlena will be eight this month."

"You have a beautiful family," the young man said as he passed the pictures back. "I apologize for not introducing myself."

"Apology accepted."

"My name is Billy Lee Long. Around here, it's Officer Long. You know how that goes. When we are by ourselves, you can just call me Billy."

"Okay then, Billy, I will do that."

"I have a few hours before I get off. If you don't mind, I would like to pull me up a chair and talk to you."

"No, Billy, I don' mind. Get yourself a chair."

Billy walked down the distance to where he usually sat to keep an eye on Samson and grabbed a chair. Once he was back with the chair, he sat it down in front of Samson's cell.

"Another thing I noticed about you is, you pray a lot. Is that because you are in this trouble?"

"As part of my belief, it is obligatory for everyone who says they believe in God. It's not a religion to my understanding because religion is man-made. I look at it to be a way of life. Are you familiar with Prophet Abraham in the Holy Bible?"

"Not really," Billy said. "I have heard that name."

"Abraham is the father of the three main religions or ways of life. However, one looks at it. He believed in the One True God, the creator of all living things. He is the only one that God called His friend. I said that to say this: Abraham was known as a *hanif*, which means he followed a monotheism way of life. The main three doctrines look up to this man and speak very highly of him. I follow the last and final revelation to all mankind that's known as the Qur'an. The name of my way of life is Islam. Islam in English means *peace*. In the Arabic language, Muslim is one who submits their will to this peace. The only true peace is God. During the time of Moses, God's revelation is what we know of today as being the Old Testament. Jews follow that part of the Bible. Christians follow the teachings of Jesus. That's the New Testament of the Bible. As Muslims, we believe in both of the books, the Old and New Testaments, the way God sent them to Moses and Jesus. The Qur'an is 1,400-plus years old.

Then it was 77,934 words in the Qur'an, and today it's 77,934. It is still in the original language. Like I said, it is the last revelation to all mankind until the return of Jesus. One reason for God to send us this message and revelation through the last Prophet Muhammad is because we as a whole have strayed away from the way of life that God prescribed and sent down to Abraham, Moses, and Jesus. Muhammad was born five hundred years after Jesus. All of them came with one universal message. The LORD GOD is one God. Don't put anyone with Him or before Him. If you believe that and follow the ways of Abraham, Moses, Jesus, or Muhammad, you will receive the promise of God: everlasting life."

"I thought you were a devil worshiper when I first saw you pray. But your actions and the way you carry yourself kept me puzzled. I have only seen good qualities in you, especially after seeing your face and the way the newspaper painted you as an evil person. I realize today that I was wrong," Billy said. "By the way, Mr. Ali, I heard that you were found guilty today."

"I was," Samson said.

"If someone here didn't tell me, I wouldn't have known. Looking at you, you can't tell. You don't act like a person facing the death penalty. I know if I were in your shoes, I might have killed myself before they did."

"Not if you are truly a believer in God and know in your heart that He has a plan for you," Samson said as Billy looked at him.

Billy became speechless.

"I need to make my rounds, Mr. Ali. I will talk to you later."

"Okay, Billy, we will talk later, God's will."

From that day on, Billy couldn't wait to get to work and talk to Samson. Samson started him to reading books that Samson I knew was filled with enlightenment for Billy. He would read them and come to work with input and questions.

CHAPTER 4

The day before sentencing, Attorney Fred Gaines went to the Jackson County Jail to visit Samson. Billy saw Attorney Gaines drive up, so he went to Samson's cell and escorted him to the visitation.

"How are you doing today, Mr. Ali?"

"I'm blessed. How about yourself, Billy?"

"I'm doing pretty good. I stayed up last night reading the book that you had me to get. It was so good that it was hard for me to put it down. I have some questions that I need to ask you after your visit, if you have the time."

"I will always have time for you, Billy."

"Okay, I will see you after your visit."

"Okay," Samson said.

"Have a good one," Billy said.

"Hopefully."

Samson went into the visitation room and waited for Attorney Gaines to come in. Attorney Gaines walked into the visitation room unaware of Samson's presence and was jarred.

"How long have you been in here?" Attorney Gaines asked.

"A minute or two at the most. My friend saw you drive up, so he went ahead and brought me in here."

"You win the hearts of people everywhere you go, huh?"

"It's not me. It's the Lord I serve," Samson said.

"As you know, we have a big day tomorrow. I would like for us to rehearse the things we are going to cover. I have interviewed all your service brothers. I'm only going to have a few of them to get up on the stand."

"Who do you have in mind?" Samson asked.

"I really don't have anyone in mind but Captain Morris right now. All of them are good. I interviewed at least fifty of them. If we were to put all of them on the stand, it would take all year for us to hear all the good things that they have to say about you."

"Inshallah [God's will], all of them will be there tomorrow, but I don't think it would help if we put one or all of them up there. Those people don't care. Their minds are already made up."

"You may be right. I can say this much. One thing I think will help is having someone from your family here."

"I could have my sister to come down, but I really don't want to send her through it."

"Whatever happens, Mr. Ali, just remember that you will always have a friend."

"Likewise, Mr. Gaines. Oh yeah, have you started working on the motion for a new trial?"

"Not yet. I was waiting until after your sentencing."

"After it is filed, how long will it take before I get back in court?"

"If a new trial is granted, it will take at least two years. I'm going to be in contact with you every step of the way."

"Mr. Gaines, do you take me to be an ignorant man?"

"No! Absolutely not. Where did that come from?" Attorney Gaines asked with an imprudent look on his face.

"You don't have to look like that. I realized that you are a traveling man a long time ago, so you can get that look off your face," Samson said with a little laughter.

"What makes it so noticeable?"

"I started noticing it in trial. After that, I kept my eyes on you, watching all your body movements. I pretty much know how the court system functions. It's mostly run by Masonics and Eastern Stars. The Klan runs Teller County. Your actions showed me that I wasn't just up against the judge and the DA. I have a whole town to fight against. I was able to see it once you figured out that I was the real victim and a man of God. You told me in so many words that you had done all you could do. You and the judge don't see eye to eye."

Attorney Gaines just nodded to what Samson was saying.

"Also, I saw you try to get the DA to ease up. He didn't understand your signs because he isn't a man of the light. Am I correct?" Samson asked.

With a smile on his face, Attorney Gaines didn't say a word.

"It's true. I know that you can't talk about it. I know that signs and symbols are for the conscious mind. When you came through the door of the visitation room when the FBI was here, I saw your hand and body movements. Both of those men are Masons. I'm a traveling man myself. I have come out of darkness into the light. I know all about Ruth, Boaz, and Tubal-Cain. Believe it or not, I am haram in the flesh. I know what the West is like. That's why I'm headed East where there is knowledge, wisdom, and understanding. One day I will know all about being a master builder. The knowledge and wisdom I have now give me the ability to understand myself and others. That's why I said I know what type of people that we are dealing with. What are you, a thirty-two or thirty-three?" Samson asked.

Attorney Gaines just looked at Samson.

"Since you won't tell me what you are riding on, I'm going to move on. Before I do so, I want you to know that the Qur'an is sufficient enough for what I am trying to achieve. That's paradise. I still would like to knock that door down for the worldly knowledge that's behind it. Keep in mind the only difference between you and I is my knowledge is free and you are paying for yours. God's will, the price don't be your soul."

"You know more than I thought you knew. That's all I want to say about that subject. So, Samson, what do you think about the jury?"

"I know we don't have a chance with the men."

"You're right. It's a toss-up. I hope that the DA doesn't put fear into the females and cause them to go against their hearts."

"Mr. Gaines, all we can do is pray for the best and look for the worst."

"That's a good way to look at it. We are fighting for your life. So let's go up in the devil's bedroom swinging. I have a couple knock-out punches. What about you?"

"God has the last say-so in my life. So we just have to play their game. Mr. Gaines, let's go in there and enjoy ourselves."

"That sounds good enough to me. We can do that."

"I'm going to wear my uniform with all my metals on it. Also, I'm going to make sure all the other brothers wear theirs as well. I want you to keep in mind, Mr. Gaines, they can't do nothing to me. So never allow failure to overcome you at any time in the courtroom. You must overcome it. Likewise, your mind must never conceive failure at anything you do. It all boils down to morality. Don't let the thought of me getting the death penalty overcome your newfound sense of true ethics. You have faith in God, right?"

"Yes, I do," Attorney Gaines said.

"Once we realize that we came from God and to Him we will return, we truly understand that concept. We no longer place a value on the life of this world. Jesus said it best in the Bible. He said, 'We can't love this world. If we do, we will cling on to it. When God calls for us, we won't be ready. The lovers of this world don't look forward to the hereafter, and there will not be any room for them in it.' As people, Mr. Gaines, we live as though there is no hereafter. Jesus also said, 'The world hates me because I am not of it.' That's how I feel, Mr. Gaines. We know the difference between right and wrong. That's something we were born with. I know that you have experienced the feeling of being watched after doing something wrong or when you did something your parents told you not to do. That guilt after doing wrong messed with your conscious. You knew no one saw you, but you still looked over your shoulders. The problem we are faced with is those people have developed habits and beliefs that have taken the place of their morality. They no longer adhere to the words of God."

"Changing habits and beliefs isn't an easy task, Samson."

"That's true, but you must know in your heart and want to confront your personality if you want to change. Knowing God gives you and me the upper hand on them. They have it in their hearts to kill me. If they could do it with their hands, tomorrow they would. They no longer look over their shoulders because they have built up a scab over their hearts. Doing wrong doesn't affect them anymore."

"That may be correct. I know that Officer Fuhrman doesn't show any remorse," Attorney Gaines said.

"The sad thing about this Mr. Gaines is they weren't born that way. Those are learned behaviors. Do you know that Satan was the first racist?"

"I have read that," Attorney Gaines said.

"The story that I am talking about is in the Qur'an surah 7:11–12. 'It is we who created you and gave you shape. Then we made the angels bow down to Adam, and they bowed down, not so Iblis [Satan]. He refused to be of those who bow down.' Allah said, 'What prevented you from bowing when I commanded you?' Satan said, 'I am better than he. You created me from fire and him from clay.' That makes them no better than Satan. That's why I like the saying 'If God guides you, no one can misguide you.' And if He allows you to go astray, surely there is no one that can guide you."

"I believe that," Attorney Gaines said.

"Mr. Gaines, I just want you to go in that courtroom and have fun, doing what you like to do."

"Samson, I thank you for those words of encouragement. I'm going to need them."

"You're welcome. Trust me, everything is going to be okay, God willing."

"By the way, has anyone heard anything from your wife and children?"

"No, not so far. My sister said that she thinks they are over my brother's house. I truly doubt that."

"Why do you doubt it?" Attorney Gaines asked.

"She knows how I feel about him and them being around him. He wasn't allowed in my home or anywhere near it."

"It wouldn't hurt for you to check it out."

"I am. I'm going to see if I can contact someone with that area and see if I can get them to go by there."

"I know that she has been watching TV or reading newspapers. You think we can count on her to pop up like what happens in movies?" Attorney Gaines asked.

"That would truly be a blessing. You know it only happens in movies, people popping up to save the day at the last minute," Samson said.

"Have you talked to her parents?"

"No, I don't know the number."

"I think we have covered everything that needed to be covered. Anything else you can think of, Mr. Ali?"

Samson thought to himself for a minute before speaking. "Yes, I need a little enlightenment, my brother," Samson asked in a joking but serious way.

Attorney Gaines caught on quickly to what Samson was asking him.

"I need to enhance my knowledge," Samson added.

Attorney Gaines smiled and said, "No."

"Well, since you won't come clean and share some of that Masonry knowledge, I'm going to share something with you, and it's free."

"I wonder what it may be," Attorney Gaines asked.

"It will help you more than anything you could imagine. Before starting your day or anything else, say, 'In the name of God.' Do you think you can do that?" Samson asked.

"Sir, yes, sir!" Attorney Gaines said, raising his right hand up to his head, saluting Samson. They both busted out laughing.

"I needed that. We have a big day tomorrow. Before I can go home,

I have some running around to do. Hopefully, I will be able to get me a good night of sleep once I am finished."

"I have a thought for the day that I am going to leave you with: 'Prayer is better than sleep.'"

"Why is that so?" Attorney Gaines asked.

"Sleep rejuvenates the body. Prayer rejuvenates the soul," said Samson.

"I agree. But right now I need some sleep. That's why when I am finished with this running around I have to do, I am going home to take a shower, pray, and go to sleep."

"So, God's will, I will see you tomorrow morning," Samson said.

The two shook hands, and Attorney Gaines left. Billy was standing there waiting for Samson to finish his visit. Billy had a lot he wanted to talk about and was very anxious to do so.

"Tell me something good, Billy," Samson requested.

"God is good for sure. I finished the book *What the World Owes Islam*. I didn't know that one man could have an effect on the whole world. It talked about how Muhammad, one man, and a handful of followers changed the whole world. That gave me a lot to think about. It makes me want to learn more about this man Muhammad. Do you have any more books that I can get that will teach me more?" Billy asked.

"Sure," Samson said. "I will write down the names of a few books for you. Stop by before you go home, and I will have a list of books for you."

"Okay, thanks," Billy said as he closed Samson's cell door and turned the key to lock it.

Samson smiled as Billy turned to walk away and gave thanks to God, *All praise are due to you, Lord. Please keep guiding the young brother Billy to a path straight. I thank you for allowing me to be a light you use to attract those whom you have opened their minds and hearts to your words. There is nothing worthy of being praised but You. Amen.*

CHAPTER 5

Time passed fast. Transport was at Samson's cell to escort him to the Teller County Courthouse for sentencing. Since it was Samson's sentencing hearing and he was facing the death penalty, two transporting officers were needed. They searched him before putting shackles on his legs and handcuffed him. The three went for their ride. Within minutes they arrived at the Teller County Courthouse.

"All, stand. The Honorable Judge Turner is presiding," the bailiff said.

Everyone stood to their feet as the judge walked up and took a seat. The judge looked over at his clerk and spoke, "Someone brief me on what we have scheduled today."

The clerk stood up and passed the judge Samson Ali's file.

"Samson Ali is scheduled for sentencing hearing," the clerk stated.

The judge took a quick look into Samson's file. Then he looked up and said, 'Okay . . . are the people of the court ready to proceed?'

"Yes, sir, Your Honor, we are," the district attorney Hernzberg said.

"What about you, Mr. Gaines? Are you ready?"

Just before Attorney Gaines could reply, twenty uniformed naval officers walked through the courtroom doors.

Mr. Gaines took a deep breath, holding it for a second before blowing it out. He then leaned over toward Samson.

"I thought that they were going to be a no-show."

"Faith, Mr. Gaines, you must have faith. God is the greatest," Samson said.

"For the courts records, I want to go over the rules of sentencing proceedings as is set by law," said the judge before moving on.

"The stages of the sentencing hearing are divided into three parts. First, the district attorney for the people will present to the court why he or she thinks that the defendant or defendants found guilty should receive the maximum penalty allowed by law for the crime or crimes they have been convicted of. The second part of the hearing gives the attorney or attorneys for the defendant the opportunity to try to convince the court to give the minimal penalty allowed by law. The third part of the hearing is given to the jury. After hearing both sides and their witnesses, the jury could request the maximum or the minimal to be given. I, as the presiding judge, may choose to agree or disagree with the jury's request. I will make my judgment after carefully looking at the facts and circumstances in the case. Also, taking great consideration to see what is best for the people and the victims. With that said, Mr. Hernzberg, are you ready to proceed?"

"Yes, Your Honor, I am."

"You may proceed," the judge said.

District Attorney Hernzberg looked down at his notes as he prepared to get started. "Ladies and gentlemen of the jury, this is a case that carries the maximum penalty of death. I am recommending the maximum penalty for the great people of this state and town. I am asking that you all recommend the maximum penalty of death on behalf of the deceased Mike McClain and his family. I would like to call Mrs. Betty McClain, the wife of the deceased officer, to the stand."

Mrs. Betty McClain stood up with her three-year-old son Jimmy McClain, who was sitting on her lap. She sat her son in the spot where she was sitting and walked up to the stand.

"Mrs. McClain, will you please raise your right hand? Do you swear to tell the truth and nothing but the truth so help you God?" the bailiff asked as she stood there.

"I do."

"You may be seated, Mrs. McClain, and for the record, will you please state your full name?" the judge asked.

"My name is Betty Ann McClain."

"Thank you. Mr. Hernzberg, you may proceed."

"Thank you, Your Honor. Mrs. McClain, will you please inform the court of your relation to the deceased officer Mike McClain?"

"He was my husband."

"How long were you two married?"

"Twelve years," she said.

"Out of the twelve years you two spent together, I am sure you and your deceased husband had children together after twelve years."

"We do! We have four."

"What are their ages?"

"Eleven, nine, seven, and three."

"Which of them do you have here with you today?"

"That's Jimmy, our three-year-old," she said as she pointed at the young child seated on the front row in the courtroom.

"Mrs. McClain, since the murder of your husband, how have things been at home for you and your four children?"

"It has been very hard for me as well as the children. I don't have the support or help that's needed to raise three boys, not to speak of our daughter. There's no way I could fill in for their father. I can't teach the boys how to be men or show them how to do manly things. I don't even know how to talk to them about the death of their father and all the stuff that's surrounding it. It's just hard for us as a whole."

"Mrs. McClain, what do you think should happen to the one responsible for the death of your husband?"

"I think that he should meet the same fate that my husband did."

"What do you mean by that, Mrs. McClain?

"He should be put to death."

"Thank you, Mrs. McClain. No more questions."

"Mr. Gaines, would you like to cross-examine Mrs. McClain?"

"Yes, sir, I would, Your Honor."

Attorney Gaines stood up and walked over nearby Mrs. McClain while she sat on the stand with her legs crossed.

"Mrs. McClain, you stated that you and Officer Mike McClain were married for twelve years. Am I correct?"

"Yes, you are."

"Out of the twelve years you were married, have you ever questioned your husband's fidelity?"

"Objection, Your Honor. That question is irrelevant to this hearing," the district attorney said as he jumped to his feet, looking up at the judge.

"Your Honor, that question gives the court as well as the jury some insight into what kind of person Officer McClain was," said Attorney Gaines.

"Objection, overruled. Get to the point, Mr. Gaines."

"Yes, sir, Your Honor. Mrs. McClain, will you please answer the question?"

"Yes . . . yes, I have," she said as she looked downward.

"Were you right or wrong about it?"

"Well . . . I was right."

"Are you saying that your husband had an affair?"

"Yes . . . that's correct."

"Mrs. McClain, how did you find out your husband was having an affair?"

"I got a letter out of the mailbox addressed from the Welfare Department for him, and I opened it."

"What did it say?"

"Objection, Your Honor, that's personal." District Attorney Hernzberg said as he stood up in the court with both of his hands outstretched.

"Your Honor, that's a part of the original question."

"Objection overruled. Answer the question Mrs. McClain," the judge said.

"The letter was to let him know that he had to be at the juvenile court to determine if the child in question was his or not."

"Was the child your husband's?"

"Yes, it was his child."

"Was that the only time you found out that your husband had been unfaithful to you?"

"No, sir, it wasn't."

"Moving on, Mrs. McClain, do you believe that there is a God?" Mr. Gaines asked as he turned to look over at the district attorney. Mr. Hernzberg rolled his eyes as he turned his head the other way.

"Yes, I do."

"Do you go to church?"

"Yes, I do."

"What's your religious preference?"

"I'm a Christian, Baptist Christian."

"Do you follow the Holy Bible?"

"Yes, I do."

"The Holy Bible says that we must forgive to be forgiven and revenge belongs to the Lord. Have you read that in it?"

"Yes, I have."

"Do you believe that?"

"I do."

"Mrs. McClain, are you prejudiced?"

"Objection, Your Honor, that's very personal. Mrs. McClain shouldn't have to answer outlandish questions," the district attorney argued.

"Mr. Gaines, rephrase that question," the judge said.

"Mrs. McClain, how do you feel about black people?"

"Objection, Your Honor, that question is inappropriate, and Mrs. McClain shouldn't have to answer such personal questions," the DA said.

"Mr. Gaines, Don't ask any more questions of that nature," the judge said.

"Okay, Your Honor. Mrs. McClain, you said that you believe in God and you are a Baptist Christian. Am I correct?"

"Yes, you are."

"You are seeking for the death penalty for the person who the district attorney Hernzberg says murdered your husband. Am I correct?"

"Yes, sir, you are."

"I take it that you live a Christ-like life?"

"I try to, to my best ability."

"After thinking about what the Bible says about revenge and forgiveness, do you still think that a man should be sentenced to death by men and that it is righteous to do so?"

Mrs. McClain looked around the courtroom and remained speechless as she held her head down in her right hand.

"Answer the question, Mrs. McClain," the judge said after a few minutes of silence.

"No . . . no, I don't," she said with tears in her eyes.

"No further questions, Your Honor."

"Mrs. McClain, you may step down. Mr. Hernzberg, you may call your next witness to the stand."

"Your Honor, I would like to call Mr. James McClain to the stand," said Mr. Hernzberg.

Before James McClain stepped up to the stand, the bailiff stopped him.

"Excuse me, sir, will you please raise your right hand? Do you swear to tell the truth, the whole truth, and nothing but the truth so help you God?"

"I do."

"You may be seated. For the record, please state your name," the judge asked.

"James McClain," he said as he leaned forward to the microphone.

"Mr. McClain, what's your relation to the deceased officer Mike McClain?"

"He was my son."

"When was the last time you saw your son alive?"

"About eight o'clock in the morning on the day he was killed."

"How would you describe the relationship that you had with your son?"

"My boy and I were very close. We always did things that a father and son were supposed to do together. Mike was a loving person. He was a people's person. He always tried to help others, make people laugh, and he was a fun person to be around."

"How did the murder of your son affect you and your family?"

"It tore us apart. My wife, his mother, wasn't able to come here today to speak out about Mike's death. None of us have healed or recuperated from what that fucking nigger did to my boy."

"Objection, Your Honor. Your Honor, that's very inappropriate and disrespectful language in a court of law and to my client," Attorney Gaines said.

"Mr. McClain, please refrain from using that kind of language in my court. You may continue, Mr. Hernzberg."

"Mr. McClain, what do you think should happen to the person who murdered your son?"

Mr. McClain sat up in his seat and looked at Mr. Hernzberg as he prepared to answer the question.

"That fucking coon should be beaten and hanged."

The people in the courtroom began shouting, "Kill that nigger!" Unable to hear Mr. Gaines's objections, the judge called for order in the court.

"Order . . . order . . . order in this court," he said as he hit the gavel down repeatedly.

Once the judge brought order back to the courtroom, he spoke, "Any more outbursts like that and I'm going to ask you all to leave my courtroom. Where were we before this interruption?" the judge said, trying to overlook the language used by James McClain that started the outbursts.

"Your Honor, I objected to the language that Mr. McClain used, which is what caused that racist interruption," Attorney Gaines said as he looked at Samson and nodded.

"Mr. McClain, one more use of that type of language, and you will be asked to remove yourself from my courtroom. Am I understood?"

"Sure, I understand you, Bobby. Excuse me, I mean, Your Honor."

"You may continue, Mr. Hernzberg," said the judge.

"Thank you, Your Honor. With the use of one word, Mr. McClain, do you believe that the murderer of your son should receive the death penalty?"

"Yes."

"That's all, Your Honor. No more questions."

"Mr. Gaines, do you have any questions for Mr. McClain?" the judge asked.

"Yes, I do, Your Honor."

"Attorney Gaines leaned close to Samson and whispered in his ear, "Watch this."

As Attorney Gaines stood up, he cleared his throat and cross-examined Mr. McClain, "Mr. McClain, have you ever lived around blacks?"

"No and won't ever if I can help it," Mr. McClain said.

"When you found out that your son was killed by a black man, what was your reaction?"

"Objection, Your Honor. Mr. McClain's feelings shouldn't have anything to do with this sentencing hearing. That's his personal right, and he should be entitled to it."

"Your Honor, the court, as well as the jury, should know why the family of Officer McClain wants the maximum penalty to be given to Mr. Ali."

"Answer the question, Mr. McClain, and remember what I said about your language."

"I wanted to kill every colored SOB that I saw."

"Why would you want to kill every black person that you saw?"

"Because they shouldn't be here."

"Mr. McClain, where should they be?" Attorney Gaines asked.

"I'm no fool. I see what you are trying to do," Mr. McClain said as he looked around the courtroom. "Mr. Gaines, that's your name, right?"

"Yes, it is," Attorney Gaines answered.

"You know, if you play with a puppy, it will lick you in your mouth."

"No further questions," Attorney Gaines said with a smile.

"You may step down Mr. McClain," the judge said.

As he walked from the stand, he threw Mr. Gaines a birdie and said a very low "Fuck you, you motherfucking trader.'

"Mr. Hernzberg, do you have any more people you would like to take the stand?" the judge asked.

"I do, Your Honor, but I don't think it would be wise."

"That's your choice and a good one, Mr. Hernzberg."

"With that, Your Honor, the state rests."

"Mr. Gaines, it's your turn. Would you like to call anyone to the stand?" the judge asked.

"Yes, sir, Your Honor. Your Honor, before I call anyone, I would like to address the jury."

"Your request is granted."

"Thank you, Your Honor. Ladies and gentlemen of the jury," Attorney Gaines said as he walked toward the jury box, "I would like for you all to take a look around you. You can't help but notice that there's only one black face in here. It might just be me and my way of thinking, but something is wrong with this picture. I felt the same way you do before I got to know my client as a person. I looked at him as though he was the enemy. Not because we had crossed paths and something happened between us but because he was the opposite color. It didn't stop there. I had hatred in my heart for a man I never knew existed. After I got to know Mr. Ali, I saw that we have a lot in common. I saw that he loves this country and is willing to die for it, a country said to be 'the land of the free.' Inside it's engulfed with hatred. This man has a family he hasn't seen since the night of October 31, 1979. Pictures are the only thing he has to remind himself of them."

Mr. Gaines spoke as he was reaching into his inside-suit coat pocket to get the pictures of Samson and his family. Slowly, one by one, Attorney Gaines passed the jury the four pictures Samson had given him of his family. Attorney Gaines gave the picture to the foreman seated on the far-right-hand corner on the first row of the jury box.

"This man is a true believer in God. He has served this country for over fifteen years. He fought in the Vietnam War. After he served our country in the Vietnam War, he kept on his uniform all the way up until the day he was arrested just because some people within this country, for which he has placed his life on the line to make safe as a whole, has prejudged him and hated him because of the color of his skin. Don't mean we all do. So don't think for one second that he is alone. A lot of white men in the courtroom love him, and don't look down on him because of the color of his skin. Today I am happy to say that I am one of them. Just because the dictionary says that black is wicked, bad, or evil and white is right, pure, and good doesn't mean it's true as far as people are concerned. I ask that you don't pass judgment on Mr. Ali simply because of the color of his skin. He once told me that the truth will knock the brains out of falsehood, and God didn't make us different colors and tribes to hate one another but to learn from one another. Godly people make righteous choices. Just as God has His believers, Satan also has his. Who do you follow?"

Samson smiled, giving his approval, and said to himself, *Alhamdulillah [All praises are due to God]*.

"Your Honor, I would like to call Sgt. Bernard Scott to the stand."

The six-foot-two-inch nicely built white male who looked younger than he was stood up and slid past the other servicemen who sat beside him on the bench. With his hat under his left arm, the young-looking man was sworn in before he respectfully took the stand.

"Will you please state your full name for the court records?" the judge asked.

"My name is Bernard Scott."

"Thank you, young man," the judge said.

Sitting in his uniform, with his back straight, he looked out into the courtroom.

"Mr. Scott, what is your occupation?"

"I am a sergeant in the naval air station of Memphis. It is a navy base."

"How long have you been serving our beautiful country?" Attorney Gaines asked.

"It will be nine years next month."

"Sergeant Scott, do you know Samson Ali?"

"Yes, I do."

"How did you get to know him?"

"He is my lieutenant."

"Did you know him before he became your lieutenant?"

"No, not really."

"What do you mean by that?"

"I didn't actually know him personally. I just heard good things about him through mutual friends."

"How long have you known him personally?"

"Over six years."

"Over six years, I would say that's long enough time to get to know someone. Would you agree?"

"Yes, sir, I agree."

"Do you see Mr. Ali as a friend?"

"Yes, I do, a close friend."

"What kind of friendship would you say you have with Mr. Ali?"

"I don't look at him as just a friend. I see him as my big brother."

"How did it make you feel when you found out about his arrest?"

"When I found out that he was charged with murder, I felt a feeling that I can't truly explain with words. I said to myself that someone had to have crossed the line."

"Why do you say that?" Attorney Gaines asked.

"The Samson Ali that I know isn't going to just up and kill someone without a just reason. After I talked to him, I knew then that the story told by the news was untrue."

"Why would you believe Samson's story over the news reporter?"

"This is a man I was around every day, not just on the base. Most of the other brothers that you see in court and I—we pray together and hang out together pretty much every day. It's like we are family. We are so close that when I am not over at his house, he's over at mine. You know when a parent can feel and know when their child has done something wrong by the way they act? The same goes for close siblings or when one brother knows the other brother. That's how we are. Just that close."

"Do you think Samson Ali committed the murder unjustifiably?"

"Objection, Your Honor, the jury has already found Mr. Ali guilty," District Attorney Hernzberg said.

"Your Honor, Sergeant Scott is entitled to his opinion."

"You may answer the question, Sergeant," the judge said.

"Thank you, Your Honor. I believe that the two officers didn't like the fact that a black man was in the car with a white woman and wanted to do something about it."

"Do you think he should receive the death penalty?"

"Hell no, I don't think that. I don't think he should be locked up," he said in a choked voice with tears in his eyes.

"Thank you, Sergeant Scott. Your Honor, that will be all."

"Mr. Hernzberg, would you like to ask Sergeant Scott any questions?"

"Yes, sir, Your Honor," Mr. Hernzberg said as he stood up.

"Sergeant Scott, do you think you can really get to know a person within six years?"

"Yes, I do."

"So you are saying that you know everything about him?"

"What's that? Some kind of trick question?" Sergeant Scott asked.

"No, no, no, not at all. Let me put it like this, Sergeant Scott. Do you really think you know everything about Mr. Ali?"

"No, I don't, and I didn't say I knew everything about him. What I said was I pretty much know what he will or will not do."

"No more questions, Your Honor."

"You may step down, Sergeant. Mr. Gaines, do you have anyone else you would like to call?" the judge asked.

"Your Honor, the next person I would like to call to the stand is Captain Brandon Morris," Attorney Gaines said with a big smile on his face.

A noticeable face that the judge and other people in the court had become aware of walked up to the stand.

"Do you swear to tell the truth and nothing but the truth so help you God?" the bailiff said.

"I affirm," Captain Morris said.

"You may be seated. Will you please state your full name and occupation?"

"My name is Brandon Lee Morris. I am a captain of the naval air station of Memphis."

"Captain Morris, how long have you been in active service?"

"Sixteen years."

"Do you know Samson Ali?"

"Yes, sir, very much so."

"Do you know him just because he serves this country with you?"

"We met during the Vietnam War, but how we got to know each other goes deeper than that."

"Will you please share that with us? Maybe that will give all of us a better understanding of who Samson Ali is."

"After we returned from Vietnam, we started traveling the world together in our earlier years of the navy. He saved my life numerous of times, and he was there for me when my family wasn't. I had no family that I could call or write, and he only had his sister Tiltyla. We bonded and became family. Not just that, about fourteen years ago, we saw something that changed the both of our lives to this very day. We accepted Islam and became believers in the one and only true God, the creator of all things. We became closer than siblings. Our faith and views are the same. I love that man with all my heart. He's one man I will lay down my life for," Captain Morris said as he pointed his finger at Samson. "I could go on and on saying many good things about him. I trust that man with my life. I'm the one who introduced him to his wife, the white lady you all see on the pictures. I paid for the whole wedding ceremony. Never once have I regretted it. I am no different than you all. I was raised to hate and look at blacks as being less than whites. That man helped change my thinking.

All praises are due to God. Today I can say that I love that man. I love him more than I love my blood brother. A good thing about it is I know he feels the same about me. I am proud to be the godfather of his two children, who call me their uncle. It hurts to go down to the Jackson County Jail and leave without him. There hasn't been a day that goes by that I don't cry and pray for him. I have to cry for him because he is too strong in his belief to do so. The first time since Samson has been locked up, he allowed tears to fall from his eyes. I know what's up with you, people," Captain Morris said as he leaned back and crossed his arms. "It's not about what happened that's giving you all the incentive to want to kill him. It is because of the color of his skin. This is something that's orchestrated by that devil sitting over there," Captain Morris said as he uncrossed his arms and pointed his finger at Officer George Fuhrman.

Officer Fuhrman smiled and rubbed his forehead with his middle right-hand finger.

"All of you can take these words to the bank. He will prevail over anything you people try to do to him. His faith lies in the hands of Allah, who has the last say-so," Captain Morris said as he raised up and stepped down and looked over at George Fuhrman and returned his smile.

Mr. Hernzberg stood up.

"Your Honor, I would like to question Captain Morris."

As Captain Morris walked past Mr. Hernzberg, he very calmly stated, "Mr. Hernzberg, I am not going to allow you to insult me today."

"No need, Your Honor," Mr. Hernzberg said as he sat back down.

"Mr. Gaines, do you have anyone else you would like to take the stand?" the judge asked.

Attorney Gaines looked over at Samson for his approval, and Samson shook his head with very little motion.

"No, sir, Your Honor."

"At this time, this court is going to take a thirty-minute recess to allow the jury time enough to decide and make a recommendation in this matter."

"All, stand. This court is in recess for thirty minutes," the bailiff said as the people stood to their feet.

Attorney Gaines looked over at Samson and said, "God has put some true friends in your life. I am going to see if the bailiff will allow them to come up here and talk to you for a few minutes."

After getting the okay from the bailiff, all twenty men walked up one at a time to embrace Samson. Everyone in the courtroom was looking and trying to listen in to hear what they were talking about. They didn't say one word about the task that Samson had before him. They joked, smiled, and laughed the whole thirty-minute recess.

"All, stand. This court is now back in session," the bailiff said as the judge walked in.

"Bailiff, will you please escort the jury back in?" the judge said.

After the jury returned, the judge continued to speak, this time directing his attention to the members of the jury.

"Have you all come up with a recommendation?"

"Yes, sir, Your Honor we have," the foreman of the jury said as he stood to his feet.

Attorney Gaines tapped Samson on his left leg with his right hand. "Look," he said to Samson. "Look at those two female jurors on the end and the one in the middle on the second row. Both of them have their heads down."

"They look as if they have been crying. Is that what it looks like to you?" Samson asked Attorney Gaines.

"Sure . . . sure, it does," said Attorney Gaines.

After the judge received the recommendation that the foreman had given to the bailiff, he looked it over with his hand over his mouth as he paused for a moment.

"I have been left with no other choice but to rule in this matter. The circumstances surrounding the murder of Officer McClain and the attempted murder of Officer Fuhrman are by quite substantial. I have not seen anything throughout the phase of the case to show me why the defendant Samson Ali should receive the minimum sentence for the crime he has been found guilty of. I have no choice but to sentence the defendant Samson Ali to death. Wherefore, the defendant will be transferred to the Tennessee Department of Corrections where he will stay until the sentence of death is carried out," the judge stated as he hit his gavel on the desk, ending the proceedings.

"All praise are due to Allah," Samson said.

"This court is adjourned," said the judge.

"All, rise. This court is adjourned," said the bailiff.

Samson's and Attorney Gaines's eyes met as Attorney Gaines checked to see Samson's reaction. Samson stood strong; he didn't look down or blink his eyes.

"We have a lot of good grounds to come back on. They violated your rights from the beginning when this whole ordeal started. I will get you back on the *Miranda v. Arizona* and on *Keenan v. United States*," Attorney Gaines said.

"God is the best of planners. He knows what is best," Samson said.

CHAPTER 6

Seven years later.

"Today is Monday, December 4, 1987. It is now nine o'clock. I would like to bring this morning group to order."

"Thank you!" the group said with a loud and united sound.

"My name is Stacy Lee, and I am the facilitator of this meeting. Let us start it off with a moment of silence for the sick and suffering addicts in and out these institutions, followed by the Serenity Prayer for those who care to join. All together!" Stacy said.

"God, grant us the serenity to accept the things that we cannot change, and the courage to change the things we can, and the wisdom to know the difference. Amen."

"Once again, my name is Stacy Lee. I would like to take this time out to acknowledge any new brothers and sisters who have entered the program. So if you are new in this program and have not introduced yourself, will you please stand and give your first name and drug of choice?"

"Hi, my name is Shanda, and my drug of choice is crack cocaine."

"Welcome to the program," the group said all at once.

"Shanda, we would like to welcome you to the Faithway Drug and Alcohol Program. We hope that you get the help here that you are searching for," Stacy said as she stood in front of the classroom of people with a smile.

"Thank you," Shanda said.

"We need a volunteer to read the daily schedule. All hands must go up."

Stacy looked over the classroom of about fifty people and chose a middle-aged black woman sitting midway down the third row of chairs.

"Joyce," Stacy said.

"Good morning. My name is Joyce, and I am an addict."

"Hi, Joyce!" the group said.

"The FDAP schedule for Monday through Friday: 6:00 a.m., wake up;

7:00 a.m., unit cleanup; 7:30–8:30 a.m., breakfast; 8:30–9:30 a.m., news hour; 9:45–10:45 a.m., morning meeting; 11:00–11:45 a.m., time to read; 11:45–1:00 p.m., lunch. Throughout the rest of the day, we have relapse prevention groups: AA, CA, and NA groups. From 7:00 p.m. to 10:00 p.m. is free time. By 10:00 p.m., lights out, bedtime, no exceptions."

"Thank you, Joyce," the group said.

"Marino, will you be kind enough to read the daily meditation for this day?" Stacy requested.

As he stood up to receive the daily meditation book from Stacy, he announced his name, "Hi, my name is Marino, and I am a cocaine addict."

"Hi, Marino," the group said.

"I will be reading from *Faith and Focus* for December 4. Taking action. As an addict, we must put forward actions by taking the message to addicts still trying to stay sober. Their internal hopes will help us to stay clean and keep us focused on Him that gives us strength. Thank you."

"Marino, what did you get out of that spectacular reading?" Stacy asked.

"What I got out of it is—first of all, today is my birthday and I read it this morning—if we desperately want to live and succeed, we have to become more active in this God-given program. This program and suggested steps must become a part of our everyday lives. We must work it one day at a time. When we work this program in with the twelve steps of AA, we will accomplish something. Also, what I get out of it is, God has given us a second chance to allow us to see where we have come from. Thank you, all."

"Thank you, brother," the group said.

"Once again, brothers and sisters, my name is Stacy. Let's wish the brother a happy birthday on the count of three—one, two, three."

"Happy birthday!" they said all together.

Stacy said, "The first thing about an addiction is you must admit that you have one and that you have become imprisoned by it. You may not be able to look around this room and see a bar or dopehouse. Like in your drug addiction, you are not able to see the barbed-wire fence, armed guards, and lots of people watching you while you watch them. There are other kinds of prisons too. We have walls, bars, and fences. Some people are imprisoned by their spouses, their jobs, bills, poverty, racism, peer pressure, or lifestyles. The list goes on and on. It's about fifty of us in this room who at one time or another were imprisoned by the desire for drugs or alcohol—some of us both. The addiction that we have has become bad for us at one time or another. It took away our wants and desires for good and healthy things. It enslaved us. The cruelest thing about it is, it forces us to devote most of our time and energy trying to fulfill the desire for it. The problem about that is it can't ever be fulfilled. There is never enough, and we always want or need more. It's like we were chasing King Kong, really thinking that we could chase him by ourselves. It's at that point that you really need help. We want help, but we are caught up so far into chasing. This is when insanity has set in. One definition for insanity is to keep doing the same thing and expecting different results. With that thinking, we no longer can make healthy choices. Now, with the help we so need, we can choose a general direction, not a direction that someone else has chosen for us. There are choices we must make if we want betterment in our life. We won't be being selfish. We will move up to the standard of life that God wants us to live. When we know that we are making healthy choices, we do what is necessary to be happy in life. Don't raise your hands unless you want to," Stacy said before asking the question.

"Who in this room was okay or happy with your life before coming to Faithway?" No one raised their hand, so she asked another question, "Who is happy with their life today?"

Tears started running down Shanda's face as she held her head down near her lap. "You all take a break," Stacy said to the group. "Shanda, do you need someone to talk to?" Stacy continued.

In a hurting voice, Shanda spoke, "I . . . I'm okay."

"I know how you feel. I have been there. This is the place where you can gain the strength that you need. Dry your eyes and come take a walk with me," Stacy said.

Shanda got up, and they both walked out the door. Stacy walked Shanda out the back door to an open yard filled with trees and fresh air. The two walked around the track as Stacy talked, "It's obvious you are now looking at your life. The thing about that is, now you have to get up and dust yourself off. That's something that happens automatically as a result of your assessment for a very simple reason. For once in a long time, your self-assessment made you quite aware of everything in your life. It probably made you focus on the pain that you caused yourself and the hurt you inflicted on others from your choices. It also made you look at the problems your addiction caused. I can see from looking at you that your injuries are mostly self-inflicted from the way you have been living your life. Shanda, this is a one-year program. Use all the tools it offers. If you need me for anything, don't be afraid to pull me to the side, okay?"

"Okay, thank you, Stacy. I needed those words of wisdom."

"You are welcome, but remember what I said about using this program to the fullest, Shanda. It will definitely help you."

"I will. Oh yes, Stacy, I don't have any family here in Memphis. I need to write my children to let them know where I am."

"Where are they, if you don't mind me asking?"

"They are living with my sister-in-law in Colorado Springs, Colorado."

"I was raised there," Stacy said with a big smile on her face.

"Get out of here. Were you really?"

"Really, I have only been here in Memphis for about five years."

"I can tell by your accent that you're not from here."

"Well, right now, we are scheduled for morning reading. I got your back, so go ahead and write your family."

"Thank you, Stacy," Shanda said.

"You are very welcome."

Shanda walked back into the building as she realized that it had been almost four years since she had seen her children or her sister-in-law with a clear state of mind. She didn't know where to even write, so she just sat with her head on her arm on the table, crying, feeling all the pain she inflicted on herself and how the night of October 31, 1979, had taken her husband, Samson, who was everything to her. She took two weeks to get herself together and gain the strength to write the children. Feeling better about herself, she wrote her sister-in-law a brief letter. Once she finished the one-page letter, she proofread it:

> Dear Tiltyla,
>
> I open this letter with love, and I hope it finds you and the children in the best of health and spirits. All praise are due to Allah. I am now in a drug rehabilitation program. It is called Faithway, a good program. I am here hoping to get the help I need to put me back on the straight path. I don't feel comfortable enough to write the children at this time. Will you please tell them I wrote and I am trying to get help? Also, let them know I love them much. Whenever I can find the strength to write them, I will. Thank you,

Tiltyla, for being there for them when I wasn't. I love you, and may Allah bless you.

Love
Shanda

After she proofread her letter, she put the address on it with a stamp and dropped it into the mailbox. Less than two weeks later, Shanda received four get-well cards and some pictures in the mail. Undecided on which one to open first, she opened the one from Tiltyla. Looking at the beautiful and thoughtful card brought tears to her eyes and a smile to her face. She opened the card and read it:

> Dear Shanda,
>
> Thank god, you are okay and trying to get some help for your problem. I didn't allow the children to write you, but I did allow them to send you a get-well card. I know you are wondering about the picture of the little boy.
>
> Shanda stopped reading the card and looked down at the letters she had lying on the bed. She picked them up and looked over the senders' names. One letter she looked at, she didn't notice the name, so she opened it. Seeing the picture of a little boy, she turned the picture over. It said Mustafa Ali, three years old. She became puzzled. She sat it down and started back reading the card from Tiltyla.
>
> I will explain the picture to you when you call. I hope you get better soon. I love you.
>
> Love,
> Tiltyla
>
> PS: Here is the new number (719) 252-6699.

Curious about the picture of the little boy she didn't recognize, she sat there and looked at it. Finally, she put the picture down and opened the other two cards. "Wow," she said after seeing how big her children had grown. Smiling and feeling good, she jumped up off the bed and ran to the telephone. After dialing the number on the card she was holding in her hand, she heard the phone ring twice before a voice of a man picked up.

"Hello."

"You have a collect call. Caller, say your name."

"Shanda, Shanda Ali."

"Do you accept?" the operator asked.

"Yes, I do," said her son Adam.

"Thank you," the operator said.

"Hello . . . may I speak to Tiltyla please?"

"Hi, Mom, she's in the restroom."

With a choking voice and tears in her eyes, Shanda responded to her son, "Baby! My god, baby, I didn't know that it was you. I love you, baby."

"I love you too," Adam said.

"Where is your sister?"

"She's at school."

"Why are you not in school?"

"All the twelfth graders graduating this year were given the last two weeks off school to prepare for college."

"What grade is Verlena in?"

"She's in the ninth."

"What are you planning on majoring in?"

"Law, criminal law."

"When are you planning on starting?"

"In a few months from now."

"What college are you going to?"

"The University of Tennessee in Nashville. Guess what, Mom?"

"What, baby?"

"Uncle Brian is going to buy me a car for graduation."

"That's good. Is he still a captain?"

"No, he's a general now."

"Have you been in touch with your father?"

"Yes, ma'am. I wrote him yesterday. We talk to him on the phone every weekend. We got a chance to go see him two months ago. He was telling us that his appeal for a new trial was denied. His attorney, Mr. Gaines, has filed something else for him."

"Did he tell you what it was?"

"I don't remember. Inshallah [God's will], I will be able to help him when I finish law school."

"Inshallah [God's will], you will," Shanda said.

"I gave him my word that I would get him out. Aunt Tiltyla said that she's going to drive us down there to get my car from Uncle Brandon when school is out. I think it will be best for us to fly. Then we could drive my car from Memphis to Nashville to visit Dad. Since I am not coming back up here, they could catch a flight from Nashville back to Colorado. I love you, Mom. Here is Aunt Tiltyla."

"I love you too, baby."

"Hello!" Tiltyla said as she picked up the phone.

"Hi, Tiltyla, first of all, thank you for taking the time to write me back."

"You're welcome. I am thanking God for putting it in your heart to write when you did. We needed to hear from you. Samson talks about you all the time. It really made him feel good. It was a big relief for him. I just told him that you were in a program trying to get some help."

"Thanks," Shanda said.

"What would help is if you would write him yourself."

"To be honest with you, Tiltyla, I don't know where to start. You know I haven't seen or talked to him since that night."

"Whenever you feel comfortable, Shanda, write him. He really needs to hear from you. He might not act like it. I know my brother. He is going through a lot right now. He tries to hide it and does a very good job of it. Just write him soon."

"I will."

"I have someone that you should know about. He's the one on the picture that I sent, with his lil bad butt stays into something."

"I was going to ask you. Whose child is he?"

"He's Verlena's baby."

"Verlena's?" Shanda said as she stopped panicking.

"Yes, Verlena's. Don't say anything yet. First, you need to sit down if you are not already."

"I am sitting down."

"How can I put this?" Tiltyla said as she took a deep breath and looked up. "Well . . . your daughter got raped."

"My god! When?"

"Right before I picked them up. She didn't tell anyone. I just noticed that she was getting bigger. This was about four or five months after they were up here, so I took her to the doctor. Came to find out she was seven months pregnant. I asked her about the pregnancy. That is when she told me that she had gotten raped by some man over at my brother Jay's house."

"What did she say happened?"

"She told me whoever he was came into the room one night while she was asleep. She said that she felt someone on top of her forcing themself into her. Whoever it was put a sheet over her head so she couldn't see him."

"Why didn't she say anything to me about it?"

"That's the sad thing about it. She didn't know how to tell you—or anyone. She did say the only time that you or Jay would come out of his room was to go to the bathroom. She still doesn't like being around men and still have nightmares every so often about the ordeal."

Tiltyla could hear Shanda crying on the other end of the phone.

"Everything is going to be all right, Shanda. She is a strong girl."

"She was only ten years old, a baby. Why would someone want to have sex with a baby? That's crazy."

"I have been raising the child myself, so she could enjoy her childhood. She still has a child's mentality. She plays with little girls her age. I think that's a good thing because most young girls with babies are forced to grow up and be mothers. So now you know the bad part. Are you ready for the good?"

"I guess so."

"Samson named him. He said that he was the chosen one, so he named him Mustafa."

"How did he take the bad news?" Shanda asked.

"Not good at all. You know how he is. He has a lot of inner strength. That makes it hard to tell if something affects him or not. He does somehow take the good with the bad. That's why you need to write him. It just might give him that extra boost that he needs. He really does need your support. He has been strong for all of us through this."

"I will. I just need some more time. It took me two weeks to write the letter I sent you."

"Mustafa is so happy when his papa calls. That boy doesn't want to give the phone up. He loves him some papa, and Samson loves him too."

"I can't wait to see him," Shanda said.

"God's will, you will see him soon. You just need to stay focused on getting yourself together. Do you need anything—money?"

"No, I'm good. They give us the things we need."

"Cool. Before I go, do you have something to write with? I can give you Samson's information."

"No, I can get something real quick. Hold on." Shanda sat the telephone receiver in the chair she was sitting in and went to get a pen and a piece of paper. "I'm back. What is it?" Shanda said.

After Tiltyla gave her Samson's information, she said, "I'm going to send a copy of the picture we took of Samson the last time we visited him."

"Okay, make sure you do that. I am not going to hold you up any longer. I love you, and Inshallah [God's will], I will see you soon."

"I love you too. I will tell Verlena that you called. Take care."

"You too."

When Shanda hung up the phone, she was filled with mixed feelings and emotions. Once again, she didn't know what to do. One thing in her mind was saying "Cry," and something else was telling her she has a reason to smile. Seeing she was still accepted by her family gave her the strength to accept her past. Now having something to look forward to, she opened up and worked the program. The first place she went after getting off the phone was to Stacy's office. She felt that Stacy was one person she could confide in. She knocked on the half-opened door to Stacy's office. Stacy looked up.

"Hi there, Shanda. Come in and have a seat. I will be with you in a moment."

Shanda walked in and took a seat, looking around the office at the pictures of Stacy's family. Stacy finished her writing.

"Okay, I'm finished. What can I help you with?"

"I just talked to my son and my sister-in-law, and they are going to support me 100 percent."

Stacy smiled and said, "That's good. Having some kind of support helps the recovery process. Shanda, you must realize that many situations that happen in life can't be fixed, repaired, or even made up. You have to start working on acceptance—accepting that life has its ups and downs. You don't have to do anything special. They love you and want to see you do better. That alone will be enough for them. Now you need to learn that there are higher and better levels of morality than the ones you have been functioning on in your addiction. You have been living the life of a female crack addict. You scratch my back, and I'll scratch yours. You know what that means? You always end up with the short end of the stick by degrading yourself."

Shanda lowered her head as the words from Stacy hit home. Stacy looked at her.

"To escape that feeling, Shanda, you must create an identity for yourself, one that will help you understand this world and your place in it. Then you will be able to accomplish real bliss. Make some accomplishable goals. Then act and think in accordance with them. That's called establishing a path for you to follow. Believe me, you will find true happiness and gain self-esteem. There is a major difference between people who are happy and successful in life than those who are unhappy with themselves before coming to Faithway. Your task now is to try to figure out the things that you really want to accomplish within the next year. Things like where you will live should be one. Where will your money come from, and how will you spend your time? If you don't plan, Shanda, it is safe to say that you're planning to fail. There is a saying: proper preparation prevents poor performance."

Shanda liked that. She smiled and said, "You're right."

"Are you planning on eating lunch?" Stacy asked.

"Yes, I am."

Stacy looked at her watch and said, "You need to get down before they close."

"It slipped my mind. I will see you later," Shanda said.

"Thanks for stopping by. Later."

"You're welcome. You will be seeing more of me," Shanda said with a smile on her face.

CHAPTER 7

Finally, after three months, Shanda conjured up the power to write her husband, Samson. The two hadn't seen or talked to each other in eight years.

> Dear Samson,
>
> I open this letter with love, and I hope this letter is one accepted by you. I haven't written or tried to contact you in eight years. Nor have I provided myself as a support system in any form or fashion. There are no words or reasons I could use to justify my actions. I realize that my hands made my life a living hell. Everything that has happened in my life since that night, I opened the door and allowed it. I don't feel I have to go through the whole details with you because you know the life your brother lives and what type of people he allows in his circle. Now, I can understand firsthand why you shielded us from him. I have come to realization since having taken the time to take a deep and full inventory of myself. When I sat down and thought about it, all I could come up with was that you know more about me than I know about myself. It all goes back to what you said when we first got married. Do you remember what you told me? You said once a person becomes an addict, they will always be one. I used marijuana and drank alcohol throughout high school all the way until we met. After we were married, I changed my people, places, and things. But I didn't. Even after I followed Islam, I didn't change my whole way of thinking. That made me vulnerable. I could sit here and go on and on pointing my finger at you, those racist cops, and the KKK who came to the house.

You know what, Samson? It will be more fitting to just point it at myself. I chose to be at Jay's house. I knew in my heart what I was doing before I did it. I just didn't know the full consequences of it. By me being open to alcohol and marijuana, it became a gateway to freebasing and crack cocaine. The reason I said that is, when I think back to that night everything happened, when I made it home that night, the first thing I wanted was something to drink. I literally had the taste for alcohol in my mouth. The whole time I was telling myself it would stop me from being so nervous if I get me something to drink, not knowing about the ripple effect it would cause. Today I have been at some high points in life and at the lowest I thought I could ever go. Samson, I have done things within the last eight years that do not sit right with me and I wouldn't dare put it in this letter. When I think about it, it makes me think less of myself. You are a very wise man, and you shouldn't have to hear me say it to know what's been going on or what went on. I don't know where your mind is, but I would like to know. Like I said, I am in a drug and alcohol program, trying to get me some help. Inshallah [God's will], I will. We are having a NA meeting tonight. I am thinking about giving a testimony. Just put it all on the table. Set it out of me so I can move on with my life. Talk about my life before and after I used crack cocaine. I want to put everything out there. Things I wouldn't dare put in this letter. Overall, I think it will help. Before I close, I just want you to know that I would like to keep writing you. I hope you don't mind. Tiltyla and the children will be down here next week to visit me Inshallah [God's will]. The plan is to leave here and drive down there to visit you. This program will not allow me to take over a six-hour pass. I have to be here for at least nine months to get a twenty-four-hour pass. To be honest with you, I cannot face you right now. I will end this letter with love. I will keep you in my prayers, and please keep me in yours. I love you.

Love, Shanda

Feeling a little at ease, Shanda started preparing herself for the NA meeting that was less than one hour away, getting all her thoughts together and watching how fast the time was passing. Time was running out. People started lining up to fill their cups with coffee. Within minutes, the multipurpose room was filled. Shanda, seeing all the people sitting around with cups in their hands, started feeling more uncomfortable.

"Hi, my name is Stacy. I am a recovering addict."

"Hi, Stacy," the audience said.

"On April 27, 1988, at seven o'clock in the evening, I bring this NA meeting to order," Stacy announced.

"Thank you!" the audience said with a loud united voice.

"Let us have a moment of silence for all the sick and suffering addicts in and out of the institutions followed by the Serenity Prayer," Stacy said.

While the Serenity Prayer was being recited, Shanda became even more nervous. Sweat beads started popping up on her forehead. She started having hot flashes. The palms of her hands got sweaty. She looked over at Stacy and wanted to walk over and tell her that she couldn't do this, knowing Stacy had stayed late at work to hear her testimony and show her support by opening the meeting for her. *I can't let her down, and I can't let myself down,* she said to herself. The thought came to her mind to ask God for the strength. *God, will you please give me the strength to stand in front of these people and give my testimony?*

"Amen," the audience said once the Serenity Prayer was over.

"Once again, my name is Stacy, and I am a recovering addict. We have a speaker for the night. I would like to welcome her personally to the front. Will you all give her a round of applause? Shanda, will you please come up?"

Shanda walked up to the front of the group as they were applauding her. When the clapping stopped, she looked over at Stacy and said, "Thank you."

"Hi, my name is Shanda, and I am a crack addict."

"Welcome, Shanda," the group said

She took a deep breath as a sign of nervousness but was quick in thinking to try to utilize the few seconds they took to welcome her.

"I need you all to bear with me. This is my first time ever speaking openly about my past or even speaking to a group of people." *Okay, I can do this,* she quietly whispered to herself. "I was born in New Jersey. My parents were very open-minded people with little money. My father was an alcoholic when I was growing up. Thank god, he is now recovering. I took my first drink when I was fourteen years old, and I will never forget it. It was on the Fourth of July. I liked the way that it made me feel. All my female friends I went to school with were already smoking weed. The night of the school jamboree, my tenth-grade year, was my first time trying it. That night, I smoked some weed and did a little drinking—not too much. This went on until my second year of college. My boyfriend got a scholarship to play football at Boulder University in Colorado. I had a family member who lived in Colorado. I used that to follow my boyfriend up there, hoping we could be together. After about a year and a half, we broke up. You know how it is when you are a star on a football team. Women come from all angles. Shortly after we stopped seeing each other, I started drinking a lot, trying to escape the thought of him lying with some other female. My cousin by marriage, Brandon, was in the navy, but they had a special unit of men training with the air force stationed on the outside of Colorado Springs, Colorado. He noticed how I started drinking myself to death, so he made me stay at his house while school was out for spring break. The next morning he told me he had someone he wanted me to meet. He said, 'You need to get yourself together. He will be over soon.' I got myself together. About thirty minutes later, I heard a knock on the door. My cousin said, 'I got it.' He opened the door and said, 'Come in, brother.' This big black man walked through the door. He said something to my cousin in another language. I said to myself, *What the F did he say?* My cousin said something back to him in that language. Then they hugged. My cousin introduced us. This was not the person my cousin was talking about he wanted me to meet. But he was. He was a very respectful and handsome man. I had never dated a person of another color or race. A lot of my friends had dated black men before. The ones who had slept with them always talked about the experience and how big they were.

"Months passed as he would drive up to BU to see me. There were days he took me out and my stuff was on fire, but he would do nothing. After six months of dating, we got married. That night, he let me know that it was worth waiting for, if you know what I mean. Being with him, I didn't have the desire to drink or smoke weed maybe because he was a Muslim, a very religious person. One reason I liked his religious side is because he never once tried to force his beliefs on me. If I didn't ask about it, he didn't talk about it. He took nothing to the extreme. He is a very beautiful person inside and out. I went thirteen years using no alcohol or marijuana. Eight years ago, on October 31, 1979, the day I relapsed, was a day I will never forget for as long as I live. This day ruined my entire life. My husband, our two children, and I were driving back from visiting my parents in New Jersey. I was stopped by two racist cops in a small town east from her. One of them came to the car after I stopped. When he looked in and saw my husband on the passenger side of the car asleep, the first thing he asked me was 'Are you all right?' I said yes without thinking."

Tears ran down Shanda's face as she stood there telling her painful story. The group heard the pain in her voice. Slowly trying to get herself together, she continued, "Before I knew it, they were making my husband get out of the car. They forced him to the back of the car at gunpoint. One held a gun on him while the other one beat him with a nightstick or blackjack—whatever you call that stick. My husband started fighting back. He ended up killing one of the officers and shot the other one in the shoulder with his gun. I called for help on their CB. When the other police officers got there, they started beating him again. By the will of God, the FBI agents pulled up and stopped them. The FBI gave me his business card and told me to go home. He had someone to follow me there. The first thing I did when I got home was drive to the liquor store, thinking something to drink would ease my nerves. I was a nervous wreck because I waited and waited for my husband to call. He never did. Two o'clock in the morning the next day, my children and I were in the bed asleep. I heard a window burst, and something hit the floor in the front room. I jumped up. What is it? I walked into the front living room. That's when I saw the brick on the floor. My front yard was lit up. I was too scared to look out the window that the brick came through, so I looked out the bedroom window. That's when I saw about twenty-five or more KKK members in my front yard burning a cross, wearing white hooded sheets over their heads. One of them had a bullhorn. He called me a nigger-loving bitch. He said if they ever catch me and my nigger kids in their town, they would kill us.

"Not thinking about the fact that I had given up my driver's license the night before, I thought the FBI who followed me home had told them where I stayed. As soon as they left, I packed up and got the hell out that house. Never again to this day have I returned. I sold that house. That's another story. Anyway, my children and I went downtown to the shelter. That's where we stayed for months. I drank heavily. I was afraid to get a job or anything in my name, thinking it would be one way they could find me. I saw one neighbor downtown one day. She gave me a business card of a man who claimed to be my husband's attorney. It was the first time I had heard anything about him since that night. So I called the number. He freaked me out with all the questions about what happened that night. I was a little drunk too—shoot. He told me that my husband was being held in the Jackson County Jail on charges of murder. I said to myself the town we were in wasn't Jackson. That made me not trust him. I went on and told him everything that happened. He kept trying to get me to tell him where I was staying. I hurried up and got off the phone. When I got off, I got the hell out of there. Thinking he had tapped or somehow he could trace the call back to where I was, I grabbed our stuff and put everything in the trunk of my car, got the children, and went straight to the bank. Once there I took a thousand dollars out. My first thought was to get a hotel room.

"I was driving down Third Street, hoping to find a hotel room when I saw my brother-in-law Jay crossing Third Street by Gaston Park. As I passed him, I blew the horn and pulled over. The first thing he said was 'Girl, the whole family has been looking for you. They are worried about ya'll. Shanda, it's been a long time since I have seen you and the kids. They have gotten big as hell. What's up with you? Where are you headed?' I said 'To try to find a hotel for me and the children.' He then said, 'Girl, you don't have to do that. Ya'll can stay with me.'

"I agreed. Satan is good, but God is the greatest. He got into the car and showed me where he lived. I asked him if he had heard anything from Samson. He said that he hadn't, only what he had seen and heard on TV and in the newspapers. He was no help. We got to his house. It was just the next street over from Third on Patton Street. I gave him $300 off the top. After that, we went grocery shopping because there wasn't anything in the house to eat. To make a long story short, I was sitting back drinking me a little some when there was a lot of traffic. Jay ran in and out the house. The people he had over with him came out the room, all buck-eyed, sweating. I didn't know what they were doing, but I knew they were high. One day I asked my brother-in-law about some weed. I had a taste for some. All he said was 'How much are you looking for?' Off the top of my head, I said, 'Twenty dollars' worth.' He said, 'Give me the money.' I gave it to him. He came back with some good stuff. This went on for a few weeks. Then they would smoke with me, but he and his girlfriend Kim never would buy any. One morning Jay's girlfriend Kim and I were sitting in the house. Jay was at work, and the children were at the park playing. I was about to roll a joint. It was like she was waiting for me to roll it up. When I pulled out the weed and papers, she said, 'Hold up.' She pulled this little white rock out of her sock and said, 'Put some of this in there.'' I said, 'What in the hell is that? It looked like one of the rocks you see in a fish aquarium. I don't want none of that,' I said. She said, 'Girl, you are going to love this high.' She didn't. I tried it and fell in love with the way it made me feel. It gave me a rush like never before. Bells rang in my ears. My lungs opened up. She turned me on to the pipe within a week after that. I hit it, and it gave me an orgasm. So you already know I was on from that point. Within eighteen months after moving in with my brother-in-law, I spent the $52,000 left in the bank. I sold the house for $95,000 and spent that. The only reason I didn't spend the children's trust fund money was because of the way my husband had it set up for them. We ran my car into the ground. We weren't even putting oil in the car, so the motor locked up. I sold it for a little of nothing. Day in and day out, we got high. I think I did good smoking in the closet, me and Kim. When Jay discovered, I got to spending all that money. Sometimes days passed before we got any sleep. He quit his job and became a full-time smoker at my expense. I was their supporter. Kim knew that I had orgasms whenever I got a good hit. One day we were in the house alone. I had some dope from the night before. She asked me to buy some so we could get a wakeup. I told her I still had a little. She said give me a wakeup. Then I pulled out the few rocks I had. For the first time I could remember, she told me to go first. I put a nice piece up on the pipe and got a good blast. She told me while I was holding the smoke in to give her a shotgun. For those of you who don't know what I was talking about, that is when you take a good hit off the pipe and blow the smoke into the other person's mouth. So I took a big hit and leaned over and put my mouth up to hers and blew the smoke into her mouth. Once I was finished blowing her the smoke, I felt the effects of the crack. She put her tongue into my mouth. As she was doing that, she put her hand down my pants and played with my clitoris. Before I knew it, she had my pants down, licking it. I wanted to stop her, but the dope and the feeling wouldn't allow me to do so. That was just the beginning of the things she and I did together. Things changed once I spent up all my money. They would get their dope and hide with it. The guy that sold Jay his dope was over one night getting Jay to rock up some cocaine for him. After Jay finished rocking the dope up, he gave Jay some for doing it. Jay gave me a little piece—I mean little too. While I was doing it, the guy whose name is RA RA, called Jay out the room so he could talk to him. A minute or two later, they came back into the room.

Jay told me he was going to the store and RA RA will stay here until he got back. I didn't think anything of it. I was high and had the cravings for more. I had my mind set to ask him for some anyway. It was good Jay was out the way, I thought. So I asked him to let me have a little something to smoke. He said, 'This shit cost. It's not free. Do you have any money?' 'If I had some, I wouldn't be asking,' I said. He said, 'I will tell you this. If you do me a favor, I got you. It will be something nice too.' 'What are you talking about?' I asked. 'Something sexually, like a blowjob. But I really would like to see what that pussy is like.' I thought about it. The cravings and the devil got to talking. I said to myself, *Samson got the death penalty over a year ago. I haven't had sex with a man in over two years.* I still tried to put up a defense, a weak one. I said, 'Jay will be back soon.'

"He said, 'Check this out.' He reached into the plastic bag he had the crack rocks in and pulled out three of the biggest rocks he had in it. They were the size of the tip of my finger. Then he said, 'I will give you these three for some head.' I said like a fool who had allowed crack to become their master, 'Can I smoke one first?' He said, 'Sure, you can get them all as long as you take care of your business.' He handed them. I took a blast and got freaky. While I was hitting the pipe, he took down his pants. I blew the smoke out and went to work. Ya'll know what I'm talking about.

'Ra Ra and I messed around for about six months. It came to a time where he wasn't able or willing to supply my rapidly growing habit. So I prostituted, walked up and down McLemore Street, to support my drug habit. I fell to my lowest. I did stuff I had never dreamed of like having sex with two men, giving one of them head while the other one was behind me. That madness went on for years. For years, I degraded myself.

"My sister-in-law came down here from Colorado Springs about four years ago and took my children back with her. I finally wrote them when I first got into this program. I found out through my sister-in-law that my fourteen-year-old daughter got raped in my brother-in-law's house right before she picked them up and took them to Colorado. At the time, she was only ten years old. Now she got a three-year-old son. The sad thing about it is, while I was getting high, someone was in the next room raping my baby," Shanda said with a cracked voice filled with sorrow.

"My sister-in-law didn't find out until my baby was seven months pregnant. Thank god, my child is doing great. My son starts law school next month, God's will. He told his father he was going to get him out. They are coming to visit me next week, God's will, before he starts college.

Today, unlike yesterday, I think that I am strong enough to face them. That's all. Thank you all for listening to me and having me as your speaker for tonight."

Everyone stood up and gave her a big round of applause.

"Shanda, you did just how I thought you would do. Great!" Stacy said.

"Thank you, Stacy," Shanda said.

"You are going to do good in your recovery."

"God's will, I hope so. Guess what, Stacy?"

"What?"

"I finally got the nerve to write my husband today. It really was a hard task for me."

"Shanda, just keep working the program like it should be worked. You will see many more doors open for you. Life is what you make it. If anyone did to you what you did to yourself, you would kill them."

"You are right. That's so true, Stacy."

"I really would like to see you get something out of this. So keep up the good work. I am going home now. I will see you tomorrow morning," Stacy said.

"Okay. God's will, I will see you tomorrow."

CHAPTER 8

"Listen up, everyone. Mail call. Joyce S., David T., Shanda A., James H., Willie J. That's all the mail for today." For Shanda, to hear her name called sent an overwhelming feeling of joy through her. She looked at the envelope to make sure that it was from Samson. Seeing his name in the upper-right-hand corner of the envelope made her heart drop to her feet and her stomach filled with butterflies. She felt uncertain with the response. She became anxious but optimistic as she opened it.

> As-salamu alaykum [may peace be upon you]. Dear, my love,
>
> It was pleasant to receive a scroll from you today. I prayed that Allah would place the thought in your heart to write. I can put myself in the mind frame of Jesus when he said that Allah [God] always answers His prayers.
>
> First of all, I would like for you to know that I am not upset with you. But I am highly disappointed. That doesn't stop me from wanting the best for you. I understand by the grace of Allah [God] that everyone that He allows to be tested will not pass. Satan is real, but you are the one who gives him the power to trap or get you caught up. He didn't mislead you. You mislead yourself by thinking you could get something for nothing. Everything in life has a price. For every action, there is a reaction. There are many of verses in the Qur'an that give us the tools to fight him off. In surah 7 *ayat* [verse] 16–17, it says, 'Satan said, "Because you have sent me astray, surely I will lie and wait for all humankind on Your straight path. Then I will attack them from their front, their back, from their right and left. You will not find most of them thankful to you."'
>
> Satan was talking to Allah [God]. That's not all of it. It

68

goes on to say that the devil [Satan] will make us promises, but he can't and won't keep them. Allah [God] is the one who makes promises and always keep them. Shanda, Satan can't answer your cries or you can answer his. He only whispered to you. You made all the choices yourself. No one forced you to do the things you did. All those cries for help—the devil didn't help because he couldn't answer them. If you would have taken it to Allah [God] from day one, you wouldn't be where you are now or feel the way you do. Satan himself lets us know that we are responsible for our actions. I am not going to kick you while you are down. I must say this: the Holy Bible teaches us that a wise man will fall down seven times and get back up. But a fool will fall down and stay down. I will keep praying for you on a daily basis. Whenever you feel like writing, write. I know you feel like you have been through hell for the last eight years. Think about what Jesus and all the prophets went through to convey the message of Allah [God]. Yours were self-inflicted. You made those choices, so you can't associate your self-infliction to hell. Don't get me wrong, my love. I believe that hell could be mental, physical, and spiritual. Allah [God] allowed me to have the strength to go through the physical aspect of hell. When I think of fire, I think of purification. We can see it work on a spiritual sense or physical one. Allah [God] made us all out of the best of molds. Look how we belittle ourselves. I have been in the physical aspect of hell for eight years, true enough, but I am not going to—and I refuse to—allow it to be anything other than that. In my heart, I feel that I made the right choice that night. Allah knows I don't regret it. If I had to do it all over again, I would. That night things happened all within seconds. Those seconds cost me and caused me to be away from my family. You didn't make it any better. Shanda, I didn't know if you all were dead or what. Allah is Akbar [God is the greatest]. Like Prophets Job and Joseph in the Bible, I am not going to give up. I believe in the same God they do, the one true living God. I knew within my heart that he wouldn't place a burden

on me greater than I can bear. I have recently come into
the true concept of being a slave of Allah [God]. I believe
that is the greatest achievement one could accomplish in
this world. Shanda, we all are slaves to something. This
world is designed for that. You allowed drugs to become
your master. You know that I am right.

Shanda felt as though Samson was right in the room preaching to her.
The things he was saying were hitting home. It sounded like he heard the
testimony she gave.

"Shanda Ali, report to visitation," one member said loudly. Unable to
finish reading the letter because her name was being called for visitation, she
folded the letter up and put it back into the envelope and put it underneath
her pillow. She tried to gather her thoughts and regroup from the letter.
Feeling a little insecure of herself and past, she walked into the visiting
room as the butterflies grew stronger.

The first one to greet her was Adam. With tears of joy in his eyes, he
hugged and kissed her on the jaw. Tiltyla was right behind him to offer her
a big hug, causing tears to build up in her eyes.

"Now, this is the Shanda Ali I know," Tiltyla said.

"Thanks!" Shanda said as she wiped the tears from her face.

Verlena picked up her son, Mustafa, who stood in front of her, watching
the new face everyone is hugging. After she picked him up, she just sat with
Mustafa on her lap, looking downward.

Tiltyla turned around and asked Verlena; "Are you going to give your
mom a big hug?" Verlena shook her head from side to side as a sign of no.

"No. What do you mean no?" Tiltyla asked.

"It's okay, Tiltyla. Let her be. I understand," Shanda said with a feeling
of disappointment. "Can I at least see my grandbaby?"

Verlena looked at her mom for a moment before she sat Mustafa on
the floor.

"Mustafa, come to Grandma."

Mustafa looked around.

"Go on to your grandma, boy," Tiltyla said.

He walked over to Shanda. She bent down and picked him up, kissed
him, and sat him down on her lap.

"Adam, how do you feel about starting college?" Shanda asked as she
played with Mustafa.

"I feel good about it, Mom. I just want to get the degree quick enough. As soon as I get educated enough on law, I could start working on Dad's case. I have been doing a lot of reading on criminal law. I was looking at the news yesterday before we got on the airplane. They were talking about blacks who had been wrongfully convicted by the court system. Ninety-five percent of the convictions are in the Southern States. I wish I could obtain the education needed overnight. Unfortunately, there isn't a magical pill I can take. It will take at least four years before I can get started on his case. That's four more years that my father has to be away from us. When I think about that night, it doesn't make me cry. It makes me mad. Through my trust and belief in Allah [God], I know the only way something could be done is to fight the law with law, so it is a must I learn it."

"You sound very sure of yourself and what you want to do," Shanda said.

"I am sure of myself," Adam said.

"How did you get here from Colorado?" Shanda asked.

"We flew," Tiltyla said.

Adam smiled.

"So you got it your way?" Shanda asked Adam.

"Something like that. It was the best plan," Adam said.

"It wasn't the best plan. I just didn't feel like driving all the way down here," Tiltyla said.

"You wouldn't have to drive all the way by yourself. I could have helped," Adam said.

"Boy, you are crazy for thinking I would go to sleep in that car while you are driving, especially on the highway." All laughed. Even Verlena got a kick out of that. To get them up off him, Adam said, "Uncle Brandon brought me the car like he said he would."

"What kind is it?" Shanda asked.

"You can see for yourself. Can you go outside?"

"Yeah, sure."

"Come on, let me show it to you."

Shanda stood up and put Mustafa on her hip, and the three walked outside. Tiltyla talked to Verlena. As they walked out the door, Tiltyla pulled her chair close to Verlena. "Why won't you say anything to your mom?"

"A mother doesn't allow things like what happened to me to happen to their children. She didn't have any time for us. She didn't even care if we ate or not. All she wanted to do is smoke that stuff. It was like she didn't care about us or Dad. She had different men coming over to Uncle Jay's house looking for her."

Tiltyla could say nothing. She was speechless.

"You are the only mother that I know of. If you only knew what we went through, you would understand. Adam had to go out and get money any way he could so that we could have something to eat. Is a mother supposed to do that to her children?"

"No, baby, I understand that you all went through hell. But you've got to learn to forgive even if you can't forget. She's your mother, and she made some bad choices that she has to live with. Your father took things the way he did because of his personal relationship with God. God performs the impossible in our lives. Your mom is trying to turn things around now. She needs your help.

"What has been keepin' your father strong are those qualities he has that can only come from God. The years your father was in your life and the way you are show me that he passed those same qualities to you and Adam. Look at what you went through and how you have maintained your sanity. Your mom didn't have those qualities when she was tested. She still can redeem herself with our help. We need to work with her, not give up on her. Let's work together where we are at today. Believe it or not, she is in a great deal of pain. The pain from what happened to you and the pain she caused herself. Verlena, baby, we are all human, and we all will make mistakes. Throughout life, we will make a lot more of them. We just have to learn from them so we won't make them again. Just give her a chance. She needs our support more than anything right now. Pray about it and give her a little time. Will you please do that for me?"

"Yes, ma'am," Verlena said.

"Just keep in mind that no successful men or women of God in the Bible or Qur'an who at one time or another didn't face obstacles they couldn't overcome themselves. That is because the things that are impossible for men are possible for God. So allow Him to slowly remove those bad feelings you have toward your mom from you."

"Okay, I will give it a try."

"Here they come," Tiltyla said.

As they walked up, Shanda said, "Tiltyla, girl, that is a nice car."

"It sure is. Oh yes, I gave Brandon this address. He said that he would be down here to see you sometime this week or no later than next week."

Shanda said nothing.

"Do you want anything out the vending machine to eat?" Tiltyla asked.

"Let me see what's in it."

"Here, here is some money." Tiltyla passed Shanda ten $1 bills.

"Does anyone want anything while I'm up here?" Shanda asked as she held Mustafa's hand as they stood up at the vending machine."

"No thanks," they said.

"That's okay. My grandbaby and I will eat us some of this junk food. What do you want, baby?" Shanda asked Mustafa.

Mustafa pointed to a bag of potato chips.

"You have good taste. I'm going to get me a bag too." Shanda put the money into the vending machine and punched the numbers. The machine released the potato chips. Mustafa opened the flap and got the potato chips out.

"I'm going to get us a soda to drink, okay?"

"Okay," Mustafa said as he nodded.

"You can talk I see," Shanda said as the two walked back to the table. Shanda had two sodas in her hands, and Mustafa held the two bags of potato chips tightly in his arms. Shanda sat down, put the sodas on the table, and then reached down and picked Mustafa up to sit him on her lap. Shanda folded the six remaining dollars up with the change in the middle. She passed the remaining money to Tiltyla. Tiltyla looked over at her and said, "Keep it. Do you need any more for your personal things?"

"No. This program supplies everything we need. We all are given a part-time job to pay for the treatment that goes on here. This is also a 50 percent government-funded program. The only time we eat sweets is when a candy company or store donates some. This $6 and change will be enough. Overall, this is a pretty good program. I'm thankful that Allah [God] put the thought in my head to get some help. I couldn't recognize myself four months ago. It feels good to be clean and have clean thoughts. I truly don't know what I am going to do when it's time to leave this program. I messed up everything. I will be able to keep the job that I have now. Maybe move up to full-time. This program will help me get a place to live. The only thing about that is I will be right back in the line of fire. I just want to be able to live up to the expectations that I have set for myself."

"You are worrying about the wrong things. You just need to stay focused on your recovery. For you to live up to any expectation that is of righteousness, you must put God in charge of all your affairs. Without

Him, nothing is possible. With Him, all things are possible. When we were growing up, my brother Samson was like a father to me. Our parents were killed when I was young. He had to take responsibility for our father. Our grandmother stayed sick. Jay is the oldest, but Samson was the one who stepped up. If he didn't, I can't imagine how things would have turned out. God allows things to happen in our lives so that we can become stronger. Now I am left with this question. What are you going to do, Shanda? That's a question that I want you to ask yourself. Verlena said that she wants to go to college and get herself master's degree in sociology or in medicine like her father. If something was to happen to me—may God forbid it—while she's off in school or even before she goes, who will take care of Mustafa while she is trying to better herself? Will she have to delay or stop going to school altogether so that she can look after the welfare of her son? You are her mother, and you know that it will be a hindrance to her accomplishing her goals. It is hard on a single parent as well as the children. That's why you need to stay focused on getting healthy. Your children need you. I am their aunt, not their mother. You are. Their father isn't here to help raise them, but he does support them. There isn't anything like a mother's love. Shanda, I know you can do it. When you get yourself together, you have a home to come to. True enough, my brother gave me the house. It's not just mine. It's ours, and you are welcome there anytime. To be truthful, girl, I need a break, a vacation or something." All laughed. Shanda felt the speech and took it as constructive criticism.

"You all think that's funny, huh? I'm serious! It's two full-time jobs dealing with Mustafa's spoiled butt."

"I'm not spoiled," Mustafa said as he smiled and lay back on his grandmother.

"Shanda, we have to go. We have to be in Nashville by three o'clock. That will give us time enough to stop by the college and look around. To get to a hotel room before it gets too dark. Tomorrow morning we are heading out to visit Samson."

"Mom, Inshallah [God's will], I will be able to drive down here to see you about once or twice a month. I also have this address. I'm going to keep you posted on everything," Adam said.

"I am going to hold you to that, son. Verlena, you haven't said one word to me today. I apologize for the pain I caused you and your brother. It will make me feel a lot better about this visit if I can at least get a hug before you go."

Verlena stood up and walked over to where her mother was. Shanda stood up and put Mustafa down on the floor and gave her daughter a big hug and said, "I love you." Not wanting anyone to see her cry, Verlena walked out the door.

"She will be all right," Tiltyla said. "Start writing her so you can try to rebuild ya'll relationship. It will take time, but it can be done."

"I see it's going to take more than overnight," Shanda said

"You're right! You have the number. Use it!"

"I will," Shanda said.

"I love you, Shanda."

"I love you too, Tiltyla. Ya'll give me a hug, starting with you, Mustafa."

All hugged Shanda. In tears of joy, she stood there as Tiltyla and the children headed out for Nashville. Once they were out of sight, Shanda went to her room to finish reading the letter she received from Samson. She went in the room and sat down on the bed and grabbed the letter from underneath her pillow. She unfolded it and picked up where she left off.

> At this point of time, Shanda, in your life, you feel like you have dug a hole so deep for yourself. The bad thing about it is, you are not for sure how you will get out.
>
> Thank Allah [God] that you haven't committed suicide. Many do. That shows me you do have the will to live.
>
> I try my best to call the children at least twice a month and write them once a week. You should do the same. That helps keep the communication line open. You will be amazed after reading their letters how knowledgeable they are. You can see their strength and their weakness. Thank Allah [God] that their strengths outweigh their weaknesses.
>
> Out of all we've been through, all praise are due to Allah. I must say fortunately we have a son who will be going off to college next week. Our daughter has surprised me with her ability to still be a child who acts her age. She is still Daddy's little girl.
>
> Shanda, Allahu Akbar [God is the greatest]. I have only received a small taste of what Prophet Job went

through. I have kept the faith, and I will not question Allah [God] in this matter.

I need not know why it had to be me. I trust and believe, when this is over, I will emerge out of this successfully.

It is time for you to be responsible. People who are truly responsible fulfill their commandments. They pay their bills on time, follow their conscience, do their job correctly, obey the law and the laws of Allah [God]. You made a commitment to me when we got married. Part of that commitment was to be a responsible mother. Shanda, it is time for you to accept total complete absolute responsibility for your life and its condition. Anything short of that will not work. If you are too weak to do that, I take it that you will be too weak to write back. I am going to end this letter with love, and I pray that Allah give you the strength that you need to one day come visit me.

Truly,
Samson

CHAPTER 9

"Good morning, ladies and gentlemen. For those of you not familiar with me, my name is John B. Roberson. I am the facilitator of this class. The year 1988 will be a good year if we make it one. I have rules in my class that I strictly follow to ensure that we have a good one. To my new students, they are new rules. To my last-year students, they are not. There are rules that make teaching and learning flow as smooth as possible. Without law, we have corruption. Corruption makes teaching and learning impossible. I get paid to teach, not to babysit or run a dating service. I love what I get paid to do," Mr. Roberson said as he paced the floor.

"This is a time in your life when you have to set aside anything that will obstruct you from achieving your goal. Believe me, there are no magical words that I can say that will make you attain a degree in law overnight. Some of you will catch on quicker than others. There is only one for sure way of gaining the education and getting a degree. That is to apply yourself. There is no free ride in here. You will have to work for what you get in this class."

Mr. Roberson picked up the stack of papers he had on the desk. Then he placed small stacks on each desk on the front row. Then he spoke, "Take one and pass the rest back. I am passing out the prerequisite along with the rules of my class. The prerequisite will cover everything you will need to know for this semester. As for the sheet with the ruler on it, I need you all to pay close attention and read them with me. There will be no exceptions. Number one, all students will show respect. I *cannot* hear you all. Number one says . . ."

All the students said in a loud tone, "All students will show respect."

"Number two."

"All students must come to class prepared."

"That's what I'm talking about. Number three," Mr. Roberson said as he walked around the classroom.

"All students must be on time."

"Number four."

"All students must do their work."

"Number five."

"All students must show proof of absences."

"Number six."

"There is no bursting out."

"Number seven."

"When wanting to be acknowledged, you must raise your hand."

"Number eight."

"No eating or drinking in class."

"Number nine."

"No profanity."

"Last but not the least is?" Mr. Roberson asked. "Number ten."

"All students must be properly dressed in my classroom."

"These rules are the law, and all ten will be strictly enforced. The objective here is to make sure you get what you came here for. You all will have homework tonight."

"Ahhh, mann!" some students said after Mr. Roberson mentioned homework on the first day of school.

"Yes, homework tonight," Mr. Roberson stated once again as he walked around the room with his ink pen in his right hand, hitting it against the palm of his left hand. The gray hair and mustache showed signs of the years he had been teaching.

"For the homework tonight, I want all of you to write down your goals. I will put them up, not just that I will hold you to them. So you must act and think in accordance with the goals you write down.

"By setting goals for yourself, you will be establishing a straight path for you to follow. It will be much easier to accomplish something that's well thought out and planned. There is a major difference in people who plan and those who don't. That is why in a court of law people who plan their crime get more time than those who don't. By you having time to think about what you are going to do and write it down, you are creating a guideline, a map so to speak, to follow. That makes the chances of you being successful greater. I know some of you have heard this saying, 'We don't plan to fail. We just fail to plan. One more is 'Proper preparation prevents poor performance.'"

"Utilize those five *P*s. Like I said, I'm going to look over your goals, and

I will discuss them with you. Your task is with this exercise. Try to figure out the things that you will want to do for the next four years. Be sure about what you write, and remember you are the one who's got to obtain them, so they must be within reason."

Before Mr. Roberson could get any more pointers out, the bell rang. Within seconds the students cleared the class. Not in so much a rush. Adam was one of the last to exit the classroom. As he was walking down the hallway, a slim white student with a nicely trimmed haircut standing an inch over six feet walked up behind him.

"Excuse me!" the nicely trimmed young man said.

Adam turned around to see who was trying to get his attention. "Are you talking to me?" Adam asked.

"Yes, excuse me! My name is Mark. I live in the room right across from you. By some coincidence, we are majoring in the same thing, and I sit right next to you."

"Coincidence, huh? Nice to meet you, Mark. I'm Adam. I don't believe in coincidences, Mark. I think everything happens for reasons."

"If you don't mind me asking, are you from Nashville?" Mark asked.

"No, I am from Colorado Springs, Colorado."

"You came all the way from Colorado to go to this school?"

"I have my reasons. Are you from here?" Adam asked.

"Born and raised."

"That's good to know. Hopefully, you can show me around, if you don't mind," Adam replied.

"Not at all. I would be more than happy to do that. If you don't have anything to do, we can get together later, and I will show you around."

"All I have to do later is write a letter. That will be all good. What time?" Adam asked.

"How about six o'clock?"

"That's cool with me."

"I will meet you by the room," Mark said.

"Okay, sounds like a plan."

Adam and Mark became best friends. When you saw one, you saw the other one. Both of them kept their heads in the law book. Adam found out that Mark's family were into law and he already had a shot waiting on him once he finished school. Every weekend Adam would take the time out to go visit his father Samson. He did the same thing every Sunday—week in and week out—for nine months. Every Sunday he would gas up and head down Highway 40 West until he got to Memphis. Once there, he would go to visit his mother, Shanda. After seeing her, he would go by his uncle Brandon's house.

Time passed quickly. It had been two years since Adam's mother, Shanda, had been released from the Faithway Drug Program. Adam still took the time out to make the trip once every other Sunday to spend time with his uncle Brandon and his uncle's wife. Within three years, Adam gained a good reputation around the campus for being a focused student. One of his female classmates who had been having a crush on him walked up to him one day as he and Mark were leaving out the classroom.

"Excuse me. Mark, can I have a word with Adam? It won't take long," said a young lady who stood five feet seven inches around 125 pounds. She had long silky black hair laid over her shoulders and reddish-brown skin.

"You can take all the time you need. I will catch up with you later, brother," Mark said as he walked off with a smirk on his face.

"Okay, bro, I will catch you later. God's will," Adam said.

"How have you been doing, Adam?" the beautiful young lady asked.

"As well as could be expected, thank god. How about yourself, Gloria?"

"Pretty good, I must say."

As they walked down the hall, the conversation grew. Gloria couldn't take her eyes off Adam. Adam tried hard to keep his cool. He would only look over at Gloria if it was necessary. He could feel her eyes all over him. He wanted to ask her why she was looking at him like she was but thought it would be best to stay focused and keep looking straight ahead.

"I noticed that you don't go to any of the parties that they have on campus. Why not?" Gloria asked.

"I have a lot that I am trying to accomplish right now. To me, that will be a waste of my time."

"So do you think it would be a waste of your time to go with me to one this Saturday?" Gloria asked.

"Saturday is a bad time. My weekends are set aside for some personal reasons. I will tell you what. If possible, I can make it up to you on another day."

Thinking Adam was about to shoot her down, she dropped her head slightly. She was not sure how to respond to his proposal. "Yeah, sure" were the only words that came to her mind. After her mind cleared, she said, "How are you planning on doing that?"

"I will think of something," Adam responded.

"When can I look forward to this date?"

"I will let you know Monday, God's will," Adam said as he looked up to her for the second time since they had been talking.

"Is that okay with you?" Adam asked.

"Sure. I am going to be mad at you if you stand me up, Adam."

"I'm not going to stand you up. I will let you know Monday what I have planned, okay?"

"Okay. Now, Adam, I am going to hold you to that."

"You don't trust me?" Adam asked.

"It's not like that!"

"Yes, it is. I'm not going to let you down."

"Okay. I will see. I'll see you later."

"Okay, Gloria, make sure you have a good day!"

"I will. You do the same."

"God's will," Adam added.

Adam went to his dormitory room and prepared himself for his weekend routine. After getting all his notes together, he wrote a short letter to his mother in Colorado. Adam got up and walked over to the window to take a peek out. He noticed that the sky was darkening as he could smell the rain. The rain had stopped, but the clouds were still dark. Just like the cloud that had been over his father's head for over eleven years. In his heart, he knew the sun will shine again. *When* is the question. Three years had passed by since he stepped his feet into law school, and nothing had changed. He knew more about law but nothing that would help his father's situation. As he looked out the window into the sky, the clouds moved to allow a single star to shine through to show there is hope. To remove those thoughts, Adam turned away from the window and walked over to his bed. As he sat down on the bed, he reached over to the nightstand by the lamp to grab the book he was reading the night before. He kicked off his shoes and lay back on his pillow.

He held the book outward from his face as he opened it and turned to where he left off. Before he knew it, he was awakened by the sound of his alarm clock. He sat up in bed peering into the darkness, wondering whether to lie there or get up and shower so he can offer his morning prayer. *Prayer is better than sleep,* Adam said to himself before he stood up on his feet. *All praise are due to you, Allah,* he said as he stumbled bleary-eyed into the bathroom. He turned on the shower before he took a seat on the toilet to relieve himself. When he was finished, he undressed and stepped into the shower. He slowly changed the water temperature from hot to warm. He stood there as the warm water fell onto his body, calculating his thoughts. Once he finished, he got out the shower, dried off, and threw on the dark-blue-and-white T-shirt and a pair of blue jeans and socks. He stood there next to his bed and offered his morning prayer. Seeing that time waits for no man, he grabbed the things he wanted to go over with his father and headed out the door. Once at the Tennessee Maximum Security prison where his father is being held Adam's diligence made his face well-known by the correctional officers; all the routine checks didn't deter him from being there every week. Most knew him by name. They knew that he's one of the dedicated visitors who came every week to visit his father. The line of people ended as he walked up to the officer in charge of the visitation room.

"Good morning, Mr. Ali," the officer said.

"Thank you, sir. The same to you," Adam replied.

After signing in, he walked over toward the table in the far-right-hand corner of the visitation room. He sat the stack of papers on the table before he took a seat. Within minutes his father, Samson, was escorted in by two black correctional officers. They looked like monsters compared to Samson. The three men walked into the visitation room laughing with enjoyment all over their faces.

"We'll talk after your visit," one officer said.

"Okay, we will do that," Samson said as he turned around with a smile on his face.

The new inmate painting caught his attention on the wall. The painting was a picture of a man holding his son within his arms. The picture was titled *A Father's Love*. As Samson walked over to the check-in desk, he thought of the painting.

"Excuse me, Officer Brown."

The clean-cut military man looked up from writing the time down that Samson arrived.

"Yes, sir, how can I help you, Mr. Ali?"

"Has anyone purchased that *Father's Love* painting or put a hold on it?" Samson asked as he pointed over at the painting.

"I can check for you," the officer said as he grabbed the inmates' work notebook from out the desk. He pulled the notebook out and sat it on top and flipped through the pages. After a few seconds of looking through the book, the respectful military man said, "No, sir, it's still on the market."

"Thank you, Mr. Brown. I would like to buy it for my son if possible. How do I go about purchasing it?"

"If you have enough money in your inmate trust fund account, all you have to do is fill out a money transfer request, and I will put a hold on the picture until it clears. Once it clears, he can pick it up."

"Do you have any of those requests?" Samson asked.

"Yes, sir, I sure do," the officer said as he reached down underneath the desk, grabbed one, and handed it to Samson.

"Thank you, sir," Samson said.

"You're welcome."

"One more thing, can I use your pen to fill out this request, Mr. Brown?"

"Sure," he said as he reached up to pull the pen from his shirt pocket.

Samson filled out the request and passed the pen back.

"Thank you once again, Mr. Brown," Samson said.

"You are more than welcome."

Samson then walked over to the table where Adam had sat to the side for them. As he walked up, Adam rose to his feet.

"As-salamu alaykum, son [May peace be upon you]."

"Wa alaykumu s-salam [My peace be upon you also]," Adam responded to his father's greeting with a smile across his face.

"How's your health and well-being, son?"

"All praise to Allah [God], I'm doing good. What about you?" Adam asked.

"Alhamdulillah [All praise are due to God]. Without Him, I couldn't be better. Allah [God] has been showing His favors on me. Neither Mr. Gaines nor I has heard anything from appeal court. Inshallah [God's will], I will be able to get a new trial," Samson replied.

"Will Mom's testimony be of any help?"

"I hope so. It's all a long shot, but Allah is Akbar [God is the greatest]."

"Guess what, Dad?"

"What?"

"Mark got me a part-time job at his family's law office here in Nashville, not too far from school. I am going to need the hands-on anyway."

"That's a blessing. When was the last time you talked to your mom?"

"I talked to her days ago. I knew I had something to tell you. If you don't already know, Verlena still hasn't decided on where she wants to go for college. I tried to convince her to move down here with me. That way, we could get us an apartment together off-campus. She wasn't going for that. She wants to be around Mustafa. So most likely she's going to enroll in one of the colleges in Colorado. For sure somewhere near. She wants to be home on the weekends. That's pretty much where she stood when she got off the phone."

"I'm not going to say anything to her about it. I am going to let her make her choice. Whatever she decides, I'm going to support her. What's been going on with you, son? Do you shoot ball or play any kind of sports?"

"Yes, sir, I can hoop a lil bit. My game is football," Adam said as he did the Heisman pose.

"Why don't you play?" Samson asked.

"I don't want anything to take my focus off me getting you out this place."

"What about females? What have you been doing to stay from them? I know they be all over you."

"As far as the girlfriend-boyfriend thing, I haven't put myself out there like that. There have been a lot of females trying to talk to me on that level, and the way I sort of brush them off, they probably think I am gay, ha-ha." They both laughed.

"Why don't you use the opportunities to share your belief with them?" Samson asked.

"They are not trying to hear anything about religion. So I see them and don't. They see me as a handsome and focused student. They only be trying to get me in bed. It's this beautiful sister who's been hitting on me. She seems to be a very nice and focused young lady. We are enrolled in the same classes. She came on to me yesterday. As we were walking, I could feel her just staring at me. I kept my glance lowered. The way she was looking at me made the hair stand up on the back of my neck. She asked me to go with her to a party on campus that they are having tonight."

"What did you say?" Samson asked

"I told her that I had something lined up."

"What do you have lined up?" Samson asked with a serious look on his face and head tilted slightly to the right side.

"I use the time that I have after I leave here to study. I did tell her that I would make it up to her and to give me until Monday to come up with something," Adam said as he leaned back and crossed his feet, with a big Kool-Aid smile on his face.

"What are you smiling for?"

"Because I think I got myself into a situation yesterday. I really think I might have put my foot in my mouth."

"Why do you say that, son?"

"I gave her my word that I would make it up to her. I just should have told her that I have something to do and left it like that. Me and my soft heart. Don't get me wrong, Dad. She is a beautiful, smart, and open-minded female."

"Son, that's just might be what you need. You need to start going out doing something. You are doing time right along with me. You must get a peace of mind. What I mean by that is you are focusing too much on getting me out and neglecting yourself in the process. You must learn to relax and allow Allah to put things in order. You can't do anything without His approval. It's His will, not yours, that your mind is open to receive the education that will be needed to get me out. Allah places people in your life for reasons. They might be an angel sent by Allah to help. So don't ever close positive people out. I don't have to tell you about the laws of Allah because you are aware of them. You know that you can't have sex before marriage and so on. Stuff like that I don't have to get into with you. You can take her out and respect yourself and her. I really would like for you to do that, son. Even if I have to pay for it myself. Go ahead and take her somewhere nice. Not to some nightclub or somewhere a lot of nonsense goes on. A nice place to eat would be just fine. Will you do that for me, son?"

"Yes, sir," Adam replied.

"Do you need any money?"

"No, sir."

"What did you say her name was again?"

"I didn't."

"You know what I mean, boy," Samson said with a smile on his face.

"Gloria."

"Son, you are twenty-one years old now. I need you to start loosening up some and realize that Allah got me here for a reason. If it's His will I get out, I will get out. If it is not His will, I won't get out. I am okay with that, for He is my creator. It's not about my will. It's His will that matters. Keep in mind what Jesus said. He said, 'The servant is not greater than the Master.' Have you thought about what you are going to do once you graduate?"

"I don't know right now what I am going to do. I can stay in school here to get my master's or go to school in Memphis and get me a job with a law firm down there. Uncle Brandon knows a lot of people down there. Those are my two choices. Staying up here near you and continue working with Mark at their firm. I think it would be the best out of the two. Transferring to Memphis State University has its good and bad points. The good ones are I would be able to get with one of the top law firms down there. Like I said, Uncle Brandon knows a lot of the heavy hitters in the law business. He said a few of their names. Right now I can't recall them. The bad ones are I will have to drive almost three hundred miles each way every weekend to visit you and get to meet new people. Inshallah [if it's God's will], I will have my mind made up by the end of this school year, Dad. I really like being up here close to you. You are the main reason I wanted to come here."

Samson just sat back and looked at himself within Adam. He understood his son's standpoint. When he was a year or two younger, he had to make the choice to stay at home with his sick grandmother and younger sister or enlist for service in the armed forces. So Samson just sat there and listened to his unsure son talk without offering his opinion in the matter.

"Dad, I was reading where it said a believer shouldn't stop one task and go to another one. Right now I am blocking everything out of my life. I have a father I love and thank Allah for every day. But my father is locked up for defending himself and his family. It might have affected me differently if I didn't see everything with my two eyes. Now I am forced to relive that night over and over. It didn't affect all of us the same way. I was left with a choice to do something about it or go through life trying to pretend like nothing happened, holding the pain inside. I'm awakened night after night from nightmares from the stuff I saw that night. Allah [God] says in the Qur'an don't oppress and don't be oppressed. I chose to act on the words of Allah. When Mom was on drugs, Verlena and I didn't have anything—I mean anything—to eat," Adam said as the tears built up in his eyes from the pain he had to incur. "I stole, swept parking lots, cut grass, and some more stuff. I made sure we stayed in school. Dirty clothes on, run-down shoes—the list goes on. Not because it was the right thing to do but because I knew that we could get two for-sure meals five days a week. I thank Allah for you. You as a father figure raised me to stand up. It's what you taught me that I acted on. When I stole, I did it because I had no other choice. I prayed for Allah [God] to help us, and He did. From the age of ten to thirteen were the worst years of my life. It also became the cornerstone of my faith. It is what I call a learning experience. I knew something had happened to Verlena because I couldn't do anything without her being all under me. She started sleeping in the bed with me. I tried to talk to her, but she wouldn't talk about it. Allah is the greatest. I knew He had answered my prayers when Aunt Tiltyla's car pulled up. I didn't even speak to her. I just walked up to her and asked, 'Are you here to get us?' She said, 'Yes, if that's what I need to do. She didn't have to say anything else. I grabbed Verlena by her hand and told her, 'Come on, let's go.' We got in her car and did not get out. I know you wanted the best for me, Dad, and I wanted the best for you. I will not feel at ease until you walk out that front gate. You used to tell me all the time, 'Whatever my mind could conceive, I could achieve.' The only way that that concept could come true is I put forward a working effort. Nothing comes to a sleeper but a dream. You have been locked up over eleven years. That's eleven years too long. I'm not going to just sit on my butt and wait on them to kill you. I have found a lot of errors in your transcripts that will get your case overturned. The case just being overturned means you will only get off death row. You will still have a life sentence. Also, the FBI was mentioned. I remember seeing them that night. They followed us home. Did they talk to you?"

"Yes, they did," Samson answered.

"The reason I asked that is because I looked through the stack of transcripts on the table. They were only mentioned by your attorney. For the FBI to be around there, they were investigating something or someone. When they got to the scene, all they did, which was a blessing, was to stop the police from jumping on you or even killing you. All they did after they stopped them was to look around. One of them talked to Mom for a moment then told her she could go. What did they say to you?"

"They came to visit me right after I was sentenced. They talked like it was possible for me to get out. What really puzzled me was they said that I was in the wrong place at the right time. Like I just said, they told me that they might be able to get me off the hook if I could provide them with the right information. I told them that your mom woke me up right before they made me get out the car. So they asked to talk to her. But she was nowhere to be found. I never heard from them again."

"Do you remember their names?" Adam asked.

"Yes, I do. I still have the business cards they gave me," Samson said.

"I need you to send me their information ASAP. In the meantime, I am going to go down to Teller County to see what I can come up with or dig up. There is a reason why the FBI was there, and we need to know why.

When you send me the FBI information, send me Mr. Gaines's too. As I was reading your transcripts, I saw that he tried to put up a fight for you."

"He did. He just didn't have enough to work with."

"Do you think he will be willing to work with me?"

"Sure, he would! He has become a good friend of mine. Whenever he gets the time, he stops by to visit me," Samson added as the two sat up, straightening their chairs, thinking.

"He gets right on top of everything I ask him to do. So call him as soon as you get his information," Samson said.

"Dad, it's time for me to go. I love you."

"I love you too, son."

"I am going to take your advice. Inshallah [God's will], I will take Gloria out some time next week."

"Enjoy yourself," Samson said with a smile on his face. "Oh yeah, son, make sure you stop up here one day this week and pick up that painting right there," Samson said as he pointed at the picture.

"Okay, I will, Inshallah [if it's God's will]."

The two hugged and said their goodbyes.

CHAPTER 10

"Good morning, students. I must let all of you know that this is one of the best classes of students, if not the best I have had within my twenty-seven years of teaching at this school. This class has been focused— so focused that you all have the highest test scores in the history of this school. Do you all know what that means for me? You all have showed this university and others that I am doing what I get paid for. I see that it will be a fight for who's going to graduate head of the class. There's one major problem that we have in this class that needs to be addressed. That problem is racism—yes, racism," Professor Roberson stated.

He looked into their eyes after capturing their attention.

"Oh yes, it is noticeable. A blind man would be able to recognize it. For the last three years, this class has been racially divided. My black students sit on one side and my white students on the other side. Look around you. You would have to be spiritually blind not to see it. This is not good at all—not for any of you. Do you all remember the goal sheets that you gave me three years ago?"

The students nodded.

"Most of you said that your goal was to get a higher education, so you could make good money. I went over all the goal sheets, and I still look over them to make sure you all are living up to them. Most of you have been following the guidelines that you set for yourself. All but one of you wrote down your reason for going into the law field has to do with money. Adam Ali's reason was the total opposite of that. I am not going to go any further into his reason because it's personal. I will say this: he wants to help someone, and he must know law to help. Now on to the new news," Professor Roberson said as he walked around the classroom with his arms locked behind his back.

"Before you are able to graduate, you will have to do a senior thesis. The paper will have a big twist from any other thesis that I have ever had my students write. This paper is important for two reasons. One is you will need to graduate. Two, it will take you a long way in life. In the field of law, you all will have to deal with other nationalities and races of people. You will not be able to just deal with your kind, your race in this world. You don't have to like others outside of your race, but it is a must that you respect them. Take a look around this classroom. This is an actual footage of segregation. To be truthful with you all, I don't like it. I am hoping that I can change it. This is the plan to try to solve this segregation problem in my class. I have forty-two students. I divided that number in half to twenty-one. I made two of each number and put them in separate bags. There are twenty-one numbers in the bag labeled black and twenty-one numbers labeled white. All my nonwhite students will pull from the bag labeled black. For my white students, you will pull from the bag labeled white. For my students who aren't either, if you don't feel comfortable pulling from the black bag, you may pull from the white bag. All I ask is that you wait until all my white students have pulled one. My aides are coming around with the bags. Please take only one number from the bag. Print your name on the back. You may want to remember the number you pulled."

One by one the teacher's aides went to each student, allowing them to put their hand down into the bag to pull a number. The number was printed on a white sheet of paper. Once the numbers were passed around, Professor Roberson continued, "My aides are on their way back around to pick up the numbers. The numbers will be posted on the board Monday when you get to class. If you are one of my white students, you will be writing a paper on African history, African American history, and how it relates to the person who has the same number as you. For my black students, you will have to write a paper on European history, European American history, and how it relates to the person who has the same number as you. You will have to get to know the person you are writing about to complete this assignment." A white female student with long brown hair, combed back into a ponytail, raised her hand. "Yes, Ms. Janice Henderson, how may I help you?" Professor Roberson asked as he looked over at her.

"Professor, what is the reason for this nonsense that you are having us to do?" she asked in sarcastic voice, moving her head from side to side.

"If you were listening, Ms. Henderson, you wouldn't be asking me that question. Once again, the reason for this is to get this class off the racial trip that it's on. I have a question for you and anyone who feels like you. It's a question you don't have to answer out loud. How do any of you expect to be good attorneys, district attorneys, or even judges with racism and hatred in your heart? It will be close to impossible for you to be just. That is a fact. We have about five minutes before the bell rings. If any of my nonblack or nonwhite students have a problem with writing this paper, you may use this time to come up and talk about it. Remember that the names and numbers will be posted Monday morning, so you will know who you will be writing your paper on. Also, starting Monday, you will have forty-five days to get to know the person who has the same number as you. Have a good weekend, and hopefully I will see you all Monday morning," Professor Roberson said as the bell rang.

The students didn't waste any time to exit the classroom so they could talk about their assignment. Gloria waited outside the classroom, knowing that Adam and Mark always were the last two to leave out.

"Excuse me . . . first of all, how are ya'll doing?" Gloria asked.

"Pretty good," they both said simultaneously.

Adam added, "Thank god," at the end of his response.

"Adam, are you and Mark about to do something personal?" Gloria asked.

"No, not really, what's up?" Adam replied.

"I just wanted to spend some time with you, if it's not a problem."

"Ya'll excused, so excuse me. I am going to let you two have some alone time. I will see you later, bro."

"Okay, Mark, I will catch up with you later," Adam said as he shook Mark's hand with a light hug.

"I will see you later, Gloria. Take care of my brother," Mark said as he walked off.

"Don't worry about him, Mark. He's in good hands," Gloria said with a smile on her face as she looked at Adam out of the corner of her eyes.

"I'm in good hands, huh?" Adam asked to start the conversation.

"No doubt," Gloria said jokingly. "N-E way, what are you planning on doing today?"

"I was planning on going to the state park and feed the ducks and maybe do some reading," Adam said.

"Would you like to have some company?"

"Sure, I wouldn't run good company away," Adam said as he thought about what his father told him six months earlier when he first told him about Gloria.

The two walked to Adam's car. Adam, being a gentleman, opened the door for her. By the time he had made it to the driver's side, she reached over and unlocked his door.

"Thank you," Adam said as he got into the car.

"You're welcome," Gloria responded.

"Do you want something to snack on while we are at the park?" Adam asked as he was pulling into the lot to buy some of the on-sale day-old bread to feed the ducks while they were at the park.

"No, I'm good. Thank you anyway."

"Okay," Adam said before getting out of the car. When he got back, he reached over and put the bag of old bread into the backseat. The two had little to say for the remaining of the short ride to the park.

"This is it!" Adam said as he reached into the backseat to grab the bag of bread.

"So this is where you come to hide out?"

"I wouldn't say I come here to hide out. When the weather permits it, I like to come here to get me a little serenity and some fresh air," Adam said as he looked over at Gloria.

"Whatever . . . you probably be coming out here to hide from me."

Adam laughed. "Come on now, you got jokes. Why would I hide from you?" Adam asked.

"I'm just playing with you. On a real note, are you going to visit your father tomorrow?"

"God's will," Adam said.

"I would like to meet him. From being around you, I know he is a good person. I bet you got your qualities from him."

"You would have to go see him, so you could make that determination," Adam replied.

"Okay, Mr. Smarty, when you go to see him tomorrow, ask him if I can come with you next weekend to visit him."

"Okay, I am going to ask him. When next weekend gets here, don't chicken out," Adam said.

"You will chicken out before I will. I have something to ask you now. Don't chicken out on me. I have been doing a lot of thinking lately. You realize we have been seeing each other for six months now. I appreciate the way you have been treating and respecting me. In return, I have learned how to respect a person's religious beliefs. I don't know about you, but sex has crossed my mind a lot, especially when I'm around you. I am not saying this to try to pressure you into marriage or into having sex with me. Adam,

I really like you a lot. I just don't wanna be thinking that we are going to be together and have a future together when we are not. No one wants to be led astray, not me anyway. School will be over in a few more months. I just wanna know what's up. What are we going to do, Adam?"

Adam wasn't expecting Gloria to come with those questions. While Adam was speechless, she asked him more questions, "Are we going to further our relationship or what, Adam? Or are we going to be just someone we knew in college?" Adam still said nothing. "If this is a bad time, Adam, I apologize."

"No . . . no . . . no! I just don't want to say anything without thinking first. Gloria, we have less than three months of school left. Let's stay focused on that and see where we go from there. Then, if it's God's will that we get married, let it be so. But I don't want to rush into anything. My father is on death row for defending his family. My main focus is on getting him out, not sex, money, or anything else. I ask that you respect that. By me having this task at hand, I wouldn't be able to give you, my wife, or anyone else in my life the quality time that I'm supposed to give."

"Adam, you are talking about things that we can do together. Two heads are better than one any day. Am I right or not?" Gloria asked.

"In some cases, you are right," Adam said.

"I know how you feel about your father, and I'm not trying to take that away from you or trying to hinder you from your goals. I just want to be a part of whatever you got going on in your life," Gloria said with a serious look on her face, trying her hardest to stop from crying.

"Gloria, I like you a lot too. Right now let's stay focused on school, and in between time, we will work on us, okay?"

"Okay, that sounds good enough to me," Gloria said as she tried to regain her composure.

"Are you hungry now?" Adam asked as he hugged her.

"Yes, sir, I am," she said as the two hugged.

"Let's go get us something to eat."

"What are you going to do with this bread?" Gloria said.

"Keep it. I will be back Sunday, God's will. I have a taste for some fish. What about you?" Adam asked.

"That will work for me."

"I know this drive-through restaurant that sells the best fillet fish sandwiches that I have had here in Nashville," Adam said.

"Do they sell salads too?" Gloria asked.

"Sure, they are pretty fresh too."

Adam drove up to the drive-through window. The two placed their orders at one window, then drove up to the next window, and received their orders. After receiving the orders, Adam pulled over and parked. The two ate and shared their opinions on the class assignment that Professor Roberson lined up for Monday. After they finished eating, Adam drove back to the school campus. Gloria softly grabbed Adam's hand as he pulled over to let her out in front of her living unit.

"Thanks, Adam. Make sure you don't forget to ask your father about next week."

"I won't forget, God's will."

"If you do, I am going to beat you up, and you don't want me to do that," Gloria said as she got out the car with a smile across her face.

"Okay, make sure you have a good night too."

Adam prepared himself for the next day. Early the next morning, he walked through the gates of the maximum prison with a large stack of papers than he had the week before. Once he made it through the checkpoints, he walked into the visitation room and up to the desk to sign in.

"Good morning," said Officer Brown, the ex-military gentleman who secures the visitation room.

"Good morning," Adam responded.

"We are running a little late for some odd reason today. We will have your father down here soon," the gentleman said as he looked Adam in his eyes.

"Okay, thanks."

Adam walked over to his favorite table, sat the stack of papers on it, and pulled a chair up a little closer so he could sit down. He sat there and thumbed through the stack of papers. He went through copies of Samson's sentencing hearing and research notes he obtained from his trip to Teller County a few days prior. His father walked up before he could get into his new discovery. The two gave their salams (greetings of peace) and hugged. Samson pulled up him a chair.

Looking at all the papers his son had on the table, Samson asked, "What do you have there, son?"

"I told you that I was going down to that small town Teller County. I finally got around to doing it a few days ago. The reason I didn't write and tell you about them is because I had not gone through them. Dad, I have a lot of good stuff here. But it doesn't add up. For some reason, I can't find the main piece to this puzzle. Mom and I talked to Special Agent Woods of the FBI on a three-way phone call on Thursday. Mom told him who she was. He remembered her but wouldn't give us a straightforward answer to any of our questions. He did say that Officer George Fuhrman is Teller County's newly elected sheriff.

"I also got to talk to Mr. Gaines, and we went over a lot of stuff surrounding your case. That's not all. When I went down to Teller County, I stopped by their local library. I was just trying my hand to see if there was any reason or anything major going on that would draw the FBI down there to that area before the night everything happened. There was a big article in the local newspaper a week before you killing that cop. The twelfth woman had come up missing along that same twenty-five-mile stretch of highway. That makes me do a little more digging. About six months before that night, a young white woman in her early twenties came forward stating that the same two officers pulled her over and put her into the backseat of their squad car. One of them drove her car to an isolated location. They followed behind him in the squad car to the same location. Once there, they forced her to perform all kinds of sexual acts with both. As I read on, she later recanted her story. From the look and sound of it, she was given a good reason to change her story."

"You are probably right," Samson said as he placed his hand up to his mouth.

As he thought more deeply, Adam talked more, "I have been trying to put two and two together, but it's not adding up. Dad, if I am not mistaking, you told me that the FBI told you that you were in the wrong place at the right time?"

"That's correct. I said that."

"Look at this," Adam said as he picked up an article and passed it to Samson.

As Samson was looking at the article on the table, Adam looked at his father's expression. "All these articles clearly state that they are alleged abductions," Adam said.

"Do you know why they are reporting them like that?" Samson asked.

"Because none of the women's bodies have been found or their cars even to this day."

"Has anything turned up?" Samson asked.

"Nothing. It's like they have vanished from the face of the earth.

What I think is those cops were pulling lone white women over along that twenty-five-mile stretch of highway, first raping them and then killing them. That was most likely what they were up to the night that they pulled Mom over. I might be wrong, but I don't think so. That's why the FBI said that you were in the wrong place at the right time. They were going to get themselves another victim that night. Ever since then, no women have come up missing. If someone other than you were in the car that night, they would have played it off. You being a black man in that car with a white woman made the racism come out of them. Mom said she felt something was wrong from the moment George Fuhrman walked up to the car and bent down. She said he looked around in the car like they needed her to be alone. The way he acted she said it sent chills through her body. So she watched him through the rearview mirror as he walked toward the back and signaled for his partner. That's when she started waking you up. The sound of her voice not only woke me up but also scared me."

"Son, with all this information we have here, in all actuality, we don't have anything or should I say enough. We can't prove anything. That's why the FBI hasn't locked him up. They know that it was someone of an authority pulling the women over," Samson said.

"You're right. That's why I am puzzled they don't have anything to go on. I can see the FBI standpoint now. It had to be someone of authority to get them to pull over in the dark."

"Right! Son, you are close but not close enough." Samson said.

"So true. I still have a lot of unfinished work to do. Before it slips my mind, Dad, Gloria wants me to ask you if she can come with me next weekend to visit you."

"Sure, it's okay with me. What about you?" Samson asked.

"It's okay with me too. She really wants to meet you. She told me if I didn't ask you if she could come, she was going to put hands on me. She didn't say it like that, but she did say she would beat me up." They both laughed.

"How do you feel about her?" Samson asked with a little laughter left in his voice.

"She's very nice. I like her. I found out yesterday that she is very serious about us starting a relationship. She is willing to help me with your case. She let it all out yesterday. I mean she let it all out too. She started crying and all. I just told her that we need to stay focused on school and we will see from there what Allah has planned for our future. I also allowed her to know my main goal is to get you out."

"Is that when she told you she would help you with my case or before?" Samson asked.

"I think it was after I told her you are my main goal. I like her and think she would make a wonderful wife. She knows I'm Muslim and respects it," Adam said.

"What kind of character does she have?"

"She has a beautiful character. Her parents taught her some good morals. She asked me if I got my qualities from you. I told her that she would have to meet you to make that determination. I will bring her up here next week so you two can meet, Inshallah [if it's God's will]."

"I'm going to be looking forward to it," Samson said.

"Okay, she is also," Adam replied.

"Have you made up your mind yet about staying or moving to Memphis?" Samson asked.

"No, sir, not really. I have been leaning more toward Memphis because of the opportunities. I want to see what Uncle Brandon has in mind and lined up for me. I am going to give him a call one day this week that's coming up. Speaking of him, Dad, here he comes now."

"As-salamu alaykum [May peace be with you]," Brandon said.

"Wa alaykumu s-salam," Samson and Adam replied simultaneously with smiles on their faces. "We were just talking about you," Samson said as the two embraced.

"I hope it was about the good things I have done and not the bad ones," Brandon said.

"All good things about you, brother," Samson said.

"Lil Brother, you are looking good with that gray in your beard," Brandon said.

"Thanks, I feel good too, all praise to Allah. I have a bone to pick with you," Samson said.

"What have I done now?"

"Why aren't you ever at home when I call?"

"I am a working man, brother. If I don't work, I won't eat. Don't you have my cell phone number?"

"No!" Samson said.

"I will write it down for you before I go."

"Will I be able to call it collect?"

"That I don't know. I will check with my phone company. The phone is a gift from the military. They gave it to me so they could keep track of me. They have me running in and out the Middle East. Since Operation Desert Storm, the United States has been using me as a liaison for America to the Kuwaitis and Saudis. My background as far as my belief, my status, and my ability to speak multiple languages gave me this headache. I will be leaving out next week."

"How long will you be gone?" Adam asked.

"For about sixty days. I will be touring all over the Middle East and some parts of Africa Inshallah."

"I still will be making it my business to drive down to Memphis to see Aunt Lisa. I can never catch up with Fatimah when I'm down there," Adam said.

"She is one busy young lady. She has her hands full with school and work. You are good if you catch her. By the way, they will be finished building my house by the time I get back into the country. Speaking of that, Adam!"

Adam looked at him closely.

"Have you made up your mind on what you are going to do after graduation?" Brandon asked.

"No, sir, not yet. I was just telling my dad that I am going to call you to see what you have lined up."

"If you do decide to move to Memphis, you could have the house that I am living in now for your graduation present if you want it," Brandon said.

Adam's eyes got big, and he opened his mouth, but no words came out.

"Ha-ha-ha!" Brandon and Samson laughed as Adam fought trying to gain control of himself.

"Alhamdu lillahi rabbil alamina [All praise are due to God, the Lord of all the worlds]" were the only words that Adam could say at the moment.

"May Allah be pleased with your giving. Thank you, Uncle Brandon," Adam finally said.

"You're welcome. How are you and that young lady coming along, the one you told me about?" Adam's uncle asked.

"Pretty good," Adam said with a million and one things going through his head.

"Are you planning on marrying her?"

"We have talked about it. Inshallah [if it's God's will] in the future. Allah knows best. Basically, I have just been trying to stay focused on Dad's case and school. I made a major breakthrough, but it's not enough. I got a lot of good information that's not vital."

"Why do you say that?" Brandon asked.

"Because the most important stuff is still out there somewhere," Adam said with a disappointed look on his face.

"Inshallah, the truth will come to the light soon. What did you find out when you went to Teller County?" Brandon asked.

"That the stuff I was just mentioning, to make a long story short, those two cops killed twelve women. If Dad wouldn't have been in the car with Mom, she would have been the thirteenth. The reason nothing has been done is because the FBI can't find the bodies or the women's cars. Now that George Fuhrman is the sheriff of Teller County, they may not ever turn up."

"What is done in the dark will come to the light. Inshallah, his past will catch up with him soon," Brandon said.

"I pray so," Adam said.

"Adam, what is the young lady's name?"

"Gloria."

"Samson, have you met her yet?"

"No, not yet. Inshallah, Adam is going to bring her up here next weekend."

"Where are you going to let me meet her, Adam?"

"When we leave here, I could take you by the campus to meet her, if you like."

"I'm in no hurry. I can do that."

"Big Brother, when was the last time you've seen Bernard Scott?" Samson asked.

"I will have to say about a month or two ago."

"I have not seen him in almost a year. He came by to let me know he had made captain," Samson said.

"He is stationed in Kuwait right now. Overall, he has been doing pretty good Alhamdulillah [all praise are due to God]," Brandon said.

"Visitation is now over. All inmates, remain seated. All visitors, you may leave and thank you all for coming," the loud voice said over the PA system.

"I'm going to try to get a special visit with you before I leave the country. Since I don't have enough time to give you my cell phone number, just call the house tonight. I will be there Inshallah. I love you, brother. God's will, I will see you later."

"I love you too, brother. Make sure you be at home. I'm going to call around eight thirty or nine. I love you, son. Inshallah, I will see you and Gloria next weekend."

"Inshallah, next week, Dad. I love you too. All that paperwork is yours. I have my copies," Adam said.

"Okay, son, I will look them over, and hopefully we will be able to talk about it next week."

"Uncle Brandon, you can follow me to UT," Adam said.

"That will work. You're the man. Lead the way."

Once Adam approached the school campus, he slowed down, hoping that he would see Gloria outside. *There she is,* Adam said to himself as he blew his horn to get her attention. Gloria and two of her female friends were walking across the grass. Once they heard the horn blowing, they turned around.

"He is blowing for me. I will see ya'll later," Gloria said as she walked toward Adam's car.

Adam pulled over and put the car in park. Brandon pulled over behind him. The two exited their cars as Gloria walked up. "Gloria, I have someone I would like for you to meet. Uncle Brandon, this is Gloria. Gloria, this is my uncle Brandon," Adam said as he walked up to Gloria.

"Hi, Gloria, how are you doing? It's nice to finally meet you," Brandon said.

"I'm doing okay, I guess. It's nice to meet you too."

"My nephew has told me a lot about you. All good things I must say."

Gloria's face lit up like a Christmas tree as she reached over and pinched Adam on his arm.

"Thank you, sir, and it's good that Adam allowed me to meet you," she said as she quickly turned her face toward Adam with a smile.

"Can I take you to somewhere nice to eat? I promise not to talk too much or ask a lot of questions." Adam and Gloria looked at each other. Adam nodded, and both agreed. The three entered into Brandon's car and went to find a nice place to eat.

CHAPTER 11

Monday morning came quickly. All the students anticipated this morning. They had no clue on who they would be writing their senior thesis on. A lot of the students didn't like the idea of associating themselves with the opposite race, knowing that they had come too far to turn back. The professor waited until all the students assembled in the classroom. Once the bell rang and all the students were seated, he turned the blackboard around so the names that he had written could be seen. The students looked at the blackboard for their names and who had pulled their same number.

"Adam Ali, you pulled number one. Janice Henderson, you pulled the same number, number one. You and Mr. Ali will have the opportunity to get to know each other." Professor Roberson said as he looked over at Janice before reading the rest of the names off the blackboard.

Janice knew that he was singling her out. She rolled her eyes at him as he turned toward the blackboard. Janice didn't like the idea of associating with blacks. When she realized that the person was Adam, she felt little comfort. Adam possessed some Caucasian resemblance and attributes that were a lot different from those of the blacks she had encountered around campus.

"For those of you who would like to start today getting to know the person you will be getting acquainted with the next forty-five days, you may use this time to do so," Professor Roberson said after reading off all the names.

Adam got up and walked over to where Janice was sitting.

"Excuse me, my name is Adam . . . Adam Ali," he said as he extended his hand toward her.

Janice acted as if she didn't see him standing there with his hand out. Adam looked at her for a moment. He wasn't the type to bite his tongue. He took a deep breath.

"I know you see me standing here, and I am okay that you don't want to touch me. We only have forty-five days to have this paper done. I would like to make the best of my time. Right now, at this point, I am not doing that," Adam said.

"So what do you mean by that?" Janice asked as she looked up, finally making eye contact.

"What I mean is we need to look over our personal differences. I'm not here to try to change the way you feel about me or people who look like me. All I am hoping is we could work together, and hopefully we can come up with something that will work for the both of us. If you don't want to do that, I think we should talk to the professor and see if he could switch us around," Adam said nicely.

Janice sat there silent as she weighed the situation.

I have two choices. One is not to do this shit. Two, to see if the professor would give me someone else, she said to herself as she sat there.

She looked up at Adam. "It doesn't matter. All of you are the same," Janice said.

Adam just looked at her and smiled as he shook his head.

"I'll tell you what, I think it would be best for us to go talk to the professor. I am quite sure he will resolve this frivolous matter."

She knew the assignment had to be done like the professor stated. She wanted to graduate, and that made her have a change of thought.

"No! We don't have to. I apologize for my egocentric behavior. We can handle this ourselves," Janice said.

"When will be the best time for you to get together?" Adam said, feeling a little relief.

"I work Friday through Monday, part-time. Any other day during the week will be good by me."

The two of them talked for the remaining of the class. Adam was the best example of a man he could be. His character was one of the things that stood out to Janice. She realized that he wasn't the human-like monkey she was taught growing up about blacks. Within those few limited minutes, the two of them started building a fellowship of respect. After the bell rang, Janice headed to work. Adam and Mark went down to the law firm. The two used their time wisely. They helped out around the office by doing a lot of the case research for the paralegals. The two left there and stopped at a fast food restaurant to get a bite to eat before heading back to the college campus.

"I will see you, God's will, in the morning, Mark."

"You can say *Inshallah*. I know what it means," Mark told Adam as he walked into his room.

At 12:30 a.m. the sound of a cell phone ringing caused Janice Henderson to sit up straight in her bed. Half asleep, she felt around in the dark until she located her phone on the table next to her bed.

"Hello," she said.

"May I speak to Ms. Janice Henderson?"

"This is she."

"Are you the Janice Henderson related to Eric Henderson?"

"Yes, I am. He is my brother. Why do you ask?"

"I would like to inform you that there has been an accident pertaining to your brother."

"What kind of accident?"

"He was shot in an apparent robbery at the convenient store where he works security."

"My god, is he okay?"

"I can't say at this time. He has been flown to the hospital in Jackson, Tennessee, where he is about to undergo surgery."

"What's the name of the hospital he was flown to?" Janice asked.

"Jackson General."

"Thank you for notifying me."

"You're welcome."

Janice hung up the phone and within minutes found herself flying down I-40 West in the fast lane. Thoughts of death ran through her head.

God, please let Eric be okay. He is all I have left. Please, Lord, let him be okay. I beg you.

Her heart rushing and mind filled with the worst, she turned into the parking lot of the hospital. She grabbed her cell phone and purse before exiting her car and running into the emergency room. As she entered the emergency room short of breath, she felt a little better to see the support from family and friends. One by one, they approached her with tears in their eyes and embraced her. Janice knew at that point that things were bad and her brother wasn't doing very well.

"Has anyone told you what happened?" a woman asked. She looked like she could be a family member by her slight resemblance.

"No," Janice answered.

"All we know is two masked men tried to rob the store where he works," the middle-aged lady said.

"Does the sheriff have anyone in custody?" Janice asked.

"Not that we know of. As soon as we heard about it, we came straight down here. All I know is what Sheriff Fuhrman said on the news."

"What did he say?" Janice asked.

"He said multiple shots were fired. They believe at least one of the robbers was shot by your brother. They are checking all the surrounding hospitals for him."

"Aunt Sarah, has anyone come out to talk to you all?" Janice asked.

"Someone came out about two hours ago asking for you. I signed the consent form for them to go ahead and operate on him."

"Thank you, Aunt Sarah."

"You're welcome, baby. I don't feel too good. I'm going home. Call me when he comes out of surgery," Aunt Sarah said.

"Okay, I will talk to you later," Janice said.

After three and a half hours of surgery, Eric was stabilized and moved to ICU. A doctor came out and talked to Janice. "Hi, I am Dr. Coleman. Your brother was lucky. If there wasn't a doctor on the scene, your brother wouldn't have been here. The quick action of the doctor on sight saved his life."

"How is he doing?" Janice asked.

"He's in stable condition. Right now, he is in a coma. There is a possibility that he will never walk again."

"Where was he shot?"

"In the upper part of his chest, near his neck. The bullet cleaved a main artery into. We were unable to remove the bullet during the operation."

"Why not?"

"He's going to need a specialist to do the very complicated operation. The bullet is pushing against his spine, and we couldn't take the chance of trying to remove it. We went in to fix the cleaved artery, so we could get him stabilized. He had a lot of internal bleeding," Dr. Coleman said.

"How long will he be in the coma?"

"That I don't know. You are welcome to stay with him if you like."

"I will be staying," Janice said.

"I will have someone to bring you something to sleep on and show you to his room."

"Thank you very much, Doc," Janice said as she waited for someone to show her to the ICU of Eric.

After about five minutes, Janice was escorted to her brother's ICU. She walked in and saw him lying in bed with tubes in his nose and mouth. She started crying from the sight of his lifeless body lying there. The thought of losing him was at the forefront of her mind. She was still trying to get over the mysterious death of her father two years earlier. She was only eighteen months old when her mother died from cancer. Eric is the only one she has left. With his life hanging by a string, she was forced to turn to God once again. She prayed and cried herself to a sleep.

Tuesday morning came quickly. Janice had to make the two-and-a-half-hour drive back to school. Running late, she rushed to class. Professor Roberson held his head up as she entered the classroom and quietly took her seat. He didn't stop talking; he just nodded to let her know that he's aware of her tardiness.

"I would like to inform you all that there are only forty-four days remaining to have your senior thesis completed and turned in. I don't want to see any last-minute work. There are only fifteen days remaining before one of the biggest examinations you will take for the year. It will cover the Tennessee Rules of Court, the Tennessee Rules of Civil Procedure, the Tennessee Uniform Commercial Code Forms, Tennessee Criminal Practice and Procedures, Tennessee Legal Forms, and the Tennessee Rules of Court, state and federal. For the next two weeks, my suggestion to you all is reread chapters 9, 10, 11, and 12. I don't think that this class will have any problems with this examination. Most of you are pretty knowledgeable. That shows me that you all have been applying yourselves. For the ones who need a little, I suggest that you get with Mark or Adam. They are just two of the students in this class who know their way around law books," Professor Roberson said as he turned and walked to his desk.

"If you all like, you could use the remainder of the class to work on your thesis or prepare for the examination coming up. Just hold down the noise."

Janice got up and moved over to the empty desk next to Adam. She spoke to Adam as she sat down. Adam looked up and saw that it was Janice.

"Hi, Janice, you look like something is troubling you! What's wrong, if you don't mind me asking?"

"My brother was shot last night."

"Is he doing better now?"

"No, not really, he is in a coma, and the doctors really don't know how long he will be in it."

"I hope and pray that he is okay and comes out of it soon . . . amen."

"Adam, I won't be able to meet with you this week. I will be at the hospital with him. I am going to need your help before I go back to Jackson, Tennessee."

"If it's within my power, I will be more than happy to help out with whatever you need me to do," Adam replied.

"No telling how long I am going to be at the hospital with him. I am going to need some books on African history. I have some books on African history."

"I can help you out with that. Once again, I pray that God be with you and your brother."

"Thank you, Adam. I need to talk to the professor. I will meet with you after class."

"Okay," Adam said.

As Janice was walking off, Gloria walked over and sat down in the same desk that Janice got up out of.

"How are you doing this afternoon?"

"I'm blessed and highly favored," Adam said.

"Show noughs?"

"Show nought how about yourself?" Adam asked.

"I can't complain. Are you ready for the big exam coming up with in the next two weeks?"

"Sure. What about you?" Adam asked Gloria.

"I'm going to reread those last four chapters to make sure I have everything down pat," Gloria said.

"I need to have a very important talk with you whenever you have time," Adam said.

"I have time now, if it's something you really need to talk about," Gloria said, thinking it was something wrong by the way Adam looked at her.

"I just want to ask you to move to Memphis with me after graduation."

"Boy, I thought you were going to say some crazy stuff. You had my heart beating fast. So is that your way of asking me to marry you?" Gloria asked.

"You can say that."

"Why don't you just ask me then?"

"We will talk about it later," Adam said.

"*Bak . . . bak . . .* you are a chicken, I told you."

"I'm not a chicken. I just want to stay focused on school until I get my degree in law."

"Why did you bring it up then? You might as well ask me today. Tomorrow isn't promised," Gloria said as she looked at Adam.

"Look at me!" Gloria demanded. Adam looked up.

"I am not going to get in the way of you getting your degree within the next few months. If you weren't going to be man enough to talk about this, you shouldn't have brought it up. I'm not going for that you can't say that mess. I want you to be man enough right now and ask me to marry you, or I am going to ask you in front of the whole class to marry me. So what are you going to do? Do you think I am playing?" Gloria said as she stood up.

"No, I don't think you are playing. Sit back down," Adam said. When she sat back down, Adam looked at her.

"Girl, you are crazy. I want it to be in the right setting when I finally propose to you. I just want you to think about what you are going to say when I do ask you to marry me."

"I already know what I'm going to say. I will say. 'Yes, I will marry you, Adam.'" Adam tried to put his hand over her mouth before she said that too loud.

"If you put your hand over my mouth, I'm going to bite you," Gloria said as she opened and closed her mouth, clicking her teeth together. Both burst out laughing.

"I told you that you are crazy," Adam said.

"I'm crazy about you, that's all," Gloria said with a smile on her face.

"My uncle Brandon told me Saturday that I could have his house, if I like, for a graduation prize. Thank God for giving me the provisions so I could get married. When we had that talk last week at the park, I didn't have the means for me to choose a wife. I must be able to provide for her. Things are beginning to manifest. All praise are due to God. When everything becomes clear, I will like for you to be my wife, if it's God's will."

Gloria just looked at Adam for a moment. She was speechless.

"Yes, I would love to move to Memphis with you, Adam. Adam, you don't have to have anything for me to be with you. We could get everything we need together, sooner or later."

"You're right. I could have asked you a long time ago. You know my father and uncle have been asking me when I was going to ask you to marry me," Adam said.

"What was your excuse?" Gloria asked.

"The same thing I have been telling you. This weekend, don't you chicken out because he would like to meet you. That brings something else to mind. When are you going to allow me to meet your parents?" Adam asked.

"The only way you can meet my family is if I introduce you as my fiancé. So you won't meet them until then. I am not going to take a man home to meet my parents and we don't have any wedding plans."

"Hummm, it's like that, huh? Well, we need to start making plans," Adam said as he looked at Gloria.

"What are you going to do after school?" Gloria asked with a smile on her face.

"Janice asked me to show her where she could buy some African history books. I'm going to put her up on some ancient African civilization books—none of that watered-down stuff. Most of the world, especially here in the Western world, only knows about Africa and how she fell from grace. A lot of blacks and whites only know what they see on TV or what they read in the Americanized books. They haven't taken the time out to see why a country rich with natural resources like Africa has people dying by the thousands of hunger or why a great continent with great countries within it like Ancient Egypt, Ancient Ethiopia, Ancient Gush, and Timbuktu, the list goes on. Gloria, it really makes a thinking person think and ask themselves how such countries fell the way they did. Even the black rulership vanished. Africans were robbed of everything even their history. That's going on as I speak."

"It is essential that we know where we come from," Gloria said.

"That's so true," Adam agreed.

"What are you going to do after you return from the bookstore?" Gloria asked.

"I don't have anything planned but my usual," Adam responded.

"The park!" both said together.

"What's on your mind?" Adam asked.

"I was hoping that we could go to the mall, walk around, and do us a little eye shopping. After that, catch us a movie or something."

"That sounds good to me. We can do that." Adam said as he moved his head up and down with his bottom lip over the top one.

"Where do you want me to meet you?" he asked.

"I will be outside waiting on you. It shouldn't take you too long. Just drive by my dormitory."

"I'm not going to drive. I am going to ride with her. So I will have Janice to drop me off at my car."

"Okay, I will see you when you get back."

After the bell rang, Adam walked over to where Janice was standing and asked her. "Are you ready to go to the bookstore?"

"Yeah, what about you?" Janice asked.

"Sure! Janice, do you mind if I ride with you?" Adam asked.

"No, I don't mind."

The two walked out to the parking lot. As they were about to get into Janice's car, Adam asked, "What did the professor say about you needing a few days off?"

"He was cool with it after I told him about my brother. Professor Roberson is pretty cool. He's just straightforward. As they say, he shoots from the hip."

The two had gotten to know each other slightly from the conversation they had in the classroom. Janice had found out more about Adam's origin. Adam let her know that his mother is white and his father is black. He went on to tell her that he has one sister and how long his parents have been married. He even pulled out his wallet and showed her their pictures.

Janice shared some of her family background with Adam. She told him how she was raised to hate blacks, Jews, and anyone who wasn't white. Her father was the head of the Klan for many years. After his death two years prior, her brother became the Grand Wizard. She understood why she was raised to hate Jews; but as for blacks, she didn't really know. She said that she was taught to hate Jews because they are the ones who killed Jesus Christ, and they are arrogant people. She admitted that she didn't know any history of blacks outside of American history. After Janice had the conversation with Adam, she started to like him as a person. His personality was outstanding. In her mind, she knew he had seen and witnessed hatred and racism from both sides. Just like Janice. Adam didn't know why whites hated blacks in America. They knew that a large percentage of Africans were brought to America and sold into slavery, and also, they were badly mistreated. Once they made it to the bookstore, Adam started showing Janice some of the same books that his father had given him to read when he was a kid.

"This book is about Africa at its best, not what you will see on TV and what they teach here in American education system," Adam said.

Janice just looked at him. "Janice, the Africa that we see today is the result of countries outside the continent taking from it and not giving back. We can say that's what's happening to that country could happen to any country. If people outside of them continue to take from it without giving anything back, over a period, that country will be broke, empty, and robbed of all its natural resources. Look at how much better life is here in America. America doesn't have nearly the natural resources that Africa has. Janice, here is something to think about. Racism and anything else that's not of God will vanish. As you can see, racism is slowly decaying. Twenty years from now, it won't be common. We will see a black man run for the highest office in this country and be elected president. Green will be the color people will notice. Don't get me wrong. It is good to be proud of your race, but you don't have to put another race down to feel that way," Adam said as he walked around the bookstore with Janice.

Adam had managed to break through a lot of years of behaviors with his personality and elegant way of explaining things. The two of them walked around the bookstore looking at books like they had known each other for years. Before Adam could locate a precise book he wanted for Janice, he got her to smile. With his attention captured by a beautiful card that was on a nearby shelf, he picked out two cards that drew his attention. One was a get-well card, and the other was a personal card for Janice. He then took the pen out of his shirt pocket and wrote on both of them. Inside the card for Janice, he wrote:

> God allows things to happen in people's lives for a reason. You don't have to worry any longer about your brother because God answers the prayers of His servants. Just stay focused on the lesson that God is trying to teach the both of you.
>
> A true friend,
> Adam

Adam walked up to the check-out counter and purchased the two cards and a book he wanted Janice to read. He had the cashier put them into a bag. Then he walked back to where she was standing.

"I found one of the books you suggested."

As she was talking, Adam reached up and grabbed a book from off the shelf and handed it to her.

"That's a pretty thick book. How many pages is this book?" Janice asked.

"It's close to eight hundred," Adam replied.

"My god, that's a lot of reading. Reading is something I don't like to do," Janice said.

"That will give you something to do while you're sitting up in the hospital. You will have these books knocked out in no time and be looking for something else to read. Trust me, those books will give you a lot to write about. Most of all, they will open your eyes to a lot of things."

"So you are telling me I will have these books read and my paper written by next week?"

"Sure, without a doubt," Adam said.

Seeing the bag in Adam's hand as the two got into the car, Janice asked, "Where did you run off to in the store?"

"I just went and got something for a friend," Adam said with a slight smile on his face.

Janice pulled up into the campus parking lot. Before the car stopped, she looked over at Adam.

"Thank you for taking out the time to show me where I could find these books. Most of all, thank you for the words of encouragement. God knows I needed them."

"You're welcome. I have something for you. I don't want you to open it until you get back to the hospital," Adam said as he passed her the bag.

"Okay," Janice said.

"Be safe. I will see you when you get back, God's will," Adam said.

As Janice was pulling off, Gloria walked up. Adam was about to get into his car when he saw her.

"You made it back quick," Gloria said.

"We just went downtown. It looks like you are ready," Adam said.

"I've been ready. That's why I walked around here."

"You have good timing," Adam said.

"Soon you will be able to feel me, just like I feel you," Gloria said with a smile on her face.

"Get out of here," Adam said.

"I can feel you trust me."

Adam opened the driver-side door and pushed the power lock so she could get in. They went to the mall and from the mall to the movies.

CHAPTER 12

Janice arrived at the hospital in Jackson, Tennessee. Before going inside, she grabbed the books she purchased and the bag she received from Adam. Once in the ICU, she walked over to her brother.

"How are you doing today?" she asked, not looking forward to a response. "I will be here until you wake up. We need to talk."

She sat the bag she received from Adam on the bed with him. Then she opened the bag to see what Adam had given her, which she had to wait to open until she got to the hospital. She reached into the bag and grabbed the two envelopes sitting on top of a book. She looked at them and sat one of them on her brother's leg. With a slight smirk on her face, she opened the envelope that revealed a colorful get-well card for her brother Eric.

"This nig—" Janice said before stopping short of saying the whole word. "This black guy who goes to school with me sent you a get-well card. If you don't mind, I would like to read it to you. It says, 'It is great prosperity in suffering for those who are wise. God grants wisdom to whom He pleases, and he to whom wisdom is granted receives indeed a benefit overflowing, but none will grasp the message but men of understanding. Eric, I pray that you are wise and grasp the message that God has sent you. Sincerely, Adam.'"

Janice looked around to escape the need to cry. The words that Adam used caused her jaws to tremble as tears rolled down. She turned back to look on to his lifeless body. With a cracking sound in her voice, she began to speak to him, "Eric, I pray that you can hear me. You are all I have. Whenever you get better things are going to have to change. We were raised to believe in God. Now it's time that we start living for Him. I truly believe now, Eric, that everything happens for a reason. Just over the last few days, I have come to understand the true meaning of the word n———. It's just not a word that applies to blacks. It's a word that could be applied to us because of the way we act. Another thing, Eric, how could we fix our mouth to say we love God but hate His creation? I just want you to think about that," Janice said as she leaned over the bedrail and kissed Eric on the forehead. "I love you," she said as she wiped the tears she had left on her lips.

She took the card and book off the bed and went over and sat down. She placed the bag with the book in it on a nearby table and grabbed one of the books she purchased. Before she started reading the book, she read the card that Adam gave her. That card made her feel better about the situation. She got comfortable and started reading her book. Hours passed, and her eyes began to slowly close. Before she knew it, she drifted off into a deep sleep. The book lay against her breast. She started seeing herself in her dream walking in the middle of the desert of Africa. The sun was at its highest point in the sky. As she was engulfed by the intense heat with no protection from the blistering sand floor, her skin started to cook. She felt like she had been out there for days without any water. Her lips began to swell with blister as she grew weaker by the second. She held her right hand above her eyes. From a far-off distance, she could see what looked like it could be a caravan of people on camels and horses. She started waving her hands. Her lips were too swollen to make a sound. Using the little strength that she had trying to stop them and get help, she gave out. Her body fell to the ground as she cried out, "Oh, God, please help me!" Lying on the burning-hot sand, she could feel herself getting weaker and weaker. She was at the point that she wanted to give up. While she lay there, she felt someone picking her up and washing the sand from her face with cool water. "Janice was put inside an enclosed wagon that looked like it could have been a stagecoach or carriage with a top on it. She looked out the opening in the back as she was being taken to a kingdom surrounded by a wall of marble and limestone. Upon their entering the kingdom, Janice could see people lining up and asking questions as the wagon passed.

"Is she all right?"

"God's will, she will be just fine," one man said with a smile.

The whole kingdom was showing true concern for Janice. As she was taken into a huge white marble castle trimmed in gold, the scene looked like something that you would only see on an animated cartoon show—a place where the mind could only imagine. Breathtaking for anyone who laid eyes on it. Janice was taken into the castle to a large room where she was laid down on a big and very soft bed; shortly after, two young black ladies walked into the huge room. While Janice was lying there weak, one of them began to speak to her.

"Janice, I need to cut your clothes off you so we can treat the sunburns."

Janice didn't say anything, just nodded and blinked her eyes. The young lady started cutting her clothes off. The other young lady walked over with a ceramic bowl filled with a yellowish-green substance. As Janice lay there, the young lady rubbed the substance all over Janice's blistered and sunburned body. She started at her face and worked downward to Janice's neck and arms.

"Where am I?" Janice mumbled.

The young lady administering the substance said, "You are in the land of Gush. You're safe. All you need to do right now is save your strength."

After the two ladies finished rubbing Janice down with ointment, another young lady wearing the color of her skin held a silver cup in her hands with a liquid in it.

"I have some nun mixed with khamr for you to drink. It doesn't taste too good, but it will give you all your strength back instantly," Toya said.

She then held Janice's head up while she placed the silver cup of liquid up to her mouth. As Janice was drinking the nun and khamr mix, she began to sit up. Like Toya said, the liquid was giving Janice her strength back with every swallow. She started thinking it was some kind of magic. Once the cup was empty, she immediately regained all her strength.

"How do you feel, Janice?" Toya asked.

"I feel much better. I wasn't sure at first when you walked into the room and said my name. How do you know my name?" Janice asked as she sat up.

"A wise man of the king told us of your coming."

"One of the females who came in told me that this is the land of Cush. I have never heard of this place. Where is it located?" Janice asked.

"We are southeast of the Red Sea and Kemet [Ancient Egypt]."

"So you are telling me I am in Africa?"

"I don't understand what you mean by Africa," Toya said with an unsure voice and look on her face.

Janice was puzzled.

"Are we near the great Pyramids of Egypt and the Red Sea that Moses and the children of Israel crossed?" Janice asked.

"Yes. So you know the stories of old?"

"Pretty much so," Janice replied.

"If you like, you can bathe now. I will get you something to wear. Dinner will be served soon. The king and queen would like for you to be there. Come, let me show you the bath area." Toya showed Janice a room right off the room she was in. The room would make you think of an oversized master's bedroom. When Janice walked into the bathroom, her eyes were captivated. Her mouth opened at the sight. The bathroom was equipped with marble floors, a sunken bathtub surrounded by marble trimmed with gold, and a golden lion's head, with water running out its mouth. It was the most beautiful bathroom setting that Janice had ever seen. Once she stepped down into the tub, she realized it was big enough to swim in. She washed off the ointment and noticed that the sunburns and blisters were gone. Just as Janice had bathed, Toya walked in with a drying towel in her right hand and a green, black, and gold silk dress across her left arm. The dress looked like it was made for a queen. Janice was used to wearing quality clothing, but never in her wildest dreams did she think she would be wearing a dress of that quality. Once she put it on, the feel of it sent chills through her whole body. All she could do was look down at it. The way that it fit her body, you would think it was tailor made for her. Toya pulled the handmade slippers from underneath her left arm and placed them on the floor for Janice to put her feet in. Once Janice was dressed, Toya escorted her to the dining room. Toya showed Janice to her seat at the royal table that looked close to a half of a street block long.

The members of the royal family walked in one by one. As they walked in, they looked over at Janice and greeted her with smiles. To let her know that they acknowledged her, they nodded downward and held the palms of their hands up. When everyone was seated, the king and queen walked in. The king and queen had on the same colors as Janice. There was a slight difference in the style of dress the queen wore. The king stood there for a few seconds to acknowledge Janice. She knew he was the king by the crown on his salt-and-pepper afro, unable to make him out, die to his very dark skin and big smile with bright white teeth. The queen, not as dark, could be recognized once she nodded at Janice and took a seat. Her skin, a glowing golden dark brown, stood out.

Right before everyone was finished eating, one servant, a big black man who stood close to seven feet tall, walked up beside Janice and leaned over next to her right ear and said, "Madam, the king would like to speak with you after dinner."

Janice nodded in response. Once everyone had finished eating, Toya, who was sitting in the seat next to Janice, got up.

"Janice, everyone will be meeting on the ballroom. If you would like to clean your teeth first, we will have to go get you some *miswaks* from the supply room."

As the two walked through the castle Janice became more amazed of its structure and layout. She noticed that everyone she passed was polite and didn't mind showing their beautiful white teeth to go with their big smiles. Toya walked into the supply room and grabbed a handful of wooden sticks and passed them to Janice. She took the sticks the size of pencils and didn't think too much of them. As the two walked off, Janice looked over at Toya.

"What am I supposed to do with these sticks?"

"Those are miswaks. We use them to clean our teeth," Toya said.

"They are for cleaning teeth?" Janice asked with an uncertain look on her face.

"Yes, they are for cleaning your teeth. Give me one so I can show you. They are really good for your teeth and gums," Toya said as Janice passed her one. Toya chewed on the tip of the miswak to soften it up. Once it was to her liking, she rubbed it up and down against her teeth. When she finished with her teeth, she rubbed her tongue with it. Then she showed Janice her white teeth. Janice liked how clean and bright they were. Janice tried it. Shortly after she finished cleaning her teeth with the miswak, she rubbed her tongue across them. She was surprised at how clean they felt to her tongue. She looked over at Toya and smiled. "They do clean your teeth. Wow, pretty nice."

Toya smiled as the two walked into the ballroom. When Janice entered the room, all eyes and smiles were on her. She could feel the acceptance of the black people.

"Follow me," Toya said as she walked through the large crowd.

The two walked through the ballroom to where they were met by the king and queen of Gush.

"Greetings, Janice. My name is Omri, and this is my queen, Leah."

Leah nodded and turned the palms of her hands upward to show their way of peace.

"Welcome to the land of Cush," the queen said.

"I would like to welcome you into our land. You are welcome to stay as long as you like. We have prepared for you a talent show. On behalf of the kingdom, we hope that you enjoy it," the king said.

"Thank you all very much," Janice said as she looked at the king and queen.

"If you would, follow me," the king said as he and the queen turned around and walked up two flights of stairs to the second level of the ballroom floor. They walked up to a place set aside for the royal family and their guest. The view of the whole talent show could be seen from the level.

Janice couldn't believe her eyes. They had chairs made of gold and animal skin—some of the most beautiful chairs made by men's hands. Janice was seated right next to the king. Before the talent show began, the king asked Janice questions, "Janice, my wise man Ziba told me that you were coming. He was also able to tell me your name and where to find you in the desert. He said that you were from a great land in the west. He didn't say the name of this great land. Could you tell me the name of this great land?" King Omri asked.

"The United States of America," Janice said.

"I have never heard of a land with such a name. Perhaps I might know your king. What is his name?"

"We haven't had a king in over 350 years. My country has not had a king or queen since we won our independence from Great Britain on July 4, 1776. The people of my country vote every four years for our leader. Our leader is called the president," Janice said.

"What did you say your leader is called again?"

"The president," Janice replied.

"Yes, yes, what is that person's name?"

"His name is George H. W. Bush."

"I have never heard of him. I see that things are much different in the west from all the other great lands that we trade with. We trade with some great lands in the west. We get a lot of leather buffalo hides and jad from them. That leather you are now sitting on came from the west. Tomorrow we are going to meet the men of King Solomon, the son of King David on the Mediterranean Sea, to send him our gifts."

"Are you talking about King Solomon, the wisest man who has ever lived?" Janice asked.

"Yes, do you know him personally?"

"No, I just have read about him in the Bible."

"We will be passing through Kemet [Egypt] as we travel up the Nile by boats. Kemet [Egypt] is the land of our great-uncle. We are the descendants of Cush. Have you been told the story of Noah and his three sons, Ham, Shem, and Japheth?"

"Yes, I have, but I don't remember the whole story. Which one of the sons of Noah did Cush come from?" Janice asked, thinking about the story she was told growing up about the curse that started the black race supposedly.

"Cush was the son of Ham. Cush had three brothers. Mizraim was given the land of Kemet [Ancient Egypt]. Put was given the land of Libya, and Canaan was given the land named after him. That's the land above Kemet [Egypt]. There came a time when our people allowed Satan to come between us. Since the reign of King Solomon, there have been many wars."

"Why the wars?" Janice asked.

"Because if any land wasn't God fearing, their king had to submit it the One True God along with his people or be destroyed. Solomon gave them the choice. No kingdom wants to go against him. A lot of people have mistaken me for being King Solomon until they take a look at my clothing. If you see him among the people, you wouldn't notice him. The only way you would realize it's him is if he was to speak. The words, once they leave his tongue, soak right into the heart of the believers of God. He is truly a prophet of the living God. I have witnessed shiploads of gold given to Solomon as gifts. He takes his gifts and helps the surrounding lands. He has accomplished more than his father, King David, in just a short time. God has allowed a lot of prophets, messengers, and great men to walk these lands. David and the prophets of old have prophesied the coming of a child by a virgin. He will be called the Messiah. God will send him as a gift of mercy from Himself. He will strengthen the Messiah with His word and His spirit. I said that to say this, Janice. God has sent you here for a reason. You have received a gift of mercy from Him. Whatever He has sent you here for, it is here for you to obtain. I will allow you to speak with my wise man Ziba. God's will, he will be able to help you get what you were sent for. The talent show is starting. After it is over, I will allow you to talk to Ziba."

People with talent came from all around the nearby lands to perform for Janice, the guest of the king of Gush. They danced, sang, played music, and performed all kinds of magical tricks. Some were so amazing they had Janice wondering how they were done.

"Ahh . . . wow," Janice said as she saw a man blow fire from his mouth like a dragon.

One female made objects disappear; another man folded himself up into a small box. For hours, they did acts that were unbelievable.

"Did you enjoy the show?" King Omri asked.

"Yes, I did. The show was spectacular. Thank you, Your Majesty," Janice said.

"You're welcome. Are you ready to meet Ziba?"

"I guess so."

"Janice, I am going to leave you with these words. God tests those who say they believe in Him. So He allows things to happen for reasons. You are not here because you got lost. You were prophesied to come. That tells me that God has a plan for you. Anything other than that is beyond my comprehension. That's why I think it will be best for you to talk with Ziba. God's will, he will be able to direct you."

The king looked off from Janice and motioned with his hand to summon one of his royal guards. The guard rushed over.

"Escort her to Ziba," the king ordered the guard.

Not knowing what to expect of the meeting with Ziba caused Janice to have butterflies in her stomach. Chills flowed through her body as the royal guard escorted her to Ziba. The wise man stood at the entrance as the royal guard walked up with Janice behind him.

"I will take it from here. Thank you," Ziba said as the guard turned around.

"You're welcome," the royal guard said.

"Hi, Janice, I'm Ziba. I have been waiting for this day."

Janice didn't say a word. She just nodded at him.

"Come in," Ziba said as he turned around to lead the way back into the room.

"Could I be kind enough to offer you a seat?" Ziba asked as he motioned his hand toward a plush chair.

"Thank you!" Janice said as she felt the softness of the chair.

"Can I get you anything to drink?"

"Yes . . . if you don't mind," Janice said.

"I only have water and herbal tea on hand. Which one would you like?" Ziba asked.

"I will have the tea."

"Good choice," Ziba said as he walked over to a nearby stand.

Ziba grabbed the silver pitcher and a matching cup off the stand. He stood there talking to Janice as he filled her cup. After the cup was full, he placed the pitcher back on the stand and walked over to Janice and handed her the cup. "This tea will help you relax and free yourself from the bondage of your mind. The mind is the universal control of the body. We were all born with the main understanding of God within us. I said that to say when someone dies, their body goes back into the ground and their soul, which came, from God returns back to Him."

As Ziba was talking, Janice started to feel the effects of the tea. Feeling relaxed, she leaned back in the chair and closed her eyes.

"Janice, you will start remembering and seeing all the most important aspects of your past. Your past is what molded you into the person that you are today. Your mind is at war right now. Your learned behaviors are at war against the true inclination of God that's within you."

As Ziba was talking, Janice flashed back to her childhood. She relived the hatred and prejudice she was taught from birth. As her past flashed before her, she became emotional.

"You didn't have a choice in the matter as a child. God doesn't pass judgment on an ignorant person. It is after knowledge has reached you and you reject it. Then you will be punished. God has blessed you by allowing you to cross paths with someone who has opened your eyes. The process of understanding and recognizing your learned behaviors has begun. God is One, and He is often forgiving, Most Merciful. Now it's on you. You can stay on the path of destruction or turn from it to the path of righteousness. Janice, you have been chosen above many. Some people live their whole lives with hatred in their hearts for a race of people that they don't know," Ziba said.

Janice saw from a distance people burning crosses, non-whites being mistreated for no reason.

"Your past was that of an artificial charade, false teachings. You were fed the seed of deception. Once inside you, that seed molded your personality and character. It cut you off from the truth or prevented you from walking away from the falsehood. You must keep fighting those foxes at work to keep you insulated from the true you. Remember when you were a child and you did something wrong you felt guilty, tensed, or timid? Now you can say bad things to people and don't care how they feel. You could do things new without remorse. That is where the devil wants I you to be.

He feels that he is in control at that point. You still feel some resentment, and that is a good thing."

"What do I have to do to make things right?" Janice asked. "You first have to see humanity as a whole. Respect all of God's creation. Respect is a foundation that we all must build on. No one has any choice in what color God made them or what path He has chosen for them. We must respect their beliefs and opinions. In your case, don't prejudge anyone. When you open your mind and heart to other races and cultures, you open yourself up to knowledge. When you meet someone in the future, it doesn't matter what color they are, if you don't agree with them on a matter, don't look down on them. It just might be that knowledge hasn't reached them. If they reject the truth, say to them, 'I worship not that which you worship, nor will you worship that which I worship. To you be your way and to me mine.' Keep in mind, Janice, everyone hasn't been through what you have. You are one of the fortunate. It is up to you now. The only limitations that you have now are those you set for yourself. Don't turn yourself back on the truth."

Janice started hearing a beeping sound. *Beep . . . beep . . . beep . . .* The sound got louder and louder as Janice's vision of Ziba started to fade.

"Ziba, what's going on?" Janice asked.

"Don't turn back from the truth. Within your inner self is where you will find God. Make every effort to identify your prejudiced attitude and avoid stereotypical attitudes toward blacks, Jews, and all people of color. Respect the elderly, people with disabilities, and children. The heavens will open up to you."

CHAPTER 13

Beep . . . *beep* . . . *beep,* the monitor sounded off. Nurses ran in from all directions to cram into the ICU by Eric's bedside. All the commotion of the nurses and the beeping sound of the monitor woke Janice up out of a deep sleep. Being not sure of what was going on, seeing all the nurses around Eric's bed, and the monitor going crazy beeping scared her. She sat up on the sofa as she looked around.

"Relax, Mr. Henderson," one nurse said as Eric tried to sit up.

Janice felt a sense of relief after hearing the nurse talk to Eric.

"Relax, Mr. Henderson. I need to check your blood pressure," the nurse said as she reached for his arm.

"Where am I?" Eric asked.

"You are in the Jackson General Hospital. Your sister is here. Just let us finish checking you out," the nurse said.

Janice stood back with her right hand over her mouth.

"Thank you, God. All praise are to you," Janice said.

"Mr. Henderson, you have a strong will to live. You're a fighter. We didn't think you would come out of the coma so quickly. Welcome back. The doctor in charge has been notified," the head nurse said as they turned to walk out.

Janice stood back as they walked out one by one. Once they were out of the way, Janice walked over with tears in her eyes and a smile on her face. She reached down and gave Eric a big hug.

"I love you," she said.

"Ahhh!" Eric hollered as Janice hugged him. "I'm sore as hell . . . I love you too," Eric said.

Startled, Janice jumped back.

"What did I do?" Janice asked as she looked at Eric's facial expression.

The look on Janice's face made Eric laugh. Janice hit him on the shoulder with the palm of her right hand.

"Boy, don't scare me like that anymore."

"I wasn't trying to scare you. My chest is sore as hell. How long was I out?" Eric asked.

"You were in a coma for three days. You best to believe I am going to kick your butt the next time you scare me like you did, Eric."

Both smiled. Eric reached and grabbed Janice's hand.

"Remember what I told you a few months ago? I was surprised no one has tried to rob that store before now."

"I don't think they were there to rob the store," Eric said.

"What makes you say that?"

"I believe that they came to kill me. Never once did they look at the cashiers. They came through the door looking for me. By the grace of God, I saw them first. Don't tell anyone I told you this. Since the death of Dad, it has been a lot of crazy stuff going on. I just can't put my finger on it yet. But it is like some of the brothers want me out of the way. Has anyone outside our family members come up here to check on me?"

"No one but your friend Tom stopped by. He is the one who talked to the Jackson County sheriff about getting you around-the-clock security on the door."

"Good! Tom and I have been talking about how most of the brothers have been acting. Other than him, have you seen anyone else?"

"No, I had to leave and go back to school to let my professor know I needed some time off. When I got back here, I noticed the flowers on the table for you. But I didn't see who left them. Eric, you need to back up. You lost me. What's been going on since Dad died?"

"Our new sheriff George wants the brothers to unite with the Aryan Nations brotherhood. He has been asking me just like he stayed asking Dad. Dad wouldn't do it because he knew that they would bring the Klan unnecessary problems. Now Dad is gone, and I'm in charge of all the brothers in this area. George has been trying hard to get me to unite us. I have been keeping Dad's wishes. Plus, those brothers are wild, crazy, into drugs and criminal activities. Him and a few—a small few—of the older brothers don't like the fact that I am in charge of them at my age. I was born in the Klan. It is starting to come together. I shot one of them after he shot me. The both of them ran out of bullets. They didn't know if I was out or not. The one I shot fell and tried to get back up but couldn't. His partner had to help him out the door. When his partner pulled him out the store by his shirt, that's when I saw the white power and swastika tattoo on his stomach. I lay there for a few minutes on the floor up against the potato chip rack. I tried to get one of the store clerks to call for help. They were too scared to look up. A n—— walked through the door looking at the shot-out glass and blood that was on the floor. And little did I know the nigger turned out to be an angel. He walked up to me and started saying something to me. I couldn't make out every word he said. My inner self wouldn't allow my mouth to tell him to get the fuck away from me. I understood him clearly when he said, 'I am a doctor. Let me help you. Has anyone called for help?' He shouted as he looked over at one clerk on the floor behind the counter. Seeing she was terrified, he said, 'Ma'am, this man is dying. I need you to snap out of it and get up and call for help.' Finally she snapped out of the trance she was in and called for help. He shined his light into my eyes and said, 'I am losing you. I need you to talk to me.' Shortly after the clerk got off the phone, he called her over. 'Talk to him until I get back,' he told her. He ran out the store to his car and came back with a black medical bag. He sat it down beside me and took off his jacket and rolled his shirt sleeve up while he talked. He pulled out a long tube, like one of these IV tubes I have in me now."

He pointed his finger at the IV tube as he continued to tell the story, "Once he put the needle in my neck and his blood started flowing through my body, I felt the oxygen in his blood going to my brain. I could feel the relief before I started fading in and out. I remember the ambulance arriving along with some officers from the Teller County Sheriff Department. The last thing I saw was them putting us in a medevac helicopter. I owe that man. If it wasn't for him, I would have died on that floor in the store. I felt like I had lost a lot of blood, but I didn't see a lot on me. That's what scared me. Janice, all my life, I was taught to despise them. I wouldn't swim in the same pool with them. I looked at them like they're the scum of the earth. It took my kind attempting to kill me to open my eyes. I have n—— blood running through my veins. Does that make me a n—— or less than white? Never in my life have I had a problem with one of them. It has always been with my kind. I wonder if I would be here today if the man knew how I felt about his kind. When I was in the coma, I kept hearing his voice calling my name. His voice guided and kept me from being pulled into the darkness. I have heard stories about people having near-death experiences. It's true. I saw the light. I was headed the other way. I felt that I was headed the wrong way, so I tried to turn around and walk toward the light. Some force that I couldn't see pulled me backward into the darkness.

The doctor's voice pulled me forward. I looked around to try to see where the voice was coming from but didn't see anyone. I was stuck in a tug-of-war. I went backward and forward. I'm blessed. If I don't change my life, I am going to hell for sure. God allowed me to live for a reason. Janice, for this first time in my life, I was scared. I saw my whole life flash before my eyes as I lay on that floor."

Janice looked at Eric and thought about the dream she had. As Eric was talking, the doctor walked in the door, causing Eric to become speechless as he thought to himself, *Not only did this man save my life, but he also came back to check on me.*

"Mr. Henderson, the way that we met, I didn't get a chance to introduce myself. My name is Dr. Skinner. How are you feeling?"

"Pretty good, I guess. How about yourself?" Eric asked.

"Better than I truly deserve. Mr. Henderson, I just wanted to stop by to check to see if you had come out of your coma. I have been calling up here periodically to check on you. On my way here, I felt that today would be the day. Sure enough, it is. The crazy thing about it is, as soon as the thought entered my mind, the hospital was paging me to let me know. It's good to see your eyes open."

As Dr. Skinner said that, he held his hand out toward Eric. For the first time in Eric's life, he touched a black person's hand. It was like he didn't want to let go of Dr. Skinner's hand. Tears built up as he looked up into the doctor's eyes.

"Thank you very much for saving my life," Eric said.

"No! Mr. Henderson, don't thank me. Thank God because it was Him and all Him. I have driven by that store every day for years without stopping until that day. I didn't have a logical reason why I stopped. God is the greatest. He stopped me for you. The timing and everything else was just right. Even when I was checking you out, your ID was turned over for me. I couldn't help but notice your blood type. The story gets even better. You needed blood, and you share the same blood type as me. Everything was too perfect. The signs showed me that it was a divine intervention, and that's the reason you are here today. So I can't take the credit. It belongs to God. After everything became clear to me, I asked the hospital to put me on your case. I am hoping you don't mind," Dr. Skinner asked.

"No, not at all, Doc. I feel for some reason that I know you. Not just that, I know I can trust you. So, Doctor, last names are used by people who don't know each other. My first name is Eric, and you can call me that. By the way, this is my sister, Janice. I was just telling her about you."

"Hi, Janice, I know you feel better now," Dr. Skinner said.

"Oh god, yes," Janice said with a smile on her face as the two shook hands. "Thank you for saving my brother's life."

"You're welcome, but like I told him, all the credit belongs to God. Eric, I was looking at your X-rays, and if you haven't realized it yet, you are paralyzed. There is no reason to panic. I believe I will be able to help you," Dr. Skinner said.

He couldn't help but see the look of panic forming on Eric's face.

"The bullet is sitting up against your spine, cutting off the circulation below your torso, mainly your legs."

"What could be done to help me?" Eric asked.

"If you allow me to perform the operation, what I will do is go in and remove the bullet. Your spine could be seriously injured or severed. The surgery I would like to perform is pretty complicated but easy. I would have to temporarily cut off the movement from your neck down. Then I would make a two-inch incision in your back, go in, and temporarily remove two of your vertebrates. Then I will slowly inject small amounts of fluid into your spine and hope that the fluid will inflate it enough. The reason I will remove two of your vertebrates is to give the bullet room enough to move back without applying pressure to the bullet from behind. That will allow the bullet to back up through the route it entered."

"Do you really think it will work?" Eric asked.

"God knows best. It's up to you. With your approval, I will be more than happy to do it."

"I have a question," Eric said.

"What is it?" The doctor asked.

"Why do you have to cut off all my movement?" Eric asked.

"We can't allow your body to move any. Any movement could cause the bullet to go into your spine. That will eliminate any chances of your ever walking again."

"If you believe this surgery will help me walk again, let's do it."

"Okay, that sounds like a go. Let me get the paperwork that I need you to sign," Dr. Skinner said.

"When will you be able to start the operation, and how long will it take?" Eric asked.

"The operation will only take a few hours. It will have to take at least a week to allow the bullet to slowly move backward away from your spine. Then I will have to go back in and remove it. That shouldn't take an hour. If you believe in prayer, that will be the time to do so. If you like, I could have you scheduled as early as in forty-eight hours."

"The sooner the better," Eric said.

"Once again, it's good to see you out of your coma. Hopefully, you will be up on your feet soon."

"Hopefully!" Eric said as he nodded.

"I know that you and your sister have a lot to talk about. Once again, Janice, it was nice to meet you."

"You too, Doc," Janice said.

"I will be back later with the papers that you need to sign in order for me to do the operation."

"Okay, I will be here," Eric said as a joke.

As the doctor was walking out, the sheriff of Teller County walked in.

"Goddamn it, Eric! Boy, we didn't think you would make it. Hi there, Janice. How do you do?" the sheriff asked.

You wish I didn't make it, you motherfucker, Eric said to himself.

"I'm doing pretty good now that I know my brother is okay," Janice said as she turned to go sit down, wanting absolutely nothing to do with George Fuhrman.

"Eric, how long will it be before you are back on your feet?" Sheriff Fuhrman asked.

"The doctor just informed me that I am paralyzed from the waist down," Eric responded.

"That's fucked up. Will your piece work?" Sheriff Fuhrman asked as he looked over at the two other officers as he laughed at his joke.

Eric just looked at him.

"You can't take a joke now?" the sheriff asked.

"It's not that. This isn't a joking matter," Eric said.

"Ahhh, shit, Eric, don't go soft on me now."

"The doctor told me that he would like to try a never-before-done-in-this-area operation on me to try to remove the bullet that's up against my spine."

"I know you are not talking about that coon that I saw walk out of here?" the sheriff asked.

Eric paused for a moment. "I want to walk again. So yes, the one—whatever you want to call him—is going to do it," Eric said with a sign of disgrace on his face.

"I know I will be one crippled motherfucker before I let that black son of a bitch touch me."

The two officers stood there with smiles on their faces like two soldiers. They didn't even take the time out to walk over and shake Eric's hand. Eric tried to get the sheriff to maintain eye contact with him.

"The brothers sent their regards," the sheriff said, talking about the Klan.

"Tell them I said thanks. George, has anyone been arrested yet?" Eric asked, just trying to see what he would say and what type of facial expression he would give.

"Yes, as a matter of fact, we have one the niggers. We believe that he's the one you shot. The getaway car caught a flat down the highway. They were heading to Summerville, Tennessee. His hand was busted up really good. He tried to tell us that he did it trying to change his flat tire. The stupid-ass nigger said the one-way tire iron slipped off, and his hand slammed up against the fender of the car. We beat the shit out of the nigger. He actually shit on himself. Ha-ha-ha!" the sheriff said, laughing.

"George, I can tell you now that you have the wrong man," Eric said.

"How in the fuck do you know?" the sheriff asked.

"The men who came into that store were not black," Eric said, making sure he didn't let him know that he knew exactly why they were there to kill him.

"Eric, how in the hell do you know that if they had masks and gloves on?" the sheriff asked and for the first time looked Eric straight in his eyes, trying to see what he knew.

"I saw the one I shot, and his skin wasn't black," Eric said, cutting himself off, making sure he didn't reveal the white power and swastika tattoo he saw.

"Fuck!" the sheriff said as he stormed out of the ICU. The two officers followed behind him.

"Did you see the way he was acting?" Eric asked Janice.

"I sure did. He couldn't look at you," Janice said.

"Something is up. I think he's in on it too."

"I wouldn't doubt it. I don't trust him. He is evil. Chills run through my body whenever he is around. Like now. Ahh, I am hungry. I'm going to get me something to eat. Do you want anything?"

"So funny. How can I eat with this tube in me?"

"Well, that's not going to stop me. I am going to get me something to eat."

"Where are you going?" Eric asked.

"Downstairs to the hospital cafeteria. They might have some good food down there." Janice walked out the room and headed down to the hospital cafeteria. When she got back, Eric was asleep. Making sure she didn't wake him, she sat down and started back where she fell asleep at in the book.

The doctor came back into the room to allow Eric to sign the papers. Janice just looked up from her book for a moment and went back to reading. After she finished the book, she started on her senior thesis. The books gave her a lot of knowledge. She wrote her paper from the little that Adam told her about himself and the books he showed her. After discovering that Eric's operation will be a success, Janice planned to return to school. "Eric, I have an exam coming up next week. I need to go study for it. God's will, you will be up on your feet next month for my graduation."

"I don't think I will. I have to go through therapy once this operation is finished. Thank god, things are going as planned. The doc said the bullet is moving backward," Eric said.

"I was just wishing that you would be able to attend my graduation."

"My heart will be there with you. I know what you can do!" Eric suggested.

"What!" Janice replied.

"You can have someone record it for me."

"You are right. The only problem is I don't have a camcorder or the money to buy one of those expensive things. I know your tight butt has the money. I will go buy one if you give me the money," Janice said.

"Go ahead. Get one. I will give you your money back," Eric said as he looked at Janice.

"You still haven't paid the last money back that you borrowed to get the stuff for your truck."

"Girl, talking about me being tight, you're the one. I promise I'm going to give you your money back."

"Okay, Eric, you know your butt can't move. I can beat you up, and you can't do anything to stop me. I will stop by the bank when I leave to get the money out to purchase one of those high-cost things. Don't act like you got amnesia when it's time for you to pay me my money back. I will bring you a receipt."

"You'll get your money back, lil sis."

"I'm about to go. I love you."

"I love you too."

Janice did what she said she would do. She stopped by the bank before she headed back up I-40 East to Nashville. As soon as Janice arrived on campus, she searched for Adam. She saw Gloria with two of her female friends standing out.

"Excuse me, Gloria! First of all, how are you doing?"

Gloria was stunned not because Janice was looking for Adam but because they hadn't spoken in three years.

"I'm doing okay, and you?" Gloria asked.

"I'm blessed," Janice said.

"If you don't mind, I would like to know why you are looking for him?" Gloria asked, trying not to sound too jealous.

"I just wanted to thank him," Janice said.

Gloria smiled. She knew the effect that Adam has on people. "He's in the library," she said.

"Thank you," Janice said before walking off toward the campus library.

Seeing Adam sitting alone at a table with his back turned toward the door, she walked up behind him and put her hands over his eyes.

"I bet you don't know who this is," Janice asked with a cheerful voice.

"My friend Janice," Adam said.

"How did you know it was me?"

"You have a one-of-a-kind voice."

"Why do you say that?"

"You sound country."

"Do I really?"

"Yes, you do."

"I see you spend a lot of time working on law cases," Janice said, seeing Adam with his father's court transcripts and law books on the table.

"This is my reason for living," Adam said as he placed his band on top of the stack of papers.

"I see. God's will, you will be a great lawyer one day."

"Thank you, Janice. God's will, I will," Adam said.

"I just wanted to stop by to let you know how much I appreciate all the things you have done for me. Just the words you put in the card hit home. Adam, you have opened my eyes and mind to life. Thank God for you. You are truly a blessing. God is real. The things you told me and your prayers got answered."

"All praise to God," Adam said.

"If you don't mind, I would like to give you a hug, and hopefully, later you let me take you out to dinner. I just want to show you a token of my appreciation." Adam stood up, and both hugged.

"So I take it that your brother is doing okay. Is he out of the hospital?"

"No, but everything is going good for him. The doctor operated on him a few days ago. The bullet was pressing up against his spinal cord. The operation went good. The bullet has started to move backward from his spine. They are still injecting fluid into his spine right now. God's will, they will be able to go back in to remove the bullet next week."

"Just keep your trust and faith in God. He will keep answering your prayers," Adam said.

"I will."

"I can see that you are thankful. Just remember that being thankful is a by-product of achieving what God has for you. You have gone through the process of achievement—the striving and the pain. Now you get to fulfill your calling. You have won the great fight that you will face yourself. I just pray that you keep allowing God to speak to your heart," Adam said.

"I will. I promise you that."

"You don't have to make any promises."

"Are you going to let me take you out to eat or what?" Janice asked.

"Do you think I'm going to turn down some free food? No way. Just let me put my legal workup. Then we can go."

CHAPTER 14

The weekend came quickly. Gloria, being true to her word, sat in visitation with Adam. The two waited on Samson to walk through the door that inmates and officers entered through for visitation. Gloria held Adam's hand as she locked her eyes on the entrance.

"Don't say anything, Adam. I'm going to see if I can pick him out," Gloria said as she eased her leg close to Adam's leg.

"I'm not going to say anything," Adam said with a smile.

Samson made his usual entrance with a smile on his face as he and the two officers accompanying him were laughing. Gloria looked at the dark-skinned man who stood at six feet four inches and a solid 245 pounds with a full beard and white kufi.

"I know that can't be him," Gloria said while Samson was signing in at the desk.

"He's Muslim, but he looks too young to be your dad."

Adam just smiled as Samson turned around and walked toward their favorite table. "As-salamu alaykum, ibn [May peace be on you, son]," Samson said to greet Adam as he walked up.

"Wa alaykumu s-salam, Dad," Adam said to wish peace back onto his father.

"You must be Gloria. Stand up and give me a hug, future daughter-in-law," Samson said.

Gloria, not sure how to respond, stood up so the two could hug. "I'm nervous," Gloria said.

"Why? I am not going to bite you."

"*Bark . . . bark . . . bark.* I knew you were a chicken," Adam said.

"Shut up. I am going to get you when we leave here," Gloria said.

"Let's sit down before the officer says something to us. So what's going on with you two?" Samson asked as he looked at them.

Both looked at each other and looked back at Samson. "Nothing!" both said in unison.

"How are the both of you going to sit here and tell me there is nothing going on with you? Have you made up your minds about getting married and moving to Memphis?" Samson asked.

"We talked about it," Adam said.

"And what did you decide?"

"Gloria agreed that she would move to Memphis with me," Adam said.

"What about marriage?" Samson asked.

Adam stuttered, "I . . . I . . ."

"Mr. Ali, I have been trying to get your son to ask me to marry him. He keeps telling me we need to stay focused on school."

Samson sat back in his chair and looked at Adam. He waited a moment before he said anything. "Gloria, why have you not moved on knowing he's not ready for a commitment?" Samson asked.

"I have asked myself the same question. What I came up with is good black men are hard to find. He isn't out trying to soar his royal oaks around campus or anywhere else. I'm cool after I got to really know Adam. I have seen how devoted he is to getting you out. It would be selfish of me to try to interfere with that. I just try to make it known that I am here for him, and if it takes me helping him with your case for me to be with him, I am willing to do that."

"What do you have to say for yourself, son?"

"I care about Gloria a lot and would love to marry her. But my heart and mind are in here with you. After school is over, I am going to ask her to marry me Inshallah [if God wills it]. We have a lot on the both of our plates. We have our final exam coming up. Also, we have our senior thesis due next month. After graduation, we will get married, if she will still marry me."

"You already know. I'm waiting on you," Gloria said.

"Dad, before we go to Memphis, we will be married Inshallah [if it's God's will]."

"I can live with that response," Samson said.

"Dad, don't want to cut this visit short, but we have a lot to do. I want to make sure Gloria got everything down pat for the final that's coming up in a few days, and we need to utilize the little time we have today in the library."

"Okay, son, thank you for bringing my daughter-in-law to see me.

Gloria, thank you for coming. I am going to be looking forward to seeing you again."

"Yes, sir, Mr. Ali, I will be back to see you if Adam brings me," Gloria said as she looked at Adam with a smile on her face.

"I love you, Dad. Inshallah, I will be back next week."

"Inshallah, son, I will see you next week. I love you too."

The three hugged and wished their peace before walking out of the visitation room.

The day of graduation, Adam asked Gloria to marry him. It was the words she was waiting to hear. The two got married a week after and moved to Memphis, Tennessee. Once in Memphis, the two worked together on Samson's case.

Two years after graduation, things shifted. Adam walked outside of the home that his uncle Brandon gave him to pick up his daily newspaper. He walked back into the kitchen where his wife was preparing breakfast.

"Good morning, my love," Adam said as he walked into the kitchen.

"Good morning, baby," Gloria said as she turned around from the stove to kiss Adam. Adam sat down at the kitchen table and flipped through the newspaper. As he read it, a small picture of his father made Adam go straight to the article that read:

> Convicted former military lieutenant lost a bid in the Tennessee Supreme Court on Friday to overturn his 1980 conviction for the shooting death of a Teller County sheriff deputy almost 15 years ago. In a unanimous decision, the state's highest court said it found no reversible errors in the trial that led to Samson Ali's conviction. The attorney for Samson Ali said he would ask the court to reconsider, and if he has to, he will appeal to the US Supreme Court. Ali, 53, was convicted in 1980 of the October 31, 1979, shooting death of Teller County sheriff's deputy Mike McClain and the attempted murder of the newest Teller County sheriff George Fuhrman. He was sentenced to death by jury. Mike McClain was killed and his partner George Fuhrman was wounded when they attempted to make a routine traffic stop. Ali was taken into custody on the scene by the Teller County sheriff. The court said the evidence, which included a statement made by

Ali and ballistics tests, would find Ali guilty. The court said it found no merit to a claim of equal protection because the country's procedures for choosing grand juries were flawed. Defense attorney Fred Gaines said that the motion to dismiss on grounds that Samson Ali's constitutional rights were violated under *Keenan v. United States* and *Miranda v. Arizona*, where a death case or any of that could receive death must be appointed at least two defense attorneys by the court. The court's decision sends a message to prosecutors and lower courts that they can violate someone's rights and there's no consequence. Ali could have an execution date set if the Supreme Court doesn't reconsider by as early as next week.

Adam immediately picked the phone up and called Attorney Gaines. Gloria noticed the look on Adam's face and the change of mood. Adam looked up with the phone on his ear and saw Gloria staring at him. He passed her the paper as the phone rang.

"The Gaines residence, may I help you?"

"Yes, may I speak with Mr. Fred Gaines please?" Adam asked.

"One moment please," the person said as she called for him. "Fred . . . Fred," the lady said.

"Yeah!" Mr. Gaines said from the background.

"Telephone," she responded.

"I will get it back here. Thank you. You can hang up. Fred Gaines speaking, may I help you?"

"Yes, sir, Mr. Gaines, this is Adam."

"How are you doing, Adam? What's up?"

"I was just reading the newspaper, and I read the Supreme Court verdict regarding my father's case. Why didn't you give me a call yesterday?"

"Adam, I apologize, but I had a lot of things to do. When I did get home, it was after eleven o'clock. As we are speaking, I am making plans to go visit your father. I was hoping that you would be there so I could let you and your father know what went on. Are you planning on visiting him today?"

"Yes, sir, I am."

"I will talk to you then, if that's okay with you?"

"That will be fine. I will see you there, God's will," Adam said before hanging up the phone.

"Was that your father's attorney?" Gloria asked.

"Yes, it was."

"What did he say?" Gloria asked.

"I wanted to know why he didn't call me yesterday to let me know what the Supreme Court said. He's going to meet me at the prison this morning so we all can talk about it. Are you planning on going this week?" Adam asked.

"I don't think that would be a good idea. You know I am about due. We will have a little one here any day now. You just go on. You can fill me in on what happened. Tell Dad I send my love, and God's will, the three of us will be down there next month," Gloria said as she rubbed her stomach.

After the two of them finished eating, Adam stood up from the table and was about to walk out the door. He took two steps and turned around.

"Baby, do you feel like ironing my clothes for me?"

"Sure," Gloria replied.

"Thank you, baby. They are lying across the bed."

Adam took a shower, got dressed, and headed out the door.

"Give me a kiss. Make sure you have your cell phone on you," Gloria said as Adam kissed her.

"You make sure you keep the cordless phone with you at all times. If you even think you're about to go into labor, call for help first. Then call me," Adam said with a smile.

"I got this. You just make sure you be careful on that highway."

"I will. I love you," Adam said.

"I love you too."

Adam walked out the door and got into his car and headed up I-40 East to Nashville. Once at prison, Adam went through the usual routine search before he entered into the visitation room. He noticed that Mr. Gaines was already there. Not sure how his father would take the bad news, he became cautious. The smile that Samson had on his face as he stood up from the table to hug him gave him ease. Not knowing what to think made him forget to greet his father.

"As-salamu alaykum, ibn. What is wrong with you, son?" Samson asked.

"Wa alaykumu s-salam. I didn't know how you would take the court's ruling," Adam said.

"How old are you, son?" Samson asked.

"Twenty-four."

"Out of the twenty-four years you have known me, have you ever known me to give up?"

"No, sir."

"God is in control, not men. Come on over here and have a seat."

"How are you doing, Mr. Gaines?" Adam asked as he sat down.

"I'm a little tired. Other than that, I'm doing pretty good. I see you made it," Mr. Gaines said as he reached out and shook Adam's hand.

"I wouldn't miss it for the world," Adam said.

Both shook hands.

"Where is my daughter-in-law?" Samson asked.

"She is just about due. The baby will be here any day now, Inshallah. It was best for her to stay home. She did ask me to deliver a message for her. She said she loves you and the three of us will be down here next month with the rest of the family."

"Did you watch the news last night or this morning?"

"I just found out this morning when I read the newspaper. What are we going to do?" asked Adam.

"That's what Fred and I were going over before you came. Fred was saying we have to wait on the Supreme Court to make the next move. They have set a date to reconsider the motion. Once they say what they are going to do, we will know what we need to do."

"You two can sit around and wait on them to make the next move or pull the trigger. In other words, I know the governor of this state personally. I went to school with his youngest son, Mark, my best friend. He came to our graduation and took us out to eat after it. He is a very open-minded person, and I believe he will help."

"Son, don't have doubt in your heart about me and this case. Allah [God] is the best of planners. That's why I don't have any doubt. I am a true believer, and I know that Allah put me here for a reason. Nothing happens by coincidence with Allah."

"I believe that, Dad, but Allah just doesn't want us to sit around on our hands and do nothing. He gave us three ways to change things, which are with our hands, mouth, and heart. He has given us the faculties. I'm not going to sit around and talk about it or hide it in my heart. That's the weakest of the three. I'm about to get out and act on this. Inshallah [God's will], I am going to take off from work Monday and drive back up here so I can talk to the governor. Dad, I'm going to leave early today so I can get back to Memphis and take care of some business. Inshallah, I will see you next week."

"Okay, son, I love you."

"I love you too. As-salamu alaykum."

"Wa alaykumu s-salam, ibn," Samson said.

"I will see you or talk to you later, Mr. Gaines."

"Okay, Adam take care," Mr. Gaines said.

Adam got up from the table and hugged his father and shook Mr. Gaines's hand before he walked out the door. Mr. Gaines looked over at Samson. "I know you are thankful to have him as a son," Mr. Gaines said.

"Yes, I am. I thank Allah [God] daily for giving me children that fear Him. I have been blessed for sure."

"When was the last time you've seen your family in Colorado?"

"It has been about three months since I've seen them. Fred, did you submit the motion to introduce the new evidence?"

"No, I haven't. I have been holding it for our ace in the hole. I'm going to submit your wife's testimony with it. I have it already drawn up. I will put you a copy of the brief in the mail on Monday. After you look over it, give me a call if you have any questions or something that you think I should add. I will be back to visit you after the Supreme Court gives their final decision on the appeal. Okay with you?" Mr. Gaines asked.

"Yes, it's okay with me. I will see you then, God's will."

The two shook hands, and Attorney Gaines walked out. Meanwhile, Adam drove home and tool care of all the things he needed to. Early Monday morning, he was back in Nashville. His first stop was Bobbitt and Nixon Law Firm, the firm owned by the governor and his sons. It's the same law firm that Adam and Mark worked at while in college. Adam walked through the door of the law office; he was greeted with open arms by the long-time friend and clerk of the family-owned law firm.

"Oh my god, look at what the wind has dragged in. Adam, it's so good to see you," the clerk said.

"It's good to see you too, Mrs. William."

"Come on over here and give me a hug. Are you coming back to work with us?"

"No, ma'am, I drove up here to see Mark and Governor Nixon," Adam said.

"You know we miss having you around here."

"I miss being around here, Mrs. William."

"Mark walked over to city hall to meet his father."

"About how long ago?" Adam asked.

"No more than ten minutes ago."

"I need to try to catch him. I will be back to see you before I leave."

"Make sure you do," Mrs. William said.

"Yes, ma'am, I will."

Adam walked about two blocks to the city hall building. As he was walking through the hallway, someone tapped him on the shoulder. When he turned around, it was Janice Henderson. "My god, Adam! I didn't think I would ever see you again. How has the married life been treating you?"

"Pretty good. I love it."

"You're looking good. You have made my day. Since I've been up here, I have seen a few of our old classmates. I see Mark just about every day. I ask him about you from time to time. He told me that you and Gloria got married and live in Memphis. I also heard you two have a baby on the way. Congratulations!"

"Thank you. I am looking for Mark. Have you seen him?" Adam asked.

"Not today."

"What are you doing up this way?" Adam asked.

"I live here now. I am working with one of the biggest law firms up here. God is good! What about you. What are you doing up here?"

"My father's appeal was turned down Friday by the Supreme Court. They might be setting him a death date soon. We are just waiting on their final decision."

"Wow. . . oh my god, I know you are not talking about Samson Ali's case?" Janice said with a stunning look on her face.

"Yes, I am," Adam said as he looked at her.

"Adam, I have known about that case since I was a little girl, and I pretty much know what happened that night."

"What?" Adam asked as heat waves went through his body. "Tell me, are you for real?"

"I am. What are you about to do now?" Janice asked.

"I drove up here to catch up with Mark, so he could go with me to talk with his father, Governor Nixon."

"If you have time, I would like to go somewhere so we can sit down and talk. I can fill you in on some things that might help your father's case," Janice said.

"Where would be a good place for you?" Adam asked as his heart was about to beat its way out of his chest.

"We can go to the coffee shop that I go to every day. It's not too far from here. When we leave there, I will show you where you could catch Mark over at the county courthouse."

"Cool," Adam said.

The two of them walked out of the city hall building.

"Where is your car?"

"On Bobbitt and Nixon's lot," Adam said.

Janice walked up to her candy-apple-red BMW and put the key into the door.

"You have good taste I see," Adam said as Janice pushed the power lock to open the passenger-side door for Adam.

"What are you thinking about, this car?"

"Sure."

"This is just a little something," Janice said as she pulled off. "This is the coffee shop that I come to every day. This is a nice place. I come here to go over my cases before I head over to the courthouse. It's a good place to come and relax," Janice said as she parked in front of the business.

"It looks like a nice place, man. The coffee sure smells good," Adam said as the two walked through the door.

"You need to try my favorite cappuccino. I believe you will fall in love with it," Janice said.

"You think so?"

"Yes, I do. *You* can go and get that table for us in the back. I got you on the cappuccino."

Adam took a seat at the table all the way in the back of the coffee shop. Within a few minutes, Janice walked over to the table with two cups in her hands.

"It's hot. Be careful." Janice said as she passed Adam one cup.

"Thank you," Adam said as he carefully took the cup.

"Go ahead and taste it," Janice said.

Adam took a sip. "Pretty good."

"I know now why you stayed in those law books in school. You were in the car that night your father killed Mike McClain, wasn't you?"

"Yes, I was," Adam said.

"So you saw everything? I bet that was a scary scene, huh?"

Adam just nodded.

"My father took me and my brother, Eric, to the funeral. I can still remember it like yesterday. I was about ten years old at the time. My father was the head of the Ku Klux Klan for Teller County and the surrounding area. I was also riding in the front seat with my father, and Eric took the backseat. After the funeral, we all headed back to the car. I opened the passenger-side door, got in, and was about to close the door when my father stopped me. He said, 'Hold up, sweetheart. I need you to get in the back with your brother. George is about to ride with us.' I got in the back. George Fuhrman got into the front seat. George hollered out the car window to the fat man who drove him to the funeral, 'I'll catch you later. Bo is going to drop me off.' When he go into the car, that's when I noticed his arm in a sling from being shot by your father. My dad asked him as we were pulling off, 'George, what in the hell happened out there the other night?' George told my father after shaking his head and taking a deep breath. I think he was trying to think of something. He knew he had to tell my father something, and he had to do it quick. The story he told my father was that 'a car shot past them in a high rate of speed, so they pulled it over.' Then he said, 'When I walked up to the car, a white female was driving. I looked into the car and noticed it was a nigger in the passenger seat asleep, with two nigger kids in the back. I thought it would be a good idea to teach them a lesson, especially the nigger, for messing with our women. When I walked back to get Mike to let him know what was going on, we got the nigger out the car with our guns on him and took him to the back of the car. I struck the nigger several times with my nightstick. Somehow the nigger managed to get the ups on us. The nigger knocked me down and rushed Mike. Somehow he took Mike's weapon and killed him. Before I could get up off the ground and get to my weapon, he shot me in my shoulder. When the other brothers showed up, the FBI was right behind them. They had him moved to Jackson.' I don't know if my testimony will help because it falls under hearsay. We might need some substantial evidence, and I know who might have some," Janice said.

Adam smiled and burst out laughing.

'Ha-ha-ha. Did I just here you say *we*? I laughed because you had a serious teammate look on your face. I didn't mean it in a negative way. I'm going to need all the help I can get . . . partner," Adam said as he sipped his cappuccino.

"I will do whatever I can," Janice said.

"So George Fuhrman told your father he pulled my mother over for speeding. That's not true. We believe that they pulled her over to rape and kill her. So happens my dad was in the car with us. The FBI told my dad he was in the wrong place at the right time, and they might be able to get him off the case. They needed to talk to my mom, but she wasn't anywhere to be found. The following night the Klan showed up at our house. They burned a cross in the front yard. My mom moved us out the very same night. I got a chance to go to the Teller County Public Library two years ago to see why the FBI was in your area. I found out what drew the FBI's attention to the town. A week before that happened to us, the twelfth white woman along the twenty-five-mile stretch of highway that goes through your town came up missing."

Janice had a stunned look across her face, with her mouth slightly open.

"Not just that, Janice. Neither the bodies of the twelve women nor their cars have ever been found. All of a sudden, the women coming up missing stopped. That's no coincidence," Adam said with his arms stretched outward toward his sides and the palms of his hands upward. "The FBI narrowed it down to the twenty-five miles that run through Teller County. One witness came forward and started that Mike McClain and George Fuhrman pulled her over, handcuffed her, and put her in the back of their squad car. One of them got into her, and they took her to a secluded place. There they made her perform all kinds of sexual acts. Shortly after, she denied anything ever happened," Adam explained.

"Do you remember her name?" Janice asked.

"No, not off the top of my head. I have the newspaper articles at home."

"My brother, Eric, was in charge of the Klan for over two years after the death of my father. He hung out around them a lot growing up. He could have witnessed or been a part of some of the lynchings and cross burnings. He knows a lot about George. He believes George tried to have him killed. We are going to need his help," Janice said.

"Why do you think he will be willing to help me?"

"My brother has changed a lot for the better. He's not the same person he was two years ago. He doesn't look at blacks the way he used to before he got shot."

"Where is he now?"

"He's at work right now. He doesn't get off until five o'clock."

"Does he still live in Teller County?"

"No, he moved up here shortly after he got out of the hospital. I will tell you what—" Janice said and paused for a moment to get her thoughts together. "I will get with him today and see what he can do to help us. Here is my address and phone number," Janice said as she passed Adam her business card. Adam pulled out his wallet from his back pocket and put her card into it. He then pulled out his business card and passed it to her.

"Okay, good, I will call you tonight and let you know something," Janice said.

"Janice, if by chance I'm not at home, call me on my cell phone or leave a message with my wife. I have a habit of turning my cell phone off during the day."

"Why do you do that?" Janice asked.

"Our judges in Memphis, down at 201 Poplar, don't play when it comes to cell phones going off in their courtrooms."

"Once again, congratulations to you and your wife. Tell her I said hi."

"I will make sure I do that."

"I got to get back over to the courthouse," Janice said as she looked at her watch.

"Okay," Adam said.

"Where is Mark's law firm? I need to hurry up and drop you off so I can get to court."

"It's right down the street. You can let me out at the red light. I can walk from there."

The two walked out the coffee shop and got into Janice's car. She drove Adam down to the light. "Are you sure you will be okay with me letting you out right here?"

"I am sure. I'm just going right down the street."

"Give me a hug. I will call you later," Janice said.

"Okay, take care. I will be waiting on your call."

Adam got out of the car and walked down the street toward the law firm of Babbitt and Nixon. When he looked up the street toward the law office, he saw Mark as he was about to enter the office's door.

"Mark!" Adam yelled down the street. Hearing Adam's voice calling his name, he turned around in the doorway to see where his friend's voice was coming from. When he saw Adam's face, a smile instantly formed on his face. As the two approached each other, they collided with a big hug.

"Man, I should kick your butt. I know you have been coming up here every week to visit your father. You haven't stopped by my house to see me in two months. What's up with that?" Mark asked as the two walked inside the law office.

"Bro . . ." Adam said as he shook his head.

"Don't shake your head. I know what it is!" Mark said.

"What is it?"

"Gloria got her foot on your neck," Mark said.

"Ahh, come on with that, brother, you know better than that."

"I can't tell, and don't use her being pregnant as your excuse."

"I call you two or three times a week," Adam said.

"Come on now, Adam, it's me you're talking to. You know talking to you and seeing you are two different things. It feels much better when I see you."

"You're right. It feels better to see you too."

"On a different note, I say your father's picture on the news Friday. What's up? What are you going to do?"

"My father's attorney said that we need to wait on the Supreme Court's final decision. They might reconsider. If they don't, they're going to set a death date. That's my reason for driving up here. I need to talk to your father. Mrs. William told me you went to meet him earlier. How is he doing?"

"He still thinks he's young," Mark said.

"So he's doing wonderful then Alhamdulillah [all praise are due to God]."

"You can say that."

"Where were you when I walked over to the city hall looking for you?"

"I probably was in his office."

"While I was over there looking for you, I ran into Janice Henderson. We talked for a minute. Come to find out, she knows all about my father's case. As a matter of fact, she went to the funeral of the officer my dad killed."

"For real?" Mark asked.

"Yeah, for real."

"Get out of here!" Mark said, surprised.

"Not just that, she's willing to testify to what she knows."

"What did she say she knows?"

"She heard George Fuhrman tell her father in front of her and her brother that they pulled my mother over and saw a nigger in the car with her. They wanted to teach him a lesson. The court believed he was in the car alone that night. She also said her brother knows more about him than she does. I hope so. She's going to talk to him and see if he is willing to help. Once she talks to him, she's going to give me a call. I was going to ask your father for help. God's will, I don't need him."

"He has been asking about you anyway."

"I'm going to take off from work and drive up here to see him and your mom one day soon. I'm going to make it my business to do that. Let me allow Mrs. William to know that I am about to go. I will keep you posted."

"Okay, bro, make sure you do that. Don't take two more months to come back and see me."

"I won't," Adam said.

CHAPTER 15

Adam paced the floor as he watched the clock on his wall.

It's almost ten o'clock. She should have called by now. Her brother must have told her he wouldn't help! Adam said to himself as he paced the floor, second-guessing Janice and himself.

He had been out all day ripping and running the streets. The whim for sleep made him go lie down. The next morning Adam got up out the bed half asleep and walked into the bathroom. After taking care of his hygiene, he came out and offered *fajr*, the Muslim's morning prayer. As soon as he finished, he walked into the kitchen.

"Good morning, my love. How are you feeling?" Adam asked Gloria.

"Good morning, baby. I feel pretty good, thank god," Gloria answered.

"Has Janice called?" Adam asked.

"No, not yet."

"Do you think she's going to call like she said she would?" Adam asked.

"I believe she will. Just pray that her brother will be willing to share what he knows," Gloria answered.

Gloria fixed breakfast, and both ate. Within minutes after Adam finished eating, he started pacing the floor again.

"Baby, come over here and sit down. You paced the floor all last night. You are starting to get on my nerves with all that walking backward and forward. You don't have to worry. Janice is going to call you. I'll tell you what, you go get the cocoa butter stick off the top of the dresser and rub some on my stomach. You haven't rubbed my stomach once this week."

Adam walked out the living room to go get the cocoa butter stick out their bedroom. When he came back, he had Gloria lie down on the couch. He lifted her blouse over her stomach. Adam then took the top off the cocoa butter stick and pushed it out a little. He took the stick and rubbed it in the palms of his hands. Then he started rubbing it onto Gloria's stomach.

"Feel right here. No, at the bottom of my stomach. That's the baby's head," Gloria said as she looked at the smile on Adam's face. "Adam, you know I love you, right?"

"Yes, I know you love me. I love you too," Adam said as he gently rubbed her stomach.

"You are a very diligent man. I will give you that much. You sometimes try to force things to work. You've got to stop that. If it doesn't fit, don't force it. Just relax and allow Allah [God] to do the work. I know in your mind you feel like time is running out. You must keep in mind God does things when He chooses to. You might think that He's running late, but He is always on time."

As she said that, the phone rang. Adam's face lit up.

"See there, that's the call you have been waiting for," Gloria said as she rubbed her hands across his face.

The phone rang again.

"Are you going to answer it?" Gloria asked.

"Ali's residence, may I help you?"

"Yes, may I speak to Adam?"

"Speaking!"

"Adam, this is Janice. First of all, I would like to apologize for not calling you yesterday like I said I would. I did talk to my brother. He would like to talk to you personally."

"For real? When?" Adam asked as the happiness filled his body.

"Yes, for real! He had to work last night. That's why I didn't call. He is off today. I only have one court case schedule for this morning. Can you meet us at the same place I took you yesterday?"

"Sure, what time?" Adam asked.

"How long will it take you to get to Nashville?"

"About three and a half hours."

"Okay, it's seven o'clock now. How about 11:00 a.m.? That gives you four hours to get here."

"That's more than enough time," Adam said.

"Oh yes, Adam, before I forget, bring everything you have on your father's case with you."

"I sure will."

"Not to rush you off the phone, but I got to go. I have to get to a meeting."

"Okay then. God's will, I will see you later."

Adam hung up the phone with a big smile on his face.

"Baby, she wants me to meet them in Nashville this morning."

"I was just telling your butt to have patience. Come here and give me a kiss. Be careful," Gloria said.

"Inshallah, I will."

Adam got up and got dressed, grabbed everything he had on his father's case, and put it into the car. He didn't look up until he saw the sign that read Welcome to Nashville, Tennessee. He picked up his cell phone and called Janice. Her phone rang three times before the answering service picked up.

"This is Janice Henderson. Sorry I can't come to the phone right now. If you leave your name and a brief message, I will get back with you. Thank you. At the sound of the beep, please leave your message." *Beeeeep!*

"Janice, this is Adam. I am in Nashville. I will be at the coffee shop waiting on you and Eric."

Adam hung up the phone and drove straight to the coffee shop. He walked through the door and stood in line.

"Welcome to Best-Tasting Coffee Shop. May I help you?" the young lady said with a smile on her face.

"Yes, you may. I would like to have a large cappuccino with a little hazelnut in it," Adam said.

"Will that be all, sir?" the cashier said.

"Yes, ma'am, for now."

After Adam paid for and received his cappuccino, he walked to the back and sat down at the table. After about fifteen minutes, his phone rang.

"Adam Ali speaking, may I help you?"

"Adam, this is Janice. We are on our way. It shouldn't take us no more than ten minutes to get there."

"Okay, I will be here," Adam said as he sat there looking over his father's case and praying in a low tone, *In the name of Allah [God], the Most Gracious, the Most Merciful. All glory and praise are due to you. I ask for your forgiveness. Verily, you are the one who accepts repentance and who forgives over and over. Forgive me, Lord, for my shortcomings. Forgive me for having lack of patience. Thank you for putting the thought of you in my heart and mind. Allah [God], I ask you to allow this day to be the day you begin to start uncovering the light of your servant and allow the truth to come forward. For you are the Best of Planner. Lord, I pray that you allow the hearts of Janice and Eric to be open to your plan. Thank you, Lord. Amen.*

Once Adam finished praying, he got up from the table and went back to stand in line for another cappuccino. Before he could place his order,

Janice and Eric walked through the door. The bell over the door rang. It made him turn around. Janice didn't notice him standing in line. Her attention was focused toward the back.

"Janice!" Adam said, holding his hand up in the air so she could see him. "That's my stuff on the back table."

"Okay," Janice said.

"You're back already. What can I get you?" the young lady at the cash register said.

"May I have three cappuccinos with hazelnut and one dozen glazed donuts?"

"Will that be all?"

"Yes, ma'am, it will."

"That will be $12.53."

Adam handed her a $20 bill. The cashier gave him his change and passed him his order."

"Thank you. Come back."

Before Adam could put the stuff he ordered on the table, Eric stood up with his hand outward. The two shook hands.

"So you are, Adam. It's nice to finally meet you. For some reason, I wanted to thank you over the last past two years for the get-well card and the wise words within it."

"You're welcome, and it's a blessing to meet you. I brought you two some of Janice's favorite cappuccino," Adam said with a smile.

"Thanks," both said.

"Also, I brought some donuts to go with the cappuccinos if you would like to have some."

"Sure . . . thanks," they said in unison.

"As you can see, I brought a lot of stuff with me. This is the most important stuff I have on my father's case. I have dissected the whole case inside and out. What I need is the cause of it all. What I mean by that is, I need to know where they were going to take my mother's body once they were finished with her. It's clear on what mind frame that Mike McClain and George Fuhrman was in the night they pulled us over. I got to prove that it's a connection between my father's case and the cases of the twelve missing women along the same twenty-five-mile stretch of highway."

"I can remember the FBI combing through the area looking for signs of those missing women. I don't know if they found anything or not. If they did, I don't remember them broadcasting it," Eric said.

"Maybe because they had their eyes on George Fuhrman and his partner Mike McClain," Adam said.

"Why do you say that?" Eric asked.

"I have a few reasons. One of them is, the FBI told my father that he was in the wrong place at the right time. They also told him that they might be able to get him off the case, but they really needed to talk to my mom. The Klan ran us off from our home, and my mom didn't get a chance to talk to them."

"The FBI really didn't have anything. When they come for you, 95 percent of the time, they have you dead to rights or they have someone telling it," Eric said.

"They knew whatever happened to those women was well planned out. To this day, none of the women's bodies, property, or cars have been found."

"Really? Where are you getting all this information from?" Eric asked.

"I went down to the Teller County Public Library and dug it up myself. Here are the articles," Adam said as he passed them to Eric.

After Eric read them, he looked up at Adam.

"This is truly a blessing you ran across this," Eric said as he looked at Adam.

"What really makes me think that those cases are related to my father's is because the missing reports stopped a week before the night my father killed Mike McClain. It took at least two people to clean up after every kidnapping. One to drive the person's car being taken and a person to drive the car they used to follow or pull the person over in. Like I told your sister, a woman came forward and stated that the same two officers pulled her over and kidnapped her. When they got her where they wanted her, they made her perform all kinds of sexual acts. She later changed her story. Here is that article," Adam said as he handed it over to Eric.

"I believe we are on to something," Eric said as he read the article.

Adam just looked at him.

"Janice, do you remember the land with the lake on it that Dad sold to George?"

"Yes, the land that Mom left," Janice said.

Eric stopped for a moment to make sure his thoughts were accurate. Janice and Adam looked at him at the same time trying to figure out what his facial expression meant. After a few seconds, Eric looked up.

"I went out on the lake one Saturday morning to go fishing. I had been out there for about two hours before Mike and George came out there pulling a car with a tractor. Once they got the car close as they could to the lake, George unhooked the rope from the tractor and got into the boat that he kept out there. He pulled off in the boat as he held on to the rope that was hooked to the car. Mike drove the tractor all the way around the lake to the other side to meet George. Once the both of them met up on the other side of the lake, they hooked the rope back up to the tractor and pulled the car into the lake. The car didn't have any door on it or have seats inside it. That's why I didn't think too much about it. So I just kept on fishing. I had a good day, come to think about it. I caught so many fish. I couldn't tote them. So I went to ask George to give me a ride home. When I got up to his house, the one he had built, I was about to knock on his door when I heard them in the garage. I walked over to the garage. The side door was slightly open. I stuck my head in the doorway to see where he was. That's when I saw them taking something out the deep freezer. Whatever it was, it was wrapped in black plastic. It was shaped like a human body. When I stepped into the door, my foot hit an empty dog's bowl sitting on the floor of the garage. It scared the mess out of them. George jumped and said, 'Fuck, Eric, you are going to get your ass shot. You don't sneak up on no one like that. You are lucky you didn't get your fuckin' head blown off.' He drew his gun. It would have been too late if I was there to do something to him. George said to me, 'The next time, Eric, you need to say something before you just walk in on someone.' 'Okay, I'm sorry,' I said. After they got whatever it was in the plastic wrapped up into the trunk of the car, Mike closed the deep freezer and George closed the trunk of the car. 'What's up?' George asked me as he was taking off his gloves. 'I need a ride home. 'A ride home? Hell, boy, you live right down the fuckin' road,' George said. I told him I had a good morning fishing. There were too many fish for me to carry all the way home. He said, 'Let me see what you got there.' He looked inside my cooler. 'Hell, boy, you caught all the damn fish. Come and look at this, Mike.' He said, 'Hell yeah, I see you did pretty damn good. I will tell you what, Eric, when I finish taking this car down to the lake, I will bring your fish to you. I need to talk to your father anyway,' he said. I looked around his garage and saw all the parts they took off the cars lying around. Come to think of it, the cars weren't old cars either. Then I didn't think too much of it. I will bet you those cars belong to those missing women. They were probably putting a body in the trunk when I walked up."

"You might have the missing piece that I have been looking for. Is there any way I could find out or get the numbers off at least one of those cars? If I could get the serial numbers, I could have them run. That will tell us who the cars are registered to," Adam said as he looked at Eric.

"If you are willing to pay for the scuba diving equipment and go with me, I will go down in the lake myself to get the numbers," Eric said.

"How much do you think it will cost?" Adam asked.

"You don't have to buy the equipment. I know a place where you can rent it for about $200."

"I can handle that. Eric, let me ask you something," Adam said.

Eric looked over at Adam.

"Why are you so willing to go out of your way to help me?"

"It's a long story. For you, I could shorten it up. I know that you remember what happened to me two years ago."

Adam nodded.

"I was shot and almost killed in a convenient store that I worked at as a security guard. The two guys who tried to kill me were from Aryan Nations. George came to visit me in the hospital when I came out of the coma. He couldn't even look me in my eyes. He told me that they caught some innocent black guy and had him in custody. I told him that he had the wrong man and the person who shot me wasn't black. I didn't tell him the whole story about the man who shot me and I shot him. I didn't tell him I saw the white power and swastika tattoo on the person's stomach. You know the sign that the Neo-Nazi uses?"

"Yeah," Adam said as he looked into Eric's eyes.

"Anyway, the whole four months I stayed in the hospital trying to learn how to walk again, he never came back. During that time, I did a lot of thinking. During that short time I was going through therapy, I realized he killed my father two years prior. My father was shot in the back of his head while he was out hunting. George knew how my father loved to go hunting. So he asked my father to take him with him. Finally, he did. They say my father's death was an accident. No one ever came forward even to this day, saying that they were out there hunting that day. The people in our town loved my father. I put two and two together. Before my father was killed, George used to always ask him to unite the Klan with the Aryan Nations. My father wouldn't do it. He said that they brought too much attention on themselves. When he told George that he didn't like it, even though he acted like he was cool with it, my father told me he wouldn't trust George no further than he could throw a baby elephant. He knew he couldn't pick one up, not to mention throw it."

The three of them started laughing.

"We can laugh at it now, but my father was for real about what he said. That's why he wouldn't put George second in command. He was pissed when he found out I was. He went around talking about how young I was and how he should be second in command because his father, who was my father's best friend, gave my father his blessing before he died. My father became the Grand Dragon of the area. Since it was his father, he thought it would be more the right to make him second in command. After the death of my father, George started making all kinds of power plays. He wanted me to give him the okay to unite the two. I stood firm on my father's wishes. That is why those two men tried to kill me. There is no reason why I shouldn't try to put him away, not to think of where he should be: dead. Should I go on?" Eric asked as he maintained eye-to-eye contact with Adam.

"No, you don't have to say any more. When would you like to do this?" Adam asked.

"Saturday night or early Sunday morning about one or two o'clock," Eric said.

"Why that time of the night?"

"George goes to church every Sunday morning. He goes in pretty early on Saturday to prepare for Sunday. All the officers and the people of Teller County are asleep by then. They know my truck, so we don't have to worry about being out of the norm. We could go right to the lake. No one should be out there. If there is, the way that we're going in, we will see them before they see us."

Adam's cell phone rang. "Adam Ali, speaking, may I help you?" When Gloria said Adam's name, Adam's heart sped up. He knew something was wrong with her. "What's the matter, baby?" Adam asked.

"My water has broken, and I'm scared. Where are you?" Gloria asked.

"I'm still in Nashville. Have you called for help?"

"Yes, I have. They should be here any minute."

"Do you have the front door unlocked so they can get in?"

"Sure, I'm in the front, waiting on them."

"They should take you to the MED. If they take you to any other hospital, have someone call me. I am on my way right now. I love you."

"I love you too. Please hurry!" Gloria said.

"We need to get off this phone just in case they are trying to call you back," Adam said.

"I don't want to. I'm scared."

"I know. We got to, baby. Everything is going to be just fine. You must stay strong and in control. Just think of God and glorify Him, okay?" Adam said.

"Okay," Gloria said as she hung up the phone.

"That was my wife. She's going into labor at home."

"Is anyone there with her?" Janice asked.

"No, she has already called for help."

"Do you know what she's having?" Janice asked.

"A girl, God's will."

"Congratulations!" Eric said.

"Thanks."

Adam leaned over and pulled his wallet out from his back pocket. Then he opened it and took two $100 bills out and passed them over the table to Eric.

"This is for the equipment that we will need," Adam said.

"Okay, hopefully, I will be able to go pick everything up Saturday and have it ready. We will have to meet up in Jackson, Tennessee, Saturday night. You will have to park your car somewhere down there and ride with me. I will give you a call at midnight straight up Sunday. You need to answer your phone," Eric said.

"You don't have to worry about that, Eric. After I leave from visiting my father Saturday afternoon, I am going to stop in Jackson and get me a hotel room. I will already be there waiting on you to call."

"That will be right on time."

"I enjoyed this meeting and would like to stay a little longer, but I've got to get back to Memphis ASAP!"

"Please be careful. Don't be flying down I-40, okay?" Janice said.

"I will take my time. Eric, I will be waiting on your call, God's will. I will see you two later."

"See you Sunday morning, God's will," Eric said.

Adam didn't waste any time. He drove straight to the hospital and the MED labor unit.

"Excuse me!" Adam said to the receptionist at the front desk.

The heavyset white lady in her early forties raised her head up from the book that she was reading.

"Yes, sir, may I help you?"

"My wife was brought in about four hours ago."

"What is her name, sir?"

"Gloria Ali."

"Your name?"

"Adam Ali."

"Mr. Ali, your wife is in maternity room 602."

"Thank you, ma'am."

"You're welcome."

Adam rushed to the room, his heart beating fast as he eased his way. Gloria was sitting up in the bed with the newborn girl in her arms. She looked up and saw Adam and started smiling.

"You can come on over here and see what Allah [God] has blessed us with," Gloria said.

Adam walked up to the bed slowly. "Here, chicken, hold your daughter."

Adam shook his head.

"What are you shaking your head for?"

"She's too small!" Adam said

"Trust me, honey, she isn't small at all. She weighs nine pounds eight ounces. She felt like she weighed more than that."

"Have you named her yet?" Adam asked.

"No, I was waiting on you to do that."

Before Adam named her, he bent down and whispered into her right ear as the mother held her, "God is the greatest, God is the greatest, God is the greatest. I testify that there is no god except Allah. I testify that there is no god except Allah. I testify that Muhammad is the messenger of Allah. Come to prayer! Come to prayer! Come to success! Come to success! God is the greatest. God is the greatest. There is no god except Allah."

After he finished, he reached into his right pants pocket and pulled out a date. He bit a very small piece off and put it into her mouth. After the baby tasted the sweet date, he kissed her on the forehead.

"Alhamdulillah [all praise are due to God], your name will be Sukita Ali," Adam said as he looked into her beautiful little eyes.

CHAPTER 16

"Good morning, my love," Adam said as he passed his sleepy wife a breakfast plate and a cup of milk while she lay in the bed.

"Good morning. Thank you. I see you are up early this morning," Gloria said.

"I have a big day today."

"All of this food is for me?"

"Yes, it is."

"You know I'm not eating for two anymore."

"I know. I just want to make sure you get full. You know I will be gone until later tonight or tomorrow."

"I know, but I can't eat all of this," Gloria said as she looked at the plate.

"Just eat what you can. I'm going to see Dad first, so I could tell him the good news, the news of his grandbaby, and I want to share with him the plans Eric and I have for tonight. Inshallah [God's will], it will be the evidence we need to put George Fuhrman in his place."

"Did you send those pictures to him?" Gloria asked.

"I sent them out two days ago.'"

"Tell him I said I will try to make the trip next week with the family if God allows it."

"Baby, once I get me a hotel room in Jackson, I will give you a call to let you know here I am."

"Okay, you just be careful." Gloria said.

"Inshallah, I will. I need to get going, baby."

"Make sure you tell Dad what I said."

"I will make sure I do that."

"Thanks for the breakfast in bed, my love. I love you."

"You're welcome, baby. I love you too."

Adam was very enthused about getting to Nashville, so he could visit his father. In his mind, he envisioned his father being home soon. He started talking to himself, *I need to make it back down to Jackson as safe and quick as possible. Allah, this is what I have been longing for, for years.*

He started feeling as though he finally discovered the piece of the puzzle he was missing. His thoughts didn't change as he arrived at the Tennessee Department of Corrections. He was eager to tell his father about the things that had unfolded within the past week. He couldn't get into the visitation room fast enough to see his father. The thoughts were entering his mind very rapidly; he thought that the security was checking visitors too slowly. After going through the search required at the institution before visitors are allowed inside, Adam looked over toward the table where they usually sat.

Good, Uncle Brandon is here too, Adam said to himself as a smile formed on his face.

He walked up to the table and took a seat as the adrenaline rushed through his body. He couldn't even think to greet them as he normally would have.

Alhamdulillah [all praise are due to God]," Adam said with a big grin on his face.

"What kind of news do you have for us?" Samson asked, knowing that something was going on with his son by the way he was acting.

"Allah is Akbar [God is great]. I have received an abundance of blessings this week. Thank Allah for you being here, Uncle Brandon, to hear this great news." Samson and Brandon looked at each other as they wondered what this news could be with Adam so cheerful. Samson looked back at Adam.

"Come clean, son, and quit holding out on us."

"I am. Just give me a minute," Adam said, showing all his teeth. "Okay, first of all, Gloria had the baby, a baby girl. I named her Sukita."

"Alhamdulillah," Samson and Brandon said simultaneously. "I also have some news that's truly amazing." The way Adam sounded and looked made Samson sit up in his chair.

"Thank Allah, I didn't sit here last week and listen to you and Mr. Gaines. I came back to Nashville Monday, like I said I would. I didn't get a chance to talk to the governor like I planned. While I was up here looking for his son Mark, I ran into a female I went to school with. Her name is Janice Henderson. It was Allah's doing because I wasn't expecting to ever see her again in life. While I was walking through the city hall looking for Mark, she walked up behind me and tapped me on the shoulder. We talked and came to find out she knows a lot about what happened that night. Her father took her and her brother, Eric, to the funeral of the officer you killed. Her father was once the leader of the Klan. George Fuhrman had to answer to him about what happened out there that night. She said George got in the car with them after the funeral. She went on to say her father asked George Fuhrman what happened. From her report, he said they were going to teach you a lesson for messing with their women, and somehow you got the ups on them." Adam smiled at them because they were intensely listening to the story.

"That sounds good, don't it?" Adam asked.

"Come on and quit playing, boy. Finish telling us the story," Samson said.

"Janice said he said they underestimated you. This story gets even better. She introduced me to her brother, Eric. I drove back up here the next day to meet with him. We talked. I told him about the stuff that I found out, like the newspaper articles. He told me how he thinks George Fuhrman had something to do with the death of his father and he tried to have him killed. Remember me saying it was a piece of the puzzle missing?"

"I remember," Samson said.

"We believe we have found it."

"What Alhamdulillah," Samson said as his heart beat faster.

"You have copies of the articles of the missing women? We believe we know where the bodies and cars are located."

"How will that help your father's case?" Brandon asked.

"Hold that thought. That's what I am about to tell you. Eric believes that he saw Mike McClain and George Fuhrman put a body in a trunk of a car, and they put the car in the lake on George Fuhrman's property. Once we prove that, we can prove Mom was pulled over for the same motive."

"He is an ex-Klan. How do you know he's telling you the truth and could be trusted?" Samson asked.

"From the look in his eyes. The eyes don't ever lie. Also, my inner self tells me that he's telling me the truth." Both nodded, agreeing with Adam.

"He's going to take me out to the lake late tonight. He is willing to dive down to the bottom of the lake to get the serial numbers off the two cars he saw them put in there."

"How did he see or witness all that and wasn't a part of it?" Brandon asked.

"He told me that he was out there at the lake early one morning fishing when Mike and George came out there pulling a car with a tractor. He said he didn't think anything of it until after he got finished fishing. He walked up to George's house to get a ride home, and that's when he heard them in the garage. He went over to the garage and saw them through the garage door getting something out of the deep freezer, and it was in the shape of a human body. It was wrapped up in black plastic. They put it into the trunk of a car. They had been stripped in the garage."

"Have you called my lawyer, Mr. Gaines, and told him about this?" Samson asked.

"No, sir," Adam replied.

"Why not?"

"I don't want anyone to know but us, and the two that this information came from. Once everything works out like we have planned it and we are for sure that the cars belong to the missing women, then we will bring in the FBI, the press, and your attorney. Right now, we don't know who George Fuhrman has on his payroll or who is in with him. We know that he is the sheriff of Teller County, the leader of the Klan and the Aryan Nations in that area. He's a powerful man down there right now."

"With all that said, how do you know Eric and his sister ain't in with him too?" Brandon asked, concerned about Adam.

"All I can say is, Allah knows best, if they are or not."

"If you need my help, call me," Brandon said.

"I will, but I don't think I will need you. Not yet anyway. Just pray that this is the missing piece of the puzzle. I truly believe in my heart that it is. I haven't felt like this since Aunt Tiltyla's car pulled up in front of Uncle Jay's house," Adam said.

"I feel the same way you do, son."

"Give me a call tomorrow morning as soon as you can, Dad."

"I will, Inshallah. I hope that you have some good news for me," Samson said.

"Inshallah, I will. You know Mom and they are on their way down?"

"They told me they were coming but didn't give me a day. I know they are planning on being here by next Saturday to visit you, Inshallah [if it's God's will]. When you call tomorrow morning, they will be there. I'm going to leave here and drive to Jackson, so I can get me a hotel room. Eric said he's going to call me at straight up midnight. From Jackson, I am going to ride with him to the lake. We should be done no later than 3:00 a.m. If I am not at home by six o'clock, something is wrong. Oh yeah, I have been so caught up in this story that I almost forgot to tell you that your daughter-in-law said, God's will, they will be here next weekend too. I mailed you some pictures. You should have received them by now."

"I haven't received them yet. Monday Inshallah."

"I will be by the house tomorrow, Inshallah [God's will]," Brandon said.

A voice came over the PA system saying visiting hours are now over. "I hope that you all had a nice visit. Please come back."

"Man, time passed by quickly. Alhamdulillah [all praise are due to God]. I love ya'll, and Inshallah [God's will], I will see ya'll soon."

"Inshallah, we love you too," Adam and Brandon said as they stood up.

"I want you to be careful down there tonight, son. If you are not going to be home as planned, call your wife and let her know what's up," Samson said as he hugged Adam.

"Yes, sir, I will."

After the three embraced, they said their greetings and departed. Adam and Brandon walked their separate ways toward their cars. Brandon stopped and turned around.

"Adam!" Brandon said.

"Sir," Adam replied.

"I'm going to stop by the meat market today and get something to put on your grill."

"It's your grill too. It's about time. It has been forever since we have put anything on it," Adam said.

"You're so right. Inshallah, I will see you then. By the way, I hope you find what you are going down there for. Don't forget what I told you," Brandon said.

"If I need you, I will call," Adam said with a smile on his face. Both smiled and walked to their cars.

Adam headed down I-40 West until he got to the Jackson, Tennessee, exit. He went to the nearest hotel off the highway. Once there, he checked into a room. After getting situated, he called his wife, Gloria, to let her know his location. As soon as he hung up the phone, he called Janice. Unable to reach her, he left her a message, letting her know he was in Jackson at a hotel. Making the best of his time, he took a shower and lay across the bed to take a nap. At 11:55 p.m., Adam's cell phone rang and woke him up from his nap.

"Adam Ali speaking, may I help you?"

"Adam, this is Eric. I'm calling to let you know that everything is going as planned. I am in Teller County now. I have been here all day, so they will be used to seeing my truck. I will be your way pretty soon. What's the name of the hotel, address, and room number?"

Adam looked around for something with the hotel's address on it. He grabbed the key ring off the table next to the bed and gave Eric the address off it.

"Thank you. I need you to be ready in forty-five minutes. I will be there to pick you up."

"Cool. I will be waiting," Adam said.

"You are in room 206, right?"

"Right," Adam said.

The two hung up. Adam got up and took his stuff out to his car. He then walked back up the stairs to his room and watched the clock on the TV. Time wasn't moving fast enough for him, so he called his wife to let her know that Eric was on his way to pick him up. Shortly after getting off the phone, he heard a knock on the door. Adam jumped.

"Who is it?"

"Eric!"

Adam quickly opened the door.

"Are you ready?" Eric asked.

"I have never been more ready in my life," Adam said.

"Let's go." Eric said.

The two walked down to Eric's black truck. *Bless me, Allah [in the name of God]*, Adam said to himself as he was stepping up into Eric's truck.

"How long have you been here in Jackson?" Eric asked.

"Since about six o'clock this evening."

"I have been in Teller County all day, making my rounds, making sure my truck is seen. I don't want to look suspicious driving around one or two o'clock in the morning."

"I see you are on top of everything," Adam said as he looked around and saw the diving equipment in the back.

"Adam, I need you to hop over the console into the backseat. I don't want anyone to be able to look into the truck and see you. I'm about to turn onto the road that leads into town." Adam hopped between the seat into the backseat and lay down across it. Eric drove through town and up a back road that led to the lake on George's property. Once there, Eric drove through some high bushes and between some trees with his four-wheel-drive Ford Bronco to camouflage it. After Eric felt his truck couldn't be seen, he stopped. Both got out of the truck and walked toward the back. Eric opened the hatchback and pulled out all the equipment.

"This is what I used your money for," Eric said as he showed Adam the rubber inflatable boat and oxygen tanks. "It has been years since I have been out here. George used to have a small rowboat out here but on the other side. I need you to grab that oxygen tank. I will get the rest of this stuff."

They walked about thirty yards to a location where they could look over the whole lake without being seen.

"A good thing about this spot is, we can hear and see them first," Eric said as Adam bent down to look around.

Eric inflated the rubber boat and then started putting on his diving suit. After the boat finished inflating, Eric made sure no one was out there.

"Let's put everything in the boat," Eric said.

Once everything they needed was placed in the boat, Eric grabbed one side. "Grab the other side. We're going to tote it out to the lake," Eric said.

Both grabbed ahold of the inflated boat with all their equipment in it and slowly carried it out to the lake. Once the boat was in the water, Eric held it. "Get on!" Eric told Adam. Eric pushed the boat outward into the lake and quickly jumped in. As the boat glided slowly across the water, Eric grabbed the boat paddle and paddled, trying to make as little noise as possible. There couldn't have been a better night, Eric thought to himself. The wind was calm, and the lake was relaxed. The sky was clear enough to count the stars. Adam couldn't believe how everything was so perfectly timed. Eric stopped the boat at the location he thought the cars might be. Adam's attention returned to the lake once Eric stopped and dropped a weight into the water, with an orange flag at the top of the rope that floated on top of the water. Eric was hoping that it would help him locate the boat from underneath the water. He picked up another long rope he put into the boat and tied it around his waist.

"Adam, I need you to hold on to the end of this rope. If something goes wrong, you hear or see anything, let me know by pulling on the rope."

"Okay, I got you," Adam said.

Eric grabbed the waterproof flashlight and underwater notepad he purchased. He then sat nearly at the boat and plunged into the lake backward. Adam held on to the rope as he lay down in the boat, making sure he couldn't be easily seen. Eric resurfaced after nearly ten minutes.

While treading the water, he passed the notepad and flashlight to Adam. He then took the oxygen tank off and passed it to Adam. Eric held his hand out toward Adam.

"Pull me up!" Eric said.

"Did you see anything?" Adam asked.

"I will tell you later. Let's get out of here first," Eric said as Adam pulled him in.

Eric pulled in the rope with the flag and weight on it. Adam paddled the boat back to land while Eric pulled the diving suit off. Once on the bank, they pulled the boat into the tall grass. Eric put the equipment in the back of his truck, while Adam deflated the boat and folded it up before putting it into the back of Eric's truck. Both jumped into the truck, and Eric drove off.

"Jesus Christ, Adam, we were right."

"What did you see?" Adam said as he looked into Eric's face.

"There are more than two cars down there."

"How many did you get the numbers off of?"

"Just four of them. What took me so long is I was trying to find a way into the trunks. The second car I swam to didn't have any seats in it. I swam inside and looked through where the backseat goes into the trunk. Do you know what I'm talking about?" Eric asked.

"Yes, I do. Go ahead," Adam said, trying to hear the rest of the story.

"I shined the flashlight up through the cutout where the seat goes. I saw the black plastic that I told you about. I reached my arm through the biggest cutout and pulled it to me. Once I got it close enough to me, I tore into it to see what was inside. We were right, Adam. It was the remains of a human inside the plastic. That fucking George and Mike were actually killing people."

"Alhamdulillah [all praise are due to God]. Thank you, Lord. You are the greatest," Adam said.

"Are you okay?" Eric said after hearing Adam use words he had never heard before.

"Sure, I was just thanking God for allowing us to uncover the handiwork of Satan."

"Adam, look in the glove compartment and get that pad and pen out for me."

Adam got the pad and pen out for Eric. "Write those numbers down off the underwater pad onto some paper. We don't have the time to run the serial numbers ourselves. Our best out is to call the FBI and give them the numbers and let them run them. I know for sure we can't trust any police or sheriff department around this area. George pretty much has this whole area in his back pocket," Eric said.

"We can go to my house and call the FBI agents who worked on the case," Adam suggested.

"We can do that. I need to drive you back to the hotel in Jackson to get your car and call Janice to let her know that everything went as planned," Eric said as he dialed her number.

"Hello," Janice said.

"Janice, this is me. I just called to let you know that everything went as planned and we were right about George."

"Where are you now?" Janice asked.

"We are on our way back to Jackson to get Adam's car. When we leave there, we are going to his house to call the FBI agents handling the case."

"So you guys found enough out there to help Adam's father's case?"

"I think so. There's human remains in at least one of the car's trunk."

"My god, are you sure what you saw was human remains?" Janice asked.

"Yes, I am sure. I will give you a call later to give you an update. I love you," Eric said.

"Okay, I love you too."

"Does your car need any gas before we get on the highway?" Eric asked Adam.

"I have enough to make it. What about you?"

"I filled up right before I picked you up," Eric said as he glanced over at his gas hand.

Eric drove Adam to his car and trailed him to the highway. Adam led the way down I-40 West to his house in Memphis.

CHAPTER 17

Two hours had passed since Adam and Eric made it to Adam's house. Adam tried several times to contact Special Agent Woods, the FBI agent in charge of the investigation of the missing women in the late 1970s. Finally, after trying the number again, someone picked up.

"Hello."

"May I speak to Agent Woods?" Adam asked.

"This is he. How may I help you?"

"Agent Woods, my name is Adam Ali. My mother, Shanda Ali, and I spoke with you four years ago about the Samson Ali case."

"I can recall that case. I told you there is nothing I can do now about his case."

"I understood that, sir. Are you still in charge of the missing-women cases from 1978 out of Teller County, Tennessee?"

"Yes, I am. Why?"

"I think we have found the bodies and cars of those missing women that you have been looking for," Adam said.

"How could you be so sure?"

"We have the serial numbers off four of the cars, and we know for a fact at least one of them has human remains in the trunk of it. If you run the numbers we have, we believe that the will match up."

"Give me the numbers," Agent Woods said.

Adam read the numbers off the pad to him one by one.

"Once I check these numbers out, I will give you a call. So stand by your phone."

"What did he say?" Eric asked as Adam laid down the phone.

"He told me to stand by. He's going to call me back once he checks the numbers out."

Adam stood up and walked over to the fireplace and picked his father's picture up.

"This is a picture of my father," Adam said as he passed the picture to Eric.

"Your father was a serviceman?" Eric asked as he looked at Samson in his uniform.

"Yes, he was a lieutenant out at the Millington Naval Base when it happened," Adam said.

Hearing voices in the house woke Gloria up. She walked into the front where they were.

"Did we wake you, baby?"

"Yep, how long have you been here?" Gloria asked.

"We have been here for about two hours. Baby, this is Janice Henderson's brother, Eric. Eric, this is my lovely wife, Gloria."

"It's nice to meet you, Gloria," Eric said.

"It's nice to meet you too, Eric. What did you two find?"

"Eric went down and got the serial numbers off four of the cars down in the lake. He looked inside the trunk of one car and saw the remains of a human body."

"You're kidding me, right?" Gloria asked. "What are you going to do now?"

"I just got off the phone with the FBI."

"What did they say?"

"He's going to call me back after he checks out the numbers I gave him from the four cars."

A light from a car pulling into the driveway flashed through the window and lit up the house. "That might be the FBI," Eric said.

The three rushed to the door, unable to see from the bright lights. "Is that them?" Gloria asked as she held her hand over the top of her eyes.

"I don't know. I can't see," Adam said.

The car lights cut off, and Verlena stepped out the passenger seat of the car.

"That's my mother and them," Adam said as he walked out toward the car to meet them.

All had smiles on their faces as Adam walked up. "What are you all smiling at?" Adam asked.

"At the way you all were looking out the door," Tiltyla said.

"You all were looking like we were the police or something," Shanda said.

"That's who we thought you all were," Adam said as he hugged his mother first then Verlena, Tiltyla, and Mustafa one at a time.

All walked up and greeted Gloria with smiles and hugs at the front door. "This is Eric. Eric, this one right here is my mother. That big man right there is my nephew, Mustafa. The skinny one right there is my sister, Verlena, and last but not least is my aunt Tiltyla," Adam said as he put his arm around Shanda's neck. With each saying their hellos, Eric returned the greeting.

"Eric and I are working on something right now. God's will, it will help Dad get out as soon as next month. You all have been on the highway. I know you would like a shower and a place to relax."

"I know I could use a shower," Tiltyla said.

"Me too," Verlena said.

"Just make yourselves at home," Adam said as they walked into the back.

Another car pulled up in front of the house just as the phone rang. Without giving it a thought, Adam picked it up and walked toward the front door to see who was out there.

"Ali's residence, Adam speaking. May I help you?"

"Mr. Ali, this is the FBI. We are in your driveway. May we come in?" Agent Woods asked.

"Yes, sir, come on in," Adam said.

Three FBI agents exited the black unmarked suburban and walked into the house. They identified themselves one by one, showing their badges and IDs. "Mr. Ali, I checked the numbers out that you gave me over the phone. They match four of the missing victims' cars. We would like to know where you got them from?" Agent Woods asked.

Adams face lit up. "Alhamdulillah. Thank you, Lord," Adam said before he introduced Eric. "This is Eric Henderson. He was helping me investigate my father's case. I was one of the children in the car that night my father, Samson Ali, shot and killed Mike McClain, the Teller County sheriff. I started investigating my father's case over five years ago. As you know, Agent Woods, my father was sentenced to the death penalty for protecting himself and his family."

"Hold up, Mr. Ali. I know where you are trying to go with this. We couldn't do anything because we had no proof or anything solid to arrest George Fuhrman or Mike McClain," Agent Woods said after cutting Adam off.

"I understand that. Just hear me out," Adam said as tears of joy built up in his eyes.

"I went to the Teller County local library and found some newspaper articles of the missing women. That's how I knew for sure why you all were in Teller County. Also, I realized at that point that was why my mom was pulled over. You all and the FBI knew that. That's why you and your partner told my father that he was in the wrong place at the right time. You wouldn't have told him that you might be able to get him out of his case if it didn't have merit. You knew he stopped there from being a thirteenth victim. It has been over fifteen years. You all left him to die. A man you all know is innocent. The United States government—that's what I don't understand. Why would you all allow an innocent man to die when you have the power to prevent it?"

"It wasn't my call," Agent Woods said.

"Well, we have the proof now, Agent Woods. I don't want to hear you say you are going to see what you can do. The Supreme Court is about to give my father a death date soon. I need your word that you are going to do something to stop it after you see for yourself that Eric and I have all the proof you need to arrest George Fuhrman like you should have years ago. By the grace of God, I met this man through his sister. I showed him the articles and other stuff I have on my father's case. I told him about the missing women and how neither they nor their cars have been found. I came to find out he witnessed George Fuhrman and Mike McClain putting two of the cars into the lake. I am going to allow him to tell you all the story himself."

"Hold up. Are you the same Eric Henderson who was shot during a store robbery a year or two ago?" Agent Garner asked.

"Yes, I am," Eric said with a smirk on his face.

"You're Klan, right?" Agent Garner asked.

"I used to be," Eric said.

"We had our eyes on you. It's good you cleaned up your act," Agent Garner said.

"If you don't mind me asking, why were you watching me?" Eric asked.

"We got word that you are the man, the leader of the Klan."

"What do you know about this, Mr. Henderson?" Agent Woods asked, cutting their conversation off.

"When I was about sixteen years old, I was out at the lake located on George's property, fishing one morning. I saw George and Mike pulling a car out to the lake with a tractor. The car didn't have any doors or seats. Once they got the car close enough to the lake, George unhooked the rope from the tractor and got into the boat. He held on to the rope while he went across the lake in the boat. Mike McClain drove the tractor around to the other side of the lake to meet up with George. They hooked the rope back up to the tractor and pulled the car into the lake. I didn't think anything of it. So when I finished fishing, I needed a ride home because I couldn't tote all the fish I caught. When I got up to George's house, I heard them in the garage. I walked over, and that's when I saw them getting a body wrapped up in black plastic out the freezer he had in his garage and put it into the trunk of a car. Up until I talked with Adam, I didn't think anything of it. We got together, and I went down to the bottom of the lake to check it out. While I was down there, I checked the trunk of one of the four I took the serial numbers off. I swam inside of the first one I saw without any seats. I looked through the back cutout with my flashlight into the trunk. That's when I saw the plastic, so I pulled it to me and tore it open. It had the remains of a human inside it."

"Are you sure what you saw was human?" Agent Woods asked.

"Yes, sir, I'm positive," Eric said.

"How many cars did you see?" Agent Woods asked.

"I didn't count them. To give or take, I will say ten."

"Good enough! Agent Blocker, I need you to call and see if you can get a judge up this morning. We need us a federal search warrant to search the person and property of the Teller County's sheriff, George Fuhrman."

"While we are waiting, Mr. Henderson, how did a Klan member—"

"Pardon me, ex-Klan member," Eric said, cutting Agent Garner off.

"Excuse me, ex-Klan member. How did you hook up with a black man and turn your back on your brothers?" Agent Garner asked.

"It's a long story, and I have to give the thanks and praise to God. If I were to tell you the whole story, we would be here all day. Anyway, after I was shot in that store by two of George's men, God sent a black man to save my life. On the same token, George killed my father or had something to do with it."

"Why would he want you and your father killed?" Agent Garner asked.

"Simple—to become the head of the Klan and to unite them with the Aryan Nations," Eric said.

"We know he has become a powerful man in that area."

"Yes, he has. Now it's time that he get down off his high horse," Eric said.

"Special Agent Woods, we are in business. Judge David Parrish will have us a warrant ready within the next thirty minutes," Agent Blocker said.

"Call the bureau and get as many agents as possible down there ASAP. We are going to need some diving specialists and heavy equipment. Most likely, we are going to need some cranes or something large enough to pull those cars out," Agent Woods said.

Agent Blocker got back on his cell phone.

"I need you two to go with us and show us the location of the lake," Agent Woods said as he looked over at Adam and Eric.

"That's no problem," Eric said as he stood up from the couch next to where Adam was sitting.

"First, let me inform my wife that I'm about to leave," Adam said before walking to the back room.

"Agent Blocker, call and get us a chopper ready," Special Agent Woods stated as Adam walked off.

"Sweetheart, I am about to go with the FBI agents to show them the location of the cars. Inshallah, Dad will be calling you this morning, and Uncle Brandon, will be over as well. Tell them what we told you and that we're going with the FBI agents to show the place to them. Watch the news. There should be some breaking news. I love you, and if you need anything, call. I will have my cell phone with me."

"I love you too. Make sure they get him, tiger," Gloria said with a smile.

"Allah is the greatest. I will fill you in on everything when I get back, God's will."

The five of them exited Adam's front door one by one. Adam and Eric got into the back of the suburban with one of the FBI agents. They stopped at the federal courthouse to meet a federal agent out in front to get the search warrant needed to search the property of Sheriff George Fuhrman. After the brief stop, they drove to a nearby school yard where a helicopter was waiting for them. Within minutes, after taking off in the helicopter, they landed near Teller County at a location that the FBI agents had set up. Agents stood around, waiting for their instructions from Special Agent Woods. The five of them exited the chopper where agents were waiting to escort them in the building that would be used as their post. Special Agent Woods and the other four men walked into the building to a room that sat off to the side of the entrance. They walked into the center of the thirty-plus men waiting for some action.

"For those of you who don't know me, my name is Special Agent Woods. I would like to thank you all for showing up on such short notice. I have a search warrant for Sheriff George Fuhrman, person and property. There will be no need to search him or his home at this time. What we are looking for is in his lake. I didn't see any of the heavy equipment that I asked for outside," Agent Woods said as he looked around the room for someone to say something.

"Special Agent Woods, they are moving a little slow, but they are on the way," one agent from the back of the room said as he pulled the cell phone from his ear.

"All I need you all to do is secure the area. I don't want any Tom, Dick, or Harry to come near the lake unless they have my approval. If Sheriff Fuhrman is on his property, do not attempt to arrest him at this time or allow him to interfere. Ask him to step back once. If he fails to do so, then arrest him for obstruction of justice. Do we have the divers here?"

"Yes, sir," a tall red-haired agent said.

"Where are they?" Agent Woods asked.

"Right here, sir," the two men said as they held up their hand.

"When you two go down, I don't need you to touch anything. Just figure out the best way for the crane to bring the cars up. Am I understood?" Agent Woods asked as he looked over at them.

"Yes, sir," the two men said at once.

"Okay, listen up! I want everyone to hear this," Agent Woods said before he briefed the men on the situation at hand. "For those of you who don't know why you are here or isn't familiar with the cases of the missing women from the late 1970s down in this area, we have good reason to believe that the cars and the remains of those twelve missing women are at the bottom of the lake that's located on Sheriff George Fuhrman's property.

"I need a perimeter set up around the lake with yellow crime-scene tape. Once again, no one is to cross it. This is Officer Eric Henderson from Nashville, and this is Adam Ali from Memphis. They are the only two who are not FBI who should be inside the taped-off area. Are there any questions?" Agent Woods asked.

The whole room shook their heads. "The heavy equipment is out front," Agent Blocker said.

"Thank you. Okay, gentlemen, we got work to do. Let's move out."

The agents moved out the doors and got into their unmarked cars. Adam and Eric got into the car with Agent Woods and Agent Blocker to show them the way. When they pulled out, all the other agents pulled out right behind them. Within ten minutes, they pulled up in front of George Fuhrman's property. All the other agents trailed behind them like they were heading to a funeral. Once on the property, all the agents stepped out of their cars.

"I need you two gentlemen to stay in the car for now," Agent Woods said as he looked from the passenger side of the seat into the back at Adam and Eric.

The two agents stepped out of the car and walked up to Sheriff Fuhrman's front door. Agent Blocker stepped to the side, while Agent Woods knocked on the door. After a few minutes of knocking with no response, Agent Woods called over the two agents. "Excuse me, I need the two of you to stand right here in case George Fuhrman shows up. Here is the search warrant to serve him if he shows up," Agent Woods said to the two young agents who looked like they were fresh out of high school.

Agent Woods and Agent Blocker walked back to their car. Agent Woods opened the back door.

"How do we get to the lake?" Agent Woods asked Eric.

"Go straight down this dirt road that we are on now," Eric said as he pointed his finger toward the road.

"Can the trucks get through?"

"Sure, once everyone moves their cars."

Agent Woods had all the agents pull their car over to the side in the grass. Agent Woods, Agent Blocker, Eric, and Adam walked in front of the trucks carrying the cranes. The other agents followed their lead. Once the trucks made it to the lake, Agent Woods ordered his men to roll out the crime-scene tape. People saw the FBI agents and trucks rolling through their town. The word spread quickly that they were there. Shortly after, the HB arrived on the scene. The townspeople came from all directions, trying to see what was going on. The divers suited up and waited for Agent Woods to give them their instructions.

"The cars are about twenty feet outward from here," Eric said as they stood on the bank, looking into the lake.

"You all heard him. Get into the boat and go out about twenty feet. Once you are there, only one of you need to go down to check it out. If you see anything, just come up and give us a thumbs-up. Then we can start unwinding the cables from the cranes."

The men got into their boat and went out twenty feet as Agent Woods and Eric suggested. One man went down into the lake. He came up within seconds with his thumb up. Special Agent Woods started lowering the cables into the lake. The two divers dove down with the cables in their hands until they reached the bottom. Once they hooked the cables to the cars, they swam back up to their boat. After they were clear from the way of the cables, they gave the signal to pull. The crane operators, one at a time, lifted the cars up from the bottom of the lake. Within seconds, the cars emerged from the water. The first crane operator stopped the car in midair over the surface of the lake to allow the fish and water to escape. After most of the water stopped running, the crane operator turned the crane around and swung the car and sat it onshore. Everyone stood at a safe distance back until the crane operator sat the car down on land. The cable was unhooked, and the second crane operator followed. Once the two cars were safely on land, Agent Garner had a locksmith on sight with his tools to open the trunks of the cars. After the trunks were opened, Agent Woods put on a pair of latex gloves and pulled out a small folded-up knife from his right front pants pocket. He leaned over into the trunk; and with his left hand, he grabbed hold of the bag. With his right, he used the knife to open up the plastic straight down the middle. The smell that reeked made him step back quickly and throw his arm across his nose. "Jesus . . . it's human. Agent Blocker, I need you to get Michael Shumpert, the forensic specialist, on the phone. Let him know I need him ASAP. Also, get him on a chopper and have someone meet him," Agent Woods said.

"Copy that, sir," Agent Blocker said.

"Why is it so important that you get him out here?"

"Hands down, Eric, he is the best in the state by far," Agent Woods said.

"Where is he from?" Eric asked.

"Memphis! This case is sixteen years old. We can't afford to blow it," Agent Woods said as he watched the cranes pull the cars from the lake one by one.

As the cars were lifted one by one out of the lake and onto the shore, the trunks were opened. Agent Woods wouldn't allow anyone to get close to the cars after the trunks were opened. The news reporters tried to get in on the action from behind the yellow tape that the FBI agents rolled out. The smell from the bodies couldn't be detected. All they could see was cars lined up side by side on the shore of the lake with the trunks open.

CHAPTER 18

A breaking-news bulletin flashed in the television screens all across the state of Tennessee and the surrounding states.

"We have breaking news out of Teller County, Tennessee. We are going live to Syeria Scott. She's located down in the Teller County area. Syeria, what's going on out there?"

"I'm not sure. I'm out here on the Teller County sheriff George Fuhrman's property. From what I can see, the FBI agents have surrounded Sheriff Fuhrman's property with yellow crime-scene tape. The FBI has twelve cars, with the trunks open, that they pulled out from Sheriff George Fuhrman's lake. Apparently, there is something big going on. The spokesman for the FBI announced that he will give a press conference shortly," Syeria Scott said.

"I'm hearing a loud noise in the background. What is it?"

"That's a helicopter landing. It looks like—in fact, it is Michael Shumpert, the top forensic specialist from Memphis, Tennessee. Like I said, Kim, something big is going on out here on Sheriff George Fuhrman's property. Hold on one second. Let's go over to where the FBI spokesman is about to give his press conference," Syreri Scott said.

"I am Special Agent James Woods of the Federal Bureau of Investigation. All I can tell you is, we have pulled twelve cars from Sheriff George Fuhrman's lake. Within the trunks of the twelve cars, there are human remains."

"Do you know who the remains belong to?" Syeria Scott asked.

"Right now, I can't release that type of information. We have brought in the forensic specialist Michael Shumpert just minutes ago. We will release more information as it unfolds," Agent Woods said as the lights flashed in his face.

"Can you tell us how long the cars have been in the lake?"

"From the looks of it, the remains and cars have been in there for a number of years."

"Do you know how the cars got there?" Syeria asked.

"That's a question I can't answer. That's all the information I can release at this time. Thank you."

"Kim, you got it firsthand. I will be here until I find out what's going on. As I get the story, I will fill you in. Back to you, Kim."

Sheriff George Fuhrman was on his way home from church when he saw the FBI agents, news reporters, and people all around his property. He turned his truck around and headed to his best friend's house. Once he made it to his friend's house, he jumped out the truck and repeatedly looked over his shoulder to make sure he wasn't being followed. He knocked once on the door and then checked to see if it was unlocked. When he turned the doorknob, the door opened, and he walked into the house.

"Frank!" George yelled out as he walked through the door.

"Yeah, I'm in the dayroom," Frank said.

George walked down the hallway to the dayroom. As he was walking in, he noticed the look on Frank's face.

"Fuck, George, I have been sitting her watching the news for over an hour. The fuckin' FBI are all over your property," Frank said.

"I know. I saw them on my way home from church. What did they say was going on?"

"They have pulled twelve cars out your fuckin' lake with bodies in the trunks of them," Frank said as he sat back on his loveseat and crossed his legs.

George placed his hand up to his mouth.

"Fuck, George, I saw that motherfuckin' Eric Henderson out there with them. Is he FBI now?" Frank asked as he looked at George.

"Hell no! That son of a bitch works for the Nashville Police Department," George said before it hit him. He remembered the day that Eric walked in on him and Mike McClain. Also, he was by the lake when they pulled one car into it. Now his mind was working overtime. He knew he had to come up with something fast. "Frank!"

"Yeah, bro!"

"I need you to call all the brothers and tell them to be at location two for a meeting tonight at eight o'clock."

Frank looked over at his friend and saw the stress all over his face.

"I will get on it right now. First of all, I need you to lay low. I am going to put your truck inside my garage," Frank said.

"That's good thinking, old man," George said.

"I told you about that old-man shit!" Frank said as he picked up his phone.

"Hello."

"May I speak with Jesse?" Frank said.

"Speaking."

"Jesse, this is Frank."

"What's up, bro?"

"I need you to round all the brothers up. We have an 8:00 p.m. meeting at location two."

"Got you, bro," Jesse said.

The two hung up the phone.

"Pass me your truck keys," Frank said once he got off the phone. "I am going to put your truck up and go into town. Just stay here."

"Okay," George said.

Later that night, all the Klan and Aryan brothers under George's leadership met up at location two out in the woods. Location two was a place they often used for their secret meetings. They used gas lamps for their lighting. Over seventy men stood around listening intensely to what George had to say.

"As you all know, the FBI has raided my housed. Things were found that could land a lot of us in prison. We have done quite a bit of shit out there on that land. The FBI has a witness who once was part of us. He must be silenced. For those of you who watched the propaganda box 'news,' you should have noticed that Eric Henderson was on the scene with the FBI. We need someone to pay him a little visit. As for the rest of you, I need you to keep your ears open. If you hear anything that could hurt the brotherhood, report it to Frank ASAP. Danny, I need you to go to the station, go downstairs, and get all the heavy weapons we have in there. If anyone asks you about me, tell them you haven't seen me. Jerry, by you being my chief of police, the news reporter will be asking you about me and my whereabouts. All you know is, I am on vacation and you have been trying to contact me. But you haven't been able to do so. Also, Jerry, I need you to look up Eric's information on the computer. Get his home address that's in Nashville. All the hard training we have been doing over the years, the time might be here for us to see what we know."

"Yeah . . . yeah!" the crowd of men said in unison loudly. George held his hand up in the air, and they calmed down. "I need three of you to go and pay Eric a visit. Do we have any volunteers?" George asked.

Eight men, five Aryans and three Klan members, raised their hands.

"Hey, bro, I really would like to be one of the three who go to pay him a visit," Rowland said as he walked up to George.

"Motherfucker, you fucked up the last time. Now look at the shit that it's caused us," George said.

"I hate that too, bro," Rowland said.

"Good. By not killing that son of a bitch when you had the chance, it's come back to haunt us. We have come too far to turn back now or to allow anyone to stop our progress. So you get your ass down there and make sure you get it done this time," George said angrily.

"Bro, if you don't mind, I would like to take a couple of the Aryan brothers with me?" Rowland asked.

"Why two Aryans?"

"I will feel a lot more comfortable with them with me."

"I can live with that. Get with Danny to get everything that you will need. Rowland, I am going to put you in charge of the two brothers you choose to take with you. You will be the one that I hold responsible. I need you and them to drive up to Nashville and stay there. You will receive a call. The call will provide you with Eric's address. Rowland, don't fail me."

"I won't, bro."

"Like I said, get with Danny for any weapons and money you all will need. Look here, Rowland, don't come back unless you have finished the job. Jerry, go on down to the station and get them Eric's information or anything you could come up with on that damn computer. I am going to end this meeting."

Rowland and the two men he chose stopped at the police station to get the things they needed from Danny. Within an hour after the meeting, Eric's cell phone rang just as he was getting off I-40 onto Nashville exit.

"Hello," Eric answered his phone.

"Eric, bro, I'm only going to say this once. Get out of your house. George has sent some men to kill you. They will be there within an hour."

"Who is this?" Eric asked.

The anonymous caller hung up. Eric couldn't recognize the voice, so he immediately called Agent Woods. "Agent Woods, this is Eric Henderson. I

just received an anonymous call informing me that George Fuhrman has
sent some men to kill me."

"Where are you now?" Agent Woods asked.

"I just got off I-40 in Nashville."

"Go straight to the local FBI substation. Do you know where it's
located?"

"Yes, sir, I do."

"I am about to get on a chopper now. I will meet you there."

As soon as Eric got off the phone with Agent Woods, he called his
wife and sister to tell them to get out the house. Then Eric drove to the
FBI substation and waited there until Agent Woods arrived. Agent Woods
briefed his men. They drove out to Eric's house and staked out all around
it and waited to see if Eric's anonymous call was for real. After almost
an hour, Rowland finally received the call he and his men had been
waiting for.

"May I help you?" Rowland asked.

"Get a pen, bro," the caller said.

"I got one," Rowland said as he pulled the black ink pen from under
his arm rest.

"It's 2207 Longstreet Drive," Rowland replied.

"Right, okay, bro," the caller said.

Rowland pulled into a local gas station to buy a map of the Nashville
area and a dollar of gas, which he put into a gas can. Rowland sat in the
car looking over the map, trying to figure out the best route to Eric's house.
His two accomplices filled glass bottles with gas. As they drove down Eric's
street, they didn't have to look hard. Eric's truck was placed in front of
his garage. As Rowland passed by Eric's house, he tapped on the brakes
slightly to slow down and make sure that it was Eric's truck.

"That's his truck," the man said from the backseat.

"I'm going to drive down the street and turn around."

"All agents, stand by. This might be our suspects," Agent Woods
said after he noticed the brake lights flash when the car passed by Eric's
house. The car went up to the end of the street and turned around. When
Rowland got back in front of Eric's house, he turned off his headlights
before he drove up on the sidewalk in the front of Eric's house. Rowland
pulled the car up close to the front door. The three men jumped out. The
man from the backseat of the car had a bottle of gas in hand with a rag
hanging from it, which he passed to the man from the passenger side who

lit it for him. He then reached back into the backseat and grabbed another one from off the floorboard of the car. He lit it and then pulled his .44 Magnum from his waistband. The two men walked down each side of the house. Rowland stood out front with a fully automatic SK assault rifle in hand.

"Special Agent Woods, the men are approaching midways the sides of the house. Should we take them down?"

"Yes, all agents, move in," Agent Woods said. All the agents staked out around Eric's property moved in.

"FBI! FBI!" the agents yelled as they rushed in on the men from all angles.

The man on the left side of the house threw his Molotov cocktail at the agents and tried to raise his .44 Magnum. Before he could get off a shot, the agents opened fire, cutting him down with multiple rounds of gunfire. He was dead before he hit the ground. The man on the right side of the house held his hands up in the air, with his weapon in one hand and the Molotov cocktail in the other one. He was unsure what to do.

"Slowly put your weapon on the ground."

The man bent down slowly and placed the weapon down on the ground.

"Now do the something with the bottle," the agent said.

Once the man put the bottle down, the agents had him lock his hands behind his head and back up. The man backed up. "Slowly! Get down on your knees." An agent walked up behind him and handcuffed him. The other agents blocked off the street to stop any chance of Rowland jumping back into his car or making a run for it.

Rowland turned to get back into his car but saw he had no place to go. The agents opened their car doors and placed their weapons between the opening of the doors and cars. Others got on the opposite side of the cars and waited for Rowland to make a false move.

"Drop your weapon now!" Agent Woods said loudly.

Rowland looked around and saw he didn't have a chance, so he complied. "Don't shoot!" Rowland said as he quickly threw his hands up, dropping the weapon. "Don't shoot! I give up," he said as he stood with his hands raised high in the air. The SK automatic assault rifle hung from his neck by the strap.

"Use your left hand to remove the strap from your shoulder and lay the weapons on the ground." Rowland slowly did as he was asked. After laying the weapon on the ground, he stepped back from it without being asked.

"Keep walking. Walk backward with your hands up," Agent Woods said. Agents moved in and rushed him to the ground. After he was handcuffed and placed in a separate car from his brother, the agents called for medical assistance.

"We need to get an ambulance out here. One of the suspects is down."

"He's dead," another agent said.

Agent Woods walked over to the first car with ID in hand as he opened the back passenger-side door. "David Webb, do you know your rights?"

"Yes, I know my rights," David said.

"Good for you. My name is Special Agent James Woods. I am going to be straightforward with you. We knew you all were coming. You could help yourself by telling me who sent you to kill Eric Henderson?"

"Fuck you, pig! Get the fuck out my face. I know my rights," David said.

"No, don't fuck me. You just fucked yourself." Agent Woods said as he slammed the car door and walked over to the car with Rowland in it. "I just tried to talk to your friend. He told me fuck me, called me a pig, and told me to get the fuck out his face. Like I told him, we knew you all were coming. I am going to give you one chance to help yourself. My name is Special Agent James Woods. You can exercise your rights and remain silent, or you too can be a hard ass and tell me to get the fuck out your face like your friend just did. First of all, I don't play games. I shot from the hip. If I tell you something, you can bank on it. Like I said, we knew you were coming. Under federal law, conspiracy to commit murder carries life. Not to mention conspiracy to kill a police officer. You won't ever see the streets again. Am I making myself clear to you?"

"If I open my mouth, I am a dead man," Rowland said softly.

"You don't have to worry about that. That's something we could help you with."

"Can you get me away from here?" Rowland asked.

"Sure, I can do that. Clear the road and get them out of here before the press comes."

Rowland and David were taken to the FBI substation to question Rowland.

"One of them is willing to talk. Let's see what he knows," Agent Woods told Eric.

David was escorted to a holding cell, and Rowland was taken to a room used for questioning suspects. Inside the room was a table with three chairs around it. In the wall sat a one-way window with overhead speakers in the ceiling. Eric, Agent Blocker, and other agents stood on the other side of the window, waiting for Rowland to be questioned by Agent Woods and Agent Garner. Rowland was seated in one chair with his hands cuffed in front of him.

"I need you to sign this waiver of your rights to have an attorney present at this time," Agent Garner said as he laid the paper down with an ink pen on top on the table and slid it over to Rowland. Rowland signed it and slid the paper back to the agent.

"I'm about to turn on this tape recorder. It is for your safety and ours," Agent Garner said before he pushed the button down.

"Hold up. Hold up one minute. You all haven't promised me anything or showed me shit in writing. Who in the hell do you think I am? I'm going to give you what you want. In return, you have to give me what I want," Rowland said.

"What are you looking for, Mr. Finch?" Agent Woods asked.

"Like I said, I could be killed for opening my mouth. If you could ensure me that I will walk free and have some protection, I will give you what you need," Rowland said.

"That really depends on what you can tell us."

"You can believe it I know a lot."

"A lot? Like what?" Agent Woods asked.

"Lynchings, murders, and the first attempt on Eric Henderson's life. The time he was shot and who ordered it. The list goes on."

"Get District Attorney Nicholas Rinzy on the phone and bring a speakerphone in here," Agent Woods said.

Agent Blocker went to grab the phone.

"If I let you hear it out of the head DA's mouth, will you be willing to talk?" Agent Woods asked.

"Yes, I will," Rowland said.

A knock at the door caused them to look over at it. Agent Woods stood up, walked over, and opened it. Agent Blocker passed him the phone he had asked for. He grabbed the phone and walked over to the table where he sat it down. He held the receiver in his hand, punching the button to turn the loudspeaker on, and sat the receiver down on the phone.

"Hello, is District Attorney Nicholas Rinzy?" Agent Woods asked as he looked over at Rowland.

"Yes, it is. How may I help you?"

"Mr. Rinzy, this is Special Agent James Woods of the FBI. I have a man in custody here who is willing to help us with numerous cases. Cases that range from lynchings, murders, and the ordered murder of a Nashville police officer. I believe that all this will tie in with the twelve missing women who were found earlier today in Teller County, Tennessee."

"What is he asking for?" asked the DA.

"Immunity and the witness protection program."

"If he gives us what we need to convict, I will agree to his demands," the DA said.

"I am going to put on loudspeaker if it's okay with you, sir."

"Sure, go ahead put him on."

"He's listening."

"Can you all hear me clearly?" the DA asked.

"Yes, we can."

"This is Nicholas Rinzy. I am the head district attorney for the Thirtieth District Federal Courts of the state of Tennessee. My name and word go a long way. I am willing to agree to your demands if the information you are willing to provide is true and helpful. I will be there tomorrow to sign your statement in front of you and put your demands in black and white. Do you have any questions?"

"No, I don't," Rowland said.

"Thank you, Mr. Rinzy, for your time," Agent Woods said.

"You're welcome."

"Okay, Mr. Finch, is that enough for you?"

"Yeah, that's good enough," Rowland replied.

"Agent Garner will be handwriting your statement, and we will also be recording it. Are you ready?"

"I guess."

Agent Garner pushed the recorder's button.

"My name is Special Agent James Woods of the FBI. My ID number is 89923. I am accompanied by—state your name and number."

"My name is Agent Bill Garner FBI ID #127025."

"We are recording the free and willing testimony and statement from Rowland Lee Finch, date of birth 7-29-68. Mr. Finch, will you please state your full name and date of birth?" Agent Woods asked.

"My name is Rowland Lee Finch, date of birth July 29, 1968."

"Mr. Finch, has anyone forced you to make this statement?"

"No, sir."

"Are you giving this statement freely and willingly?"

"Yes, I am."

"Mr. Finch, what do you have to tell us?"

"A little over two years ago, David Webb and I were ordered by George Fuhrman to go into the store where Eric Henderson worked and kill him, most of all to make it look like a robbery, not a hit."

"What role did you play in the shooting?"

"I'm the one who was shot and who shot Eric Henderson."

"Where were you shot?" Agent Woods asked.

"In my left hand and in my chest near my right shoulder. The next day or the same day, a nigger was picked up on the highway changing his flat tire and charged with attempted robbery and attempted murder of a police officer. Eric came out of the coma. So George drove over to Jackson County Hospital to see him and to let him know that we had one of the niggers who shot him in custody."

"Excuse me, we need you to clarify something. You said George? What is his full name?" Agent Garner asked.

"George Fuhrman."

"You may continue," Agent Garner said.

"Somehow Eric saw that it wasn't a nigger who came in to the store for him. Later that night, George had the nigger released from jail so we could pick him up and lynch him. That night we got him shortly after he walked out of the Teller County jail. We beat him half to death and hanged him from a tree on George's property. His body is buried with another nigger's body we killed a few months before him. I can show you the place where we buried them. George called a secret meeting tonight at eight. The meeting was to let us know that Eric is working with you all and to make sure someone shuts him up before a lot of us end up in prison. He also gave us the order to prepare for war. That's when he sent the three of us up here to finish the job as he put it."

"What do you know about those human remains found this morning?" Agent Woods asked.

"All I know about that is what's been in the news."

"Did you hear George Fuhrman say anything about it in one of his meetings?"

"No, if he did, I wasn't there to hear it personally. He did say that he had to get rid of Bo, Eric's father, to unite us."

"What do you mean *unite us?*"

"The Aryan brothers and the Klan together as one."

"What are you?"

"I'm Aryan Nations."

"Why did George Fuhrman order the killing of Eric Henderson two years ago?"

"He said that he was weak and needed to be out of the way. I have only known George for about ten years. That might be a long-enough time to get to know a person, but for George, it's not. He is a man of few words. He can smell the weakness in a person like a shark can detect blood in water from miles away. If he detects any weakness or you show any sign, you become his prey. The only reason he allowed me to get up on him is because of my uncle and my uncle's son Jimmy. He and my uncle were best friends. My uncle was killed by a nigger in the late seventies."

"What was your uncle's name?"

"Mike McClain."

"Did he ever talk to you about what happened to him."

"No, not really."

"Do you know what happened that night?"

"Only what I was told by friends and family members."

"What were you told about it?"

"George and my uncle pulled a car over. A nigger was lying back in the passenger seat. So they wanted to teach him a lesson about messing with our women. Somehow the nigger got the ups on them and killed my uncle and shot George in the shoulder. The stupid-ass nigger called for help. The FBI showed up before they could kill him."

There was a knock on the door. Agent Woods walked over and opened it. Agent Blocker leaned over close to Agent Woods and whispered in his ear.

"Have him lift up his shirt to see if he has a tattoo on his stomach that says *white power* with a swastika underneath it."

Agent Woods closed the door and walked over to Rowland. "Stand up!"

Rowland, slow to his feet, stood up. Standing in front of him, Agent Woods raised up his shirt.

"What's this about?" Rowland asked.

"We need to see your stomach," Agent Woods said. Agent Woods turned toward the window and nodded.

"That's him!" Eric said to Agent Blocker on the other side of the one-way window.

"Mr. Finch, you can sit down. I did mention to you earlier that part of this agreement is you might have to get on the stand and testify against George Fuhrman," Agent Woods said.

"I know that much. Can I have a cigarette and something to drink?" Rowland asked.

"You sure can. Someone get him something to drink," Agent Woods said as he reached into his top-left shirt pocket with his right hand and passed Rowland a cigarette. Rowland put the cigarette into his mouth and waited for Agent Woods to light it.

"We will need all the main people who played a part in the lynching later." Rowland nodded as a sign of agreement.

"Would you like to read over your statement before you sign it, Mr. Finch?" Agent Garner asked.

"Yes, I would. May I have another cigarette?" Rowland asked as Agent Garner pushed the statement across the table.

"You sure can, young man," Agent Woods said before he reached back into his shirt pocket to grab the pack of cigarette.

"Mr. Finch, is there anything else that we need to know?" Agent Woods asked as he lit his cigarette.

"Nothing that I could think of right now."

"Do you have any questions?" Agent Woods asked.

"Yeah, how long will it be before I can get out?"

"We first have to bring George Fuhrman in, and then it will be up to the court system to prosecute him. That really depends. I have seen cases take as long as two years or more. We are going to place you in a holding cell until the US marshals come and transport you to Mason, Tennessee."

"What's in Mason, Tennessee?" Rowland asked.

"That's where you will be held until we get this matter cleared up. I will be down there to see you soon."

"How soon?"

"Within the next few days. We will need you to show us the location of those bodies you told us about."

"Okay."

"Agent Garner, I need you to fax a copy of Mr. Finch's statement to the Attorney General and District Attorney Nicholas Rinzy. Also, get me a warrant for George Fuhrman's arrest," Agent Woods said.

"Yes, sir, I will get right on top of that."

CHAPTER 19

"Also, in today's news, the FBI has been swarming the Teller County area looking for the Teller County sheriff George Fuhrman. He hasn't been seen since yesterday morning. Yesterday afternoon the FBI pulled twelve cars with human remains in the trunks from the lake on his property. We are going to go live to Syeria Scott to see if we can find out any more information to share with you all. Syeria, have you found out anything on Sheriff Fuhrman's whereabouts?"

"No, I haven't. I have been out front of the Teller County Sheriff's Department for over an hour. Finally I got a chance to talk to Sheriff Jerry Gram not even three minutes ago. He wouldn't speak on camera, but he did say that the sheriff is on vacation and he can't speak on anything that he has no knowledge of. The word in town is that the bodies found are of the missing women from the late 1970s. Until yesterday, neither the bodies nor the cars had been found. Once the forensic test results return, the FBI will release more information to the public. For right now, we have got to play the waiting game. This is Syeria Scott reporting to you live from the Teller County Sheriff's Department."

"Thank you, Syeria! We will have more for you as this story—"

Chief Jerry Gram jumped into his county-issued squad car and drove the long way around to make sure that he wasn't being followed. He drove up the road that led to the compound where George was hiding. George watched him out of the upstairs window with an AK-47 automatic rifle in his hands. He pulled a walkie-talkie from his back pocket to let his ten-men team know that it's Jerry.

"It's only Jerry," George said into the walkie-talkie as he held it up to his mouth.

"Copy that," one man said.

Jerry drove down the road in a high rate of speed, sending a cloud of dust and rocks into the air behind the automobile. Once he made it to the house, he jumped out the squad car while the motor was still running and walked toward the front door. He turned around to make sure no one was behind him before he walked up the steps onto the front porch. George opened the door and started to walk out.

"Don't walk out here," Jerry said.

George backed up as Jerry walked into the house, slightly looking back over his shoulder.

"George, bro, you're not going to believe this shit!"

"What is it?" George asked.

"A reliable brother from Nashville called me and said that the FBI got Rowland and David. Tony is dead. He was killed by the FBI last night outside of Eric's house."

"Fuck! How in the hell did the FBI find out that they were going to pay that son of a bitch a visit?" George asked as he put his hands up to his head and walked toward the window.

"The hell if I know!"

"Someone from the meeting last night called them. From now on, Jerry, now one knows about my whereabouts but you, Frank, and the ten brothers here with me. We have a rat among us. So, Jerry, be careful about what you say and who you say something to. What's the latest talk around town?"

"Nothing that you don't already know. The FBI is everywhere you look. The reporters are doing what they do best—asking a lot of questions. The FBI is just riding around. They haven't said anything yet. Knowing them, they might have the phones tapped. I couldn't take the chance. That's why I drove out here. If I were you, I wouldn't make any calls to the station even with the cell phone of one of the other brothers. If anything comes up, I will be back out here personally. If you need me for anything, just send word by one of the brothers. I will see you later, bro. I need to get back to the station. I'm looking for the FBI to show up any minute now. I want to be there when they do. If something doesn't look right, that's the only way I will call. Do you need anything?" Jerry asked.

"No . . . not right now," George said.

"I will see you later, bro."

"Okay."

Jerry left out the door and jumped back into his squad car and took off back down the road he came in on. George pulled the walkie-talkie out his back pocket and called the ten men together for a meeting. All of them assembled together in the house.

"Listen up! Someone has informed the FBI that Rowland and the other brother he took with him were on their way to Nashville last night. The FBI has Rowland and David in custody. Tony is dead. I know it wasn't one of us. From this point on, no one is to know where we are. Brothers or not, it doesn't make any difference."

George's cell phone rang. It startled him. He didn't know if he should answer it or not. He took a deep breath and answered it.

"Hello!" George said, expecting the worst.

"Bro, the FBI are on your property digging up the bodies."

"What bodies?" George asked, trying to recognize the voice.

"The bodies of the two nigger out there."

"I don't know what the hell you're talking about," George said and hung up the cell phone.

"What's up, bro?" one man asked after seeing George's face turn beet red.

The other men just stood in silence.

"Motherfuckers. The fucking FBI is on my property digging up the bodies of the niggers we buried out there. Whoever is telling is telling every damn thing."

George looked around the room into every one of the men's faces.

"It can't be Eric because he didn't know anything about the niggers being out there. Whoever it is, is trying to get all of us locked up. I am ready to go to war and die before I go to prison for the rest of my life. What about you all?"

"War, brother," they said in unison.

"That's what I want to hear. But it did sound like everyone is in agreement. If you are not ready for war, raise your hand."

No one raised their hand.

"Good for you, because if any one of you would have attempted to raise your hand, I would have killed you. I have a plan. We have brothers in Cañon City, Colorado, and in Montana. They own a lot of land up in the mountains. We will have a better chance up there with them. When night falls, we are going to take our chances on going into town to get all the things we need. I need to get to a phone so I can make some calls. I can't take any chances on making a call from my cell phone. As a matter of fact!" George said as he slammed his cell phone into the floor, bursting it open. The impact sent pieces flying in every direction.

"My face can't be seen in or out of town. The main focus is on me. Joe, I need you to be the driver. Four of us can ride in your truck and not be seen behind your tinted windows. Dennis, I need you to go by Barry's house. Tell him I need him to go out to my house in his light, gas, and water truck tomorrow morning about eight thirty. Most likely, the FBI will have someone posted out front. If they say anything to him, tell him to say the same thing he told me Friday about the temporary gas cap that he put on my gas line. The FBI will see the freshly dug gas line trench that's running to my house. Listen up good, Dennis. Tell him to go in my house, go straight to my bedroom's closet, and remove the carpet from the closet floor. He will need to take a flathead screwdriver with him so he can pop the plywood up from the closet floor. I have $3 million under there. Get it. Tell him to keep fifty for himself and leave the rest of it in the bed of the truck. Park the truck behind the light, gas, and water department. Can you remember all of that?"

"Sure, bro," Dennis said.

Meanwhile, in town, twenty FBI agents stormed the Teller County Sheriff's Department.

"Hey . . . hey . . . hey . . . may I help you all?" the officer sitting at the front desk said.

"Who are you?" Agent Woods asked.

"I'm Sergeant Oaks," The man said.

"I need to talk to whoever is in charge."

The sergeant picked up the phone.

"Chief Gram, the FBI is here at the front desk, and they would like to speak to you."

Within seconds, Chief Gram walked out from the back.

"I am Chief Jerry Gram. May I help you?"

"Chief Gram, my name is Special Agent James Woods of the Federal Bureau of Investigation. I have a warrant for Sheriff George Fuhrman and to search this department."

"May I see the warrant?" Chief Gram asked.

Agent Woods passed him the warrant that he held in his hand. Chief Gram read the warrant while all the Teller County Sheriff deputies stood there facing off and ready to try to stop the FBI from entering any farther than the front lobby.

"Advise your officers to move back," Agent Woods said calmly.

"Stand down, gentlemen, and move back," Chief Gram said.

The men stood there for a moment. Then one by one, they started moving out of the way.

"What in the hell is this about?" Chief Gram asked.

"You read the warrant. Your sheriff is wanted for questioning," Agent Woods said.

"Questioning for what if I may ask?"

"For the twelve bodies pulled from his lake yesterday and the two bodies found today on his property."

The chief didn't say anything, just looked.

"Chief Gram, do you remember having a black man here in this jail a little over two years ago by the name of Marvin Turner?" Agent Woods asked.

"I can't recall," Chief Gram said as he stood with his arms crossed, watching the FBI's every movement.

"Maybe I could refresh your memory. He was the man brought in and held for the shooting of Officer Eric Henderson."

"Am I under arrest?" Chief Gram asked.

"Did I say you were?" Agent Woods replied.

"You are questioning me like I am."

"You don't have to worry about being arrested right now anyway. Agent Garner, make sure you check their computer and arrest files to see if they have Marvin Turner in there somewhere."

"Yes, sir."

"Mr. Turner's family reported him missing two days after Eric Henderson was shot. Agent Blocker, I need you to go through the phone records. I don't think it would be necessary. Most likely, they didn't allow him to make a call."

"I found something, sir," Agent Garner said.

"What do you have?"

"The computer shows that Mr. Turner was held in here from April 19, 1992, to April 26, 1992. He was released according to this at 7:56 p.m." Agent Garner said as he pointed at the computer monitor.

Agent Garner looked up from the computer at Chief Gram and said to Agent Woods, "He knows something."

"Hell, the whole damn town pretty much knows what's going on around here."

"I can believe that," Agent Garner said.

"Let's make sure we go through this shithole with a fine-tooth comb. Everyone spread out and see what you can come up with."

"Breaking news from Teller County Sheriff's Department. Let's go live to Syeria Scott. Syeria, what's going on?"

"I'm not sure. About fifteen minutes ago, the FBI stormed the sheriff's department. From what I can see, all the Teller County Sheriff's deputies are standing outside the building. As we know, earlier the FBI found two more bodies buried on Sheriff George Fuhrman's property. Nothing has been said, and we still are in the dark on the other bodies found yesterday. I will deliver the news as I get it. This is Syeria Scott reporting to you live from in front of the Teller County Sheriff's Department."

The FBI agents ransacked the sheriff's department, looking for anything to help build their case against George Fuhrman.

CHAPTER 20

"You have been gone a long time," George said.

"I have been sitting at Barry's house waiting on him to get back from Jackson."

"Did you talk to him?" George asked the tall long-haired man with a skin disorder.

"Sure, after waiting over three hours. He said he did just like you suggested. The FBI wouldn't buy the story. So he went back after those two agents changed shift. They still wouldn't let him in there."

"Fuck!" George said and turned around and kicked the table over.

The men sitting around with weapons in their hands jumped. Rage filled up in George as he paced the floor, stopping by the front window that overlooked the front of the property. After standing there a few seconds, he reached into his top-right shirt pocket and pulled out a cigarette pack. He shook the pack until one came forward. He then lifted the pack up to his mouth and put the filter of the cigarette into his mouth, pulling it the rest of the way out. He then placed the pack back into his pocket. He stood there and took a big drag off the cigarette while it was between his fingers as silence filled the room.

"Motherfuckers!" George said as he stood in the window with the cigarette between his fingers as he ran them through his blondish-gray hair. After a few minutes in the window, he turned around and looked at Joe, an overweight man in his midforties.

"Hell, Joe, help me out here. Fix me a shot of that fucking whiskey. Fuck it, just pass me the whole bottle," George said, walking over to snatch the bottle out of Joe's hand. After he snatched the bottle, he walked upstairs using all kinds of vulgar language. He walked into the room he slept in and sat on the bed. The days passed without George saying or eating anything. While he sat in a chair with a new bottle of whiskey beside him and watched TV, a breaking news from Teller County, Tennessee, captured his attention.

"The FBI is about to give a press conference," Syeria Scott said.

"I am Special Agent James Woods of the FBI. The forensic test has determined that the remains found last week on the property of George Fuhrman are, in fact, that of the twelve women who have been missing since 1978 and 1979."

"What are the names of those women?" Syeria asked as lights flashed and microphones moved closer toward Agent Woods's face.

"As soon as the families are notified, that information will be released."

"Are there any ideas on the cause of death?"

"No . . . not at this time."

"What about the two other bodies found on the property the next day?" Syeria asked.

"We are still waiting on the forensic tests to be returned on them. Once that information is available, it will also be released."

"Do you think that Sheriff Fuhrman had knowledge of those bodies being there on his property?"

"At this time, we can't say. No one has been ruled out. I can say this: we need to talk to sheriff. George Fuhrman, if you are watching, will you please give us a call? We need to talk with you. If anyone sees Sheriff George Fuhrman, please call 1-800-34Crime. Your name will remain anonymous."

Lights flashed from the news reporters' cameras as Agent Woods stepped down off the stand set up for the press conference.

"Now at least the families of the victims could finally get some kind of relief after so many years of wondering, grieving and worrying about the whereabouts of their loved ones. This is, Syeria Scott reporting to you live on News Channel 6 in Teller County."

"That's fucking bullshit!" George said as he grabbed his AK-47 from off the floor next to the chair he was sitting in and headed out the bedroom back down the stairs.

"Joe, Danny, Chris, I need you all to help. Be my eyes. I am going to get my damn money so we can get the fuck out this town. Chris, you and I will have to put in the work on those fucking FBI agents in the front of my house. This is the plan! I need you three to listen up closely. We can't afford to fuck this up. Joe, I need you to be the driver. Drive up the road that leads to my house. If you see more than one car, keep going. We will catch them another day. If there's only one car with two or three agents in it, we can take them with ease. Whatever angle their car is parked, I need you to get on your left-hand side. If you have to back up beside their car, do it. Have your window already rolled down before you pull up on them. When you lock eyes with the driver, speak. If you have to, blow smoke up his ass just to get him to relax. Once you get him talking, ask him these key questions. Hell, Joe, remember these words now. The keywords are, have you heard anything from the sheriff yet? Let me hear you say that, Joe," George asked.

"Have you heard anything from the sheriff yet?" Joe replied.

"Good. Don't forget that. I will take it from there."

"What do you need me to do?" Danny asked with the look of a child on his face.

"Just watch my back. Any car pull up while I am in the house, make sure it doesn't move. Kill everything in it," George said as he tossed him a bulletproof vest. "Put it on," he said and put on his hunting gear.

George handed the other two bulletproof vests and grabbed his AK-47. The four walked out of the house to Joe's dark-green Ford King Cab truck. George and Chris hopped into the cab of the truck and lay facedown with their weapons on their sides. Joe and Danny covered them with a tarp and got inside the truck. Before Joe pulled off, he pulled out his walkie-talkie from his back pocket.

"Brothers, we are leaving out for a minute. We will be back shortly."

"Copy that," someone responded over the walkie-talkie.

Joe pulled off and made a left turn on to the rocky road heading toward George's house. As he got close to George's house, he noticed the FBI agent's car parked in front of the house.

"Fuck! The son of bitch has pulled their car up in the yard."

"I know what to do!" Joe said out loud like he was talking to Danny, but the words were meant for himself.

He passed by George's driveway and stopped the truck in the middle of the road. Then he backed up into the driveway. Two FBI agents were parked on the right side of the driveway in the grass. Joe backed his truck up to the driver's side of their unmarked car. The passenger watched the green truck from over his left shoulder as it backed up.

"We have some visitors. They are backing up."

"I see them," the other agent said from the driver's seat of the car.

The two agents reached for their weapons simultaneously. After pulling them from their holsters, they lowered them as the truck backed up. Joe backed until he and the agent in the driver's seat locked eyes. From the height of the truck, Joe saw into the agent's car. Immediately he detected that the agent on the passenger side had his weapon drawn but down between his leg and the car door. Since the driver was left-handed, he wasn't able to see his weapon down by the driver's side door.

"Good evening. How are you gentlemen doing?" Joe asked. "We've seen all the gruesome findings from out here on the news. That was some crazy stuff, I would say. What about you, gentlemen?" Joe asked.

"Yes, it was," the driver said responding to Joe's comment.

"Have you heard anything from the sheriff?"

The driver looked over at the passenger. Before he could turn back around and say anything, George had already jumped up and thrown the tarp off his head with his left arm as he took aim with his AK-47 in his right hand. The first round he released caught the driver in the face. He was dead before the words he was about to say formed in his mind. The force of the bullet pinned his head to the headrest, and his brain scattered across the backseat. When George saw his blood and brains fly through the air, he worked his way across the windshield into the other agent's chest on the passenger side. Seeing that he had subdued his targets, he jumped from the cab of the truck onto the hood of their car and released more rounds through the windshield into their corpses. Then he turned around and looked over Chris's head as he stood in the back of the truck with an AK in his hands.

"If anyone drives up, kill them," George said before he hopped down from the hood of the car onto the ground.

"I got you," Chris said.

"I will be right back."

He rushed into his house and went straight to his bedroom closet. With the strap to hold the AK on his shoulder, he grabbed the large duffel bag from the top shelf of the closet, took the pry-bar out, and pulled back the carpet. He stuck the pry bar between the closet wall and the floor to open the secret compartment. After he opened it, he threw the plywood floor out of his way and filled the duffel bag with all $100 stacks. After he finished stuffing the money into the bag, he looked over his house to get some of the other small things he wanted and needed. As he walked out the door and down the steps, he looked around. Then he sat the duffel bag of money down on the ground. He walked in a fast pace over to his garage. He came out with a gas can and doused gas onto his house. When he was finished, he took a handkerchief from his back pocket and soaked it down with gas. Then he stuffed it inside the gas can and lit it and tossed it into his front door. He picked up the duffel bag and walked to meet Joe as he backed up the truck. He sat the bag in the cab of the truck.

"What are we going to do about them?" Joe asked as he shifted his head toward the dead FBI agents.

"What do you mean?" George asked as he jumped into the cab of the truck.

"Do you want us to burn them?" Joe asked.

"No! That's a message for the rest of them sons of bitches," George said before he pulled the tarp over him and Chris as they lay down in the bed of the truck. Joe pulled off as the smoke from the house rose high into the sky. The heavy cloud of smoke in the air could be seen in town.

"Agent Woods, there's a large cloud of smoke in the air, and it's coming from the direction of George Fuhrman's property," an agent said as he looked up in the air.

"Get on your radio and ask Norvell and Hooker if they can see where it's coming from," Agent Woods asked. The agent radioed for the two agents but got no response back.

"Sir, there is no response."

"What are you saying, Montas?"

"They are not answering their radio, sir." Montas said.

"Get someone out there ASAP to see what's going on," Agent Woods said.

"Yes, sir."

Within minutes agents were at George Fuhrman's property. "Agent Garner to Special Agent Woods, come in."

"This is Special Agent Woods. Go ahead," he said as he held his radio up toward his mouth.

"You are not going to believe this, sir," Agent Garner said with a crushing tear-filled voice.

Agent Woods knew something was wrong from the sound of Agent Garner's voice.

"What is it?" Agent Woods asked as he prepared himself for the bad news.

"Agent Norvell and Hooker are DOA, sir. From the looks of it, they were ambushed."

Agent Woods dropped his head. "Is that where the smoke is coming from?"

"Yes, sir. Whoever had done it torched the house."

"I am on my way. Don't let anyone touch anything."

George called all his men inside. He knew the message he sent would force the FBI's hand.

"The reason I called you all in is because the first thing they will do is fly overhead looking for anything out of the norm," said George. He had played out the scenario in his mind for two days before he acted on it. When Agent Woods arrived on the scene, it brought tears to his eyes after seeing the two agents' badly disfigured bodies. "Fuck! Get choppers and more agents out here. We will find this motherfucker. He has declared war, and we will give him what he's looking for. Close off every exit. I want to know what goes out and what comes in," Agent Woods said.

"Grab all the ammunition you can. I'm going to give everyone $100,000. When we get where we are going, you can do whatever you choose with it. Just remember, we don't know whose name will come out in the indictments or what they have told the FBI," George said as he reached inside the duffel bag and pulled out $25,000 stacks wrapped with rubber bands around them. One by one, he gave his ten men four stacks each. Most had never seen that much money in their lives. To have it in their hands brought a smile to their faces. But George didn't think it was nothing to smile about. The only reason he gave his money away was because he knew carrying $3 million and his weapons on a foot pursuit would be hard for him. Also, it would give them a reason to die for his cause. His mind was set on getting away; he could always take the money back.

"Sir, the choppers are ready," an agent said. Agent Woods, Agent Blocker, and Agent Garner boarded one chopper.

"I know he is somewhere around here hiding out. I want us to make a sweep over the whole town," Agent Woods said to the pilot.

"Yes, sir. I copy that," the pilot said. Agent Woods sat up front with the pilot. Agent Blocker and Agent Garner sat in the back. The men looked out the windows with headphones on to communicate.

"Agent Woods to Agent Chism, come in."

"This is Agent Chism. Go ahead."

"Have you done a sweep over the southeast of this town?"

"Yes, sir, I did."

"Did you see anything that we should check out?"

"No, sir. I think it would be best to do a ground sweep. I think we would have a better chance of finding him," Agent Chism said.

"Why do you suggest that?"

"This town has a lot of farms. That alone makes it hard to determine anything. Right now it's easy for him to hide. We have agents set up at every exit. We need to close in on him before he finds a way out."

"I agree. We shouldn't talk about it too much over the air. He might be listening," Agent Woods said.

"Too late, motherfuckers. George, the mother fuckers have closed off all the ways out," Carl said over the walkie-talkie.

"They most likely will be checking the back of trunks and everything else," Joe said.

"If you don't mind, George, I have a suggestion," Lil Jimmy said.

"Aw, hell, the boy is starting to think," Joe said as a joke, but no one laughed.

"Go ahead, Jimmy. We are going to listen to what he has to say," George said with a half of a smile on his face.

"George liked Lil Jimmy a lot. He reminded George of his best friend Mike McClain, Lil Jimmy's father.

"I think it would be best for us to wait until dark falls and travel through the fields on foot to one of the nearby towns. When we get there, we could have some brothers waiting for us," Lil Jimmy said as he stood there surrounded by men twice his age.

"Jimmy, that sounds good, but that's a lot of fucking walking," George said.

Lil Jimmy held hatred in his heart for blacks because of what happened to his father. George always took time out with him and his other siblings. Lil Jimmy had always been George's favorite since he was a baby. George always told him when they were alone together. "I am going to let you kill a nigger when you get bigger." On April 26, 1992, George honored his words. After Eric Henderson said it wasn't a black man who shot him, George planned for the black man he held in jail.

Lil Jimmy was walking home from high school when George pulled up beside him and two of his friends. "Jimmy!" George called his name as he was walking and joking with his friend.

"What's up, George?" Lil Jimmy asked as he walked over to the truck.

"I need to talk to you," George said.

"I will see you all later," Lil Jimmy told his friends before he got into George's truck.

"Do you still want to do it?" George asked as he pulled off.

Lil Jimmy looked a little puzzled and didn't understand what George was talking about.

"You got me. I don't know what you are talking about."

"Do you still want to kill you a nigger?"

"Sure," Lil Jimmy said, not knowing that the time had come.

"Be ready tonight at seven thirty. I'm going to pick you up."

"George!" Lil Jimmy called his name, bringing himself out of his deep thought of the past. "That's the only way I could see us making it out of this town other than shooting our way out," Lil Jimmy said.

"That's what we need to do, just kill all of them motherfuckers," George said as he looked over at Lil Jimmy.

The other men thought it was a joke and laughed, not knowing that George was dead serious. George got up out of the chair and grabbed his duffel bag off the floor. As he walked past Lil Jimmy, he placed his hand on his shoulder. "I'm going to think about your suggestion, Jimmy. I will be upstairs if anyone needs me."

He walked up the stairs and went into the bedroom, thinking back to the night he saw the killer instinct in Jimmy. He took a seat in the chair and drifted off into his thoughts of when he pulled up into his driveway with Lil Jimmy in the truck.

"When you get out, Jimmy, grab that ax handle out the back of the truck." Jimmy grabbed the ax handle, and the two walked down by the lake where the others were waiting for George to get back. As they walked up, Lil Jimmy saw the black man lying on the ground with his hands tied behind his back and ankles tied together.

"What the fuck have you all done to him?" George asked, seeing the blood on the side of the man's mouth.

"We didn't do anything to them, bro," Rowland said.

"Don't lie to me. You did something to him. His fucking mouth is busted. Jimmy, the nigger is all yours."

Lil Jimmy wasted no time. He moved in quickly as he drew back the ax handle and delivered the first blow to the top of the man's head. As he drew back for the second one, blood shot everywhere. The second blow splashed blood all over Lil Jimmy. Lil Jimmy wiped the blood from his face with his left forearm and drove the ax handle deeper into the man's skull. The third blow cut the man's last crying prayer short as he lay there unconscious. That's when George saw the killer instinct in Lil Jimmy. Lil Jimmy drew back again only to be stopped by George. The way Jimmy looked back sent chills through George's whole body.

"It's me, Jimmy," George said as he held the ax handle.

"The nigger isn't dead yet," Lil Jimmy said.

"I know. I can't let you kill him. I want you to see him hanged. You will like it," George said with a smile.

All the men standing around just looked at Lil Jimmy.

"Rowland, do you have the rope ready?" George asked.

"Sure, bro, it's in the tree waiting on him."

"Someone get a bucket of water from the lake and wake this nigger up."

"Little cousin, I see you got it in you too," Rowland said to his younger cousin Lil Jimmy as he placed his arm around his neck.

"Pick the nigger up!" George said after they tossed the water on the man and woke him up.

"Please . . . please . . . oh god, please don't kill me," the man cried out.

"Put the rope around his fucking neck, so he can shut the fuck up," George said.

"No . . . no . . . ple—"

George looked over at Lil Jimmy only to witness the smile he had across his face. The man's eyes turned blood shot red, and his legs shook as he choked to death.

Chapter 21

"Verlena, Mustafa is riding in the car with me to visit Dad. I am sure he doesn't want to be in the car with all you females anyway," Adam said.

"I'm going to ride with you too," Verlena said.

"No, you're not. We have some manly stuff to talk about, and we don't want you all up in our conversation, ain't that right, nephew?"

Mustafa nodded with a smile on his face.

"I don't want to ride in your raggedy mobile anyway. As for you, Mustafa, I'm not going to let your lil stanky tail sit next to me on the way back."

"Yes, she is, nephew. She doesn't have a choice. Where else are you going to sit?" Adam said.

"Okay, don't let your uncle trick you into turning against me," Verlena said as she walked off.

"Ladies, Mustafa and I are about to go. We will see you slowpokes when you all get to Nashville, Inshallah. Mom, are you driving first?" Adam asked.

"No, your aunt is going to drive up there. I'm going to drive back," Shanda said.

"It's going to take you all forever to make it up there," Adam said, marking Tiltyla's slow driving.

"Whatever, boy. You can wait for us. Your wife is the one slow poking around," Tiltyla said.

"I have to get dressed. Adam knows he could have helped me get the baby dressed or pack her pamper bag for me," Gloria said.

"I asked you if you needed help. You said you had it," Adam said.

"You still could have helped. That's okay. Now I'm ready." Gloria said as she picked the baby up off the bed.

Tiltyla, Shanda, Verlena, Gloria and Sukita loaded up in Tiltyla's car.

Adam and Mustafa got into his car. Adam backed out the driveway and headed for I-40. Tiltyla kept Adam within her eyesight as the two cars drove down the highway to the Tennessee Department of Corrections in Nashville. Once in the facility visitation room, they waited for Samson to be escorted in.

"Are you okay, Mom?" Adam asked.

"I'm okay. I just hate being locked in this place," Shanda said.

"Papa!" Mustafa said as he jumped up and ran to meet his grandfather Samson. Samson picked him up, hugged, and kissed him on the jaw.

"As-salamu alaykum, Mustafa," Samson said.

"Wa alaykumu s-salam, Papa. I missed you."

"I missed you too, big man. You must be glad to see me?"

"Yes, sir," Mustafa said with a smile.

"Boy, you are getting big fast. I got to put you down. You're heavy. As-salamu alaykum," Samson said as he approached the table where the family was waiting.

"Wa alaykumu s-salam," the family said in unison.

Verlena got up and hugged him first. Then the others followed behind her.

"All praise are due to Allah, you all made it safely. As-salamu alaykum, Gloria," Samson said with a smile on his face.

"Wa alaykumu s-salam," Gloria said, wondering why Samson greeted her twice.

"I see that you fear Allah," Samson said.

"I do. What made you say that?" Gloria asked with a puzzled look on her face.

"You are being obedient to Allah and His Prophet by wearing your hijab [head covering] out in the public and covering up like a female should. Unlike my wife, daughter, and sister," Samson said as he looked around the table at them.

"Please don't start, Samson!" Tiltyla said as she twisted her mouth and turned her head to the side.

"I am just giving Gloria a compliment and telling you what Allah and His Prophet say. She has only been Muslim for a couple years, and she's showing fear of Allah, Alhamdulillah [all praise to God]."

Gloria looked over at Adam and smiled. Adam smiled back.

"Shanda, we have had this conversation many times, haven't we?"

"Samson, baby, we didn't come up here for this."

"You didn't answer my question."

"Yes, we have had this conversation before."

"I understand that you all didn't drive up here for this conversation. But it is my duty as a Muslim to convey Allah's message. Like it's your duty as well if I see a Muslim or believer doing something that's sinful or disliked, and it could lead him or her to sinning, and I turn my head like I didn't see it. Do you know what will happen to me or anyone who says they believe in Allah on the last day?" No one said anything. They just nodded and looked at Samson.

"We will have a share of the punishment with them. We as Muslims are supposed to forbid what is wrong and do what is right. Also, we should love with Allah's love and hate what He hates. That's being obedient to Him and His Prophets. No one ever wants to hear the truth. It's not what I say. It's what Allah and His Prophet say in the Qur'an. In surah 24, ayah [verse] 31, surah 33 ayahs 53–59, they tell us why Allah wants us to lower our gazes and guard our modesty. Also, that surah says in English, 'O, Prophet tell your wives and daughters and the believing women that they should cast their outer garments over their persons [when out abroad]. That is most convenient, that they should be known [as such] and not molested. Allah is oft-forgiving Most Merciful.'

"Think about it. When a woman passes by a man, what do most men look at or look for? Don't act like you all can't talk. You know they look at the women's shape or breast or try to see if she has a nice butt. If he's a sick man and likes the way she looks, he may try to rape her. When the opportunity isn't there to lust off, he has no choice but to challenge the females' mind. Allah knows best. I am going to say this and leave it alone. The rule of modesty applies to men as well as women. A brazen stare by a man at a women [a child or even at another man] is a breach of refined manners. Women looking at women goes with it too. So we must safeguard our children as well as ourselves from sexual predators. Covering up, not wearing tight revealing clothing, and teaching them to guard their modesty from a young age will help prevent a lot of the rapes and molestations. With that said, I have done what was required for me as a Muslim. Now it's on you all. You can accept the truth or reject it." Silence filled the table, and everyone just looked around at one another.

"Dad, this has been a good but hectic week. Have you been watching the news?" Adam asked to break the silence.

"Yes, I have," Samson said.

"I found out why the FBI told you that you were in the wrong place at the right time."

"Why did they say that, son?"

"If you weren't in the car with Mom, she would have been the thirteenth victim," Adam said as he looked over at his mother.

"Son, now you see for yourself that everything happens for a reason. It took the death of that officer to stop the madness. There's no telling how long the killings would have gone on. I know it wasn't any coincidence that the FBI told me that I was in the wrong place at the right time. Allah [God] is the best of planners. I was a tool that He used to bring that mess to an end. I am thankful to have a son like you. Satan had planted the seed of deception in their heads. They really thought by putting them bodies in that lake, no one would ever find them. As long as they were living anyway. Satan planted that seed, but Allah [God] is the greatest planner. He put it in our hearts to uncover Satan's seed, and that's what you have done. Thank you, son, for being open for Allah to use you."

"You're welcome! Dad, everything is slowly coming to the light. You will be home soon, Inshallah [if it's God's will]. I am going to call Agent Woods when I leave here to see what steps are going to be needed to get you out of here," Adam said.

"Inshallah, son, I will be out soon. Right now, son, they are trying to find George Fuhrman. I don't think he's going to go easy. He has killed two FBI agents, and he will kill more. May Allah forbid he does, but I don't see him going down without a fight."

"I can believe that," Adam said.

"Believe it because he won't be taken alive."

"They should have enough to help you now. So it shouldn't matter if they catch him or not."

"Just have patience, son, and let it stay in Allah's hand. He hasn't guided us this far for nothing. You have been dedicated to getting me out. Now the seed of deception has been uncovered, relax and look at the big picture. You're not just helping me. You have helped fourteen other victim's families—families who have been going through hell for the last fifteen years thinking about their loved ones. The feeling of not knowing where your loved ones are hurts. I went through that feeling for years, wondering about all of you. Justice might be blind, but Allah isn't. I have been in the belly of the beast for over fifteen years. I have watched you for the last past six years grow into a man. Through you, son, I will live on, Inshallah."

"Dad, I'm never going to give up faith. Everything that I have ever prayed for, Allah has given me. So if I have to pray a little harder to get you home a little sooner, that's what I will do."

Samson laughed and sat up in his seat. "Prayer is good. Get your prayer on, son."

"I have been watching a report out of Teller County on Channel 6 News. Her name is Syeria Scott. She's the one who's been covering the story on George Fuhrman. I was thinking I should give her a call and let her know how the can of worms got opened. Inshallah, that will get the ball rolling and push everything out into the light. I know for a fact that it will make the federal court take a closer look into it."

"Did you get a chance to talk to the governor?"

"No, sir, I got sidetracked by Janice. That turned out to be a blessing within itself. I'm going to talk to him today, Inshallah. I'm going to let him know what's really going on in his state. I really believe he is going to be our ace in the hole. Within the next few weeks, we should know something."

"Inshallah, ibn [If it's God's will, son]."

"I will see you next week, Dad, Inshallah."

"Okay, son, I love you."

"I love you too. I will see the rest of you all when I get back to Memphis, Inshallah."

When Adam left the prison, he couldn't wait to get into his car. The first thing he did was call Agent Woods. After he dialed the phone number, he placed the phone up to his ear as it rang.

"Hello."

"Agent Woods, this is Adam Ali."

"How are you, Adam. What's up?"

"I'm blessed. What I want to ask you is, since all the evidence has come forward, how long do you think it will take before my father is home?"

"I haven't had time to talk with anyone about your father. I have been focused on trying to capture George Fuhrman."

"Excuse me, sir!" an agent said, trying to get Agent Woods's attention while he was on the phone with Adam.

"Hold on Adam. Yeah!" Agent Woods said.

"Sir, we just received a call over the radio that agents have been ambushed. Four are down, and the others are under heavy fire."

"Where?" Agent Woods asked.

"West of here, sir."

"Adam, I got to go. I will get back with you later," Agent Woods said with a sense of urgency in his voice.

"Okay, we will talk later."

Adam knew something serious was going on. He hung up and called Brandon Morris.

"General Morris speaking, may I help you?"

"Uncle Brandon, you told me to call you if I needed some help."

"I did. What's going on, Adam?"

"I just got off the phone with Agent Woods of the FBI. It seems to me that they are going to need some help down in Teller County to catch George Fuhrman. I just overheard four agents were down and others were under fire."

"I have been keeping up with it since last Sunday. I had a feeling that they would need help. Give me his number. I will give him a call," Brandon said.

Adam gave him the number.

"That sheriff has gone crazy. What you were just telling me about is on the news. Listen, I'm going to put my phone up to the TV."

"Four FBI agents are dead and two others have been rushed to the hospital with serious injuries after being ambushed while conducting a check on a road that leads to I-40 just minutes ago."

"Did you hear that, Adam?" Brandon asked after he lifted the phone from the TV.

"Yes, sir," Adam said.

"That's four more to add to the other two agents who were killed two days ago."

"They should have been on full alert," Adam said.

"They weren't looking for it to happen like it did, I guess."

"They put agents on every road that leads out and in. So they know that he would be trying to get out of town."

"You're right. From the looks of it, he's not going to allow them to take him alive."

"I don't think so either. Looks like he has no problem at all showing them that. Let me get off this phone so I can call my friend Mark to see if his father is in town."

"Okay, I am going to call Agent Woods and see what I can do to help get George Fuhrman into custody."

"Inshallah, Uncle, I will talk to you later. As-salamu alaykum, Uncle."

"Wa alaykumu s-salam, nephew."

Adam clicked his phone over to clear the line and called Mark.

"Hello."

"What's up, brother?" Adam said.

"Nothing much. What's up with you?" Mark asked.

"Is your father in town?"

"Yeap, he's at home. Would you like for me to call him on my three-way?"

"No. I need to see him and talk to him face-to-face. I am five minutes from your house now. Are you dressed?"

"Sure."

"I'm on my way to pick you up. Be ready."

"I got you," Mark said.

Meanwhile, General Brandon Morris finally got through to Agent Woods on the phone.

"Agent Woods speaking, may I help you?"

"Yes, sir, my name is General Brandon Morris of the United States Naval Air Station Base in Millington, Tennessee."

"How may I help you, General?"

"First of all, I would like to offer my condolences for the men you have lost. From the looks of it, the sheriff isn't planning on being taken alive. He has been living in that town all his life, and he knows it like he knows the back of his hand. If you and your men are not careful, he's going to kill all of you one by one."

"What's your point, General?" Agent Woods asked.

"My point is, sir, you have the power to call for martial law. That will open the door and allow me and my men to assist you."

"Who in the hell do you think you are? My men and I are more than capable of handling this situation ourselves."

"This isn't the time for you to be bullheaded. Your men are dying at the hands of George Fuhrman. I don't want to take over. I just want to work with you. I have the power to help you close up all the outlets and stop this maniac from escaping. You still will have total control. Also, my men are trained for war. Yours are not."

"I could live with that. Come on, let's do what needs to be done," Agent Woods said.

"I'm on my way."

"I will see you when you get here, General."

Adam pulled around to Mark's driveway that ran from the street up to the side of his one-and-a-half-acre front yard. As Adam pulled around the driveway to the entrance of Mark's $750,000 home, Mark stepped out into his front door. He walked between the two large pillars that supported the roof of the front entrance. Before Adam could make a complete stop, Mark was there at his car. He opened the passenger door and got in the car.

"Brother, have you been watching the news?" Mark asked.

"Not today. What's up?" Adam asked, trying to see what Mark already knew.

"All hell has broken loose down in that little town. Four more FBI agents were ambushed and killed not long ago."

"I know about that. I was talking to Agent Woods on the phone when one of his men told him about it."

"Man, that sheriff ain't nothing nice. While I was watching the news, I couldn't help but see how your dedication has paid off. I have learned a lot from you. I know now that a person could achieve whatever they put their mind and heart up to do. One thing I don't understand about you is, you have been driving this same car your uncle gave you. That was six years ago. I know for a fact you make enough money to buy you and your wife new cars. You don't have any outstanding bills. What's your problem, brother?"

"I like my car. It runs good, and it's paid for. I have a question for you. Why should I put myself in debt when there's no need for me to do so?" Adam said.

"I feel you, but have you ever seen a U-Haul at the graveyard?"

"No, I haven't. You need to keep in mind. We should live like there is tomorrow. That's why we should observe and learn from the ant, not the grasshopper. All summer long, while the getting is good, the grasshopper lives large. When the winter rolls around, he has nothing. With nothing put back for the hard times, he dies and becomes prey to the earth. On the other hand, the ant works all summer while the getting is good, and he stores it for the hard times ahead. I'm not going to be young all my life. There will come a time when I can't work, but I will have all the food I need. Also, if something happens to me, my wife and children will have something. Right now, I am this close to opening my law firm," Adam said as he held his right thumb and index finger up with a little space between them. Mark nodded with what Adam said.

"I must agree with you, brother, because it does make a lot of sense.

Also, my father has been telling me pretty much the same things for the longest. Hearing it come out of your mouth puts the icing on the cake. Make a right on the next street." After Adam made the right turn, Mark said, "Look to your left up on the hill." Adam turned his head and looked over the wooden fence that ran around a large piece of land with horses roaming on it.

"Man, that's nice. One day, God's will, I will have he some land like that," Adam said.

"My father just had that house built."

"That's really nice."

"You haven't seen nothing yet. Just wait until you see the inside. Make a left on the next road." After Adam made the left turn, he was stopped by a security gate and guard who walked out the small red brick booth when he saw them coming up the road.

"Roll down your window," Mark said. "Mr. Jenkins, it's me and my friend Adam."

"Okay, Mark, I'm going to let your father know you and a friend are on the way up."

"Okay, thank you, sir," Mark said as the security gate opened.

Adam drove up to the governor's red half-bricked nine-bedroom mansion on 150 acres. As Adam drove closer, his eyes were captured by the four huge white pillars that stood out front of the mansion. "Man! Now this is a nice crib. Where do I park?" Adam asked Mark as he looked up at the mansion.

"Keep going on around to the back. We are going to park in the garage. I have my parking spot," Mark said. Both laughed. That discussion carried on from inside the car into the house. The two walked straight through the garage door into the kitchen where Mark's mother was cooking.

"Hi, Mom!" Mark said as he walked up to kiss her on the cheek.

"How are you doing, baby? Who's the stranger you have with you?" Mrs. Nixon asked with a smile on her face and arms open to receive a hug from Adam.

"How are you, Mrs. Nixon?" Adam asked.

"I'm doing pretty good, stranger. How about yourself?"

"I'm blessed," Adam said.

"Mom, where is Dad?"

"He's upstairs in his office on that dog-gone computer. I am beginning to think he loves it more than he loves me. Anyway, Adam are you staying for dinner?" Mrs. Nixon asked as she turned her head from Mark to Adam.

"Yes, ma'am."

Mark and Adam walked down the hallway and up the stairs to the second floor that led to the governor's home office. "What are you doing, Pop?" Mark asked.

"I just finished taking care of my taxes. I have some new software that's really nice to have," Mr. Nixon said as he swung around in his chair.

"How are you doing today, Mr. Nixon?" Adam asked as he shook the governor's hand.

"I can't complain. If I did, no one would listen anyway. How are you, family man?" the governor said, talking about Adam's new child.

"All praise are due to God, I'm good. I have this problem I have been having for fifteen years. I came here to see you today, hoping that you would help it go away," Adam said.

"What is it, son?"

"This problem started when I was ten years old. My father and mother took my sister and me to visit our grandparents in New Jersey. On the way back, my mother was pulled over in Teller County, Tennessee, by George Fuhrman and Mike McClain. At the time my mother was being pulled over, my father was asleep. I recently found out my mother was pulled over by the same two sheriffs who had killed twelve women along the twenty-five-mile stretch of highway that runs through that town."

"Excuse me, Adam, for cutting you off. Does this have anything to do with what's going on down there now?" the governor asked.

"Yes, sir, it does."

"Have a seat and finish the story. You were saying that the same two officers also pulled your mother over?" the governor said as Adam took a seat.

"They pulled my mother over. One of them walked up to the car. After he looked in and noticed that my mother, a white woman, had a black man, my father, in the car with her, he asked my mother if she was all right. She said yes and gave him her driver's license. The officer walked to the back of our car and signaled for his partner. My mom felt something was wrong. She said that she watched them through the rearview mirror and read his lips. He told his partner that it's a nigger in the car with her. The look on their faces made her wake up my father. Before he could open his eyes, they had his door open with their weapons out. They hollered, 'Get out the car, nigger!' Their hollering and my mother's screaming woke me and my little sister. After my father was out of the car, they forced him to the back at gunpoint. That's when one of them started beating him with a nightstick across his back and legs. After that went on for a few minutes, the officer who held the gun on him put it back into the holster. I guess my father saw him because once the gun was back into its holster, my father turned and locked eyes with me as he slowly pulled himself up on our car. The officer who was behind him with the nightstick hit him again and again one after another until he was out of breath. That's when my father got some strength from somewhere. He turned around with a swinging elbow across the officer's face. The elbow knocked him off his feet onto the ground. Before it could register in the other officer's mind what had just happened, my father rushed him. The both of them fell to the ground and fought over the officer's gun. I heard a shot sound off. My father got up with the gun in his hand. The other officer was getting up at the same time. He went for his weapon, and my father shot him in the shoulder. Then my father called for help. When help got there, they were about to kill my father, and by the grace of God, the FBI pulled up and stopped them. The next night the Ku Klux Klan came to our house and told my mom not to come back to that town or they would kill her. We moved out that night and went to a shelter. From the shelter, we went to live with my father's brother. My mother started using drugs and spent all the money my father had in the bank that she could get to. My sister was raped at the age often by a man who was over at my uncle's house, getting high. By the grace of God, my aunt came down from Colorado and took us back with her. After we were in Colorado for about six months, we found out that my little sister had gotten raped and was pregnant. With the support of my father from prison and our aunt, we were able to live like normal children again. I did have to steal and ask for food to feed me and my sister. My father had money saved in an account for our schooling. I made a covenant to do whatever it took to learn law so I could help my father get out of prison. By the grace of God, I was able to meet the right people in school," Adam said as he looked over at Mark with tears in his eyes.

"My last year of school, I was finally able to actually get to know one of the females we had shared the same classroom with for four years. I came to find out her father was the head of the Klan down in Teller County, Tennessee. Her father took her and her brother to the funeral of the officer my father killed. In front of her and her brother, George Fuhrman told their father that they were trying to teach my father a lesson about messing with their women. George Fuhrman, the sheriff all over the news, had their father killed and tried to have her brother, Eric Henderson, killed so he could become the leader of the Klan. I got a chance to talk with her brother, Eric, last week. As we were talking, I told him about my father's case and how I believe George Fuhrman had something to do with the twelve missing women from the 1970s. I read a newspaper article of the woman who stated that the same officers pulled her over on the same highway. They took her off and made her perform all kinds of sexual acts. That really lets me know that my father's case was tied with the missing women. Eric thought about what I told him for a moment, and then it came to him. When he was sixteen years old, he saw George Fuhrman and Mike McClain putting a fairly new car into the lake, while he was out there fishing. To make a long story short, after he finished fishing, he went to George's house. That was when he witnessed them putting a body wrapped up in plastic into a trunk. Last week Eric and I went out to the lake to make sure. Eric dove down into the lake and got the serial numbers off four of the cars that were in there. While he was down there, he thought to look into one of the trunks. Sure enough, he discovered the remains of a human body in it. We drove to my house and called the FBI. They went out there to George Fuhrman's property and pulled the twelve cars from his lake. Since the truth has come to the light, George Fuhrman has been going all the way out, and in the process, he has killed and shot over six FBI agents."

While Adam was telling his story, the governor paid extra attention to him. He kept his eyes on Adam as he leaned back with his arms folded. After Adam was finished, he hit the arm of his chair and shook his head as a sign of being upset.

"Adam, son, that's one helluva story. From what I have gathered, I know now that you are the son of Samson Ali. Am I correct, son?"

"Yes, sir, you are."

"From what I could remember about this case, he has been on death row for over fourteen years now. Adam, son, I am going to give you my word. I'm going to look into this matter, and I can assure you of that."

CHAPTER 22

Riot tanks rolled in, and military helicopters flew in over Teller County like it was a war zone. The sound of it put the town into panic and uproar. The military police a.k.a. MPs marched in by units to help the FBI agents secure all outlets leading in and out of town. Any outlet that could be used to flee from town was closed. For the first time, General Brandon Morris and Agent Woods got the opportunity to officially meet. General Morris—at six feet five inches and 225 pounds, a commanding yet trim man—emerged from the passenger side of the drab olive military-issued Humvee decorated with all his accomplishments. He walked into the sheriff station. As he entered the double-glass doors, Agent Woods, a twenty-seven-year veteran of the FBI, met him.

"I don't have to ask who you may be because you carry yourself the same way you spoke over the phone—with elegance." Agent Woods said before introducing himself.

"So you must be Agent Woods?" General Morris asked.

"Yes, I am."

The two maintained eye-to-eye contact as they shook hands. "It's a pleasure to meet you," General Morris said.

"Likewise," Agent Woods replied.

"The remarks you make on the phone, I didn't know whether to take it as a compliment or insult." Agent Woods looked at General Morris; and his head turned to the right side, trying to figure out what General Morris was talking about. General Morris smiled. His smile made Agent Woods smile.

"I just want to show a little sense of humor."

"That's a good thing," Agent Woods said.

"Right now, if you don't mind me asking, what do you have planned?"

"Follow me and let me brief you on what is going on," Agent Woods said.

The two men walked into a room used by the Teller County Sheriff's

Department for meetings. Agent Woods walked up to the front of the room and pulled down a map of Teller County over the blackboard. Then he reached and pulled a pen from his left shirt pocket. Flipping it through his fingers, he pointed to the top at the location where the agents were ambushed.

"This is the location where George Fuhrman and his men tried to get through. We believe he is communicating with radio or cell phones to his men," Agent Woods said.

"How many men does he have with him?" General Morris asked.

"We are not sure. My agents said that at least fifteen of them ambushed them."

"What type of firepower are they carrying?"

"For sure, we know they have AR-15s, AK47s, and M-16s. Those are the biggest we think they have. We looked over this station, and the weapon room is just about empty. Most of the men he has with him are ex-military. The other ones with him. He personally trained them f."

"What kind of profile have you come up with on him?"

"He's ex-military with some kind of special training. I want to say Green Beret. He was a Navy SEAL or Green Beret. In other words, he is a real kick-ass. He and other members of his unit were kicked out the armed forces because they got drunk and went into a black nightclub and started a fight that left one man dead and another one paralyzed. Like I said, he's a real badass, and he won't be easy for us to take down," Agent Woods said.

"I would like to read over his profile to see what I can come up with on him. Maybe he has an outstanding weakness we can use against him."

"I'll get it for you."

"What was used to kill the two agents in the front of his house?"

"An AK-47, the same shell type, was found on the scene where my other agents were ambushed. One of my agents reported that all of them carried fully automatic weapons, and they are wearing body armor. From the looks of his property, it was used as a training camp."

"It is set up like a military training camp?"

"Yes, we can go out there later, so you can see it for yourself."

"If you don't mind, I would like to get his files and go up there now. I don't want to give him too much time to put together another attack plan. We got to outthink him. Keep in mind this is his backyard, and we don't want to fall into any of his traps and be forced to lose any more men. With his profile and the camp, hopefully, it will give me an understanding of what we are dealing with," General Morris said clearly.

"Okay, let me grab his files, and then we could head out the door."

While General Brandon Morris, Agent Woods, three agents, and five MPs headed out to George's personal training camp on his property, George and his men watched the MPs unit and riot tanks move in from a distance through binoculars. George motioned for his men to fall back from their location. If you didn't know the men were lying in the high grass, you would have looked right over them. Wearing camouflage clothing and brush left them nearly undetectable.

After receiving the signal from George, three snipers slowly emerged from their location. One by one, they fell back with their earpieces in, high-power rifles with silencers and scopes in their hands. The teamwork and coordination showed they were well trained. They walked into their nearby hideout. George spoke words of encouragement to them, "Brothers, the good book talks about a great day that is to come—on that day when the true children of God will be tested by defeat. I say that to ensure you that the words of God are true. In Romans 8:25, the pure white God that we serve lets us know all things work together for the good to them who love God, to them who are called according to His purpose. That purpose is to make sure that all niggers and Jews stay in their place. It's not us. It's our kind who has fallen in love with the niggers and has become willing to help them get rid of us. But what they don't know is if God is with us and for us, who can be against us?"

"NO ONE! NO ONE, BROTHER!" they said in unison.

"We should always know and lay down the following principles as long as we live. One, niggers should be treated like horses or less. If they won't work, kill them. Two, like a horse, they must be broken. Three, keep in mind both of them are dangerous—a wild horse and a nigger. We don't always have to kill them, but we must put the fear of God in them. Let's give praise to God of the pure white."

All his followers said in a serene voice, "No one especially niggers and Jews all praise to the God of the pure white. We are justified for what we do. It is our duty to stay on top of the children of Satan—the niggers who fight for rights.'

"What rights?" George asked.

"The rights to be good slaves again," the men said.

"They are slowly trying to take the power away from the children of

God. It's our job not to allow it and do as our God tells us. The nigger lovers have sheltered the niggers too long. It's time for them to be shipped back to where they belong. Since they won't go by choice, we are going to apply force. Do you all agree?" George asked.

Those words of encouragement brought them all to their feet as they said, "We do agree."

"Brothers, let us do the work of the Father even if we lose our lives in the process. If we have to, we are going to kill every FBI and military police on the face of the earth. The information that I gathered from the news is the town is now under martial law, and the military has come in to help secure the borders of our town. After sundown, no one is allowed on the streets. We have got to use the night coverage to ambush the borders. Once we get out of town, we have brothers waiting on us in Jackson, Summerville, Brownsville, and Memphis to escort us out of the state. I need two or three teams to go out early in the morning. I want you all to dress normal. I will make sure that the weapons are there waiting for you. I need you all to carry a weapon that you can conceal. Team one is my best shooters: JR, Brant, and you, James. You three will go out together early tomorrow morning to post up on top of the old fire station downtown. The first small unit of MPs you see patrolling, catch them sitting at one of the stop lights. You need to communicate with one another. Make sure someone picks the driver, someone picks the passenger, and someone gets the one in the backseat. You all can decide that yourselves. Once you get your man isolated and in between your crosshairs, check and make sure the others are ready. If everyone is ready, Brant, you give a three count, and all three of you take your shot at the same time. Quickly break down your weapons and clean off your fingerprints. Once you have done that, get out of there. Team two—Chris, Dennis, and Danny—I need you to separate and get somewhere to post up. Make sure that you can maintain eye contact with one another. If anything happens and things don't go as planned, make sure that they get out of the building. Once you three are out, separate into twos and go to Frank's Funeral Homes before they know what hit them. When you get there, stay inside. We will maintain contact by radio. Do you all copy that?" George asked.

"Copy!" the six men said in unison. From the sound in the room, the men were more than ready for their task.

"Jimmy, I need you to drive over to Jerry Gram's house to deliver him this message. If he's not at home, tell his wife, May, to call him for you.

Don't discuss anything with him over the phone. Just say brother business. He will know what you are talking about. You come straight back here. If he is at home, tell the chief that I need him to go down to the old fire station this evening before the sun goes down or early tomorrow morning as the sun is coming up. Tell him I need him to put three sniper rifles with silencers and scopes on them in the top room. Also, make sure the back door is unlocked when he leaves," George said, knowing he could trust Lil Jimmy and need not repeat himself.

"I got you, bro," Lil Jimmy said.

"Jimmy don't let the sun go down on you out there."

"It won't. I'll be right back," Lil Jimmy responded.

George smirked at the young child he had seen grown into manhood. Sometimes George called him Mike because he looked and acted like his father so much. Over the years, George treated Lil Jimmy like he was his son. In his heart, he knew that Lil Jimmy would die for his cause and would kill for his cause. Early the next morning right before the sun came up, the six men were up and got ready for the task. Team two dressed up like businessmen, concealing their weapons inside their suits. Team one needed no weapons, so they put on regular clothing, something that would blend in with the downtown morning bustle. George walked into the room after the men were dressed and ready to go.

"Joe is going to take team one into town, and Jimmy is going to take team two. Once they drop you all off, you all know what to do. Frank's Funeral Homes is just two streets over from the fire station. It shouldn't take three minutes to get there. Let me know by blowing into the radio three times. You all get out of here before they wake up," George said.

The men got into different cars and moved out. Once they were near their locations, they were let out of the cars. Acting on the plans that George had given them, team one slipped into the back door of the old fire station undetected by the people who walked up and down the nearby street of slow-moving traffic. Team two spread out. One man walked into the nearby park and took a seat on the first bench across the street from the fire station at a location where he saw and heard everything. The second man walked halfway down the street into a coffee shop and ordered a cup of coffee and a newspaper. He walked out of the store and took a seat at one of the four small tables out front and opened his newspaper and sipped his coffee as he watched the traffic pass by. The first man took his seat at the bus stop where he maintained eye contact with the other two men. The men chose their locations and waited. Team one made it through the back door undetected and up five flights of stairs to a door. Lying in front of the door were three sniper rifles equipped with silencers and scopes. The men walked through the door onto the roof of the building. The building gave them a 360-degree view of the town. A sniper's dream. The men took their time and got themselves positioned where they saw members of team two and the street below. While the men waited, they looked through their scopes down at the people who walked up and down the sidewalks.

"They have no idea that their lives are in danger," Brant said.

"They wouldn't even know that they are dead," JR said as the three men laughed.

"Our ducks are coming down the street," James said as he ran back to his position and picked up his weapon.

"It's four of them in the jeep. I'll take one in the backseat," James said as the four MPs cruising down the street were unaware of the presence of the three men on the rooftop.

"I got the driver," Brant said as he focused on the helmet on the MP's head.

"Thank you, all. I have a choice between two—eeny, meeny, miny, moe," JR said as he shifted the rifle back and forth from the passenger side to the MP behind the passenger side.

"They are closing in on the red light. Are you all ready?" Brant asked.

"Yeah," the other two men said.

"One, two, three," Brand counted as the men squeezed their triggers simultaneously.

Before the driver could pull off, the driver and the two in the back were struck in the back of the head, sending their bodies forward. The bullet went through the back of the driver's head out his right eye and through the windshield, shattering it as his blood and brains slid down. The bullet hitting the MP in the back passenger side went through the backseat and struck him in the lower back. The passenger looked over at his partner and took cover as the jeep slowly rolled into the onto oncoming traffic with the MP slumped over the steering wheel. "I think I got two with one shot," JR said as the men wiped the weapons down.

The town was in total chaos as they looked into the jeep of the MPs. Team two slowly got up from their positions and walked toward the fire station. Team one ran down the stairs. When they got to the exit, they slowed down as they stepped out the door.

"Break off into twos," Brant said as the men walked off in twos while unnoticeable in separate directions to Frank's Funeral Homes.

CHAPTER 23

"A small town in the state of Tennessee has been turned into a battleground. The Teller County sheriff George Fuhrman and members of his white supremacy followers have dealt another gruesome blow. Within the last week, this town has witnessed the death of six FBI agents, and just moments ago, four military police were gunned down, apparently by snipers. Three died instantly, and one is in stable condition."

"Syeria, do they know where the shots came from?"

"At this time, they are checking all the rooftops in this area for any kind of lead."

"Has anyone seen or talked to Sheriff George Fuhrman?"

"Not that I know of. I'm heading over now to see what General Morris has to say about the deaths of his men," Syeria Scott said.

The five-foot-eight-inch 130-pound nicely built middle-aged brunette with a classic walk strolled over to where General Morris and Agent Woods were standing. Before she made it to their location, she turned back around toward her cameraman. "Hold up for a moment, Tony. I need to get myself together," Syeria said as she passed him the microphone.

"Syeria, what are you about to do, girl?" the cameraman Tony asked.

She winked her eye at him while she made sure her clothing was intact.

"How do I look?" Syeria asked.

"You will do," Tony said with a smile on his face. After Syeria finished patting on herself, she walked over to where the two were standing.

"Excuse me, gentlemen. If you don't mind, Agent Woods, I would like to have a few words with the general," Syeria said.

"No, I don't mind," Agent Woods said.

"Thank you."

"I will be across the street," Agent Woods said to General Morris as he walked across the street.

"My name is Syeria Scott, and I'm a reporter for Eyewitness News 6."

"You have been a regular face on TV lately. It's an honor to meet you, Ms. Scott. I am Brandon Morris. Is there anything I can help you with?"

As she looked into his eyes, her words and thoughts didn't quite come together promptly. When the words finally came out, they were all bunched together. General Morris laughed.

"That's not funny!" Syeria said as she stood with a big smile on across her face.

"I apologize, ma'am."

"I see that a man of your status has humor."

"Am I not supposed to have any?" General Morris asked.

"That's a question I can't answer."

"Why not?" General Morris asked.

"Because from watching TV, a person with your rank is always stern, and most of them are buttholes. When it came time for me to approach a very handsome man like yourself, I didn't really know what to expect. Out of respect, I came over to ask you for an interview instead of just running up on you putting a microphone and camera all up in your face. That usually pisses people off, and I sure wasn't going to run up on you like that. Most of all, I want to show some kind of respect for the three men you lost today. My prayers go out to them and their families."

"Thank you," General Morris replied.

"Within the last week or so, this whole town has been turned upside down. The sad thing about it, General, is, I have lived here practically all my life, and I truly don't know what in the hell is going on. The FBI won't tell me anything. It is my job to let the people know what's going on, and I can't. I need your help. How often do you see a female walking up to a man and asking him if she could buy him lunch? I remember this story from years ago. It just died down over the years. I love journalism, and I'm a great writer. I could see this being a best seller, believe it or not. And having Marino Scott Hester to be interested in the story should tell you something."

"So this is more than just your job?" General Morris asked.

"However you would like to put it, but it has become very personal to me."

"I feel the same way you do. This is personal to me as well," General Morris said.

"I figured that. I don't know too much about your field of work. But I do know whenever martial law is proclaimed, the military steps in. When have you ever seen or read of a general being on front line especially in this day and time?" General Morris said nothing. He just nodded.

"Your look tells me that it's personal. Yesterday you had on a white suit decorated with gold and silver. Today you're dressed for combat."

The general smiled. "You are good. I see you're very observant. I like that. What are you about to do now, Ms. Scott?" General Morris asked.

"I was trying to take you to lunch."

"A cup of coffee would be nice."

"That's good enough," Syeria replied.

"We are set up down the street. One moment," Syeria said as she motioned for her cameraman Tony with her right hand up in the air and index finger out. She then walked over to meet him. "Tony!" she yelled, looking over at the cameraman across the street.

"What's up, girl?" he said with smoke from a cigarette gushing from his mouth.

"I will see you later. I'm about to go have a cup of coffee with the tall, big, and handsome general."

"You go, girl," Tony said with a feminine-sounding voice and a waving of the hand. "What do you want me to tell the station?" Tony asked.

"What I just told you," Syeria said.

"Okay, enjoy yourself."

"I will," Syeria said with a big smile on her face.

General Morris and two MPs escorted Syeria down to the hotel they were using as a naval air station men post. Once at the post, General Morris walked into the lounge area. "How do you like your coffee?" General Morris asked.

"A little sugar and cream."

"I see you are not really a coffee drinker."

"No, not really. How did you know?" Syeria asked.

"Because you're altering the taste," General Morris said, pouring Syeria a cup of coffee. He grabbed a handful of sugar and creamer packs. He walked over and sat the cup along with the condiments on the table. Then he reached over and pulled a napkin from the box, lifted the coffee cup up, and placed it underneath.

"Anything else?" General Morris asked as he walked over and poured himself a cup of coffee.

"No, this will be good. Thank you."

"Slowly he made his way over to the sofa placed directly across from the couch where Syeria was sitting. He sat there with his legs crossed and cup in his hand as the two maintained eye-to-eye contact. Never once did his eyes leave hers.

"You can take the tape recorder out of your purse and put it on the table," General Morris said.

"Oh my god! How did you know I have a recorder?"

"A professional journalist comes prepared. You don't have anything in your hands to take notes. Anyone with common sense would know that no pen, no pad, equals recorder."

"You truly demand your respect."

"God is the best of planners, but I think this story really needs to be publicized. With that said, I want you to know for this story I would like to have something in return. In other words, this story has strings attached to it."

Syeria looked and smiled, thinking he was talking about something sexual.

"What if I disagree?" Syeria said with a smirk on her face.

"It won't be told. The story that I'm willing to tell you could actually be made into a movie. Marino Scott Hester, Sean Penn, or any big producer would love to hear what I have to say."

"If this story is what I think it is, I will agree to whatever terms you have. So yes, sir, you have a deal. What do we need to do, shake on it?"

"Your word is good enough for me," General Morris said.

"You have my word. I will do whatever it is to get this story," Syeira said with the thought of something sexual on her mind.

"How long have you been into journalism?"

"A little over twenty years. I've done a lot of those years in Nashville before I decided to move back home. I covered a fundraiser for Oprah Winfrey personally. She told me to give her a call whenever I needed her."

"For fifteen years, I have felt the ripple effects of this maniac, so I know how the families of the twenty-four victims feel," General Morris said.

"That's a lot of people." Syeria added.

"You said that you have lived here practically all your life. Do you remember the Samson Ali trial?"

"I remember it, but I am vague on what happened."

"He's the black man who killed Mike McClain and shot George Fuhrman in the shoulder. He received the death penalty."

"I remember now. I had finished school and was working in Nashville when that happened. The Supreme Court should be handing down their final decision any day now."

"Are you going to take the tape recorder out?"

"I don't have to. It's on and picks up pretty good from inside my purse," Syeria said as she pointed to her purse.

"How long has it been on?"

"From the time you sat my cup of coffee on the table and turned around."

"You know, two weeks ago, the Supreme Court denied my brother's motion for a new trial. By the grace of God, his son, Adam, dedicated his life to trying to get him out. Last week Adam and Eric Henderson made a major breakthrough. Fifteen years ago, Shanda Ali was pulled over by George Fuhrman and Mike McClain. She would have been the thirteenth victim if Samson Ali wasn't in the car that night. They thought it was just her, a white female in the car. When they got up on the car, they saw a black man in there with a white woman and two mixed children. What has never been publicized about the case is not only was the case racially motivated, but it also stopped them from killing their the thirteenth victim and the trend of murders."

"Let me make sure that I understand you. Samson Ali's wife is white?" Syeria asked.

"Yes, she is."

"This was an interracial family driving through Teller County in 1979. The wife was driving, and the rest of the family was in the car but couldn't be seen."

"They were asleep," General Morris added.

"Okay, they were lying down, asleep. The two officers thought that she was alone and they had their next victim pulled over. To their surprise, it was a black man in there with her. Their attention diverted from her to him. So you are saying that Samson Ali's son is the reason why the sheriff's Pandora's box has been opened?"

"Yes, exactly. He couldn't do it without the help of Eric Henderson. I'm sure that's his name," General Morris said.

"Are you talking about Eric Henderson from here, Teller County, who was shot a couple of years ago?"

"Yes, that's him."

"This is a great story to cover. I would like to talk to Samson's son.

You referred to Samson Ali as your brother earlier. I take it that you know him?"

"I do."

"How could I get an interview with his son?"

"I could arrange that."

General Morris pulled his cellular phone from off his waist and called Adam. Adam picked up on the second ring.

"Adam speaking, may I help you?"

"Adam, this is Brandon. I'm sitting down here in Teller County with a reporter by the name of Syeria Scott. She's sitting here right in front of me. I told her about your love and dedication for your father and how it helped to bring the sheriff of this town to the light. She would like to have an interview with you."

"Allah [God] is the greatest. I was thinking about giving her a call. May I speak with her?"

"Sure," General Morris said as he passed Syeria the cell phone.

"Hello."

"Ms. Scott, how are you doing?" Adam asked.

"I'm doing okay. I will be doing a lot better if you and I could get together and talk about what's going on in this town. To tell you the truth, I am still in the dark of what's really going on around here. What's your name again?"

"Adam . . . Adam Ali."

"Mr. Ali, if you don't know it, I am a news reporter for Channel 6 News."

"Yes. I am already aware of that. I was about to give you a call," Adam said.

"General Morris was just telling me about your quest for justice. I know a lot of people, and without a doubt, I can get this story out to the mainstream media and to the public."

"I will be more than willing to sit down with you and share this critical story with you. But you must assure me that the people will get the whole story. I don't want anything to be taken out or added."

"I promise you that it will get out to the people the same way you give it to me," Syeria said.

"I can live with that. When will be the best time to get with you?"

"Right now, Mr. Ali, this town is being torn in two. It's not safe for you or anyone to be here. I have a pen. Give me your number and address. I am going to see if General Morris will escort me out of town. Hopefully, we can meet at your home or any place you choose."

"That sounds good enough. My address is 22 Longstreet Drive, Memphis, Tennessee, 38114, and my number is 901-327- . . ."

"We will talk later," Syeria said before passing the cell phone back to General Morris.

"Nephew, that's all I wanted. If anything else comes up, I'll give you a call."

"Okay. Thanks, Unc, as-salamu alaykum."

"Wa alaykumu s-salam, nephew. Ms. Scott, now since you owe me, this is what I would like for you to do. Run a story on Samson Ali and how his case ties in with what's going on."

"That's all you want?" Syeria said, hoping there was something else.

"Yes, that's all."

"Since the final decision of the Supreme Court hasn't been passed down, I would just do what you said. Run an ad to let the people know that George Fuhrman is tied in with this case and Samson Ali's son helped uncover it," Syeria said.

"You know what to say and how to say it. I just want you to shine some light on his case."

"I will go right to work on it. I told Adam that I would ask you to escort me out of town so I could do the interview with him."

"That's no problem, but I can't do it right at this minute. I have to make sure that it's safe. You know George Fuhrman is up to something. Right now, I just don't know what it is. Give me about two hours and come back here."

"That's good enough. I have to stop by the station anyway," Syeria said with a smile across her face.

CHAPTER 24

Late the next evening before the sun could begin its journey downward, George had worked on his plan to get out of town. One of his top men and lifetime friends drove a hearse from his funeral home to the hideout. George and his four remaining men prepared to load up in the back of the hearse.

"Jimmy, ride up front with Frank. The rest of us are going to ride in the back," George said. The men stood outside the hearse with their weapons over their shoulders. Each had backpacks with money and extra ammunition in them. All prepared for war if something happened on the way to their destination. George supplied all four men with bulletproof vests.

"Listen up, brothers. We have to make our move now if we are planning on making it to Frank's before sunset. Make sure you have everything you need because we won't be back. Tomorrow morning, before noon, the FBI and military are going to allow the family and friends of our brothers Willess who's gone home to be with the Lord through the checkpoint to be buried in Summerville, Tennessee. Frank has his body. I can pass for Willess with some makeup, a clean shave, and my hair died. They will be looking for anyone who fits the description of the picture of me that they have been showing on every fuckin' news channel. You all don't have to worry yet. All you will need is some ID. I seriously doubt they have indictments for any of you this soon. They are mainly looking for me. So are you all ready to move?"

"We're ready, bro!" the men said in unison.

"Are you ready, young man?" George asked Frank.

"Whenever you are."

George tossed his duffel bag of money into the back of the hearse and climbed up inside the black-tinted hearse and positioned himself where he could have an all-around accurate shooting position. The other three men climbed in and lay down with their weapons next to them. George, feeling good about his plans, repositioned his body with the AK-47 at his side. His heart rate picked up. He took a deep breath and slowly let the oxygen flow back out through his nostril as he looked around into the faces of his expendable men. Frank closed the back door of the hearse and walked around the passenger side of the car. As he passed Lil Jimmy looking like a kid, Frank cracked a smile at the young killer as he walked toward the front of the hearse and looked through the windshield, trying to make sure none of the men could be seen by approaching drivers. Then he walked around and got into the driver's seat.

"Terry," Frank said.

"Yeah!"

"Make sure you stay flat down. Any movement you do could be noticed through the front of the windshield," Frank said as he put on his seatbelt.

"Got you, bro."

Frank started up the car and pulled out the driveway to the gravel road and turned to the left. Frank took the gravel road until he approached a black paved road where he turned west into oncoming traffic. He reached up and pulled down his visor to block the sun from shining into his eyes. Lil Jimmy followed suit. Within fifty yards from the four-way stop that led into town, Frank rolled over a sharp object in the road. *POW!* was the sound heard when the tire blew. The sound jarred the men, causing them to jump.

"Fuck!" George said as chills flowed through his body, causing him to clench his weapon tightly.

The object plunged into the front right-passenger-side tire, ripping the tread off the rim, sending pieces of the tire underneath the hearse out the back into oncoming traffic. Frank maintained control as he quickly pulled over to the side of the road.

"Motherfucker, I got a fucking blowout," Frank said as he hit the steering wheel with the palms of his hands.

"Call Steve," George said, thinking.

"What's his number?" Frank asked as he grabbed the car phone while waiting to receive the number.

"523-0303," George said quickly. Speedily, Frank dialed the number. The phone rang twice, while it felt as if it was taking forever for someone to answer.

"Steve's Wrecker Service, may I help you?"

"Steve, this is brother's business. Can you talk?" Frank said.

"Sure, bro, what's up?" Steve replied.

"We need you to stop whatever you are doing and get here fast with one of your tow trucks."

"Where are you, bro?"

"We are on State Road about fifty yards east from the four-way stop at Main and State," Frank said.

"I'm on my way right now, bro," Steve said.

Frank hung up the phone and looked into his side driver's door mirror. He noticed that a military police jeep had pulled up behind them. The driver was already out of the jeep and about to approach the driver's side of the hearse. He was just waiting for traffic to pass.

"Frank, get out and go to him, so you can lead him around to the passenger side," George said.

Frank unfastened his seatbelt and jumped out, missing a passing car by inches with his door. The sixty-two-year-old hopped out like he was a young man. Seeing it was an elderly man exiting the hearse, the MPs felt at ease. Frank stopped the young MP before he got midways down the side of the hearse, diverting his attention from trying to look through the tinted windows into the back of the hearse. The young MP was greeted with a smile of a killer.

"Hi there, young man, how do you do?" Frank asked.

"I'm good. What's wrong with your hearse?"

"I ran over something in the road, and it blew my tire."

"Do you mind if I take a look at it?"

"No, sure don't," Frank said. Frank nodded at the second MP who stood outside the passenger side of the jeep with his assault rifle in his hands. Frank and the young MP walked around the passenger side of the hearse. Hearing Frank and the MP walking and talking beside the car, Terry turned over. An approaching car from the west with FBI agents observed his movements through the front windshield.

"Did you see that?" the FBI agent driving asked the passenger next to him.

"See what?" the other agent asked, oblivious to the movement.

"I saw some movement in the back of that hearse."

"Are you sure?"

"Yes, I'm sure," the driver said as he swiftly grabbed the radio. "Agents, need assistance!"

"Where is your location?"

"We are about fifty yards east on State off Main Street," the driver replied.

"Copy that. Help is on the way."

The driver drove down the street and made a U-turn in front of oncoming traffic.

"I'm going to pull over in front of them," the driver said as he pulled his unmarked car in front of the hearse.

"No one move! An FBI car has pulled up in front of us," George said.

"Don't look that way when you get out. Just act like you are directing traffic," the driver told the passenger. Being an old veteran, Frank read the FBI agents' lips as he watched them through their back window. The MP kneeled down to look at the flat tire.

"Do you have a spare tire in this thing?" the MP asked.

"There is no need for one now," Frank said above a whisper that only the young MP could hear. Frank grabbed the twenty-one-year-old around his neck. Before the kid knew what hit him, Frank went into his front pants pocket and pulled out a closed four-inch blade. With one swift motion, he pulled the folded pocket knife out and opened it with one hand before he was half the distance to the MP's throat. The FBI agent in the driver's seat saw the MP fall in slow motion as his blood sprayed from his neck. Frank dropped the knife so he could remove the MP's M45 from his side before the agent could get his head out of the car. Lil Jimmy released multiple rounds through the passenger-side windshield, stopping the agent in his tracks, forcing him to dive back into the car. As the agent directing traffic turned around, Frank caught him in the face with the MP's, 45 knocking him into oncoming traffic.

At the same time Frank shot the FBI agent, George let off multiple rounds through the back of the hearse window, hitting the MP who stood up in the jeep on the cheekbone. He was unable to see the MP who stood beside the passenger side of the jeep. George knew he was there but was unsuccessful in lying cover for Frank. The MP took aim and pierced a hole in Frank's back, causing a catastrophe by blowing through his chest. The hole was big enough to see through. Unable to see the MP, George released multiple rounds across the side and back of the hearse, shooting in the direction where the shots came from, forcing the MP to run to the back of the jeep and take cover.

Lil Jimmy opened the passenger-side door, pushing the MP's body out of the way as he jumped out. With his eyes focused on the FBI driver, he stepped over the two bodies lying on the ground as he released several rounds through the back window into the backseat of the agents' car. Two of the rounds from Lil Jimmy's AK-47 hit the agent. Badly wounded, he lay across the front seat before rolling over onto the floorboard. Lil Jimmy let off multiple rounds as he engaged toward the agents' car. Once he got up to the car, he released more rounds into the agent's wounded body as he lay on the floorboard of the car. George stopped shooting and hollered, "Terry, take cover!"

Terry sat up and lay cover while the other three climbed over the backseat and out the passenger-side door. The outnumbered MP lay low. George tossed his duffel bag over the backseat and followed it. He exited the hearse and ran over toward the FBI agents' car. Before he could move the dead agent lying across the floorboard, he looked up and saw all the backup coming their way. Like an eagle over its prey, a helicopter appeared out of nowhere over their head. George raised his AK-47 and released three rounds into it, forcing the pilot to pull up.

"Pull back," General Morris told the pilot. "No one engage. They don't have anywhere to go."

"This is Special Agent Woods. Obey that order."

George and his four men were left with no other choice but to run into the soybean field to their right that offered them no coverage. The FBI and MPs were ordered not to engage in gunfire. General Morris knew they had nowhere to go, and he didn't want innocent bystanders to get caught in the crossfire.

"We got him. He's boxed in. They are going to try to find a location to take cover. Set up units in all four directions. He is an ex-military man. He will realize that it's over. Get your men to clear the street," General Morris said to Agent Woods.

Agent Woods picked up his radio. "All agents, this is Special Agent Woods. I need you all to clear the streets. If anyone refuses to move, take them into custody."

George and his four men moved back in twos. He led the way while the others would run ten paces, drop, and give cover. George made it to a ditch that ran through the middle of the field. He jumped down into the ditch and gave cover. Terry and Joe jumped down in the ditch with George and helped cover for Lil Jimmy and Phil. The last two jumped down into the mud and rock with the other three. All the men made it to the ditch for cover with no gunfire being exchanged.

"We must keep moving. They are trying to box us in," George said.

The sun that had been used as a patriot had within minutes became their enemy. Twenty-five minutes remained before the sun completely went down. It was more than enough time to set snipers and limit our movement. "Move, move!" George shouted as the men moved northeast through the ditch.

Hearing movement from a distance made George stop and raise his left hand to stop his men while putting his AK-47 up to his shoulder so he could look down the sight as he turned to scan the area. Out of nowhere, a helicopter appeared.

"Sheriff George Fuhrman, my name is General Brandon Morris of the United States Naval Service. You and your men have run out of running room. As you can see, you are sitting ducks. There is no reason for unnecessary bloodshed. I'm going to give you the chance to make the right call."

"Fuck you, motherfuckers!" Terry said as he released two rounds at one helicopter. *Pow! Pow!*

General Morris looked over at his sharpshooter in the chopper with him and nodded. The pilot swung the chopper around, so the sniper could see Terry. While Terry was talking, the sniper placed his head between the crosshairs.

"Terry, get the fuck down!" George said loudly.

But it was too late. The sniper shot Terry once through his head, sending his brains along with bones and hair flying through the air onto the young kids, Phil and Joe, who kneeled down not too far behind him. They looked over at Terry's disfigured head. Phil wiped the blood from his face as he looked down at Terry's body. Terry's head looked to him like it exploded. All the blood and brain matter sent the kid into shock.

"Sheriff Fuhrman, once again, there is no need for any more bloodshed. Order your men to put down their weapons and surrender!" General Morris said loudly with the bullhorn.

George looked closely around and saw he couldn't win. He looked down at Phil, the young kid in shock and fear on his face. He then pulled the duffel bag of money off his shoulder, letting it fall into the muddy water. As a sign he was about to surrender, he dropped his AK-47 into the murky water stream that ran through the ditch. He unzipped his bulletproof vest and reached into the inside and pulled a pack of Marlboro cigarettes out of his shirt pocket. After taking one from the pack and placing it into his mouth, he patted his front pants pocket, checking for his lighter.

"George, what are we going to do?" Joe asked after seeing George light a cigarette.

"There is nothing we can do. You have two choices. One is you can go out like Terry, or two, you can give up and live to fight another day. They will kill us without a doubt, and we won't be able to kill no more of them. I suggest you all go ahead and throw down your weapons," George said before pulling on the cigarette.

"Are you sure?" Lil Jimmy asked as he looked at George.

Unable to look Lil Jimmy in the eyes, George nodded. In his mind, he respected Lil Jimmy's courage, but he wasn't just any kid. He had grown to love Lil Jimmy and looked at him as his son.

"Joe, grab the kid. You and Jimmy get the fuck out of here."

"What about you, George?" Lil Jimmy asked.

"I can't go to prison. I will die first," George said as he looked at Jimmy.

"I'm with you. It's whatever. I am not afraid to die for our cause. It's death before dishonor for me," Lil Jimmy said.

George smiled and said, "I know, Jimmy, and I don't doubt you. I need you to carry the bloodline. I love you too much to allow you to die for this cause."

"I love you too, bro," Lil Jimmy said as he walked over to hug George.

Joe and Lil Jimmy dropped their weapons. Joe bent down and grabbed Phil's legs and lifted him up onto the bank of the ditch. Then Joe and Lil Jimmy climbed out.

"Turn around backward with your hands on top of your heads. Walk slowly backward," Agent Woods said from the loudspeaker. General Morris didn't take his eyes off George Fuhrman. He quickly moved from the front seat of the helicopter into the position where the sniper was sitting. "Excuse me, let me see your weapon. You can move up front," General Morris said as he relieved the marksman of his weapon. "He has something up his sleeves. If he's contemplating suicide, it won't happen today." General Morris put the scope's crosshairs on George Fuhrman and waited for him to make any false move.

George watched as the FBI moved in on his men. They took them to the ground before handcuffing them. In the back of George's mind, he tried to figure out where he had seen General Morris's face before.

"What are you about to do?" Agent Woods asked General Morris after he relieved the sniper from his weapon.

"He is thinking he's going to get off easy. Just watch him," General Morris replied.

Once George finished his cigarette, he flicked it into the bloody water. With no hesitation, George pulled out his sidearm and lifted it up to his head. Before he could pull the trigger on the 45 Colt, General Morris released a round into his right shoulder, hitting him in the same location that Samson Ali did. The force of the bullet knocked him backward into the bank of the ditch. His weapon flew up into the air and fell into the bloody, murky water. He dropped to his knees, holding his shoulder.

"All units move in!" Agent Woods said.

Feeling the pain from the bullet and seeing the FBI and MPs moving in, George started feeling around in the murky water with his left hand, trying to find his weapon. The FBI jumped down into the ditch and grabbed him before he could locate it.

Agent Woods patted General Morris on the shoulder. "Great shot!" Agent Woods said with a smile.

"Take us down," General Morris told the pilot.

"Breaking news. Sheriff Fuhrman and three of his followers have been taken into custody after a gruesome gun battle that left six men dead. Let's go live to Syeria Scott for an in-depth story. Syeria, can you tell us what just happened moments ago?"

"Yes, I can. From the information I gave gathered, two military police officers and two FBI agents were killed along with two unknown gunmen acting under the orders of Sheriff George Fuhrman. George Fuhrman was shot in the shoulder after attempting to shoot himself, according to known sources," Syeria said.

"How did it all get started?" Kim asked.

"Well, Kim, all the men were in the back of the hearse that you see behind me. After they caught a flat, the military police pulled up to help out, not knowing that they were walking into a trap. From the way things are looking, the sheriff and his men felt trapped once the FBI agents' car pulled up in front of them. They opened fire on the FBI agents and MPs. Hopefully, this is the end of Sheriff George Fuhrman's escapade. Kim, we must give thanks to Adam Ali, Eric Henderson, and Janice Henderson. Without them, we still would be in the dark. This story dates back to October 31, 1979, one week after the twelfth woman came up missing in

Teller County. Adam Ali at the time was ten years old and witnessed his father, Samson Ali, who is currently sitting on death row for defending himself and his family, shoot George Fuhrman and kill Mike McClain. His wife would have been the thirteenth victim if he hadn't fatally shot and killed Mike McClain and shot George Furman in the shoulder. Adam Ali vowed to get his father out. He went to college to study law. By the grace of God, he met Janice Henderson, a Teller County native. The two—along with her brother, Eric Henderson—uncovered and brought an end to a sixteen-year-old unsolved mystery concerning the twelve missing women. The women's bodies were found in the trunks of their cars in George Fuhrman's lake. After finding out that the FBI had found the missing women's bodies and two other bodies he had on his property, George Fuhrman refused to give himself up. He made it clear to the authorities by going on his second killing spree that left eight FBI agents and five military police dead. This is a case we will be waiting to see how the courts handle. We have a man who's caught up in the middle of it on death row. The Supreme Court denied his motion for a new trial two weeks ago. Where is the justice? Is she really blind? By all rights, something must be done as soon as possible. A man's life depends on it. I'm Syeria Scott reporting to you live from Teller County, Tennessee."

"Tony, are we off the air?" Syeria asked.

"Girl, yes," Tony said as he grabbed the microphone and wrapped everything up.

"I will see you later. I need to catch up with the general before he leaves," Syeria said.

General Morris was headed toward the military helicopter when he heard his name being called. He turned around to see who was yelling his name.

"General Morris!" Syeria yelled as she trotted in a fast pace. If you didn't know any better, you would think she was running. "Jesus, you need to get your ears checked. I have been calling your name for the longest," she said, short of breath, as he stood there talking.

"I apologize. My mind was elsewhere. What's up?"

"I just wanted to say thank you and to let you know that I sent a clear message out. Make sure you watch the 10:00 p.m. news and give me a call to tell me what you think. Oh, before I forget, I spoke with Oprah Winfrey this morning. She said once this madness is over with and Samson Ali is out, she would like to have us on her show. If you talk to Adam before I do, will you please let him know?" Syeria asked.

"God's will, I will do that. I'm on my way home now. I will call him and fill him in on what went down tonight. I will tell him what you said as well. I will see you again. Take care."

"You take care of yourself too, General."

"God's will, I will. You do the same, Ms. Scott."

Syeria saluted General Morris. He saluted her back with a smile.

"Before you go, I would like to thank you for your help," Agent Woods said to General Morris as the two stood outside the military helicopter.

"No. Thank you for allowing me to come in to help bring that madman down."

"You had some kind of personal interest in this. Am I right?" Agent Woods asked as he looked up at General Morris.

"Yes, sir, you're right, I do," General Morris said as he turned around to get into the helicopter.

"I will see you around," Agent Woods said as the helicopter lifted off.

CHAPTER 25

George Fuhrman was the last of the four to enter a United States federal courtroom in Jackson, Tennessee. He was escorted by five armed FBI agents. The six-foot-one-inch 135-pound George Fuhrman walked in with a Martin chain locked to the handcuffs and leg irons. The FBI agents didn't allow the floor and courtroom to be open to the public, only to a few known news reporters. George looked around the courtroom at all the extra security. His eyes met the eyes of Joe, Phil, and Lil Jimmy. Once his eyes met Lil Jimmy, he smiled and nodded. All the men were seated right next to one another. George was seated on Lil Jimmy's left side. Phil was at Lil Jimmy's right and then Joe.

"Your Honor, we have finally been able to get George Fuhrman into your courtroom," the district attorney said.

"What took so long to get him in here?" the judge asked.

"Mr. Fuhrman is a high-security-risk inmate. We didn't have enough agents on hand to escort him."

"He doesn't look all that dangerous," the judge said as he looked at the fifty-seven-year-old George Fuhrman.

"Looks can be deceiving, Your Honor," the district attorney said.

"Are all the attorneys here for the defendants?" the judge asked as he looked over at the DA.

"Yes, Your Honor, they are present," the DA said.

"Mr. Henry, are you ready to proceed?" the judge asked.

"Your Honor, it is still not clear on all the charges against the defendant George Fuhrman and whether we are going to add the other three defendants to the indictment. I have a meeting with the head district attorney of Teller County Tennessee, Mr. Hernzberg, at noon today."

"What does Mr. Hernzberg have to do with this case?" Judge Beifuss asked.

"We are debating whether the cases concerning the twelve bodies of the missing women from the late seventies are federal or state. The bodies were found on Mr. Fuhrman's property. We know that only one of the defendants was old enough at the time to have played a part in their kidnap and murders," the DA explained.

"We have to have them arraigned today, Mr. Henry," the judge said with emphasis.

"We can go ahead and arraign them on what we have at hand. If anything changes after my conversation with Mr. Hernzberg, I will supersede the indictments, and we can give them an arraignment on the charges this afternoon," DA Henry said.

"When I call your name, will the defendant please stand? Mr. Phil Springer, Mr. Joe Funn, and Mr. Jimmy McClain. Gentlemen, you all are indicted on a nineteen-count indictment. At this time, I am arranging you three on nineteen counts of conspiring to commit first-degree capital murder, seventeen counts of first-degree murder, and two counts of attempted first-degree murder. If found guilty of the charges that have been filed against you, you could receive a possible sentence of—" the Judge stopped and looked up at Mr. Henry, the head prosecutor in each of the cases.

"Mr. Henry, their cases carry the death penalty. What are you seeking?" the judge asked.

"In their cases, Your Honor, I am not seeking the death penalty," DA Henry stated.

"So, gentlemen, you all are facing a minimum sentence if found guilty on the charges that I read off in the indictment. How do you plea?"

One by one, the attorneys of the three defendants stated that they would like to enter a plea of not guilty on behalf of their clients.

"Gentlemen, you all will be held without bond. You may be seated. Next, Mr. George Fuhrman, will you please stand?" the judge asked.

"I don't feel like no goddamn standing. You can say what you have to say while I am sitting here," George said as he looked up at the judge.

"Mr. Fuhrman, do you know I can charge you with contempt of court?" the Judge asked.

"Does it carry life or death?" George asked.

"No, it doesn't," the judge responded.

"Well, I don't give a fuck," George said. The agents walked over toward George. The judge cleared his throat. The sound made them stop in their tracks and back up. George smiled as he looked into their faces.

"Mr. George Fuhrman, you are indicted on a forty-eight-count indictment. At this time, I will be arraigning you on them. Mr. Fuhrman, you are charged with being the mastermind of the nineteen counts of capital murder: eight federal agents, nine military police, and two African Americans. Also, four counts of attempted first-degree murder, two counts of kidnapping, two counts of hate crime that ended up in death, and twenty-three counts of conspiracy, one on each of the charges I just read out to you. If found guilty, the prosecutor is seeking the death penalty. Mr. Fuhrman, you have been formally arraigned on the charges that the United States government have brought against you. How do you wish to plea?" The Judge asked.

One of the two attorneys appointed to George Fuhrman spoke up, "I would like to enter a plea of not guilty for my client, Mr. George Fuhrman."

"Good enough. I am going to resume this case at two thirty this afternoon," the judge said as he pounded his gavel down and walked out.

The four men were escorted to holding cells. George was placed into a holding tank by himself, and the other three were put into one tank together.

"Hey, bro!" Lil Jimmy hollered over the bars to the holding tank next to them.

"Yeah, what's up, Jimmy?"

"We've seen Rowland," Lil Jimmy said.

"Where did you see him?"

"He's down in Mason, Tennessee, with us. They have him in protective custody. I wish he was over here with us. I would kill his punk ass. Where do they have you, bro?" Jimmy asked.

"They are holding me in the Jackson Jail. Watch what you say in here. I need you all to listen up," George said.

The men moved up to the bars. "I need you all to tell them the truth. Tell them I gave you all a $100,000 to help me get out of town the evening before Terry and I killed those FBI agents and the military police. You don't know anything about anything else. I sent Terry to pick you up that day. Am I understood?" George asked.

"Yeah, bro," the men said in unison.

Back in Teller County, everything seemed normal.

"District Attorney Jim Hernzberg's Office, may I help you?"

"May I speak with Mr. Hernzberg please?"

"May I ask who's calling?" the receptionist asked.

"Tell him it's Chris White."

"Hold on one moment."

"Hey, Chris, what's up, bro?" DA Hernzberg asked.

"Did you get the business I asked you to do taken care of?" Chris White asked.

"I am working on that now as we speak. I have a meeting with the United States federal prosecutor that is handling their case in Jackson, Tennessee, at noon. I am trying hard to get him to allow me to prosecute the cases of the missing women in state court. I know that I am not going to be able to try him here. I am going to let him know that we are planning on having the trial in Jackson, Tennessee."

"I need him to be placed somewhere within our system. If the feds get ahold of him first, we would have a chance to get him," Chris White said.

"I talked to his attorney yesterday, and I told him to tell George that if I can get the federal prosecutor to agree with me, I will need him to plead guilty at his preliminary hearing so that I can get him out of federal custody. I will find a way to tell him myself if I have to. Once he knows for sure that I have the case and I need him to plead guilty to life without the possibility of parole to avoid the death penalty, he will cooperate. Also, allow him to know that once he is out of the fed's custody, I will get him back down here in court as soon as possible," DA Hernzberg said.

"I don't care how you do it. Get it done. Have I made myself clear?" Chris White said.

"Sure, bro. I will give you a call when I get back from this meeting in Jackson."

"Okay, you do that."

District Attorney Hernzberg left out of his office and drove to the federal courthouse in Jackson, Tennessee, to meet up with the United States federal prosecutor. Mr. Hernzberg walked into the building down the hallway to his office.

"Mr. Hernzberg, come on in. Can I get my receptionist to get you something to drink?" DA Henry asked.

"No, thank you. Nice office."

"Let's get down to business," DA Henry said.

"First of all, I would like to say that you were right. I looked up the case law that you sent me by fax. It does say that the federal government can step in if they deem it necessary. With or without the case, you have more than enough to bet what you want. Don't be greedy. Your plate is already full. Allow the good people of my town to have a piece of him too," DA Hernzberg asked.

"If I were to allow you to prosecute the case—and I'm not saying I will—where would you try him, and what would you be seeking?" DA Henry asked.

"I will have all counts heard here in Jackson, and I would be seeking the death penalty as well," DA Hernzberg said as he looked DA Henry in the eyes.

DA Henry nodded at the straight forward answer that he didn't think he would receive.

"What about his three accomplices?" DA Henry asked.

"We have an eyewitness, Eric Henderson. He is ready to testify that he saw him and Mike McClain putting at least one body in one of the cars into the lake. I don't think he will fight it. He most likely would take the life without the possibility of parole. So as for his accomplices, they are all yours," DA Hernzberg said.

"I guess I'll share the headache with you. I am going to have a field day with the forty-eight-count indictment I have on him. If you can go ahead and get a conviction, it will make it a lot easier for me to prove my case against him," DA Henry said.

"Thank you, Mr. Henry. I can make plans to get him a TV arraignment so I can get him a preliminary hearing date," DA Hernzberg said, feeling good about getting his way.

"I need to go and let the judge know that we are not going to need them this evening. I will be talking to you later," DA Henry said. The two shook hands, and DA Hernzberg walked out of the office.

"We would like to welcome you all to Channel 6 News at noon. Hi, I am Kim Jones. First in news today: we are going to go live to Syeria Scott in Jackson. Syeria, can you tell us what's going on there in Jackson, Tennessee?"

"Today the United States federal prosecutor handed George Fuhrman down a forty-eight-count indictment. The forty-eight-count indictment ranged from conspiracy to commit murder to murder and hate crimes that ended up in death. The prosecutor is seeking the death penalty if he is found guilty. As for his accomplices—Phil Springer, Joe Funn, and Jimmy McClain—they were handed down a seventeen-count indictment that ranged from conspiracy to commit first-degree capital murder to attempted first-degree murder. The prosecutor isn't seeking the death penalty in their cases. If they are found guilty, they could receive life in a federal prison. The men are being held without bond. I will have more for you at the five o'clock news. I am Syeria Scott reporting to you live from the United States Federal Courthouse in Jackson, Tennessee."

CHAPTER 26

"Two weeks ago, former sheriff George Fuhrman was arraigned here in Jackson, Tennessee, in state court. He was arraigned on twelve counts of kidnapping and murder. Just like the prosecutor in the federal cases, they are seeking the death penalty. The head district attorney Jim Hernzberg is seeking the death penalty if George Fuhrman is found guilty. This morning he is scheduled to have a preliminary hearing. The court will determine if they have enough evidence against George Fuhrman to send the cases to the grand jury. If the cases make it to the grand jury, they will examine accusations of the charges against him. At that point, they will make their formal charges that he will be tried on at a later date. This is a day that the victims' families have been looking for. I saw the key witness Eric Henderson walk into the courthouse earlier. I will provide you the information as it unfolds. I am Syeria Scott, reporting live from Jackson County Courthouse."

Family and friends of the victims filled the courtroom, along with news reporters and bystanders. District Attorney Hernzberg walked over to the defense table where George Fuhrman was sitting with his attorney. "Mr. Tillman, may I speak with you and George?" DA Hernzberg said.

Attorney Tillman looked over at George. "Jim knows he can talk to me unless something has changed between us that I don't know about," George said.

"No, George, nothing has changed between us. Did you get my message I sent through your attorney?" DA Hernzberg asked.

"Yes, I got it." George replied.

"And . . . what are you going to do?"

"I want to hear what you said out of your mouth."

"I said I'm going to need you to plead guilty to life without any possibility of parole today. Once I get you out of the custody of the feds,

I can get you back down this way," DA Hernzberg said with his hand covering his mouth so no one could read his lips.

"Is there any other way?" George asked about him getting out.

"No, not the way things are looking. Eric Henderson is here, and he is prepared to say under oath that he saw you and your deceased partner, Mike McClain, putting at least one body into the trunk of a car and pull another one into your lake. The FBI is going to use him to testify for them. If they give you a death sentence, this case won't mean shit. I will never be able to help you, bro. This is the only way I can see us getting you out of their custody. If we prolong this too long, the federal prosecutors may come back and take this case from me. You know there is a conflict of interest anyway. If all of that comes to light, my hands will be tied and I won't be able to help you."

"What do I have to do?" George asked.

"Today you will plead guilty to all twelve counts of aggravated kidnapping and first-degree murder. I will try to get you a sentencing date within the next thirty days. You have to tell the judge what you did for him to accept your plea."

"That's bullshit, Jim. I don't think I can do that," George said with a serious look on his face.

"Do you want another shot at your freedom? People will want to write books about you and your story. You are considered a legend now. The story itself will get you your money back. Oh, by the way, you have a nigger for a judge," DA Hernzberg said.

George leaned back and thought about it. *A legend, huh? A free legend sounds better,* he said to himself.

"Let's do it! Where do I sign?" George said, feeling good about one day having his freedom again.

District Attorney Hernzberg smiled as he passed George Fuhrman's attorney the plea agreement to read over and get George to sign.

"All, stand. The honorable judge Hester James is presiding," the bailiff said as the judge made his way to the stand.

"First on the docket, we have a preliminary hearing scheduled for Mr. George Fuhrman. Are you ready, Mr. Hernzberg?" the judge asked.

"Your Honor, Mr. Fuhrman is prepared to waive his preliminary hearing and enter a plea of guilty."

"Mr. Hernzberg, are you sure about that?"

"Yes, sir, Your Honor, I am sure."

"Does Mr. Fuhrman fully understand what he is pleading guilty to?"

"Yes, he does, Your Honor."

The judge had never seen anyone with a serious case as this one plead out so fast. The people in the courtroom were taken by surprise.

"Mr. George Fuhrman, will you please stand?" the judge asked as he looked over at him.

George thought about not standing for a minute. Freedom crossed his mind, and he stood up. "Mr. Fuhrman, do you understand that by waiving your rights to a preliminary hearing that you are giving up your right to protest any evidence the prosecuting attorney will send to the grand jury?" the judge asked.

"Yes, I do," George said.

"Has anyone forced you to do this?"

"No."

"Are you under the influence of any drugs or medications?"

"No."

"I have no choice but to accept your waiver. I will set you a date for your sentencing hearing forty-five days from today."

"Your Honor, I was hoping that you could give him a much earlier date," DA Hernzberg said.

"I was hoping in two weeks, Your Honor."

"I won't be here in two weeks. How about in three weeks from today?" the judge asked.

"That will be good enough for me," DA Hernzberg said.

"Defense attorneys for the defendant, what do you have to say?" the judge asked.

The two attorneys looked at each other and then to George. George nodded, agreeing to it. "That's good enough for us, Your Honor," Attorney Tillman said.

I wonder what George and District Attorney Jim Hernzberg got going on. Whatever it is, it doesn't look good at all, Eric Henderson said to himself as he walked out of the courtroom. As Eric walked down the steps in front of the court building, he grabbed his phone off his hip and dialed numbers. He then placed the cell phone up to his ear as it rang.

"Adam speaking, may I help you?"

"Adam, this is Eric. You are not going to believe this."

"What is it?" Adam asked.

"That damn George waived his preliminary hearing and entered a plea of guilty," Eric said.

"When is he scheduled to be sentenced?" Adam asked.

"Three weeks from today."

"How much time is he facing?"

"The DA told me he was asking for the death penalty if he is found guilty, and if he cops a plea, he is facing life without any possibility of parole. I'm not talking about that. There's something going on. He talked to George for over ten minutes before the judge walked in. Also, I know for a fact that the two are cool. I think they got something going on," Eric stated.

"You might be right, Eric. If I'm not mistaken, Hernzberg, if I'm saying it right, is the same one who prosecuted my father," Adam said.

"Most likely he was. He has been around as long as I can remember," Eric said.

"We will see what happens at his sentencing. God's will, I will be there, and I'm going to see if my uncle Brandon will come with me to his sentencing. He has to admit to his role in the murders. The question is what will he say?" Adam asked.

"I don't see him coming all the way clean," Eric said.

"We will see in a few weeks. After he is sentenced, I can start counting down the days until my father comes home. Once he's home, we are going to Chicago to be on the Oprah Winfrey show. I want you and Janice to come also. Without God and you two, none of this would be possible. Once again, I want to thank you for going out of your way to help me," Adam said.

"You're welcome, and when the airplane leaves out for Chicago, I want to be on it," Eric said.

"I have to go, Eric. I have court. I will call you later."

"Okay, Adam, I'll talk to you later."

CHAPTER 27

"Today is another big day for George Fuhrman. Yesterday he was given a preliminary hearing, unlike three weeks ago in a state court. He didn't waive it or plead guilty to any of the charges filed against him. Since I have been standing here, I have seen a multitude of people going in. Among them I saw Eric Henderson, Adam Ali, and General Brandon Morris. People like me want to see what George Fuhrman is going to say at his sentencing hearing. I will fill you in on details after it's all over with. This is Syeria Scott reporting live from the Jackson County Courthouse."

As people crammed into the courtroom, George was still undecided what to say on the stand. He leaned over to his attorney and whispered in his ear.

"Go get Jim for me," George asked his attorney.

His attorney got up from the defense table and walked over to District Attorney Jim Hernzberg while he was sitting at the prosecutor's table, talking to his assistant.

"Excuse me, Mr. Hernzberg, my client would like a word with you," Attorney Tillman said as DA Hernzberg looked up at him. DA Hernzberg nodded at Attorney Tillman to let him know he heard him.

"Excuse me, Mr. Winston, I will be right back," DA Hernzberg said as he stood up from the table and walked over to the defense table. "What do you need George?" DA Hernzberg asked, thinking George had changed his mind about getting up on the stand.

"I need some assurance," George said.

"Assurance for what, George?" DA Hernzberg asked.

"I don't want anything I am about to say used against me in the future."

"What can hurt? Hell, I might be able to use it to help get you back down here. You know what I mean?" George thought about it and then nodded at the district attorney as he thought to himself that it did make sense.

"Jim, I am trying to get the other brothers cut loose. Do you have any tips of what I can do?"

"All you can do is have your attorney draw up an affidavit stating what you want to say and have your attorney get with theirs."

"I have already done that," George said.

"That's all that can be done. They are in between a rock and a hard spot."

"All, stand. The Honorable Hester James is presiding," the bailiff said as the judge walked into the courtroom and up to the stand.

"Today on the docket we have a sentencing hearing scheduled for Mr. George Fuhrman. Defense for the defendant, are you ready to proceed with the hearing today?" the judge asked.

Attorney Tillman stood up. "Yes, sir, Your Honor we are."

"Unhandcuff Mr. Fuhrman," the judge said to the bailiff. The bailiff walked over to George. George stood up and turned around so the bailiff could take the lock off the chains around his waist. That was when his eyes locked on Eric's. He noticed beside him were a mixed-breed kid and the man from in the helicopter who shot him. Then it came to him that General Morris was the same man who came to court with Samson Ali fifteen years ago. If looks could kill, all three would be dead. General Morris smiled. George turned red but kept his cool. He just shot General Morris the bird on his right hand before he turned and walked up to the witness stand with iron shackles on his legs. He was stopped by the bailiff.

"Will you please raise your right hand? Do you swear to tell the truth, the whole truth, and nothing but the truth, so help you, God?"

"I do," George Fuhrman said as he stood with his hand up in the air.

"You may step up, Mr. Fuhrman," the judge said.

George got up on the stand and took a seat as he glanced over at Eric. *I will kill you myself when I get out,* he thought to himself.

"Mr. Fuhrman, will you please state your name?"

"George Fuhrman."

"Mr. Fuhrman, has anyone forced you to enter a plea of guilty?" the judge asked.

"Has anyone promised you anything in return for your guilty plea?"

"No."

"Are you under the influence of any medications?"

"No."

"Do you understand that you are giving up your rights and chances to ever have a trial by a jury in the future?"

"Yes."

"Do you understand that I have the right to grant or deny your plea?"

"Yes, I do."

"The only reasons I would deny any agreement that you and the district attorney have agreed to is, one, I don't feel you are being totally honest on the stand, and two, I feel that your plea doesn't fit the crime. Am I clear on that, Mr. Fuhrman?"

"Sure."

"Did your attorney advise you of the amount of time that you will receive if I accept your plea?"

"Yes, he did."

"Is this your signature on this plea agreement, and is that the amount of time you agreed to?" the judge asked as he passed George the sheet of paper.

George grabbed the piece of paper and looked at it and then passed it back.

"Is that your signature and what you agreed to?"

"Yes, it is."

"Mr. Fuhrman, with all that said, I would like for you to tell me and the court your reason for pleading guilty to twelve counts of kidnapping and twelve counts of murder. Also, tell us what happened."

George looked down at the floor for a moment, then took a deep breath, and blew it out as he raised his head back up. "I'm pleading guilty because I am guilty of the kidnapping, the rapes, and the murders of those twelve women. I also plead guilty to shorten this process and to escape from receiving the death penalty," George said and looked around at what kind of effect his statement had on people.

Some made sibilant sounds; others shook their heads and covered their mouths. George kept his head up and looked them in their faces.

"I don't remember all the details. Will that effect the plea agreement?" George asked as he looked up at the judge.

"Just tell us what you can remember," The judge said.

"Well, I guess it all began in 1976 or 1977. My partner and I were sheriffs working for the Teller County Sheriff's Department. We pulled over a car for speeding. After we stopped the car and I walked up to the driver's side door, I smelled a strong odor of marijuana coming from the car. I had her get out of the car, and I placed her into the back of our squad car. My partner and I searched her car. During the search, we found a large sum of money, marijuana, and heroin. After we found it and I returned to the squad car to call it in, she propositioned me. She said that she would do anything sexually and give us $10,000 each not to arrest her. I told my partner, and we both agreed. We let her follow me back to my house where we did any and everything that we could do sexually with her. When it came time for her to pay us so she could go, she gave us the $9,000 that we found inside the car. Then she went outside to her car and opened up a stash spot to a really large sum of money that we looked over. My partner asked her how much money it was in there, and she said $1.5 million. We demanded much more than $10,000 each. She wouldn't give it to us. She said that she had given us her pay for transporting the drugs and money. So we took all of it. She threatened us by saying that she was going to the authorities to file rape charges on us. So we killed her and sat around trying to figure out what to do with the body and car. Then it came to me, 'The lake!'" George's penis got hard talking about the past enjoyment he had experienced. "That one time is all it took for my partner and me. If we saw a female we liked driving by and wasn't from Teller County, we pulled her over. One of us would drive her car, and the other would drive her inside the squad car. After we got through raping them, we would strangle them to death, wrap the bodies up with plastic, and put them in the deep freezer that I had inside my garage. Once we got through taking all the parts that we wanted off the cars, we placed the bodies inside the trunk and pulled the cars out to my lake and dumped the cars in the lake. This went on for about two years. I didn't keep count of them. That's what I did."

"Mr. Fuhrman, I have one question," the judge said. George looked up at the judge.

"Why did you and your partner stop after two years?" George took a deep breath and wiped his dry mouth. "My partner was killed," George said and lowered his head as he thought about his friend.

"Thank you. Mr. Hernzberg, do you have any questions for Mr. Fuhrman?"

"Yes, sir, Your Honor, I have one," DA Hernzberg said as he stood up. "Mr. Fuhrman, for the court's record, when you told us the story of what happened, you mentioned that you had an accomplice. You referred to him as your partner. The court needs to know the name of this accomplice."

George looked at District Attorney Hernzberg with an evil eye, thinking, *What the fuck is wrong with this motherfucker. The nigger didn't say anything about it. Why in the hell has he brought it up?*

"Answer the question, Mr. Fuhrman," the judge said. Knowing he had come too far to turn back, George said, "Mike . . . Mike McClain." He looked at the DA sideways. "Mr. Fuhrman, it is a great possibility that the district attorney's office will be filing additional charges for rape," District Attorney Hernzberg said. "That will be all, Your Honor."

"Defense, do you have anything to say?" the judge asked.

"No sir, Your Honor. We just ask that you accept the plea agreement that's on the table."

George looked over at DA Hernzberg, trying to figure him out. *It better be a good reason he asked me that shit,* George thought to himself.

"Mr. Fuhrman, I am very disappointed at you. You used your badge to lure your victims to you. If we can't trust the people who have been set in place to enforce the law, we will think twice about the system that we look at for justice. You give good officers a bad name. I know that a lot of people will feel that the system has failed them once again by allowing you to live and not sentencing you to death. I am not God or that type of judge. I am going to be a man of my word and sentence you to twelve life sentences without any possibility of parole. Each sentence is to be run consecutively. You will serve out those sentences in the Tennessee Department of Corrections."

"Your Honor, will you please order that he be transported immediately due to him being a security risk?" District Hernzberg asked.

"I order that Mr. George Fuhrman be transported to the Tennessee Department of Corrections immediately."

The district attorney looked over at George and nodded.

"Breaking news: we are going live to Syeria Scott in Jackson, Tennessee at the county courthouse."

"The story has been told. George Fuhrman put it all on the table. The mystery is now over with. George Fuhrman told the court that he and his deceased partner Mike McClain kidnapped, raped, and strangled those women to death. For two years, the madness went on. It was finally stopped on October 31, 1979, the night that they pulled the wife of Samson Ali over in Teller County. Mike McClain was killed by Samson Ali in the process of protecting himself and his family. Just moments ago, George Fuhrman was sentenced to twelve life sentences without the possibility of parole.

The twelve life sentences were run consecutively. The judge gave George Fuhrman a break. He lectured him in Court right before sentencing him. He told George Fuhrman that he was disappointed in him for using his badge to lure his victims in. He went on to say that if we can't trust the people who have been set in place to enforce the law, we will think twice about the system that we look to for justice. That was a true statement. Look at Mr. Ali. He is a victim of the system, and it shows that it has flaws. Hopefully, after fifteen long years, he will be able to regain his freedom off death row and go home to his family who has fought long and hard for his freedom. I am Syeria Scott reporting to you live from the county courthouse in Jackson, Tennessee."

CHAPTER 28

Six days after George Fuhrman was sentenced to twelve life sentences with no chance of parole, he and six other inmates were escorted from the transport bus into the River Bend Maximum State Prison intake in Nashville, Tennessee. The men slowly walked into the building with their hands bound with handcuffs and iron shackles. Inmates stood in their windows and at the tall wire fence, watching the new fish as they walked in. The sound of the phone rang out.

"Hello."

"You have a collect call from . . . Billy, an inmate at the Tennessee Department of Corrections. If you would like to accept the call press #1. If you decline, press #5." *Beeeep!* It was the sound heard through the receiver of the phone as the buttons were being pressed. "This call is subject to monitoring and recording. Thank you for using Down South."

"Hello."

"May I speak with Chris please?"

"Speaking."

"Hey, bro, this is Billy. You wanted me to call you as soon as George Fuhrman got here."

"How long has he been there?" Chris White asked.

"He just got off the bus five minutes ago," Billy said.

"I need you to make sure that nothing happens to him. I don't want to hear or read about one of those niggers in there getting the enjoyment of killing him. You will receive a note tonight letting you know what I need done, okay?"

"Sure, bro."

"Billy!" Chris said comely.

"Yeah, bro."

"It will be brothers' business. I need you to take care of it, just like the note says."

"Okay, bro, brothers' business, I got you. Later, bro."

"Later, Billy."

"As-salamu alaykum [Peace be with you]," a man said as he walked up to Samson's cell.

"Wa alaykumu s-salam [May peace be with you]," Samson said to return the greeting of the inmate in charge of cleaning up Samson's unit.

"How are you doing today, Brother Samson?"

"All praise are due to Allah, I'm good. How about yourself, Dawud?" Samson asked with a smile on his face.

"Thanks to Allah, I can't complain," Dawud said. Dawud had changed his name since he had been in prison serving a life sentence for killing a security guard in a bank robbery. David converted to Islam and changed his name from David to Dawud.

In the Arabic language, Dawud means David. He and Samson became close over the years. Samson saw he just was a young kid without guidance when he came to prison at seventeen. Dawud was a likable man around prison and was also Samson's eyes and ears. Nothing went on without him knowing about it firsthand. Dawud and Samson spent a lot of time talking about Islam and other religions. Dawud enjoyed the stories about the times Samson fulfilled his last pillar in Islam: pilgrimage to the Muslim's holy city, Mecca.

"I came over here to tell you that the Teller County sheriff made it here today. The brothers want me to ask you if you want them to handle it for you."

"No, let him be," Samson said as he looked up at Dawud.

"Let him be? Why?" Dawud asked curiously.

"Allah is the best of planners."

"Are you sure you want me to tell them that?"

"Yes, I'm sure."

"Okay, I will let them know. Salam [peace]."

"Salam, brother," Samson said.

The news of the new arrivals spread fast. Everyone talked about the high-profile serial killer who became sheriff. Within minutes the whole Nashville State Prison inmates knew about it. Extra security was called in and others put on standby to make sure nothing racial happened. The seven inmates were escorted to classification where they took showers and were given all new clothing. Once they got dressed, they were fingerprinted and pictures were taken. An inmate walked around passing out booklets of the written rules of the facility.

"What you just received is an eighteen-page handbook of all the rules that you must follow during your stay here at my facility," Sergeant Reed said before giving his speech.

"My name is Sergeant Reed, not Reed, Jack, or anything else. I'm here to enforce the rules of this institution and babysit you along with fifteen hundred more inmates like you. The book that you have in your hand, a lot of it is a bunch of crap and won't mean jack to a lot of you t heading to death row or have all day and some. Respect will get you a long way around here. You have the choice to make things easy or hard. I'm going to tell you now you won't win, so don't try it. As long as you are in the classification unit, you will be required to wear the orange jumpsuit that you have on. You will be in the classification unit for at least thirty days. You are not to have anything in your cell other than books and the items that you have on the desk in front of you now. For the next thirty days, you will be on twenty-three and one. One, our recreation, twenty-three hours in your cell. All your soap, deodorant, shampoo, and tissue will be given to you as needed. If you have or think you may have any predators you think are here or you feel like your life could be in danger out in population, I have a form for you to fill out for protective custody."

The five-ten, 185-pound, low-cut muscle man stood in the front of where the new arrivals were sitting, waving the PC forms in the air.

"Are there any questions?" Sergeant Reed asked as he looked at the men.

"Yes, sir, I have one," an inmate said as he raised his hand.

"You don't have to say sir to me. For one, I work for a living. Two, that makes me feel older than what I am," Sergeant Reed said.

"When will we be able to receive visits?" the inmate asked.

"We have the forms for you to send to your family to fill out and sent back. It will take about three or four weeks before they are approved. So as quick as you get them sent out and they come back in, the better off you are. Any more questions? No questions? Okay, make yourselves at home. Line up, so I can escort you to your cells for the next thirty days."

All the new arrivals were placed in two-man cells. After all the inmate movement had stopped and they were locked down in their cells with the lights off, a correctional officer on the midnight shift slid a small white envelope that contained a letter underneath Billy's door. Billy got up out the bunk from where he was watching his personal TV to walk over and picked up the envelope off the cell floor. The next morning a crowd of supporters gathered outside the front walls of River Ben Maximum State Prison, awaiting the release of Samson Ali. Samson was unaware that the day before, Governor Nexon of Tennessee signed the paper to pardon and release him from prison after fifteen long years.

"One week after George Fuhrman entered a plea of guilty to escape the death penalty, Samson Ali is finally being released from prison after fifteen years. George Fuhrman will be taking his place on death row if he is found guilty on the forty-eight-count indictment that he is facing in federal court. I will have more on this breaking story after Mr. Ali is let out the gate. I am Joyce Ann Brown reporting live at the River Ben Maximum Prison in Nashville."

Samson Ali's cell door was rolled open as two correctional officers stood with smiles on their faces. "You said this day would come. Sure enough, here it is," the taller of the two officers said.

"A lot of you people come here and claim that they are innocent. From the beginning, I believed the story you told me. Finally, everything has come to light for you. That truly is a blessing," the other officer said as he stuck his hand out.

"Yes, it is truly a blessing. I know it was coming, but I didn't know that today was the day until I saw it a few minutes ago on the news," Samson said as he shook the officers' hands.

"Are you ready to go?" the shorter officer asked.

"I have been ready for over fifteen years," Samson said as he walked out the cell with a big box of legal work and personal mail.

"What about your other stuff?" the short officer asked.

"When Dawud comes around to clean out the cell, tell him he can have the books and to write me. As for the TV, radio, and hot pot, give it to the unfortunate."

As the two officers who always escorted Samson to visits and other places in the facility were walking Samson out, the men in the death row unit chanted, "Ali! Ali! Ali!" The sound of his name being called made him respond, "All praise are due to Allah [God] and Allah alone." And he walked down the walkway with tears in his eyes.

"Captain Davise, I need you to do me a favor," Samson asked.

"What is it?"

"I would like to walk around to see George Fuhrman. Please hear me out before you say anything. I give my word that I am not going to say anything to him. I just want to look him in his eyes once again."

Captain Davise looked at Samson for a moment before nodding, saying, "I can make that happen for you." The two officers escorted Samson around to the classification block. Captain Davise took the ring of keys off his side and unlocked the door to the range. "He's in cell 15," Captain Davise said.

Samson walked down the walkway until he got to cell 15 and stopped. He then walked up as close as he could to the bars and just stood there. George looked over toward the bars from his bunk, where he was lying back with his fingers interlocked behind his head. Samson stood there looking at George until he noticed him standing there smiling at him.

"What the fuck are you looking at, nigger?" George asked.

Samson just kept smiling and walked off. George Fuhrman's celly looked down from the top bunk and said, "That's him!"

"Him who?" George asked.

"The nigger you had put in here."

George jumped up from his bunk and ran over to the door. "I should have killed you, motherfucker, fuck!" George yelled through the bars into the hallway. George became so filled with rage he kicked the steel cell bars and hit the wall with his fist. He hit it so hard that it hurt his injured shoulder. Samson didn't look back but kept walking with a smile on his face. The officers escorted him to the front gate of the prison.

"Take care, Samson. It was quite a privilege to meet you," Captain Davis said with a smile on his face.

"Likewise," Samson said back to the captain. "You take care of yourself, Sergeant Jones."

"I will try. You take care," Sergeant Jones said as the two shook hands for the last time.

The captain gave the signal for the officer in the tower to open the gate. As the gate opened, Samson walked out into the awaiting crowd of family, friends, and supporters. In the crowd he stopped and dropped to the ground face-first and gave praise to God. When he got up, his daughter, Verlena, ran and jumped up in the air into Samson's arms.

"I love you, Daddy," she cried.

"I love you too, baby," Samson said as he held her in his arms. After Verlena, all the rest of the family and friends moved in. Adam stood back with tears in his eyes.

meant for you will never pass you by. If it wasn't meant for you, you'll never get it."

"The next question is for you again, Samson," Oprah said as she read from the card. "This question is from Susan. Susan is from Rockford, Illinois. Her question is, 'What did you learn from the entire experience of being locked up on death row?'"

"The one thing I did learn is to have patience. I also learned to never question God's reasoning," Samson said.

"The next question is for Mr. Gaines," Oprah said as she looked over at the low-key attorney. The question is from Jacquelyn. Jacquelyn is from Jackson, Mississippi. Her question is for you, Attorney Gaines."

"What made you trust and believe in Samson?"

"His character, for one thing, is impeccable, and his background just didn't fit what they were saying about him. What put the seal on it is, after T talked to his wife, whom he himself had not spoken with since that night, related the same story to me that he did," Attorney Gaines said.

"The next question is for you, Eric, Adam, Janice, and General Morris. How do you feel about being a part of a historical event and exploring George Fuhrman? Like Samson said earlier in the show, shedding some light on the seed of deception that he thought no one knew about?"

The four looked at one another, seeing who would speak first.

"Ladies first," General Morris said.

Everyone smiled and looked over at Janice.

"It feels good being a part of it. Just bringing some kind of peace to the families of those women feels good. On the other hand, it hurts me to think about how I was caught up in that seed of deception," Janice said.

"I feel pretty much like she does. For a lot of years, I was blinded by hatred, racism, and ignorance. I had to be at the brink of death to realize that some major changes had to be made in my life. So when my sister, Janice, told me about Adam's story, it hit home. I know about a lot of things that George had done to me and others. Over the years, the seed was embedded in me deep—so deep I knew he had done a that it clouded my judgment. Even though he has done a lot of bad things to me and others, I couldn't go against the Klan or anything the Klan stood for. I fought with myself for a long time to do the right thing for the right reasons. I lost my father to hatred, racism, and ignorance. Sometimes things like that must happen for a person to have their eyes opened. I feel good today knowing that I played a major role in shedding light on his dark past," Eric said. The audience clapped once Eric finished.

"Change does come with a price," Oprah said.

"You go ahead, Adam. I will go last," General Morris said.

"In the beginning, my focus was only on getting my father out. After I told him about the discovery Eric and I made, I started trying to rush things. He told me that it wasn't all about him anymore. We had helped many others by finding their loved ones after so many years. What he said to me had to sink in. I still didn't get it until I went to visit him, and he reiterated how he went years without knowing if we were dead or not. Then it hit home, and I started feeling better about our achievement," Adam said.

"I gave all praise to God. He made it possible. He placed me in the right place. I feel good because I was there and didn't allow him to get off easy. If he would have killed himself, the families of the people murdered by him and his cause would not have received justice. My prayer goes out to all of them and their families. I was willing to do whatever it took to get my brother Samson out. If it would have cost me my life! Finally, after fifteen years, I have peace. So I feel good about it," General Morris said as he reached over and placed his arms around Samson's neck.

"I would like to thank you all on behalf of my audience for answering their questions," Oprah said.

"You're welcome," they all said in unison.

"I have a couple of questions I would like to ask. This question is for you, Samson, and I have one for you as well, Adam. Which one of you wants to be first?" Oprah asked. Both looked at each other for a few seconds. Then Samson nodded to Adam.

"I'll go first." Adam said.

"Okay, Adam, where do you see yourself in the future?" Oprah asked.

Adam smiled and thought about the question before he answered it, "Well, Ms. Winfrey—"

"You can call me Oprah!" she said, cutting him off.

"If you say so, Oprah, you said it best in a saying of yours. You said, 'When I look into the future, it's so bright it burns my eyes,'" Adam said.

"Oh my god, not too many people remember me quoting that," Oprah said.

"I am a huge fan of yours. I admire your heart, your diligence to promote change, and self-improvement."

"Thank you," Oprah said.

"Where do I see myself in the future? I see myself fighting for those who don't have the power or financial means to help themselves. My father is just one victim of the criminal system's injustice. There is a saying that goes like this: 'It's not what you know. It's what you can prove.' Lots of times you can't prove you are innocent. The court says that you are innocent until proven guilty. That's not true. You are guilty until you can prove yourself innocent. The reason I say that is, when they lock you up and you cannot make bond or hire an attorney willing to work for you and not sell you out, you have a chance because it doesn't stop there. If the police lie or plant evidence on you or you have a criminal history that could be used against you to support their lies, the system will force you into a plea bargain. It's sad to say, but a person of color doesn't have a chance in the courtroom. Please don't go in there and ask the court to appoint you a public defender. They should call themselves public pretenders. Don't get me wrong, Oprah. A lot of good attorneys work in the public defenders' office. However, they are given too many cases to handle. They don't have the time to investigate or look into the case, and the system knows it. My wife and I are only two people in one. We will help fight the ones we can. Don't mix it up. We fight for the innocent, not the guilty."

"Okay, I like that. Well, Adam, I wish you and your wife the best in your quest for justice," Oprah said as she moved on to the question for Samson. "Samson, what are your plans?"

"If it's God's will, I would like to reach out to the young men who have made bad choices that cost them their freedom. I want to go back to the prisons to not only promote Islam but also to help instill some sense of inner freedom. During the fifteen years I lived on death row, I met a lot of good and beautiful people, officers and inmates alike. I met this young man who received life for a choice that he made when he was only sixteen years old. He was seventeen when he made it to prison—still a child. He didn't know his father, and his mother was on drugs. The kid turned to the streets to support himself, and one thing led to another. Now he is doing life in prison. Did he break the law? Yes! Does that make him a bad kid? No! By the grace of God, he was placed around Muslims and not around wolves. He accepted Islam and recently changed his name. He is a really respectable kid who was dealt a bad hand. There are others like him in there and out on our city streets. If we don't reach out to help them, society will fail them too. God's will, my goal is to help the children who can't help themselves. Most of their parents are on drugs. They have no choice but to turn to the streets where they die or go to prison. We need some kind of support system in place to help them."

"I see that you and your son are pretty much thinking along the same lines," Oprah said.

"I give God thanks all the time for him. He truly is me all over again. It's truly a blessing to have a son like him."

"Samson, I have something for you that you will like, and I want to give it to you as a token of my appreciation. It's a five-bedroom, three-bathroom house in German Town, Tennessee. That's right—outside of Memphis, Tennessee. Also, I have you a new car to go with your new house," Oprah said as she passed Samson an envelope.

"Thank you, Oprah," Samson said as he got up and shook her hand.

"No, thank you. Thank you for allowing my show to be the first to extend your story to the world."

The audience stood up and gave a round of applause. "I would like to offer a special thanks to Syeria Scott for making this all possible. Also, I would like to thank Governor Nixon, the governor of the state of Tennessee, for showing his support, along with the Ali family. Once again, I would like to thank all the guests for sharing with us their role in bringing the madness that George Fuhrman relinquished on the small town in Tennessee to the end. I would like to thank you all for supporting the show, and last but not least, I would like to thank all of my staff here at the show for the great job they do. I am Oprah Winfrey, and until the next time you all be safe. Goodbye, everybody."

CHAPTER 30

Inside the walls of River Ben State Prison in Nashville, Tennessee, all the new arrivals were lining up, preparing to be escorted from classification to population.

"George Fuhrman, I need you at the front of the line. You will fall out first. You are housed in A unit B-Block cell 223," the correctional officer said as the men stood in line with their bed linen in their hands.

As the new inmates were escorted from the classification to their housing units, inmates watched out of their windows as the new arrivals walked by.

"George Fuhrman, this is your stop," the officer said as he showed George the unit and lift his radio up to his mouth to let the unit know. "Rover to Alpha unit control."

"Alpha unit, go ahead."

"You have one 216 outside your door."

"Copy that," the Alpha unit control officer said as the front door was buzzed open and George walked inside.

When George Fuhrman walked through the door, a crowd of inmates met him. Most of the ones who stood at the front door were white supremacy members. Bystanders wanted to see the notorious serial killer. They stood in and outside their doorways and along the rail on the second tier, trying to see the new fish in the tank.

"What's up, bro? My name is Billy. I am over all brothers in this facility," Billy said as he walked up to George with his hand extended out toward him.

"Nice to meet you, bro," George said.

"The same to you. I pulled a few strings to get you over here with us, bro," Billy said.

"I take it that you know me?" George asked.

"Come on, bro, who don't know you by now?" Billy asked with a half smile on his face.

George didn't know how to take what Billy just said. He hoped it was a good thing to be well-known in prison. "What cell did they put you in?" Billy asked.

"223!" George replied.

"I know that this isn't the place to be welcoming any brother but welcome. I will have the brothers to get you a care package together, just something to help you out until you get your own," Billy said.

"Thank you," George said.

"Pete, show the brother to your cell. We will get together and talk once you get settled in."

"Sure, bro. We will get a chance to talk later," George said.

All the white supremacists walked up to shake George's hand and introduce themselves. "Hey, bro, my name is Pete. I'm your cellmate. Let me show you our cell."

As the two were walking up the stairs, Pete looked at George. "You have been the talk of this place for the last thirty days. That nigger was on the Oprah Winfrey talk show yesterday. She had him, his family, Eric Henderson, his sister, and the naval guy who shot you in there with him," Pete said as they were walking.

"I don't want to talk about that shit. Do you smoke?" George asked as he cut Pete short.

"Yeah!"

"Do you have any?"

"Yeah," Pete said as he bent down after entering into the cell and pulling his right pant leg up, getting the pack of cigarettes out of his sock. Then he stood back up and reached into his top shirt pocket to pull out a book of matches and passed them to George. "They may not be your brand. We go to the commissary tomorrow. If you have money in your inmate account, you will be able to order you some. If not, I can let you get some out the care box. Whenever you are able, just replace what you get. We give all new brothers some soap, shampoo, food, and shower shoes to hold them until they can make it to the store."

A beep sounded over the intercom. "What was that beeping sound?" George asked.

"That was the fifteen-minute warning before the doors are opened for chow. Here is where all the brothers go out the door together. We have our tables that we sit at. If anything kicks off, that will be the place where it will happen or on the yard. Are you ready to go eat?"

"Yeah."

"Make sure you have your ID. You will need it." George checked his pockets to make sure his ID was still in there as both walked back out the cell. "When we get back, bro, we can switch bunks since you're the oldest," Pete said.

"I was going to say something about that," George said as they strolled down the walkway. The brothers were waiting for them downstairs. Once the two made it down to where Billy and the other eight were standing, George looked around and said, "There's a lot of niggers in here."

"This is a good place for them," Billy replied as the others laughed at George's remark.

"We may be outnumbered, but we are the strongest and run this motherfucker. We have something that they don't have: unity. We try to stay off the racial trip because both sides realize that the government is our biggest enemy," Billy said as he looked over at George.

"Where is Jeff?" one man asked in the crowd.

"He's on the way. He had to take a shit," Jeff's cellmate Willie said. "Here he comes now. He shits more than any motherfucker I know."

"What's wrong with him?" Jeff asked

"Here he comes now," Willie said.

"Bring your shitty ass on," Billy said. Everyone laughed.

"Fuck you, bro," Jeff said as he walked down the stairs. When Jeff caught up, Pete called his name, "Jeff!"

"What the hell do you want, shit for brains?" Jeff asked.

"Did you take it or leave it?" Pete asked, marking Jeff about him using the restroom.

"What! What the hell are you talking about?" Jeff asked as he looked over at Pete.

"The shit?" Pete said.

"I left it, you fucking dickhead," Willie said as he shoved Peter's shoulder with his right hand.

The twelve of them walked out the door laughing and joking with one another. George had so much going on in his mind that he didn't crack a smile or take anything that was being said to be amusing. He just watched their movements as they walked down the walkway to the chow hall. Once inside, he looked around at the correctional officers posted around the wall and on the upper catwalk with shotguns in their hands, waiting for anything to jump off. The twelve men walked through the line to get their trays. One at a time, they grabbed their tray and walked over to their tables. Two other housing units were already in there when they got there.

After everyone was seated, Billy introduced George to all the other white supremacy brothers. "This is George. George!" Billy said, calling his name loudly.

"Yeah!" George said as he was pulled back from a deep thought.

"Damn, bro, where did you go that quick? Listen up, bro! We don't do nothing around here by ourselves. Wherever you go, make sure you have at least one brother with you. That way, someone will have your back and you will have theirs. Four or more eyes are better than two. We usually take showers around the same time. If you just have to take a shower, make sure you let the brothers know so we can watch your back."

Before Billy finished talking to George, he announced, "Since the time went back an hour for daylight savings time, I don't think we will be able to meet up on the yard today. We might have to meet up tomorrow morning in the gym. As a matter of fact, we will just meet up for the morning yard. Everyone needs to be there, so let the rest of the brothers know."

"We got you, bro," two men from the other units said in unison.

After everyone finished eating, they headed back to their units. Once everyone was back in the unit, they got settled. George walked up to the cell and lit himself a cigarette. He just stood in the doorway looking at the movement in the unit while he smoked on his cigarette. Everyone maintained their daily routines of playing cards, chess, and slamming dominoes. George finished his cigarette and flushed the filter down the toilet. He paced the cell floor for a minute before grabbing his laundry bag and taking out a change of clothing. He laid all the things he needed to take with him to the shower on the bed and walked out the cell. He took his time and watched his surroundings as he walked down the walkway. He just stood at the top of the stairs looking around before he walked down them to the first floor. He walked over to the table where Billy and some of the other brothers were sitting around playing cards.

"What's up, bro? You want next?" Billy asked George.

"No, I pass. I came down here to see if I can get someone to watch my back. I need to get in the shower before it gets too late," George stated.

"Sure, let me get you some security," Billy said, looking over his shoulder at Mike, who was just standing around, trying to learn how to play pinochle by watching.

"Mike, go get Rick and Bo so three of you can A&A the brother."

George gave Billy a funny look. Billy instantly picked up on the look George shot him. "A&A means *aid and assist*," Billy said as he looked up at George. George nodded.

"What are you still standing here for? The brother is ready to get in the shower," Billy said to Mike as he stood with his arms crossed. Mike walked off and returned with the other two within minutes. When the three walked up, Billy said, "I need all three of you to stand security for George while he takes a shower."

"Cool," they said in unison as they nodded.

"Are you ready, bro?" Bo asked.

"Yeah, I just need to get my stuff out of the cell." The four walked up the stairs to George's cell. George opened the cell door with his key, walked in, and grabbed the soap, shampoo, and a change of clothing he had lying on the bed, making sure that he had everything before he walked out the door where the three brothers were waiting. The four then walked down to the end of the tier to the shower. The shower sat to the right side, which was a blind spot for the correctional officer who sat in the control center up toward the front of the housing unit. The shower is a rapist's and murderer's paradise. That's why no one takes a shower without some security to watch their back. The three men walked into the shower with their shanks out in their hands to make sure that no one was waiting on the inside of the shower. As they entered, two men were walking out. They looked around to make sure that they were the only two. After they secured the shower, they walked back out and stood in the front right outside the shower.

"You can go ahead, bro. We will be right out there to make sure no one comes in," Bo said.

"Okay," George said as he nodded and walked into the shower.

A few minutes later, Billy and the rest of the brothers walked up while they stood there.

"Rick, you and Mike keep the lookout for us. Come on with us, Bo," Billy said. The nine men walked into the shower and spread out. George had just squeezed some shampoo into his hands and sat the bottle down on the shower floor. He noticed them after he had rubbed the shampoo in his hair. Seeing that something was about to go down, George put his back up against the shower wall and clenched his fist tightly.

"What the fuck is this supposed to be?" George said as he used his left forearm to wipe the running shampoo from his forehead.

Billy just smiled as he looked at George standing there in his birthday suit with his fist balled up. "You bunch of pussies want to get me while I'm in the shower, huh?" George asked.

"Grab that old motherfucker," Billy said. Two rushed George. George got off a few blows. He knocked one of them down and slowed the other down a little. Two more men rushed in, and George swung two more punches, but they weren't enough. The men overpowered him quickly.

George hollered for help, "Help! Help! Help!" A third man moved in as George was hollering and hit him with a powerful blow to the stomach, silencing him as his breath was knocked out. The man hit him so hard that blood filled his mouth as he clenched his teeth together. George realized there wasn't anything he could do. He pled.

"What's up, bro? What the fuck is going on?" George asked after he caught his breath.

"Chris White sends his regards," Billy said as he unzipped his pants.

"Who in the hell is Chris White?" George asked.

"He's not just the Grand Dragon of the South. He is the father of one of those twelve sisters you raped and killed, you sick motherfucker."

"Bend his ass over. Bo, pass me your belt."

George tried to make another attempt to get loose, but the men who held him were too big and strong for him. They bent him forward. After hearing Billy spit into the palm of his hand behind him, George screamed, "Aaah! HELP! HELP! HELP! HELP ME! SOMEBODY HELP ME!"

Billy spit into his hands rubbed it on his penis and forced it into George's rectum. George hollered out loud as he felt the tear. "Aaah . . . motherfucker!" George said as Billy was pushing into his ass. Billy then wrapped Bo's belt around George's neck, while he moved in and out of George's ass. Billy pulled on the belt tightly while it was around George's neck. "Do you remember how your sick ass did those sisters?" Billy asked as he pumped harder and pulled upward on the belt. "If it was up to me, I would kill you, bitch," Billy added as he raped George. His eyes rolled into the back of his head.

"Pass me the towel," Billy said right before he pulled his penis out and ejaculated onto George's towel. "He has some good tight ass for an old man. One of you might fall in love with him. Who wants to go next? Just make sure that no one nuts up in him," Billy said. One by one, they raped and choked George. After the first four men, George was too weak to fight back, so they no longer had to hold him.

"Damn, Dave, loosen up the belt before you choke him to death. We don't want to kill him," Billy said as he stopped Dave from choking him.

George was so weak that he passed out. That didn't stop them, though. Once they all had their enjoyment, they left George lying on the shower floor with blood running from his rectum and mouth.

Two days later, George woke up in the medical ward. The thought of them having their way with him and the pain from his neck and rectum rushed him all at once. He sat up and looked around to see where he was. He wasted no time before he got up and pulled the sheets off the bed. He twisted the sheet up and made a loop in it to go over his head. He climbed up on the bed with the sheet in hand. He tied the sheet around the sprinkler system pipe that ran across the ceiling. Then he looped the other end of the sheet and placed it over his head, pulling it tightly around his neck. One security guard was beating on the glass window while the other one opened the door with his key. George looked at them and then jumped off the bed. The security guard got through the door and rushed over and grabbed George around his legs, holding him up.

"Get something to cut the sheet," the guard holding George's legs said.

"I think we are too late. The jump broke his neck," the other officer said as he looked around for something to cut the sheet with.

"Man, just get up on the bed and take the sheet off his neck!" the guard said loudly.

George's face had already turned purple. His tongue hung from his mouth, and his eyes were bloodshot red.